Vanishing Acts

JODI PICOULT

Vanishing Acts

HODDER &
STOUGHTON

First published in the United States of America by Atria Books
A division of Simon and Schuster
First published in Great Britain in 2005 by Hodder and Stoughton
A division of Hodder Headline

3

A CIP catalogue record for this title is
available from the British Library

Hardback ISBN 0 340 83548 6
Trade Paperback ISBN 0 340 83869 8

Typeset in Plantin Light by
Palimpsest Book Production Limited,
Polmont, Stirlingshire

Printed and bound in Great Britain by
Mackays of Chatham Ltd, Chatham, Kent

Hodder Headline's policy is to use papers that are natural,
renewable and recyclable products and made from wood grown
in sustainable forests. The logging and manufacturing processes
are expected to conform to the environmental regulations
of the country of origin.

Hodder and Stoughton Ltd
A division of Hodder Headline
338 Euston Road
London NW1 3BH

This one is for Katie Desmond,
who fed me Oreos for breakfast on my wedding day,
appreciates the fashion sense of blue suede shoes,
and knows just how many people died that first night
out on the *QEII*. Every once in a while, a person's lucky
enough to make an unforgettable friend:
you're it, for me.

ACKNOWLEDGMENTS

As always, I didn't do this alone. My first huge thank you is to Sergeant Janice Mallaburn of the Maricopa County Sheriff's Office, a dynamo who probably didn't realize what she was getting into when she volunteered to help me after meeting me during my visit to the Madison Street Jail, and who is the first (and last) research guru to ever call me Tastee Freak. Thanks to the helpers in other branches of the law: Chris and Kiki Keating, Allegra Lubrano, Kevin Baggs (and Jean Arnett), David Bash, Jen Sternick, Detective Trooper Claire Demarais, Chief Nick Giaccone, and Captain Frank Moran. Judge Jennifer Sobel gets her own special shout-out for accompanying me to jail for a day, if only so that someone would believe me when I came home with all those great stories. New Hampshire State Trooper James Steinmetz and his dogs Maggie and Greta, as well as Rhode Island State Trooper Matt Zarrella, showed me firsthand why search-and-rescue dogs are so impressive. Thanks to the medical and psychiatric professionals, for rendering advice on scorpions, tracheostomies, hysterectomies, and repressed memory: Doug Fagen, Jan Scheiner, Ralph Cahaly, David Toub, Roland Eavey, and Jim Umlas. For speedy transcription, as always, thanks to Sindy Follensbee. For letting me steal mercilessly from their lives: Jeff Hastings, JoAnn Mapson, and Steve Alspach. For being the best first reader ever: Jane Picoult. For their dedication to my writing: Carolyn Reidy, Judith Curr, SarahBranham, Karen Mender, and everyone else at Atria who makes my head swell. For reminding everyone else to be dedicated to my writing: the indomitable Camille McDuffie. For our fifteen-year anniversary and more, Laura Gross. For being the best cheerleader and ringmaster an author could ask for, Emily Bestler. And for just being: Kyle, Jake, Samantha, and Tim.

What other words, we may almost ask, are memorable and worthy to be repeated than those which love has inspired? It is wonderful that they were ever uttered. They are few and rare indeed, but, like a strain of music, they are incessantly repeated and modulated by memory. All other words crumble off with the stucco which overlies the heart. We should not dare to repeat these now aloud. We are not competent to hear them at all times.

> – Henry David Thoreau, 'A Week on the
> Concord and Merrimack Rivers,' 1849

Vanishing Acts

Prologue

I was six years old the first time I disappeared.

My father was working on a magic act for the annual Christmas show at the senior center, and his assistant, the receptionist who had a real gold tooth and false eyelashes as thick as spiders, got the flu. I was fully prepared to beg my father to be part of the act, but he asked, as if *I* were the one who would be doing *him* a favor.

Like I said, I was six, and I still believed that my father truly could pull coins out of my ear and find a bouquet of flowers in the folds of Mrs. Kleban's chenille housecoat and make Mr. van Looen's false teeth disappear. He did these little tricks all the time for the elderly folks who came to play bingo or do chair aerobics or watch old black-and-white movies with sound-tracks that crackled like flame. I knew some parts of the act were fake – his fiddlehead mustache, for example, and the quarter with two heads – but I was one hundred percent sure that his magic wand had the ability to transport me into some limbo zone, until he saw fit to call me back.

On the night of the Christmas show, the residents of three different assisted-living communities in our town braved the cold and the snow to be bused to the senior center. They sat in a semicircle watching my father while I waited backstage. When he announced me – *the Amazing Cordelia!* – I stepped out wearing the sequined leotard I usually kept in my dress-up bin.

I learned a lot that night. For example, that part of being the magician's assistant means coming face-to-face with illusion. That invisibility is really just knotting your body in a certain way and letting the black curtain fall over you. That people don't vanish into thin air; that when you can't find someone, it's because you've been misdirected to look elsewhere.

I

I think it is a matter of love: the more you love a memory, the stronger and stranger it is.

— Vladimir Nabokov

Delia

You can't exist in this world without leaving a piece of yourself behind. There are concrete paths, like credit card receipts and appointment calendars and promises you've made to others. There are microscopic clues, like fingerprints, that stay invisible unless you know how to look for them. But even in the absence of any of this, there's scent. We live in a cloud that moves with us as we check e-mail and jog and carpool. The whole time, we shed skin cells – forty thousand per minute – that rise on currents up our legs and under our chins.

Today, I'm running behind Greta, who picks up the pace just as we hit the twisted growth at the base of the mountain. I'm soaked to the thighs with muck and slush, although it doesn't seem to be bothering my bloodhound any. The awful conditions that make it so hard to navigate are the same conditions that have preserved this trail.

The officer from the Carroll, New Hampshire, Police Department who is supposed to be accompanying me has fallen behind. He takes one look at the terrain Greta is bulldozing and shakes his head. 'Forget it,' he says. 'There's no way a four-year-old would have made it through this mess.'

The truth is, he's probably right. At this time of the afternoon, as the ground cools down under a setting sun, air currents run downslope, which means that although the girl probably walked through flatter area some distance away, Greta is picking up the scent trail where it's drifted. 'Greta disagrees,' I say.

In my line of work, I can't afford not to trust my partner. Fifty percent of a dog's nose is devoted to the sense of smell, compared to only one square inch of mine. So if Greta says that Holly Gardiner wandered out of the playground at Sticks & Stones Day Care and climbed to the top of Mount Deception, I'm going to hike right up there to find her.

Greta yanks on the end of the fifteen-foot leash and hustles at a clip for a few hundred feet. A beautiful bloodhound, she has a black widow's peak, a brown velvet coat, and the gawky body of the girl who watches the dancers from the bleachers. She circles a smooth, bald rock twice; then glances up at me, the folds of her long face deepening. Scent will pool, like the ripples when a stone's thrown into a pond. This is where the child stopped to rest.

'Find her,' I order. Greta casts around to pick up the scent again, and then starts to run. I sprint after the dog, wincing as a branch snaps back against my face and opens a cut over my left eye. We tear through a snarl of vines and burst onto a narrow footpath that opens up into a clearing.

The little girl is sitting on the wet ground, shivering, arms lashed tight over her knees. Just like always, for a moment her face is Sophie's, and I have to keep myself from grabbing her and scaring her half to death. Greta bounds over and jumps up, which is how she knows to identify the person whose scent she took from a fleece hat at the day-care center and followed six miles to this spot.

The girl blinks up at us, slowly pecking her way through a shell of fear. 'I bet you're Holly,' I say, crouching beside her. I shrug off my jacket, ripe with body heat, and settle it over her clothespin shoulders. 'My name is Delia.' I whistle, and the dog comes trotting close. 'This is Greta.'

I slip off the harness she wears while she's working. Greta wags her tail so hard that it makes her body a metronome. As the little girl reaches up to pat the dog, I do a quick visual assessment. 'Are you hurt?'

She shakes her head and glances at the cut over my eye. '*You* are.'

Just then the Carroll police officer bursts into the clearing, panting. 'I'll be damned,' he wheezes. 'You actually found her.'

I always do. But it isn't my track record that keeps me in this business. It's not the adrenaline rush; it's not even the potential happy ending. It's because, when you get down to it, I'm the one who's lost.

I watch the reunion between mother and daughter from a distance – how Holly melts into her mother's arms, how relief binds them like a seam. Even if she'd been a different race or dressed like a gypsy, I would have been able to pick this woman out of a crowd: She is the one who seems unraveled, half of a whole.

I can't imagine anything more terrifying than losing Sophie. When you're pregnant, you can think of nothing but having your own body to yourself again; yet after giving birth you realize that the biggest part of you is now somehow external, subject to all sorts of dangers and disappearance, so you spend the rest of your life trying to figure out how to keep her close enough for comfort. That's the strange thing about being a mother: Until you have a baby, you don't even realize how much you were missing one.

It doesn't matter if the subject Greta and I are searching for is old, young, male, or female – to someone, that missing person is what Sophie is to me.

Part of my tight connection to Sophie, I know, is pure over-compensation. My mother died when I was three. When I was Sophie's age, I'd hear my father say things like 'I lost my wife in a car accident,' and it made no sense to me: If he knew where she was, why didn't he just go find her? It took me a lifetime to realize things don't get lost if they don't have value – you don't miss what you don't care about – but I was too young to have stored up a cache of memories of my mother. For a long time, all I had of her was a smell – a mixture of vanilla and apples could bring her back as if she were standing a foot away – and then this disappeared, too. Not even Greta can find someone without that initial clue.

From where she is sitting beside me, Greta nuzzles my forehead, reminding me that I'm bleeding. I wonder if I'll need stitches, if this will launch my father into another tirade about why I should have become something relatively safer, like a bounty hunter or the leader of a bomb squad.

Someone hands me a gauze pad, which I press against the cut above my eye. When I glance up I see it's Fitz, my best friend, who happens to be a reporter for the paper with the largest circulation in our state. 'What does the other guy look like?' he asks.

'I got attacked by a tree.'

'No kidding? I always heard their bark is worse than their bite.'

Fitzwilliam MacMurray grew up in one of the houses beside mine; Eric Talcott lived in the other. My father used to call us Siamese triplets. I have a long history with both of them that includes drying slugs on the pavement with Morton's salt, dropping water balloons off the elementary school roof, and kidnapping the gym teacher's cat. As kids, we were a triumverate; as adults, we are still remarkably close. In fact, Fitz will be pulling double duty at my wedding – as Eric's best man, and as my man-of-honor.

From this angle, Fitz is enormous. He's six-four, with a shock of red hair that makes him look like he's on fire. 'I need a quote from you,' he says.

I always knew Fitz would wind up writing; although I figured he'd be a poet or a storyteller. He would play with language the way other children played with stones and twigs, building structures for the rest of us to decorate with our imagination. 'Make something up,' I suggest.

He laughs. 'Hey, I work for the *New Hampshire Gazette*, not the *New York Times*.'

'Excuse me . . . ?'

We both turn at the sound of a woman's voice. Holly Gardiner's mother is staring at me, her expression so full of words that, for a moment, she can't choose the right one. 'Thank you,' she says finally. 'Thank you so much.'

'Thank Greta,' I reply. 'She did all the work.'

The woman is on the verge of tears, the weight of the moment falling as heavy and sudden as rain. She grabs my hand and squeezes, a pulse of understanding between mothers, before she heads back to the rescue workers who are taking care of Holly.

There were times I missed my mother desperately while I was growing up – when all the other kids at school had two parents at the Holiday Concert, when I got my period and had to sit down on the lip of the bathtub with my father to read the directions on the Tampax box, when I first kissed Eric and felt like I might burst out of my skin.

Now.

Fitz slings his arm over my shoulders. 'It's not like you missed out,' he says gently. 'Your dad was better than most parents put together.'

'I know,' I reply, but I watch Holly Gardiner and her mother walk all the way back to their car, hand in hand, like two jewels on a delicate strand that might at any moment be broken.

That night Greta and I are the lead story on the evening news. In rural New Hampshire, we don't get broadcasts of gang wars and murders and serial rapists; instead, we get barns that burn down and ribbon-cuttings at local hospitals and local heroes like me.

My father and I stand in the kitchen, getting dinner ready. 'What's wrong with Sophie?' I ask, frowning as I peer into the living room, where she lays puddled on the carpet.

'She's tired,' my father says.

She takes an occasional nap after I pick her up from kindergarten, but today, when I was on a search, my father had to bring her back to the senior center with him until closing time. Still, there's more to it. When I came home, she wasn't at the door waiting to tell me all the important things: who swung the highest at recess, which book Mrs. Easley read to them, whether snack was carrots and cheese cubes for the third day in a row.

'Did you take her temperature?' I ask.

'Is it missing?' He grins at me when I roll my eyes. 'She'll be her old self by dessert,' he predicts. 'Kids bounce back fast.'

At nearly sixty, my father is good-looking – ageless, almost, with his salt-and-pepper hair and runner's build. Although there were any number of women who would have thrown themselves at a man like Andrew Hopkins, he only dated sporadically, and he never remarried. He used to say that life was all about a boy finding the perfect girl; he was lucky enough to have been handed his in a labor and delivery room.

He moves to the stove, adding half-and-half to the crushed tomatoes – a homemade recipe trick one of the seniors taught him that turned out to be surprisingly good, unlike their tips for helping Sophie avoid croup (tie a black cord around her neck) or curing an earache (put olive oil and pepper on a cotton ball and stuff into the ear). 'When's Eric getting here?' he asks. 'I can't keep this cooking much longer.'

He was supposed to arrive a half hour ago, but there's been no phone call to say he's running late, and he isn't answering his cell. I don't know where he is, but there are plenty of places I am imagining him: Murphy's Bar on Main Street, Callahan's on North Park, off the road in a ditch somewhere.

Sophie comes into the kitchen. 'Hey,' I say, my anxiety about Eric disappearing in the wide sunny wake of our daughter. 'Want to help?' I hold up the green beans; she likes the crisp sound they make when they snap.

She shrugs and sits down with her back against the refrigerator.

'How was school today?' I prompt.

Her small face darkens like the thunderstorms we get in July, sudden and fierce before they pass. Then, just as quickly, she looks up at me. 'Jennica has warts,' Sophie announces.

'That's too bad,' I reply, trying to remember which one Jennica is – the classmate with the platinum braids, or the one whose father owns the gourmet coffee shop in town.

'I want warts.'

'No, you don't.' Headlights flash past the window, but don't turn into our driveway. I focus on Sophie, trying to remember if warts are contagious or if that's an old wives' tale.

'But they're green,' Sophie whines. 'And really soft and on the tag it says the name.'

Warts, apparently, is the hot new Beanie Baby. 'Maybe for your birthday.'

'I bet you'll forget *that,* too,' Sophie accuses, and she runs out of the kitchen and upstairs.

All of a sudden I can see the red circle on my calendar – the parent-child tea in her kindergarten class started at one o'clock, when I was halfway up a mountain searching for Holly Gardiner.

When I was a kid and there was a mother-daughter event in my elementary school, I wouldn't tell my father about it. Instead, I'd fake sick, staying home for the day so that I didn't have to watch everyone else's mother come through the door and know that my own was never going to arrive.

I find Sophie lying on her bed. 'Baby,' I say. 'I'm really sorry.'

She looks up at me. 'When you're with *them,*' she asks, a slice through the heart, 'do you ever think about *me?*'

In response I pick her up and settle her on my lap. 'I think about you even when I'm sleeping,' I say.

It is hard to believe now, with this small body dovetailing against mine, but when I found out I was pregnant I considered not keeping the baby. I wasn't married, and Eric was having enough trouble without tossing in any added responsibility. In the end, though, I couldn't go through with it. I wanted to be the kind of mother who couldn't be separated from a child without putting up a fierce fight. I like to believe my own mother had been that way.

Parenting Sophie – with and without Eric, depending on the year – has been much harder than I ever expected. Whatever I do right I chalk up to my father's example. Whatever I do wrong I blame squarely on fate.

The door to the bedroom opens, and Eric walks in. For that half second, before all the memories crowd in, he takes my breath away. Sophie has my dark hair and freckles, but thankfully, that's about all. She's got Eric's lean build and his high cheekbones, his easy smile and his unsettling eyes – the feverish blue of a glacier. 'Sorry I'm late.' He drops a kiss on the crown of my head and I breathe in, trying to smell the telltale alcohol on his breath. He hoists Sophie into his arms.

I can't make out the sourness of whiskey, or the grainy yeast of beer, but that means nothing. Even in high school, Eric knew a hundred ways to remove the red flags of alcohol consumption. 'Where were you?' I ask.

'Meeting a friend in the Amazon.' He pulls a Beanie Baby frog out of his back pocket.

Sophie squeals and grabs it, hugs Eric so tight I think she might cut off his circulation. 'She double-teamed us,' I say, shaking my head. 'She's a con artist.'

'Just hedging her bets.' He puts Sophie down on the floor, and she immediately runs downstairs to show her grandfather.

I go into his arms, hooking my thumbs into the back pockets of his jeans. Under my ear, his heart keeps time for me. *I'm sorry I doubted you.* 'Do I get a toad, too?' I ask.

'You already had one. You kissed him, and got me instead. Remember?' To illustrate, he trails his lips from the tiny divot at the base of my neck – a sledding scar from when I was two – all the way up to my mouth. I taste coffee and hope and, thank God, nothing else.

We stand in our daughter's room for a few minutes like that, even after the kiss is finished, just leaning against each other in between the quiet places. I have always loved him. Warts and all.

When we were little, Eric and Fitz and I invented a language. I've forgotten most of it, with the exception of a few words: *valyango,* which meant pirate; *palapala,* which meant rain; and *ruskifer,* which had no translation to English but described the dimpled bottom of a woven basket, all the reeds coming together to form one joint spot, and that we sometimes used to explain our friendship. This was back in the days before playtime had all the contractual scheduling of an arranged marriage, and most mornings, one of us would show up at the house of another and we'd swing by to pick up the third.

In the winter, we would build snow forts with complicated burrows and tunnels, complete with three sculpted thrones where we'd sit and suck on icicles until we could no longer feel our fingers and toes. In the spring, we ate sugar-on-snow that Fitz's dad made us when he boiled down his own maple syrup, the three of us dueling with forks to get the sweetest, longest strands. In the fall, we would climb the fence into the back acreage of McNab's Orchards and eat Macouns and Cortlands and Jonathans whose skin was as warm as our own. In the summer, we wrote secret predictions about our futures by the faint light of trapped fireflies, and hid them in the hollow knot of an old maple tree – a time capsule, for when we grew up.

We had our roles: Fitz was the dreamer; I was the practical tactician; Eric was the front man, the one who could charm adults or other kids with equal ease. Eric always knew exactly what to say when you dropped your hot lunch tray by accident and the whole cafeteria was staring at you, or when the teacher called on you and you'd been writing up your Christmas list. Being part of his entourage was like the sun coming through a plate-glass window: golden, something to lift your face toward.

It was when we came home the summer after freshman year in college that things began to change. We were all chafing under our parents' rules and roofs, but Eric rubbed himself raw, lightening up only when we three would go out at night. Eric would always suggest a bar, and he knew the ones that didn't card minors. Afterward, when Fitz was gone, Eric and I would spread an old quilt on the far shore of the town lake and undress each other, swatting away mosquitoes from the pieces of each other we'd laid claim to. But every time I kissed him, there was liquor on his breath, and I've always hated the smell of alcohol. It's a weird quirk, but no stranger than those people who can't stand the scent of gas, I suppose, and have to hold their breath while they fill up their cars. At any rate, I'd kiss Eric and inhale that fermenting, bitter smell and roll away from him. He'd call me a prude, and I started to think maybe I was one – that was easier than admitting what was really driving us apart.

Sometimes we find ourselves walking through our lives blindfolded, and we try to deny that we're the ones who securely tied the knot. It was this way for Fitz and me, the decade after high school. If Eric told us that he had a beer only every now and then, we believed him. If his hands shook when he was sober, we turned away. If I mentioned his drinking, it became my problem, not his. And yet, in spite of all this, I still couldn't end our relationship. All of my memories were laced with him; to extract them would mean losing the flavor of my childhood.

The day I found out I was pregnant, Eric drove his car off the road, through a flimsy guard rail, and into a local farmer's cornfield. When he called to tell me what had happened – blaming it on a woodchuck that ran across the road – I hung up the phone and drove to Fitz's apartment. *I think we have a problem,* I said to him, as if it was the three of us, which, in reality, it was.

Fitz had listened to me speak a truth we'd taken great pains never to utter out loud, plus a newer, magnificent, frightening one. *I can't do this alone,* I told him.

He had looked at my belly, still flat. *You aren't.*

There was no denying Eric's magnetism, but that afternoon I realized that, united, Fitz and I were a force to be reckoned with as well. And when I left his apartment armed with the knowledge of what I was going to have to say to Eric, I remembered what I had written down during that backlit summer when I was trying to guess the rest of my life. I'd been embarrassed setting the words to paper, had folded it three times so

Fitz and Eric wouldn't see. Me – a tomboy who spent hours in the company of boys pretending to be a swashbuckling privateer, or an archaeologist searching for relics, a girl who had been the damsel in distress only once, and even then had rescued herself – I had written only a single wild wish. *One day,* I'd written, *I will be a mother.*

As one of Wexton's three attorneys, Eric does real estate transfers and wills and the occasional divorce, but he's done a little trial work, too – representing defendants charged with DUI and petty thefts. He usually wins, which is no surprise to me. After all, more than once I have been a jury of one, and I've always managed to be persuaded.

Case in point: my wedding. I was perfectly happy to sign a marriage certificate at the courthouse. But then Eric suggested that a big party wasn't such a bad idea, and before I knew what had happened, I was buried in a pile of brochures for reception venues, and band tapes, and price lists from florists.

I'm sitting on the living room floor after dinner, swatches of fabric covering my legs like a patchwork quilt. 'Who cares whether the napkins are blue or teal?' I complain. 'Isn't teal really just blue on steroids, anyway?'

I hand him a stack of photo albums; we are supposed to find ten of Eric and ten of me as an introductory montage to the wedding video. He cracks the first one open, and there's a picture of Eric and Fitz and me rolled fat as sausages in our snowsuits, peeking out from the entrance of a homemade igloo. I'm between the two boys; it's like that in most of the photos.

'Look at my hair,' Eric laughs. 'I look like Dorothy Hamill.'

'No, *I* look like Dorothy Hamill. You look like a portobello mushroom.'

In the next two albums I pick up, I am older. There are fewer pictures of us as a trio, and more of Eric and me, with Fitz sprinkled in. Our senior prom picture: Eric and I, and then Fitz in his own snapshot with a girl whose name I can't recall.

One night when we were fifteen we told our parents we were going on a school-sponsored overnight and instead climbed to the top of Dartmouth's Baker Library bell tower to watch a meteor shower. We drank peach schnapps stolen from Eric's parents' liquor cabinet and watched the stars play tag with the moon. Fitz fell asleep holding the bottle and Eric and I waited for the cursive of comets. *Did you see that one?* Eric asked. When I couldn't find the falling star, he took my hand and guided my finger. And then he just kept holding on.

By the time we climbed down at 4:30 A.M., I had had my first kiss, and it wasn't the three of us anymore.

Just then my father comes into the room. 'I'm headed upstairs to watch Leno,' he says. 'Lock up, okay?'

I glance up. 'Where are my baby pictures?'

'In the albums.'

'No . . . these only go back to when I'm four or five.' I sit up. 'It would be nice to have your wedding picture, too, for the video.'

I have the only photo of my mother that is on display in this house. She is on the cusp of smiling, and you cannot look at it without wondering who made her happy just then, and how.

My father looks down at the ground, and shakes his head a little. 'Well, I knew it was going to happen sometime. Come on, then.'

Eric and I follow him to his bedroom and sit down on the double bed, on the side where he doesn't sleep. From the closet, my father takes down a tin with a Pepsi-Cola logo stamped onto the front. He dumps the contents onto the covers between Eric and me – dozens of photographs of my mother, draped in peasant skirts and gauze blouses, her black hair hanging down her back like a river. A wedding portrait: my mother in a belled white dress; my father trussed in his tuxedo, looking like he might bolt at any second. Photos of me, wrapped tight as a croissant, awkwardly balanced in my mother's arms. And one of my mother and father on an ugly green couch with me between them, a bridge made of dimpled flesh, of blended blood.

It is like visiting another planet when you only have one roll of film to record it, like coming to a banquet after a hunger strike – there is so much here that I have to consciously keep myself from racing through, before it all disappears. My face gets hot, as if I've been slapped. 'Why were you *hiding* these?'

He takes one photograph out of my hand and stares at it long enough for me to believe he has completely forgotten that Eric and I are in the room. 'I tried keeping a few of the pictures out,' my father explains, 'but you kept asking when she was coming home. And I'd pass them, and stop, and lose ten minutes or a half hour or a half day. I didn't hide them because I didn't want to look at them, Delia. I hid them because that was *all* I wanted to do.' He puts the wedding picture back in the tin and scatters the rest on top. 'You can have them,' my father tells me. 'You can have them all.'

He leaves us sitting in the near dark in his bedroom. Eric touches the photograph on the top as if it is as delicate as milkweed. 'That,' he says quietly. 'That's what I want with you.'

It's the ones I don't find that stay with me. The teenage boy who jumped off the Fairlee-Orford train bridge into the Connecticut River one frigid March; the mother from North Conway who vanished with a pot still boiling on the stove and a toddler in the playpen; the baby snatched out of a car in the Strafford post office parking lot while her sitter was inside dropping off a large package. Sometimes they stand behind me while I'm brushing my teeth; sometimes they're the last thing I see before I go to sleep; sometimes, like now, they leave me restless in the middle of the night.

There is a thick fog tonight, but Greta and I have trained enough in this patch of land to know our way by heart. I sit down on a mossy log while Greta sniffs around the periphery. Above me, something dangles from a branch, full and round and yellow.

I am little, and he has just finished planting a lemon tree in our backyard. I am dancing around it. I want to make lemonade, but there isn't any fruit because the tree is just a baby. How long will it take to grow one? *I ask.* A while, *he tells me. I sit myself down in front of it to watch.* I'll wait. *He comes over and takes my hand.* Come on, *grilla, he says.* If we're going to sit here that long, we'd better get something to eat.

There are some dreams that get stuck between your teeth when you sleep, so that when you open your mouth to yawn awake they fly right out of you. But this feels too real. This feels like it has actually happened.

I've lived in New Hampshire my whole life. No citrus tree could bear a climate like ours, where we have not only White Christmases but also White Halloweens. I pull down the yellow ball: a crumbling sphere made of birdseed and suet.

What does *grilla* mean?

I am still thinking about this the next morning after taking Sophie to school, and spend an extra ten minutes walking around, from the painting easel to the blocks to the bubble station, to make up for my shoddy behavior yesterday. I've planned on doing a training run with Greta that morning, but I'm sidetracked by the sight of my father's wallet on the floor of my Expedition. He'd taken it out a few nights ago to fill the tank with gas; the least I can do is swing by the senior center to give it back.

I pull into the parking lot and open the back hatch. 'Stay,' I tell Greta, who whumps her tail twice. She has to share her seat with emergency rescue equipment, a large cooler of water, and several different harnesses and leashes.

Suddenly I feel a prickle on my wrist; something has crawled onto my arm. My heart kicks itself into overdrive and my throat pinches tight, as it always does at the thought of a spider or a tick or any other creepy-crawly thing. I manage to strip away my jacket, sweat cooling on my body as I wonder how close the spider has landed near my boots.

It's a groundless phobia. I have climbed out on mountain ledges in pursuit of missing people; I have faced down criminals with guns; but put me in the room with the tiniest arachnid and I just may pass out.

The whole way into the senior center, I take deep breaths. I find my father standing on the sidelines, watching Yoga Tuesday happen in the function room. 'Hey,' he whispers, so as not to disturb the seniors doing sun salutations. 'What are you doing here?'

I fish his wallet out of my pocket. 'Thought you might be missing this.'

'So that's where it went,' he says. 'There are so many perks to having a daughter who does search and rescue.'

'I found it the old-fashioned way,' I tell him. 'By accident.'

He starts moving down the hall. 'Well, I knew it would turn up eventually,' he says. 'Everything always does. You have time for a cup of coffee?'

'Not really,' I say, but I follow him to the little kitchenette anyway and let him pour me a mug, then trail him into his office. When I was a little girl, he'd bring me here and keep me entertained while he was on the phone by doing sleight-of-hand with binder clips and handkerchiefs. I pick up a paperweight on his desk. It is a rock painted to look like a ladybug, a gift I made for him when I was about Sophie's age. 'You could probably get rid of this, you know.'

'But it's my favorite.' He takes it out of my hand, puts it back in the center of his desk.

'Dad?' I ask. 'Did we ever plant a lemon tree?'

'A *what?*' Before I can repeat my question he squints at me, then frowns and summons me closer. 'Hang on. You've got something sticking out of . . . no, lower . . . let me.' I lean forward, and he cups his hand around the back of my neck. *'The Amazing Cordelia,'* he says, just like when we did our magic act. Then, from behind my ear, he pulls a strand of pearls.

'They were hers,' my father says, and he guides me to the

mirror that hangs on the back of his office door. I have a vague recollection of the wedding photo from last night. He fastens the clasp behind me, so that we are both looking in the mirror, seeing someone who isn't there.

The offices of the *New Hampshire Gazette* are in Manchester, but Fitz does most of his work from the office he's fixed up in the second bedroom of his apartment in Wexton. He lives over a pizza place, and the smell of marinara sauce comes through the forced-hot-air ducts. Greta's toenails click up the linoleum stairs, and she sits down outside his apartment, in front of a life-size cardboard cutout of Chewbacca. Hanging on a hook on the back is his key; I use it to let myself inside.

I navigate through the ocean of clothes he's left discarded on the floor and the stacks of books that seem to reproduce like rabbits. Fitz is sitting in front of his computer. 'Hey,' I say. 'You promised to lay a trail for us.'

The dog bounds into the office and nearly climbs up onto Fitz's lap. He rubs her hard behind the ears, and she snuggles closer to him, knocking several photos off his desk.

I bend down to pick them up. One is of a man with a hole in the middle of his head, in which he has stuck a lit candle. The second picture is of a grinning boy with double pupils dancing in each of his eyes. I hand the snapshots back to Fitz. 'Relatives?'

'The *Gazette*'s paying me to do an article on the Strange But True.' He holds up the picture of the man with the votive in his skull. 'This amazingly resourceful fellow apparently used to give tours around town at night. And I got to read a whole 1911 medical treatise from a doctor who had an eleven-year-old patient with a molar growing out of the bottom of his foot.'

'Oh, come on,' I say. 'Everyone's got something that's strange about them. Like the way Eric can fold his tongue into a clover, and that disgusting thing you do with your eyes.'

'You mean this?' he says, but I turn away before I have to

watch. 'Or how you go ballistic if there's a spider web within a mile of you?'

I turn to him, thinking. 'Have I always been afraid of spiders?'

'For as long as I've known you,' Fitz says. 'Maybe you were Miss Muffet in a former life.'

'What if I were?' I say.

'I was *kidding*, Dee. Just because someone's got a fear of heights doesn't mean she died in a fall a hundred years ago.'

Before I know it, I am telling Fitz about the lemon tree. I explain how it felt as if the heat was laying a crown on my head, how the tree had been planted in soil as red as blood. How I could read the letters *ABC* on the bottoms of my shoes.

Fitz listens carefully, his arms folded across his chest, with the same studious consideration he exhibited when I was ten and confessed that I'd seen the ghost of an Indian sitting cross-legged at the foot of my bed. 'Well,' he says finally. 'It's not like you said you were wearing a hoop skirt, or shooting a musket. Maybe you're just remembering something from *this* life, something you've forgotten. There's all kind of research out there on recovered memory. I can do a little digging for you and see what I come up with.'

'I thought recovered memories were traumatic. What's traumatic about citrus fruit?'

'Lachanophobia,' he says. 'That's the fear of vegetables. It stands to reason that there's one for the rest of the food pyramid, too.'

'How much did your parents shell out for that Ivy League education?'

Fitz grins, reaching for Greta's leash. 'All right, where do you want me to lay your trail?'

He knows the routine. He will take off his sweatshirt and leave it at the bottom of the stairs, so that Greta has a scent article. Then he'll strike off for three miles or five or ten, winding through streets and back roads and woods. I'll give him a fifteen-minute head start, and then Greta and I will get to work. 'You pick,' I reply, confident that wherever he goes, we will find him.

Once, when Greta and I were searching for a runaway, we found his corpse instead. A dead body stops smelling like a live one immediately, and as we got closer, Greta knew something wasn't right. The boy was hanging from the limb of a massive oak. I dropped to my knees, unable to breathe, wondering how much earlier I might have had to arrive to make a difference. I was so shaken that it took me a while to notice Greta's reaction: She turned in a circle, whining; then lay down with her paws over her nose. It was the first time she'd discovered something she really didn't want to find, and she didn't know what to do once she'd found it.

Fitz leads us on a circuitous trail, from the pizza place through the heart of Wexton's Main Street, behind the gas station, across a narrow stream, and down a steep incline to the edge of a natural water slide. By the time we reach him, we've walked six miles, and I'm soaked up to the knees. Greta finds him crouching behind a copse of trees whose damp leaves glitter like coins. He grabs the stuffed moose Greta likes to play catch with – a reward for making her find – and throws it for her to retrieve. 'Who's smart?' he croons. 'Who's a smart girl?'

I drive him back home, and then head to Sophie's school to pick her up. While I wait for the dismissal bell to ring, I take off the strand of pearls. There are fifty-two beads, one for each of the years my mother would have been on earth if she were still alive. I start to feed them through my fingers like the hem of a rosary, starting with prayers – that Eric and I will be happy, that Sophie will grow up safe, that Fitz will find someone to spend his life with, that my father will stay healthy. When I run out, I begin to attach memories instead, one for each pearl. There is that day she brought me to the petting zoo, a recollection I've built entirely around the photo in the album I saw several nights ago. The faintest picture of her dancing barefoot in the kitchen. The feel of her hands on my scalp as she massaged in baby shampoo.

There's a flash, too, of her crying on a bed.

I don't want that to be the last thing I see, so I rearrange the memories as if they are a deck of cards, and leave off with her dancing. I imagine each memory as the grain of sand that the pearl grew around: a hard, protective shell to keep it from drifting away.

It is Sophie who decides to teach the dog how to play board games. She's found reruns of *Mr. Ed* on television, and thinks Greta is smarter than any horse. To my surprise, though, Greta takes to the challenge. When we're playing and it's Sophie's turn, the bloodhound steps on the domed plastic of the Trouble game to jiggle the dice.

I laugh out loud, amazed. 'Dad,' I yell upstairs, where my father is folding the wash. 'Come see this.'

The telephone rings and the answering machine picks up, filling the room with Fitz's voice. 'Hey, Delia, are you there? I have to talk to you.'

I jump up and reach for the phone, but Sophie gets there more quickly and punches the disconnect button. 'You *promised,*' she says, but already her attention has moved past me to something over my shoulder.

I follow her gaze toward the red and blue lights outside. Three police cars have cordoned off the driveway; two officers are heading for the front door. Several neighbors stand on their porches, watching.

Everything inside me goes to stone. If I open that door I will hear something that I am not willing to hear – that Eric has been arrested for drunk driving, that he's been in an accident. Or something worse.

When the doorbell rings, I sit very still with my arms crossed over my chest. I do this to keep from flying apart. The bell rings again, and I hear Sophie turning the knob. 'Is your mom home, honey?' one of the policemen asks.

The officer is someone I've worked with; Greta and I helped him find a robbery suspect who ran from the scene of a crime. 'Delia,' he greets.

My voice is as hollow as the belly of a cave. 'Rob. Did something happen?'

He hesitates. 'Actually, we need to see your dad.'

Immediately, relief swims through me. If they want my father, this isn't about Eric. 'I'll get him,' I offer, but when I turn around he's already standing there.

He is holding a pair of my socks, which he folds over very neatly and hands to me. 'Gentlemen,' he says. 'What can I do for you?'

'Andrew Hopkins?' the second officer says. 'We have a warrant for your arrest as a fugitive from justice, in conjunction with the kidnapping of Bethany Matthews.'

Rob has his handcuffs out. 'You have the wrong person,' I say, incredulous. 'My father didn't kidnap anyone.'

'You have the right to remain silent,' Rob recites. 'Anything you say can and will be used against you in a court of law. You have the right to speak to an attorney, and to have an attorney present during any questioning—'

'Call Eric,' my father says. 'He'll know what to do.'

The policemen begin to push him through the doorway. I have a hundred questions: *Why are you doing this to him? How could you be so mistaken?* But the one that comes out, even as my throat is closing tight as a sealed drum, surprises me. 'Who is Bethany Matthews?'

My father does not take his gaze off me. 'You were,' he says.

Eric

I'm almost late to my meeting, thanks to the dump truck in front of me. Like a dozen other state vehicles in Wexton in March, it's piled high with snow – heaps removed from the sidewalks and the parking lot of the post office and the banks pushed up at the edges of the gas station. When there is just no room for another storm's bounty, the DOT guys shovel it up and cart it away. I used to picture them driving south toward Florida, until their load had completely melted, but the truth is, they simply take the trucks to a ravine at the edge of the Wexton Golf Course and empty them there. They make a pile of snow so formidable that even in June, when the temperature hits seventy-five degrees, you'll find kids in shorts there, sledding.

Here's the amazing thing: It doesn't flood. You'd think that a volume of precipitation that immense would, upon melting, have the capacity to sweep away a few cars or turn a state highway into a raging river, but by the time the snow is gone, the ground is mostly dry. Delia was in my science class the year we learned why: snow disappears. It's one of those solids that can turn directly into a vapor without ever going through that intermediate liquid stage – part of the process of sublimation.

Interestingly, it wasn't until I started coming to these meetings that I learned the second meaning of that word: to take a base impulse and redirect its energy to an ethically higher aim.

The truck makes a right onto an access road and I swerve around it, speeding up. I pass the deli that has changed hands

three times in the last six months, the old country store that
still sells penny candy I sometimes bring to Sophie, the poultry
farm with its enormous shrink-wrapped hay bales stacked like
giant marshmallows against the barn. Finally I swerve into the
parking lot and hurry out of my car and inside.

They haven't started yet. People are still milling around the
coffee and the cookies, talking in small pockets of forced
kinship. There are men in business suits and women in sweatpants, elderly men and boys yet to grow a full beard. Some
of them, I know, come from an hour away to be here. I approach
a group of men who are talking about how the Bruins are
doing their damnedest to lose a spot in the playoffs.

The lights flicker and, at the front of the room, the leader
asks us to take our seats. He calls the meeting to order and
gives a few opening remarks. I find myself sitting next to a
woman who is trying to unwrap a roll of LifeSavers without
making any noise. When she sees me watching, she blushes
and offers me one.

Sour apple.

I work on sucking the candy instead of biting it, but I've
never been a patient man, and even as I imagine it getting thin
as an O-ring I find myself crunching it between my teeth. Just
then there is a pause in the flow of the meeting. I raise my
hand, and the leader smiles at me.

'I'm Eric,' I say, standing. 'And I'm an alcoholic.'

When I graduated from law school, I had a choice of several
employment options. I could have joined a prestigious Boston
firm with clients who would have paid $250 an hour for my
expertise; I could have taken a position with the public
defender's office in a variety of counties and done the human-
itarian thing; I could have clerked with a State Supreme Court
justice. Instead, I chose to come back to Wexton and hang a
shingle of my own. It boiled down to this: I can't stand being
away from Delia.

Ask any guy, and he can tell you the moment he realized

that the woman standing next to him was the one he'd be spending his life with. For me, it was a little different: Delia had been standing next to me for so long, that it was her absence I couldn't handle. We went to college five hundred miles apart, and when I'd call her dorm room and get her answering machine, I'd imagine all the other guys who were at that very second trying to steal her away. I'll admit it: For as long as I could remember, I was the object of Delia's affection, and the thought of having competition for the first time in my life put me over the edge. Going out for a beer became a way to keep myself from obsessing about her, but eventually, that one beer became six or ten.

Drinking was in my blood, so to speak. We've all read the statistics about children of alcoholics. I would have sworn up and down, when I was a kid, that I'd never turn into the person my mother had been – and maybe I wouldn't have, if I hadn't missed Delia quite so much. Without her, there was a hole inside me, and I suppose that to fill it, I did what came naturally in the Talcott family.

It's funny. I started drinking heavily because I wanted to see that expression in Delia's eyes when she looked only at me, and it's the same reason I quit drinking. She isn't just the person I'm going to spend the rest of my life with, she's the reason I have one.

This afternoon I am meeting a potential client who happens to be a crow. Blackie was wounded when he fell out of a nest, or so says Martin Schnurr, who rescued him. He nursed the bird back to health, and when it kept hanging around, fed it cold coffee and bits of doughnuts on his porch in Hanover. But when the crow chased a neighbor's kids, the authorities got called. Turns out, crows are a federally regulated migratory species, and Mr. Schnurr doesn't have the state and federal license to keep him.

'He escaped from the place where the Department of Environmental Services was holding him,' Schnurr says proudly. 'Found his way back, ten whole miles.'

'As the crow flies, of course,' I say. 'So what can I do for you, Mr. Schnurr?'

'The DES is going to come after him again. I want a restraining order,' Schnurr says. 'I'm willing to go to the Supreme Court, if I have to.'

The likelihood of this case going to Washington is somewhere between nil and nevermore, but before I can explain this the door to the office bursts open and there is Delia, frantic and crying. My insides seize. I am imagining the very worst; I am thinking of Sophie. Without even a glance at the client, I pull Delia into the hall and try to shake the facts out of her.

'My father's been arrested,' she says. 'You have to go, Eric. You *have* to.'

I have no idea what Andrew might have done, and I do not ask. She believes I can fix this, and like always, that's enough to make me think I can. 'I'll take care of it,' I say, when what I really mean is: *I'll take care of you.*

We didn't play inside my house. I made sure to get up early enough so that I was always the one knocking on Delia's door, or Fitz's. On the occasions that we settled at my place, I did my best to keep everyone outside, under the backyard deck or beneath the sloping saltbox roof of our garage, and that's how I managed to keep my secret until I was nine.

That was the winter Fitz started to play league hockey, which left Delia and me alone in the afternoons. She was a latchkey kid – her father was always working at the senior center – something that never bothered her until we happened to see a TV movie about a twin who died and had his ring finger sent to his brother in a velvet box. After that, Delia didn't like being by herself. She started to come up with reasons to hang out at her house after school – something I was more than happy to do, if only to get out of my own. I always stopped off at home first, though. I had a hundred ready excuses: I wanted to drop off my backpack; I had to grab a warmer sweatshirt; I needed my mother to sign a report card. Afterward, I would head next door.

One day, as usual, Dee and I split up at the fork in the side-walk that divided my driveway from hers. 'See you in a few,' she said.

My house was quiet, which wasn't a good sign. I wandered through it, calling for my mother, until I found her passed out on the kitchen floor.

She was sprawled on her side this time, and there was a puddle of vomit under her cheek. When she blinked, the insides of her eyes were the color of cut rubies.

I picked up the bottle and poured the bourbon down the sink drain. I rolled my mother out of the way so I could clean up her mess with paper towels. Then I got behind her and braced myself hard, trying to lever her weight so I could drag her to the living room couch.

'What can I do?'

It wasn't until I heard Delia's quiet voice that I realized she had been standing in the kitchen for a while. When she spoke, she couldn't meet my eyes, and that was a good thing. She helped me get my mother to the couch, onto her side, where if she got sick again she wouldn't choke. I turned on the TV, a soap I knew she liked. 'Eric, baby, would you get me . . .' my mother slurred, but she didn't finish her sentence before she passed out again. When I looked around, Delia was gone.

Well, it didn't surprise me. It was, in fact, the reason I'd kept this secret from my two best friends; once they saw the truth, I was sure they'd turn tail and run.

I walked back to the kitchen, each foot a lead weight. Delia stood there, holding a sponge and staring down at the linoleum. 'Will carpet cleaner work even if it's not used on carpet?' she asked.

'You should go,' I told her. I looked down at the floor and pretended to be fascinated with the little blue dot pattern.

Delia came closer to me, seeing the freak I truly was. With one finger, she traced an *X* over her chest. 'I won't tell.'

One traitor tear slicked its way down my cheek; I scrubbed

it away with a fist. 'You should go,' I repeated, the last thing in the world that I wanted.

'Okay,' Delia agreed. But she didn't leave.

The Wexton police station is like a hundred other small-town law enforcement agencies: a squat cement building with a flag-pole planted out front like a giant tulip stalk; a dispatcher so infrequently bothered that she keeps a portable TV at her desk; a nursery school class mural spread along the wall, thanking the chief for keeping everyone safe. I walk inside and ask to speak to Andrew Hopkins. I tell the dispatcher I am his attorney.

A door buzzes, and a sergeant comes into the hallway. 'He's back here,' the officer says, leading me through the pretzeled hallways into the booking room. I ask to see the warrant for Andrew's arrest, pretending, like any defense attorney, to know far more than I actually do at this minute. When I scan the paper, I have to do my best to keep a straight face. *Kidnapping?*

Indicting Andrew Hopkins for kidnapping is like charging Mother Teresa with heresy. As far as I know he's never even gotten a traffic ticket, much less been implicated in criminal behavior. He's been a model father – attentive, devoted – the parent I would have killed to have when I was growing up. No wonder Delia's so rattled. To have your father accused of living a secret life, when, in fact, he's been about as public a figure as humanly possible – well, it's insane.

There are two lockups in Wexton, used mostly for DUIs who need to sleep off a bender; I have been in the one on the left myself. Andrew sits on the steel bench in the other. When he sees me, he gets to his feet.

Until this moment, I haven't really considered him to be an old man. But Andrew is almost sixty, and looks every year of it in the shallow gray light of the holding cell. His hands curl around the bars. 'Where's Delia?'

'She's fine. She's the one who came to get me.' I take a step forward and angle my shoulder, blocking our conversation until the sergeant leaves the room. 'Listen, Andrew, you have nothing to worry about. Obviously this is a case of mistaken identity. We'll contest it, set everything straight, and then maybe even get you some money for emotional damages. Now, I—'

'It's not a mistake,' he says softly.

I stare at him, speechless. He starts to repeat his confession, but I stop him before I have to hear it again. 'Don't tell me,' I interrupt. 'Don't say anything else, all right?'

Part of me has shifted into automatic defense attorney mode. If your client confesses – and they almost always want to – you put in earplugs and go about doing your job. Whatever the vice – felony or misdemeanor, murder or, *Jesus Christ*, kidnapping – you can still find a way to make a jury see the shades of gray involved.

But part of me is not an attorney, just Delia's fiancé. A man who needs to hear the truth, so that he can tell it to her. What kind of person steals a child? What would I do to the son of a bitch who took Sophie?

I look down at the arrest warrant again. 'Bethany Matthews,' I read out loud.

'That . . . used to be her name.'

He doesn't have to explain the rest; I know in that instant we're talking about Delia. That she is the little girl who was stolen a lifetime ago.

I know better than most people that a criminal isn't always a thug in a black leather jacket with a big brand on his forehead to warn us away. Criminals sit next to us on the bus. They pack our groceries and cash our paychecks for us and teach our children. They look no different from you or me. And that's why they get away with it.

The lawyer in me urges caution, remembers that there are mitigating circumstances I don't yet know. The rest of me wonders if Delia cried when he took her. If she was scared. If her mother spent years searching for her.

If she still is.

'Eric, listen . . .'

'You'll be arraigned tomorrow in New Hampshire on the fugitive charges,' I interrupt. 'But you've been indicted by an Arizona grand jury. We'll have to go there to enter a plea.'

'Eric—'

'Andrew' – I turn my back on him – 'I can't. I just can't, right now.' I am about to exit the lockup, but at the last moment, I walk back toward the cell. 'Is she yours?'

'Of course she's mine!'

'Of *course?*' I snap. 'For God's sake, Andrew, I just found out that you're a kidnapper. I have to tell *Delia* you're a kidnapper. I don't exactly think it's an unreasonable question.' I take a deep breath. 'How old was she?'

'Four.'

'And in twenty-eight years you never told her?'

'She loves me.' Andrew looks down at the floor. 'Would you risk losing that?'

Without answering, I turn and walk away.

When I was eleven, I realized that Delia Hopkins was female. She wasn't like ordinary girls: she didn't have the dreamy, loopy handwriting that reminded us of soap bubbles lined up in a row; she didn't giggle behind her hand in a way that made us wonder what we'd done wrong; she didn't come to school with neat braids twisted like French crullers. Instead, she spoke to frogs. She could make a slap shot from the blue line. She was the first one to cut her palm with Fitz's Swiss army knife when we three made a blood vow, and she didn't even flinch.

The summer after fifth grade, everything changed. Without even trying, I smelled Delia's hair when she sat near me. I noticed how her brown summer skin stretched tight over the muscles of her shoulders. I watched her tilt her face to the sun and felt an answer in my own body.

I kept these thoughts a secret through the first half of sixth grade, until Valentine's Day. It was the first time in school that we weren't forced to bring in a card for everyone in the class, including the kid who picked his nose and the Missing

Link, who had so much hair on her arms and back you could practically braid it. Girls flitted around the cafeteria like butterflies, alighting long enough to plant kisses on the bright cheeks of boys they liked. When it happened, you'd pretend to be disgusted, but there would be a coal burning inside you.

Fitz got a card from Abigail Lewis, who had just gotten glow-in-the-dark braces and, it was rumored, invited select boys into the custodian's closet to watch them light up. In my own back pocket was a folded pink heart that I'd glued to a square of red construction paper. *When I'm with you, bells go off in my head,* I had written, and then added: *Like a moving truck that's backing up.*

I was going to give it to Delia, but a thousand times that day, the moment hadn't been right – Fitz was with us, or she was too busy rummaging in her locker, or the teacher came by before I could pass it across the aisle. I slipped it out of my pocket just in time to have Fitz grab it out of my hand. 'You got a card, too, didn't you?' He read it aloud, and he and Delia started to laugh.

Angry, I snatched it back. 'I didn't get it from someone, you jerk. I'm *giving* it.' And because Delia was still sort of laughing, I marched right past her and up to the first girl I saw, Itzy Fisher, carrying a hot lunch tray. 'Here,' I said, and I shoved the card between her napkin and her slab of pizza.

There was absolutely nothing special about Itzy Fisher. She had long frizzy hair that nearly touched her behind, and she wore gold-rimmed glasses that sometimes caught the light in class and made little reflections dance on the blackboard. I had barely said three words to her all year.

'Itzy Fisher?' Delia accused when I sat back down. 'You like *her?*' And then she got up and ran out of the cafeteria.

Groaning, I flopped my head down on my arms. 'I didn't make that card for Itzy. It was for Delia.'

'*Delia?*' Fitz said.

'You wouldn't understand.'

Fitz stared right at me. 'What makes you think that?'

In the thousands of times I have replayed this moment over the years, I realize that what happened next could have gone a different way. That had Fitz been less of a best friend, or more competitive, or even more honest with himself, my life might have turned out very different. But instead, he asked me for a dollar.

'Why?'

'Because she's pissed at you,' he said, as I fished into my lunch money. 'And I can fix that.'

He took a Sharpie from his binder and wrote something across George Washington's face. Then he creased the bill the long way. He brought up the bottom edge and then the halves, turned it over, and tucked in both sides. A few more maneuvers and then he handed me a dollar folded into the shape of a heart.

When I found Delia, she was sitting underneath the water fountain near the gym. I handed her Fitz's heart. I watched her open it, read the message along with her: *If all I could ever have is you, I'd be a billionaire.*

'Itzy might get jealous,' Delia said.

'Itzy and I broke up.'

She burst out laughing. 'That's the shortest relationship in history.'

I glanced over at her. 'You're not still mad at me, are you?'

'That depends. Did you write this?'

'Yes,' I lied.

'Can I keep the dollar?'

I blinked. 'I guess.'

'Then no,' she said. 'I'm not mad.'

I waited for years to see Delia spend that dollar on something – every time she pulled out money to buy candy or ice cream or a Coke, I'd scan it for Fitz's words. But as far as I know she never spent it. As far as I know, she has it, still.

When I go into Andrew's house, it's quiet. I call for Delia, but there's no answer. Wandering around, I check the bathroom and the living room and the kitchen, and then I hear noise coming from upstairs. The door to Sophie's room is closed; when I open it she is on the floor, playing with the Crime Scene Dollhouse. Delia and I got to calling it that when Sophie would leave the rooms with the contents overturned, a Barbie or two spread-eagled on the floor of the kitchen or bathroom. 'Daddy,' she says, 'did you bring Grandpa home?'

'I'm working on it,' I tell her, ruffling her hair. 'Where's Mommy?'

'Out back with Greta.' Sophie holds a Ken doll up to the front door. *'Open up. It's the police,'* she says.

When I look at Sophie, I see Delia. Not just in the physical features – Delia's dark hair and rosy cheeks are duplicated in our daughter – but their expressions are identical. Like how a smile unfurls across both their faces, a sail caught in a rip of wind. And the habit they have of separating the food on their plates into similar colors. Or the way, when they look at me, I so badly want to be who they see.

I watch Sophie for another moment, thinking about what I would do if someone took her away from me, how I'd upend the earth to find her. And then I hesitate, and wonder what might make me be the one to run away with her in tow.

Downstairs, I find Delia deep in thought on the outside deck. Her legs are propped up on Greta, a lightly snoring ottoman. When she sees me she startles. 'Did you—'

'I can't get him out until the arraignment tomorrow.'

'He has to spend the night at the police station?'

I weigh the cost of admitting that, actually, her father will spend the night in the Grafton County Jail, and decide against it. 'First thing in the morning, we can go to the courthouse.'

She glances up at me. 'But they'll let him go, won't they? They're looking for someone named Bethany Matthews. That's not me. That was never me. And I wasn't kidnapped. Don't you think I'd remember something like that?'

Taking a deep breath, I ask, 'Do you remember your mother dying?'

'Eric, I was practically a baby—'

'Do you remember it?'

She shakes her head.

'Your father told you your mother was dead, Delia,' I say bluntly. 'And then he brought you to New Hampshire.'

Her chin comes up. 'You're lying.'

'No, Dee. *He* was.'

Just then Fitz bursts onto the deck. 'Why aren't you answering the phone? I've been trying to get in touch with you for an hour!'

'I've been a little busy trying to get my father out of police custody.'

'You found out,' Fitz says, his jaw dropping. 'About the kidnapping.'

'How the hell do *you* know about it?' I ask.

Fitz sits down across from Delia. 'That's why I've been trying to call you. You remember how we were talking about past lives the other day? Well, I started to think about how people reinvent themselves all the time. And that maybe there was a more logical explanation to the whole lemon tree memory than the fact that you used to be a citrus farmer in eighteenth-century Tuscany. So I jumped online and Googled your name. Come on inside; I'll show you.'

We follow Fitz to Delia's computer, buried under topographical maps of New Hampshire and Vermont and catalogs from K-9 supply companies. Fitz starts to type, and a minute later, a screen is filled with stripes of search results. The first few links are *Gazette* stories about Delia and Greta, making a missing-person rescue. But Fitz clicks on a different link, and a page from the *St. Louis Post-Dispatch* fills the screen. 'CORDELIA LYNN HOPKINS,' it reads. '*Daughter of Margaret Ketcham Hopkins and the late Andrew Hopkins, was born in Maryland Heights on March 16, 1973 . . .*'

'That's my birthday,' Delia says.

'*. . . in Clarkton and died March 8, 1977, at the age of four as a result of complications from an automobile accident that also* *claimed the life of her father. Survivors include her mother; her grandparents, Joe and Aleda Ketcham; and a brother, Lloyd. Funeral services will be conducted at 11 AM on Saturday, at the Malden Baptist Church with Reverend Thomas Monroe officiating. Interment will follow at Memorial Park Cemetery in Malden.'*

'She had the same name, the same birthday. Her father died in the same car crash. And the accident happened the same year that you showed up with your father in Wexton.'

'Type in Bethany Matthews,' I tell Fitz.

The screen glows green with a new list of articles, all from the *Arizona Republic.* '*CHILD ABDUCTED DURING CUSTODY VISIT. MOTHER VOWS TO FIND MISSING DAUGHTER. NO NEW LEADS IN SCOTTSDALE KIDNAPPING CASE.*' Fitz clicks on one link.

June 20, 1977 – Investigators continue to search for clues in the disappearance of Bethany Matthews, 4, of Scottsdale, who was last seen in the company of her father, Charles Matthews, 33, during a routine custody visit. Police in Albuquerque, acting on a tip, raided a hotel room that had been paid for with Mr. Matthews's credit card, but turned up no positive results. Meanwhile, the girl's mother, Elise Matthews, has not given up hope that her daughter will be found and returned safely. 'There is nothing in this world,' Mrs. Matthews vowed yesterday at a televised press conference, 'that can keep me away from her.'

Mr. and Mrs. Matthews divorced in March, and shared custody. Matthews was last seen picking up his daughter from the home of his ex-wife at 9 AM on Saturday, where he indicated that he would return before 6 PM on Sunday. When he didn't bring Bethany back, and Mrs. Matthews was unable to reach him via telephone, she involved the police. An initial search of Mr Matthews's apartment suggested that the subject had permanently vacated the premises.

Volunteers who would like to contribute time or materials

to the search effort should report to the Saguaro High School
gymnasium. Any tips regarding the whereabouts of Bethany
Matthews or Charles Matthews should be directed to the
Scottsdale police, at 555-3333.

Delia puts her hand over Fitz's, where it rests on the mouse.
She clicks a single word at the end of the article: *photo*. Twin
head shots fill the computer screen – one of a little girl who
looks frighteningly like Sophie; the other of a younger, grinning Andrew Hopkins.

A minute later she runs out the door and into the woods,
Greta bounding off at her heels. We both know enough to let
her go.

'This is all my fault,' Fitz says.

'I think Andrew might be a little more to blame.'

He shakes his head. 'I didn't know her name . . . her real
name. After I saw the obituary on Cordelia Hopkins, I started
thinking of who might steal an identity, and why. Delia
mentioned some weird memory about a lemon tree . . . so I
narrowed down my search by figuring out where they'd grow.'
Fitz starts counting off on his fingers. 'Florida. Southern
California. Arizona. Only one of them had a well-publicized
kidnapping case in 1977. I called the number in the article for
the Scottsdale Police, and asked about Bethany Matthews. It
took a while to find someone who knew what I was talking
about – all of the officers who'd worked on the case had retired.
They asked me where I was calling from.'

'And you *told* them?'

Fitz grimaces. 'I had to say I was a journalist, didn't I? The
thing is, Eric, I never told them Delia's new name.' He gets
up from the chair and faces the window, scanning the woods
as if he might be able to see her. 'My guess is that someone
from Scottsdale heard the words *New Hampshire Gazette,* did
a little digging on the Internet. Andrew's a town councilman,
you know how many times his picture's been in the paper?
Not to mention *Delia's?*'

'He hid in plain sight,' I murmur. It seems remarkably fast for a law enforcement agency to have connected the dots – and yet, I know that it's an illusion. A warrant for Andrew's arrest has been sworn out for nearly thirty years; the police just didn't know where he was so they could serve it.

Fitz turns away, his hands in his pockets. 'You have to go find her.'

'*You* go. *You're* the one who brought in the cops.'

'I know,' Fitz admits. 'But I'm not the one she wants.'

By the time the end of sixth grade rolled around, boys had mustered up the nerve to ask girls out. This meant absolutely nothing, except that the duo would sit next to each other at lunch in the cafeteria, and occasionally talk on the phone. By this criterion, Delia and I were practically married – we spent far more time together than any couple in the Wexton Middle School – that is, until Fitz officially asked Delia to go out with him.

I knew it meant nothing – rumors about who liked whom flew around like gypsy moths in August – but all the same, I spent too much time wishing that I was Fitz, holding on to Delia's hand when we balanced on the railroad tracks or lying next to her on the damp grass when we tried to look at the solar eclipse through a pinhole in a shoebox. After a while, Fitz stopped calling me, and then Delia; and I tried to convince myself that I'd never needed either of them.

I went stag to the end-of-school dance. I was listening to the boasts of Donnie DeMaurio, a twelve-year-old who had a mustache and a pack of bootleg cigarettes, when Delia appeared, crying. 'Fitz broke up with me,' she said.

I couldn't imagine why; later he told me the truth. *I'd rather have both of you,* he said, in that easy way of his, *than just one.* But at that moment, Fitz was absent and Delia was so close that the hair on my arms was reaching toward the heat of her. 'I guess I could go out with you,' I said.

'You *guess* you could go out with me?' she repeated. 'Gee, thanks for making the sacrifice. Don't do me any favors.'

I knew her well enough to understand that when Delia pushed you away, it was her way of making sure she didn't get shoved first. I grabbed her arm before she could run away. 'I would very much like to go out with you,' I said more carefully. 'Is that better?'

'Maybe.'

'So what do we do?' I asked.

She chewed her bottom lip. 'We could dance. If you want.'

I had never danced with a girl before, and even though Delia and I had grown up skinny-dipping in ponds and sleeping so close in a pitched tent that we had to share each other's air, it felt unreasonably new. My hands skimmed over Delia's spine to settle on her hips. She smelled like peaches, and beneath her knit dress I could feel the thin elastic of her underwear.

She talked for both of us. She talked about how, on the phone one night, Fitz had asked her out, and how she didn't know whether to say yes or no and yes had just slipped out. She talked about how she fully intended to get back her Dwight Evans baseball card, which she had given to Fitz as a way of saying she really liked him.

When the song ended, Delia didn't pull away. She stayed there, maybe even moved a tiny bit closer. 'You want to keep talking?' I asked.

'No,' she said, smiling into my eyes. 'I think I'm done.'

When I find her, she is ten feet above my head, in the scarred elbow of an oak tree. Greta sits at the bottom, whining. 'Hey,' I say, pushing aside some of the smaller branches and leaves. 'You okay?'

Above me, the stars are coming out, a bright-eyed audience. 'What if this was all my fault?' Delia asks.

'How could it be?' I reply. 'You don't even remember it happening.'

'Maybe I do and I've blocked it out. Maybe my father hid that from me, too.'

I hesitate. 'I'm sure he's got an explanation for what happened.'

Delia drops down from the tree, landing like a cat beside me. 'Then why didn't he give it to me?' she says, her voice striped with scars. 'He had twenty-eight years. Don't you think that's long enough to mention, maybe, that Delia Hopkins is a dead girl from Missouri? You know, "Delia, honey, can you pass the Cheerios, and did I ever tell you that when you were four I stole you away from your mother?"' Suddenly, Delia's face goes white. 'Eric,' she asks, 'do you think I still *have* a mother?'

'I don't know,' I admit. 'We'll find out once we get to Arizona.'

'Arizona?'

'After your father is arraigned on fugitive charges in New Hampshire, he'll be extradited to Arizona. That's where the . . . crime allegedly occurred. If it goes to trial, you'll probably be called as a witness.'

She seems horrified by this. 'What if I don't want to be one?'

'You may not have that choice,' I admit.

She takes a step closer to me, and I fold my arms around her. 'What if I wasn't meant to grow up here . . . like this?' she says, her voice muffled against my shirt. 'What if there was a different cosmic plan for Bethany Matthews?'

'What if there was a different cosmic plan for Delia Hopkins, one that got ruined because of a car crash?' I search my mind frantically for the right thing to say. I try to think of Fitz, of what he would tell me to tell her. 'You could have been Bethany Matthews, Delia Hopkins, Cleopatra – it wouldn't matter. And if you'd grown up with a thousand lemon trees in the middle of the desert, with a cactus instead of a Christmas tree and a pet armadillo . . . well, then, I would have gone to law school at Arizona State, I guess. I would have defended illegal aliens crossing the border. But we still would have wound up together, Dee. No matter what kind of life I had, you'd be at the end of it.'

She smiles, just a little. 'I'm pretty sure I was never Cleopatra.'

I drop a kiss on her forehead. 'Well,' I reply. 'That's a start.'

We were fifteen and drunk and in the bell tower of Baker Library at Dartmouth, watching a meteor shower that, the newscasters said, would only be this vivid once in our lifetimes, although that was hard to believe, feeling as we did that we'd live forever.

We played games to pass the time: I Spy, and Twenty Questions. Anyone who didn't get the answer had to chug. By the time our corner of the world turned to face the meteor shower, Fitz was snoring with his mouth open and Delia was having trouble zipping up her sweatshirt. 'Here,' I said, and I did it for her, just as a fireball chased the moon across the sky.

Delia watched the midnight show, and I watched her. Sometimes she smiled, or laughed out loud; mostly her mouth just made a wondrous *O* as the night changed before her eyes. When some of the activity died down, I leaned forward until our lips touched.

She drew back immediately, stared hard at me. Then she wrapped her arms around my neck and kissed me back.

I remember that we didn't really know what we were doing, that I felt two sizes too big for my skin, that my heart was beating so hard it moved the denim of my shirt. I remember that for one moment, I believed I was hitchhiking on one of those comets, falling so fast that I'd surely burn away before I ever hit the ground.

At nine o'clock the next morning, Delia and I take a seat close to the defense table at the Wexton District Court. It is a rotating habitat for public defenders and hired guns like myself, a new one warming the chair each time the judge calls for a new case. Arraignments are a rubber-stamp process, the prosecutor riffling through a big box of files as defendant after defendant is brought in. We watch a woman get arraigned for stealing a toaster oven from Kmart, a man brought in for violating a restraining order. A third defendant, one I recognize as a hot dog stand vendor in town, has been arrested for the felonious sexual assault of a minor.

It reminds me that there are people in this world who have done worse things than Andrew Hopkins.

'Do you know the prosecutor?' Delia whispers.

Ned Floritz was the leader of my AA meeting yesterday, but recovering alcoholics are always in the business of keeping one another's secrets. 'I've seen him around,' I say.

When our case is called, Andrew is brought in wearing a bright orange jumpsuit that says GRAFTON COUNTY DEPARTMENT OF CORRECTIONS on the back. His hands and legs are shackled.

Beside me, Delia gasps; her father's incarceration is, after all, still new to her. I stand up and button my jacket, carry my briefcase down to the defense table. Andrew's eyes roam the courtroom. 'Delia!' he yells out, and she stands up.

'Sir,' the bailiff says, 'please face front.'

I can feel sweat breaking out on my forehead. I have been in court before, but not for a case of this magnitude. Not for a case where I have a personal stake in the outcome.

Beside me, Andrew touches my arm. 'Make them take the chains off. I don't want her to see me like this.'

'It's inmate policy in the courtroom,' I answer. 'I can't do anything about it.'

The judge is a woman relatively new to the bench. She comes from a public defender's background, which is a plus for Andrew, but she is also the mother of three small children. 'I have before me a complaint alleging that you are a fugitive from justice with kidnapping contrary to the laws of Arizona. I see that you have an attorney with you, so I'll address my remarks to him. You have two options today. One is to waive extradition and go to Arizona to meet the charge. The other option is to contest extradition and require the State to seek a Governor's Warrant.'

'My client chooses to waive extradition, Your Honor,' I say. 'He's looking forward to dealing with this charge quickly.'

The judge nods. 'Then bail won't be an issue. I assume you're going to allow us to incarcerate Mr. Hopkins until he can be transferred to Arizona.'

'Actually, Judge, we'd like bail to be set,' I say.

The prosecutor is out of his seat like a shot. 'Absolutely not, Your Honor!'

The judge turns toward him. 'Mr. Floritz? Is there something you'd like to add?'

'Your Honor, the two primary considerations for bail are the safety of the community and risk of flight. The defendant is just about the biggest flight risk you could ask for – look at what already happened.'

'Allegedly happened,' I interject. 'Mr. Hopkins is a valuable member of the Wexton community. He has served for five years as a town councilman. He's almost single-handedly responsible for the creation of the current senior center, and he has been nothing less than an exemplary parent and grandparent. This isn't a man who's a menace to society, Your Honor. I urge the Court to consider the admirable citizen he has been before rushing to any hasty judgment.'

Too late, I realize what I've done wrong. You never, never, ever infer that a judge might be hasty in his or her decision-making; it is like pointing out to a wolf that it has bad breath while it is considering ripping out your carotid. The judge looks coolly at me. 'I believe that I have more than adequate information to make a legitimate ruling here . . . swift though it may be, Counselor. I'm setting a one-million-dollar cash-only bail.' She bangs her gavel. 'Next case?'

The bailiffs haul Andrew out of the courtroom before he even has a chance to ask me what happens next. The seniors erupt in a slow-motion flurry of activity, crying foul and then being shuffled by another bailiff into the hallway. The prosecutor gets up from his seat and walks toward me. 'Eric,' he says, 'you sure you're ready to get involved in something like this?'

He isn't questioning my legal abilities but my tolerance for stress. Although he's been dry for twenty years, I'm a neophyte. I give him a tight smile. 'I've got it under control,' I lie. Recovering alcoholics are good at that, too.

I relinquish my table to a public defender who is getting ready for the next arraignment. I'm not looking forward to Delia's disappointment, now that she knows Andrew will have to stay overnight in jail again, that I have already failed. Resigned, I turn to the spot where we were sitting, but she's disappeared.

Six years ago I drove my car off the road while I was trying to open a bottle of Stoli and steer with my knees. By some miracle the only casualty was a sugar maple. I walked to a bar, where I had to consume a few drinks before I felt calm enough to call Delia and tell her what had happened. The next week, I found myself waking up in places I had no recollection of going to: the living room of a fraternity on the Dartmouth campus; the kitchen of a Chinese restaurant; the cement divider of the Wilder Dam. It was after one of these benders that I found myself in the backyard at Delia and Andrew's house, asleep in their hammock. What woke me was the sound of crying; Delia was sitting on the ground beside me, shredding pieces of grass with her hands. 'I'm pregnant,' she said.

My head was swimming underwater, my tongue was as thick as a mossy field, but immediately, I thought: *She's mine, now*. I stumbled out of the hammock and onto one knee. I tugged the ponytail elastic out of Delia's hair and doubled it up, then reached for her hand. 'Delia Hopkins,' I said, 'will you marry me?' I slid the makeshift ring onto her finger, and turned up the wattage on my smile.

When she didn't answer – just curled up her knees and buried her head against them – I began to feel the butterfly beat of panic in the pit of my stomach. 'Delia,' I said, swallowing. 'Is it the baby? Do you want to . . . to get rid of it?' The thought of a part of me taking root in her was miraculous to me, like finding an orchid growing in the cracks of a broken tenement sidewalk. But I was willing to give that up in return for Delia. I would do anything for her.

When she looked at me, there was nothing in her eyes, as if she'd pulled free from her life the strand that was me. 'I want the baby, Eric,' she said. 'But I don't want you.'

Delia had complained about my drinking before, but since she hardly drank herself, it seemed impossible for her to be able to know what exactly constituted too much. She claimed she didn't like the smell of alcohol, but I thought it was loss of control she couldn't handle; and that seemed to be her hang-up, not mine. Sometimes she got angry enough to take a real stand, but it was a vicious cycle: Every time she swore she'd leave me, it would only send me spiraling down into a bottle, and eventually she'd come help me crawl back out to consciousness, swearing up one side and down another that it would never happen again, when we both knew that it would.

This time, though, she wasn't leaving on her own behalf, but someone else's.

For a long time after she walked away, I sat on the lawn in her backyard, balancing the truth between my shoulders like Atlas's weight. When I finally headed home, I looked up the information for Alcoholics Anonymous, and went to a meeting that night. It took me some time, but eventually I realized why Delia said no to my proposal. I had asked her to spend the wrong life with me, but at any moment, a person might start over from scratch.

I would like to take the time to find Delia, but right now I can't. I make one phone call: to the prosecutors in Arizona. The canned voice I reach informs me that the Maricopa County Attorney's office hours are from nine A.M. to five P.M. I glance at my watch, and realize that in Arizona it's only seven in the morning. I leave a message, informing whoever needs to know that I am representing Andrew Hopkins, that he has waived extradition here in New Hampshire district court in return, we hope, for a speedy transport.

Then I head downstairs to the sheriff's office, where Andrew is temporarily occupying a six-foot-square space. 'I need to see Delia,' he says.

'That's not an option right now.'

'You don't understand—'

'You know, Andrew, as the parent of a four-year-old . . . I honestly don't.'

This brings back yesterday's conversation, and his confession. Andrew, wisely, changes the subject. 'When do we leave for Arizona?'

'It's their call. It could be tomorrow; it could be a month from now.'

'And in the meantime?'

'You get luxurious accommodations provided by the State of New Hampshire. And you get to meet with me, so we can figure out what we're going to do in Phoenix. Right now, I have no idea what evidence the prosecution has. Until I can put together the pieces, we'll just enter a not guilty plea and figure out the rest later.'

'But,' Andrew says, 'what if I want to plead guilty?'

In the history of my career, I have met only one defendant who didn't at least want to tell his side of the story. The man was seventy, and had served thirty years in the state penitentiary. He held up a bank fifteen minutes after his release, then explained to the teller that he'd be waiting out front on the curb for the police. All he'd wanted was to get back to an environment he understood, which is what makes Andrew's comments even stranger. For all intents and purposes, a man who once resorted to crime in order to have a life with his daughter should want to continue to spend it in her company.

'Once you enter a guilty plea, Andrew, it's over. You can always switch your plea from "not guilty" to "guilty," but you can't go the other way around. And after twenty-eight years, their evidence has to be sketchy; their witnesses might not even be alive anymore – there's a good chance you'll be acquitted.'

Andrew looks at me. 'Eric, are you my lawyer?'

I am completely unequipped to be Andrew's attorney; I don't have the experience or the wits or the confidence. But I think of Delia, begging; believing that someone who was once a failure might still be a candidate for a hero. 'Yes,' I say.

'Then don't you have to do what I ask?'

I don't answer that.

'I knew what I was doing twenty-eight years ago, Eric. And I know what I'm doing now.' He exhales heavily. 'Plead guilty.'

I stare at him. 'Did you bother to think how this might affect Delia?'

Andrew looks over my shoulder at something for a long moment. 'That's all I ever think about,' he replies.

Once, when we were seventeen, Delia cheated on me. I was supposed to meet her at a bend in the Connecticut River where we liked to go swimming – there was a swatch of cattails and reeds that hid you from the eyes of anyone on the road, should you feel like making out with your girlfriend. I rode my bike down there, a half hour late, and heard Delia talking to Fitz.

I couldn't see them through the grasses, but they were arguing about the origin of the O. Henry bar. 'It's named after Hank Aaron,' she insisted. 'That's what everyone used to say when he hit another home run.'

'Wrong. It's the writer,' Fitz said.

'No one names a candy bar after a writer. They're all base-ball players. O. Henry, Baby Ruth . . .'

'*That* was named after Grover Cleveland's daughter.'

I heard a shriek. 'Fitz, don't . . . don't you dare . . .' A splash, as he tossed her into the river and fell in himself. I pushed through the screen of reeds to jump in along with them. But when I had almost reached the bank, I saw Fitz and Delia in the water, wrapped around each other and kissing.

I don't know who started it, but I do know that Delia was

the one who stopped. She pushed Fitz away and ran out to grab her towel, then stood shivering three feet away from my hiding spot. 'Delia,' Fitz said, coming out of the river, too. 'Wait.'

I didn't want to stay and listen to what she had to say; I was afraid to hear it. So I retreated in silence, and then ran back to my bike. I rode home in record time, and I spent the rest of the afternoon in my room with the lights off, lying on my bed and pretending that I hadn't spotted what I had.

Delia never confessed to kissing Fitz, and I didn't bring it up. In fact, I never mentioned it to anyone. But a witness is defined through what he sees, not what he says. And just because you keep something a secret doesn't mean it never happened, no matter how much you want that to be true.

I find Delia watching a flock of kids alighting on a jungle gym. 'You know how I hate to swing?' she says.

'Yeah,' I say, wondering where this is going.

'Do you know why?'

Delia broke her arm once on a swing set when she was eight; I always figured it had something to do with that. But when I tell her so, she shakes her head. 'It's that moment when you've gone too high, and the chains go slack for a half-second,' Delia says. 'I was always afraid I was going to fall.'

'And then you did,' I point out.

'My father promised he'd catch me if that happened,' she says. 'And because I was a kid, I actually believed him. But he couldn't be there all the time, no matter what he'd said.' She watches a little girl hide under the long silver tongue of the sliding pond. 'You didn't tell me he was in jail.'

'It's going to get worse before it gets better, Dee.'

She pushes away from the fence. 'Can I go talk to him, now?'

'No,' I say gently. 'You can't.'

She is unraveling before me. 'Eric, I don't know who I am,' she says through tears. 'All I know is that I'm not the person

I was yesterday. I don't know if I've got a mother somewhere. I don't know if I was being hurt in some way I don't even want to think about. I don't know why he thought that what he did would hurt me any less. Why would he lie to me, unless he wasn't so sure I'd forgive him?' She shakes her head. 'I don't know if I can trust him now. I don't know if I ever will, again. But I also don't . . . I don't know who else I'm supposed to ask for the answers.'

'Sweetheart—'

'Nobody just steals a child,' she interrupts. 'So what godawful thing happened that I can't remember?'

I settle my hands on her shoulders; I can feel everything inside her spinning like a top. 'I can't tell you that yet,' I say, 'but neither can your father. Legally, I'm the only one who's allowed to talk to him.'

Delia lifts her face, fierce. 'Then you go ask him what happened.'

Although it's unseasonably warm for March, she's shivering. I take off my jacket and drape it over her. 'I can't. I'm his attorney,' I say. 'This is exactly why I think someone else should—'

'Should represent him?' Delia asks. 'Someone who only knows my father because he's a name on a manila folder? Someone who could care less whether he gets convicted or acquitted, because it's all just in a day's work?'

On the playground, a teacher calls out to the class. She unravels a white rope with little interval loops for each child to grab hold of, a miniature chain gang taking the safest measures back to their school. 'He intends to plead guilty,' I say uncomfortably.

'What will that do?'

'Get him sent directly to jail.'

Delia looks up, stunned. 'Why would you want *that?*'

'I wouldn't. I told him to take a chance on a trial, but it's not what he wants.'

'What about what *I* want?'

If I show up in court in Arizona at Andrew's side, the judge will ask *me* how we plead, not Andrew. To say 'not guilty' means subverting my client's request. It means Andrew could fire me and wind up with a lawyer who'd gladly enter a guilty plea, because it is the path of least resistance.

To say 'not guilty' means a big, difficult trial, in which Delia will serve as a material witness.

As the only other person who was with Andrew at the time of the kidnapping, she will be courted by the prosecution as well as the defense. And in spite of the fact that she is my fiancée, I can be sent to jail for telling her any details about her father's case. It is a felony to consciously or unconsciously influence what a witness says in court.

But is it a crime for her to influence what *I* say?

I smooth my hand over her hair. 'Okay,' I promise. 'Not guilty.'

Andrew

Does it really matter why I did it?

By now you've already formed your own impression. You believe that an act committed a lifetime ago defines a man, or you believe that a person's past has nothing to do with his future. You think I am either a hero, or a monster. Maybe knowing more about the circumstances will make you think differently about me, but it won't change what happened twenty-eight years ago.

There have been nightmares. Sometimes I have picked up the phone and heard Elise's voice in the pause before the telemarketer's brain kicks in. Whenever I pass a police car, I sweat. I was thrown into a panic when one of the seniors submitted my name for election to the Wexton Town Council, until I realized that the easiest place to take cover is in plain sight; no one ever looks twice at someone who acts like he has nothing to hide.

Believe what you want, but be prepared to answer this question: In my shoes, how do you know you wouldn't have done the same thing?

Believe it or not, there is a relief to finally getting caught. The moment I gave up my clothes for a baggy orange jumpsuit I also peeled off the skin of the person I've pretended to be. In a strange way, I belong here more than I did out there. Like me, everyone in jail has been living a lie.

For twenty-three hours a day, I stay in my cell. That last hour, I am granted a shower and a turn around the exercise yard, where I do my best to breathe in deep and get the smell of jail out of my nostrils.

I have asked twice now to call you; I thought that everyone was given a phone call upon arrival, but it turns out that's only true on television. I wait for Eric, but he hasn't come yet either. I imagine there are all sorts of knots made out of red tape he has to untangle before we are shipped off to Arizona.

The last time I was there, it was a state unlike anything in the Northeast. A place where the soil was the color of blood, where snow was a fantasy, where the plants had skeletons. Just falling off the abrupt edge of Scottsdale could land you in towns that consisted of a handful of people and a gas station; back then the West was still a haven for lawless rebels. I hear those towns are now the enclaves of the rich, who have built multimillion-dollar houses into the inhospitable red cliffs, but I imagine the part of Phoenix I will be seeing is still peopled with lawless rebels, the ones who have been arrested.

It never gets dark in jail, and it never gets quiet. The sound is a symphony: the wheezing snore of the guy one block down; the creak of a door being opened. Rain on the roof and the viper hiss of the radiator. The ping-ping-ping-ping of metal on metal as a corrections officer walks down the corridor side by side with his attitude, hitting his keys against the bars of a cell to wake up all the nearby occupants.

The only way I am able to stand it is to think about you. This time, the memory that spreads across my mind is of the autumn weekend we drove to Killington and took a chairlift up to the top. It was October, and you were only five. When we got to the peak, the ring of Killington's mountains rose to our left and right; the valley below was a lavish tapestry of reds and golds and emeralds, studded with church spires that looked like fallen stars caught in the folds of the landscape. The Ottauquechee River scalloped a blue seam down the center, and the air already smelled of snow.

It looked just about as different from Arizona as humanly possible. And I began to understand what New Englanders say, what I had learned long before I took refuge in New Hampshire: You never forget your first fall.

When you're a parent you find yourself looking at the unknown that is your child, trying to find a piece of yourself inside her, because sometimes that is what it takes to stake a claim. I remember watching you making muddy mixtures in the sandbox, and wondering if a love of chemistry was something you might be born with. I remember listening to your tearful recollection of the monster in your nightmare, trying to see whether it resembled me.

What I saw most in you, though, was your mother.

You had an uncanny ability to find things: the diamond earring Eric's mother lost somewhere in her driveway; the old stash of comic books hidden behind a loose panel of wood in the basement; a buffalo-head nickel caught between the cracks of the sidewalk. Unlike Elise, who could discover parts of a person they didn't even know were absent, you specialized in the tangible, but that, I feared, was only a matter of time.

When you were seven, you found a chickadee's egg that had fallen out of a nest. The egg was cracked and the bird, still embryonic and developing, was pink-skinned and pale, oddly humanistic. You and I lined a matchbox with tissues and held a private burial. 'Wilbur,' you intoned, 'lived a short life, full of danger.'

Not unlike your own.

You cried for a week over that damn bird – the first time that finding something, for you, became equated to loss. That was when I realized that I could take you to the far ends of the earth, but I couldn't keep your mother from surfacing. Elise was in your blood; Elise was printed upon you. And, like Elise, I was terrified that if you grew up able to find whatever it was that hollowed out a person's heart, you would wind up feeling just as empty as she had.

God forbid, maybe you'd try to fill yourself the same way.

I made a few phone calls and took you to meet a policeman

who happened to be the son of one of the seniors who played mah-jongg every Tuesday at the center. Art was a state trooper who had a German shepherd named Jerry Lee, known for his search-and-rescue ability. He let you play hide and seek with Jerry Lee, who always won. By the time we drove home that day, you knew what you wanted to be when you grew up.

There is a fine line between seeing something that's lost as missing, and seeing it as something that might be found. The way I figured, it was my job to make sure that you were focused correctly. In high school, I got you an apprenticeship with a local vet. In college, you adopted a hound from a shelter, and trained it for search and rescue. As a senior, you made your first big rescue: a little boy who had wandered off at a county fair. You began to get a reputation for hard work and diligence; you were called in to work with K-9 units all over New Hampshire and Vermont. I have heard you tell the story of how you got started in this business over and over to reporters and to grateful victims; you always say it began when you found a bird.

I'm not even sure you remember anymore that it was dead.

Sometimes parents don't find what they're looking for in their child, so they plant seeds for what they'd like to grow there instead. I've witnessed this with the former hockey player who takes his son out to skate before he can even walk. Or in the mother who gave up her ballet dreams when she married, but now scrapes her daughter's hair into a bun and watches from the wings of the stage. We are not, as you'd expect, orchestrating their lives; we are not even trying for a second chance. We're hoping that if this one thing takes root, it might take up enough light and space to keep something else from developing in our children: the disappointment we've already lived.

Last night, before my arraignment, I started shaking. Not shivering, but the palsied kind of seizure that even made the guards bring me to the infirmary for a free nurse's check, not that she could find anything wrong. It was the sort of tremor that astronauts get when they come back to earth, that a hiker suffers after coming back down from the crest of Kilimanjaro – a bone-deep chill that has nothing to do with cold and everything with being moved from one world to another. It continued the whole time the guards snapped on handcuffs and led me underground to the court building next door; it continued while I waited in the sheriff's department cell there; it continued until the moment I saw you in the courtroom and called your name.

You couldn't look me in the eye, and that was the first time I ever had doubts about what I did.

'Hey,' my cellmate says. 'You gonna eat your bread?'

A twenty-year-old awaiting trial for armed robbery, my cellmate's name is Monteverde Jones. I toss him my bread, which is stale enough to be classified as a weapon. We are fed in our cells, given an unappetizing array of blots on a plastic tray that blend together like Venn diagrams.

Because Monte has been here longer than I have, he gets to eat on the bunk. Me, I have to sit on the toilet or the floor. Everything is based on hierarchy and privilege; in this, jail's a lot like the real world. 'So,' he says, 'what do you do on the outside?'

I look up over my fork. 'I run a senior citizens' center.'

'Like a nursing home?'

'The opposite,' I explain. 'A place for active seniors to come and socialize. We had league sports and chess tournaments and season tickets to the Red Sox.'

'No shit,' Monte says. 'My grandma, she's in one of those places where they just give her oxygen and wait for her to die.' He takes out a pen that he has whittled to a sharp point, a makeshift knife, and begins to run it under his nails. 'How long you been doing that?'

'Since I moved to Wexton,' I tell him. 'Almost thirty years.'

'Thirty years?' Monte shakes his head. 'That's, like, forever.'

I look down at my tray. 'Not really,' I say.

★

If I had been allowed to make my phone call to you, this is what I would have said:

How are you? How's Sophie?

I'm fine. I'm stronger than you'd think.

I wish it hadn't happened this way.

I will see you in Arizona, and explain.

I know.

I'm not sorry, either.

Fitz

I'm not prepared for what I see when I turn the corner onto the street where I grew up. Two news vans from the Boston area are parked in the driveway of what used to be Eric's childhood home. In front of Andrew Hopkins's little red Cape is a lineup of television reporters, each facing a cameraman whose job it is to carve out a small square of background and make it look as if no other journalist has stumbled onto this grand story. This is a plum assignment, and under any other circumstance I might find myself sitting alongside the others, bumming cigarettes and thermoses of coffee while we wait for the Victim to peek out the front door.

I park the car and circle around the media into my former backyard. A gay couple lives here now, with their adopted daughter – the gardens are far more manicured than anything my parents were ever able to pull off. But there's still a corner of the chain-link fence behind the rhododendrons that's bent up, just high enough for you to squeeze underneath into Delia's yard – a secret passage where we'd leave each other notes and treasures. I walk up the back door and let myself inside. 'Dee?' I call out. 'It's me.'

When there's no answer, I wander into the kitchen. Delia is dressed in jeans and one of Eric's sweaters; her hair is a wild black tangle around her face and her feet are bare. She is hunched over the counter, with the phone pressed to her ear. Underneath the kitchen table, Sophie sits in her nightgown, lining up plastic farm animals into military formation. 'Fitz!' she says when she sees me. 'Guess what? I couldn't go to school today because all the cars were in the way.'

'Could you check again?' Delia says into the phone. 'Maybe under E. Matthews?'

I kneel beside Sophie and hold my finger up to my lips: *quiet*. But Delia slams down the phone instead and swears like a sailor – the same Delia who once nearly took my head off for saying the word *damn* in Sophie's presence when she was only three months old. When she looks up at me, her eyes are full of tears. 'They must have told her about me . . . about *us* being here in New Hampshire, but she hasn't called, Fitz.'

There are all sorts of excellent reasons for this: Delia's mother doesn't live in Arizona now, and hasn't been told yet of Andrew's apprehension; she's not even alive anymore. But I don't have the heart to point these out to Delia.

'Maybe she's afraid you won't want to talk to her, with your father's arrest and all,' I say after a minute.

'That's what I thought, too. So I figured . . . maybe I'll just call *her*, instead. The thing is . . . I can't find her. I don't know if she's remarried or if she goes by her maiden name. . . . I don't even know what her maiden name *is*. She's still a total stranger.'

I stick my head under the table. 'Soph,' I say, 'I'll give you a dollar if you go upstairs and find Mommy's purple nail polish before I finish counting. One, two, three . . .'

She is off like a shot. 'I don't wear nail polish,' Delia says wearily.

'No kidding.' I step toward her. 'What have you told Sophie, anyway?'

'She saw the police take her grandfather away in handcuffs. What was I supposed to say to her?' Delia shakes her head. 'I told her it was just a game, like the one we were playing when the cops came.' She closes her eyes. 'Trouble.'

'Where's Eric?'

'At the office. Filing paperwork to try a case in Arizona.' Her voice stumbles over the words, and she sinks into a chair. 'You want to hear something funny, Fitz? I used to wish every night that my mother was still alive. I'm not talking about when I was a kid, I mean as recently as a week ago. You know . . . like when Sophie was a tooth in the school play and I wished my mother could have seen her, or when I had to pick out the dishes for the main course at the wedding and I couldn't even pronounce half of the ones on the caterer's list. I used to pretend that there had been some hospital mix-up, and that my mother would show up saying it had all been an awful mistake. Well, look at what happens when you get what you ask for: I have a mother, but I have no idea who I am. I don't know my actual birthday. I don't even know if I'm really thirty-one. And I thought I knew my father . . . but it turns out that was the biggest lie of all.'

'He's the same man you grew up with,' I say carefully, treading over a minefield full of false comfort. 'He's the same man he was yesterday.'

'Is he?' Delia retorts. 'I've been through some pretty awful situations with Eric, but I never thought about picking Sophie up and stealing her away so that he'd never see her again. I can't imagine a person ever getting to that point. But my own father apparently did.'

I could tell her from personal experience that when people we love make choices, we don't always understand them. But we can go on loving them, just the same. It isn't a matter of comprehension. It's forgiveness.

But all this took me a lifetime to discover, and where has it gotten me? To the point where, if Delia asks me to jump, I strap on my moon boots. Some lessons can't be taught, they simply have to be learned.

'I'm sure he had a reason for doing what he did,' I say. 'I'm sure he wants to talk to you.'

'And then what happens? Are we supposed to go back to the way it used to be? I don't quite see us meeting my mother for dinner every other Sunday and laughing about old times. And I don't know how I'm ever supposed to be able to listen to what he says without wondering if he's telling me the truth.' She starts to cry. 'I wish this never happened,' she says. 'I wish I'd never found out.'

I hesitate a second before hauling her into my arms – touching Delia is something I am always careful about; it comes at such great cost to me. I feel her heart beat hard against mine, two prisoners communicating through a cell-block wall. I understand better than she'd imagine that history is indelible. You can mask it; you can patch it smooth and clear; but you will always know what's hidden underneath.

I find myself selfishly leaning closer, so that I breathe in the scent of her hair. Delia taught me that human scents are like snowflakes – each one's different. Blindfolded, I could find Delia by smell alone: She is lily-milk and snow, fresh-cut grass in summer, the perfume of my childhood.

She shifts, so the softest skin below her ear brushes against my lips, and that's all it takes for me to jump back as if I've been burned. I know what it's like to wake up thinking you will be able to cast the people who play the starring roles in your life, only to realize that you have to watch it from the audience. For Delia, the whole play has changed in the middle, and the least I can do is to be her constant. She had always trusted me to fix what's wrong: a dead car battery, a flooded basement, a broken heart. This time, I am out of my league, but I try to rescue her anyway. I'll be the hero now; soon enough Delia will realize that there's reason to think of me as the villain.

'Sophie!' I yell. 'Time's up!' She appears breathlessly at the bottom of the stairs.

'Mommy doesn't have—'

'Get your coat,' I say. 'You're going to school.'

Sophie is still young enough to be delighted by this news. She runs off to the mudroom, while Delia glances out the window into the driveway. 'Did you happen to notice the jackals outside?'

I push aside the image of what Delia will think when she sees tomorrow's paper. 'Yeah,' I say, keeping my tone light, 'but I'm one of them, and we don't eat our own.'

'I don't want to go out—'

'But you need to,' I say. The last thing Delia should do is sit around waiting for the phone to ring, letting her mind wander enough to wonder why her mother might not be calling – none of which will lead to the outcome she's dreamed of her whole life.

Sophie skids to a stop in front of me, and I squat down to zip up her coat. 'We're dropping her off,' I tell Delia, 'and then we're going directly to jail.'

This morning I was called into the business offices of the *New Hampshire Gazette* by my editor, a woman named Marge Geraghy who smokes Cuban cigars and insists on calling me by my full godawful name. 'Fitzwilliam,' she said, 'take a seat.'

I sank into the ratty armchair across from her desk. The *New Hampshire Gazette* is exactly what you'd imagine of a paper you can, literally, read in its entirety during a visit to the bathroom – dingy gray walls, fluorescent lights, thrift-store furniture. There is a decent reception area and one nice conference room, for the one time a year when the governor of New Hampshire graces our offices for an interview. It's no wonder that most of the reporters choose to work from their homes instead of their cubicles.

'Fitzwilliam,' Marge repeated. 'I want to talk to you about this kidnapping case.'

On her desk she has the paper spread open to my article – page A2, because yesterday there was also a murder-suicide down in Nashua. 'What about it?' I asked.

'Your piece was missing something.'

I raised a brow. 'It's all there. The facts, the history to date, and the plea. If you're looking to make an arraignment more sexy, you'll have to watch *The Practice*.'

'I'm not criticizing your technique, Fitzwilliam, just your effort.' She blew a smoke ring into my face. 'Did you ever wonder why I pulled you off the Strange But True story to cover this instead?'

'Sheer human mercy?'

'No, because of what you could bring to the piece. You grew up in Wexton. Maybe you even crossed paths with this family – at church, at a school graduation, whatever. You can make this personal . . . even if you have to make it all up. I don't want the legal crap. I want the family drama.'

I wondered what Marge would say if she knew that not only did I grow up in Wexton, I grew up next door to Andrew Hopkins. That, all drama aside, Delia *is* my family. I wondered if she would understand that sometimes being close to an issue is not a good thing for a writer. That sometimes it means you can't see clearly.

But then Marge lifted up an envelope. 'An open e-ticket,' she announced. 'I want you to follow this guy to Arizona and get the exclusive.'

And that, really, was what made me agree. After all, I am a man who has never gotten very far from Delia Hopkins, no matter how I've tried. You can widen the feet of a compass, but they are still attached at the top; you can spin them away from each other, but you always wind up where you started. If Andrew is extradited to Arizona, and Delia follows, I am going to wind up there sooner or later. The *New Hampshire Gazette* might as well foot the bill.

I plucked the envelope out of Marge's hand. I would figure out, later, how to explain to Delia that I was writing an exposé on her heartache. I would figure out, later, how to explain to my boss that, for me, Delia will never be a story, but a happy ending.

Delia and I walk Sophie into the classroom because she's late, and because the teacher is brand new, having just taken over for Sophie's regular teacher while she's on maternity leave. I hang Sophie's coat on a little hook near her cubby and take her lunchbox out of her knapsack. A teacher who seems small enough, and nearly young enough, to be a student gets up and approaches Sophie, squatting down to her level. 'Sophie! I'm glad you could join us.'

'There's television people in my driveway,' Sophie announces.

Amazingly, the teacher's smile never wavers. 'Isn't that interesting!' she says. 'Why don't you join Mikayla and Ryan's group?'

As Sophie runs off, already focused on what's next, the teacher draws us aside. 'Ms. Hopkins, we read about your father's arraignment in the paper. All of us here want you to know that if there's anything we can do to help . . .'

'I'd just like Sophie to stay busy,' Delia replies woodenly. 'She doesn't really know what's going on with my father.'

'Of course,' the teacher agrees, and she glances at me. 'She's lucky to have two supportive parents right now.'

Too late, she realizes this is probably not the smartest comment, given the circumstances. She blushes a deep red, then an even deeper hue when both Delia and I hasten to explain that I'm not Sophie's father.

There have been times, I'll admit, that I wished I was. Like when Delia put my hand on her belly so that I could feel Sophie kicking inside, and I thought: I should have been the one to make that happen. But for all the nights I lay in bed as a teenager, imagining what it would be like to be Eric, with the freedom to touch her whenever I wanted, or breathing in the smell of my pillow after she'd sprawled on my bed studying for a test on *Hamlet,* or even feeling my pulse jump when we were both patting Greta after a find and our hands brushed – for all those times, there were a thousand others that did not belong to me.

By now, the teacher is so tangled up in the kite strings of her embarrassment that she couldn't fly straight if she wanted to. 'We have to go,' I say to Delia, and I drag her out of the classroom. 'I thought I'd save the poor woman before she put both of her feet in her mouth at once,' I explain. 'How old is she? Eleven? Twelve?'

'I didn't get to say good-bye to Sophie.'

We stop for a moment at the plate-glass window, watching Sophie make a block pattern out of colored circles and squares.

'She'll never know.'

'I bet the teacher noticed. She'll probably tell the school guidance counselor that I just picked up and left. They're all waiting to see how far the apple falls from the tree, you know.'

'Since when do you care what anyone thinks about you?' I ask. 'That's the kind of crap I'd expect to hear from Bethany Matthews, not Delia Hopkins.'

I hear Delia suck in her breath at the sound of that forbidden name.

'Bethany Matthews,' I continue blithely, 'is always the first one parked at the curb to pick up her daughter. Bethany Matthews thinks that the pinnacle of personal success is being president of the PTA for four consecutive years. Bethany Matthews never serves frozen pizza for dinner because she's forgotten to defrost.'

'Bethany Matthews would not have gotten pregnant before she was married,' Delia says. 'Bethany Matthews wouldn't even let her daughter play with a child who was the product of that kind of broken household.'

'Bethany Matthews still wears velvet headbands,' I laugh. 'And baggy granny underwear.'

'Bethany Matthews throws like a girl.'

'Bethany Matthews,' I say, 'is no fun to be around.'

'Thank God I'm nothing like her,' Delia replies, and then she turns to me and smiles.

I dated Delia first. We were in middle school and it didn't mean anything at all – if you said you were going out with a girl, it basically meant that you walked her to her bus at the end of the school day. I did it because everyone else seemed to be asking girls out, and Delia was the only one I really talked to. I broke up with her because as cool as it had been to have a girlfriend the week before, it was uncool to have one the following week. I told her that maybe we should spend a little time hanging out with other people.

I realized too late that the look on Delia's face when I did it was one I had never seen before – and with good reason: It was the first time in our lives that any of us three wanted to ration the amount of time we spent in one another's company. In a fit of conscience, I went to find Delia in the gym. I was going to tell her that I didn't mean it, that words without thought behind them were like deflated balloons, unable to go anywhere, but instead I spied her dancing with Eric. He had his arms around her, with an easy confidence I didn't have. He touched her as if parts of her belonged to him, and maybe, after all these years, they did.

On Eric's face I saw my own mistake. It brightened his eyes and narrowed his focus so much that I thought of yelling *Fire* to see if he'd even hear. He looked the way I felt around Delia: as if a second sun was growing underneath my breastbone, a secret I could barely conceal. The difference, though, was how Delia was looking back at *him*. Unlike the hours we'd spent as an alleged couple – when we'd argue who would be the starting pitcher for the Sox, or whether Spider-Man could kick Batman's ass in an arm-wrestling competition – Delia had nothing to say when she was staring up at Eric. He took away all her words, and I had never been able to do that.

There were times, when we were getting older, that I thought of telling her how I really felt. I convinced myself that even if I lost Eric's friendship forever as a result, I'd still have Delia to make up for it. But then I'd remember that moment when she and Eric were swaying in the middle school gym, with streamers caught on the bottoms of their shoes and a DJ playing REO Speedwagon; and I'd realize that even if all three of us had grown up, Delia and Eric still looked at each other as if the rest of the world had fallen away, myself included. I could lose one of them, but I didn't think I could stand to lose both.

Once, I slipped – I kissed her when we were horsing around on the shore of the Connecticut River. But I made a joke of it, the way I did when anything came too close for comfort. If I'd said what I really wanted to when she was floating with me in the reeds, her hands tight on my shoulders and her mouth a flower beneath mine, I might have wound up with her staring speechless at me, too. But what if it wasn't because I took her breath away? What if it was because she couldn't say back to me the things I said to her?

When you love someone, you want her to have everything she wants.

In Delia's case, that has always been Eric.

The Grafton County Correctional Facility hunches like a sleeping bear at the end of Route 10 in Haverhill, yoked at the neck to its sister building, the courthouse. As we drive up and park my car, I can feel Delia's eyes go straight to the razor wire at the top of the fence.

I get out of the car and open Delia's door. She squares her shoulders and marches toward the entryway, a squat little addition with a heavy wooden door that makes me think of the ogre's cottage in a fairy tale. The correctional officer at the desk looks up from the *MAXIM* he's reading. 'We've come to see an inmate,' I say.

'You a lawyer?'

'No, but—'

'Then come back Tuesday night during visiting hours.' He turns his attention back to his magazine.

'I don't think you understand—'

'Nope, I never do,' the CO answers dully.

'My father was brought in here two days ago—'

'Then you can't see him, period. It'll be a few weeks before he's approved for visitation.'

'My father won't be here in a few weeks,' Delia says. 'He's being sent to Arizona.'

This, finally, gets his attention. There just aren't all that many people in the Grafton County Jail who are on the short list for extradition to another state. 'Hopkins?' the CO says. 'You couldn't meet with him even if I let you. He left this morning for Phoenix.'

'What?' Delia says, stunned. 'My father's not here? Does his lawyer know?'

The CO turns as a door is slammed nearby, followed by the sound of Eric cursing. 'He does now,' the guard answers.

Eric sees us standing in front of the CO's booth and does a double-take. 'What are you doing here?'

'Why didn't you tell me my father was leaving today?'

'Because no one told *me,*' Eric says, shooting a dirty look at the CO who led him out. 'Apparently, neither the Arizona prosecutor nor the Grafton County Jail thought it might be important to let me know that my client's been extradited.' He pulls out his wallet and digs through it. 'You have any cash? I'm going to drive straight to the airport.'

I give him forty, Delia gives him fifty. 'Do you even know where you're going?'

'I have a seven-hour trip to figure it out,' Eric says. He stamps a kiss on Delia's forehead. 'Listen, I can handle this. In the meantime, find someone to watch the house for a while. Get tickets to Arizona for you and for Sophie. Bring a few of my suits and the box marked "Andrew" that's sitting on the desk at my office. I'll call you on your cell as soon as I know more.'

The three of us walk outside, where it is still cold enough for the promises we are making to crystallize in the air. Eric heads to my car and tucks Delia into the passenger seat, leaning close to speak to her for a moment out of my range of hearing. I imagine him telling her that he loves her, that he will miss her, that when he closes his eyes on the plane her face will be what rises inside him – all the things I would be saying to her, in his place. After he closes the door, sealing her safely inside, he comes around the back of the car to talk to me. 'I can't handle this,' he says.

'You just said—'

'Well, what the hell was I supposed to tell her? Fitz, I'm totally screwed. I honestly don't know what I'm doing,' Eric confesses. 'I can count on one hand the number of felonies

I've tried. I should have made her find another attorney. A real attorney.'

'You *are* a real attorney,' I say. 'She wanted you because she knows you'll do everything to get Andrew out of this mess.'

He rubs a hand down his face. 'Then what am I supposed to do when he gets convicted and Delia blames me?'

'Make sure you never have to find out.'

'I'm screwed,' Eric repeats, and shakes his head. 'I have to go. Take care of her, okay?'

He gives Delia to me as if she were a jewel to be smuggled, a prayer to be whispered between heretics. A pawn. Eric is halfway across the parking lot by the time I answer. 'I always do,' I say.

II

How little remains of the man I once was, save the memory of him! But remembering is only a new form of suffering.

– Charles Baudelaire, *La Fanfarlo*

Delia

When I was little, I used to imagine the ways my mother would come back to me. I would be ordering a milkshake at a diner, and the woman sitting on the stool next to me would turn and our eyes would connect like lightning. Or I'd open the door and instead of the mailman, my mother would be standing there with her arms open. I'd go to my first driver's-ed class in high school and slip into the car and find her waiting with a clipboard in the passenger seat, just as surprised as I was. In all these daydreams, death was not the absolute it is supposed to be, and we always found each other by accident. In all of these daydreams, my mother and I recognized each other without a single spoken word.

It is strange to think that, sometime in the past twenty-eight years, she might have been standing in line behind me at the grocery store. We might have passed each other in a bus station or on a crowded street. We might even have talked politely on the phone, *No I'm sorry, you have the wrong number.* It is strange to think that we might have crossed paths, and still not have known what we were missing.

You can boil your life down to a single suitcase, if you desperately have to. Ask yourself what you *really* need, and it won't be what you imagine – you will easily toss aside unfinished work, and bills, and your daily calendar to make room for the pair of flannel pajamas you wear when it rains; and the stone your child gave you that is shaped like a heart; and the battered paperback you revisit every April, because it was what you were reading the first time you fell in love. It turns out that what's important is not everything that you've accumulated all these years, but those few things you can carry with you.

Sophie presses her face to the tiny window of the plane, waiting for takeoff. It is her first flight. As far as my daughter knows, we are going on a spontaneous adventure. A vacation. I've told her that where we're headed, it's warm. That Eric is already there waiting for us.

Maybe my mother is, too.

She still hasn't called. Maybe, like Fitz said, she's afraid; maybe her attorneys have told her not to. Eric has explained to me that just because the State of Arizona is prosecuting after all this time doesn't mean that my mother is pushing for it, or even that she's still alive. An outstanding warrant is an outstanding warrant, period.

Every now and then I let myself think the darkest thought: that the reason she hasn't contacted me is because she doesn't *want* to. I cannot reconcile that mother with the one I've pictured for years.

But then again, if my mother was as perfect as I've always imagined, why would my father have run away with me? I've never doubted his love for me, but for that to still be true, given what I now know, do I have to doubt my mother's love for me? And if I can't, if I *won't*, then don't I have to admit to myself that my father has done something wrong?

When I told all of this to Eric, he said I'd find out soon enough if my mother is still living in Arizona, that I should just stop analyzing it to death, because it's only going to make me crazy.

But if it were me, and Sophie, and it had been years . . . I wouldn't listen to lawyers; I wouldn't pay attention to misgivings. I would walk halfway across the world to stand on my daughter's doorstep; I'd wait for her to answer the bell and hold her so close that nothing could come between us, not even the narrowest sliver of regret.

'Mommy?' Sophie asks. 'Will they give Greta a seat belt?'

'She's in a special crate,' I assure her. 'She's probably asleep by now.'

Sophie considers this. 'Does she ever dream?'

'Sure,' I reply. 'You've seen her running in her sleep.'

'I had a dream last night,' Sophie tells me. 'Grandpa was taking me for ice cream, but no matter what you asked for, you got strawberry.'

'He hates strawberry,' I say quietly.

'But in my dream,' Sophie says, 'he ate it anyway.' She twists in her seat to face me. 'Will Grandpa be on the other side?'

She means in Arizona, but that isn't how I hear it. I'd always thought of my father and me as a unit, a team, but now I'm not sure. On the one hand, I was his child, and he must have been doing what he felt he needed to do. On the other hand, I'm a mother now, and he committed my worst nightmare.

Sophie snuggles against me, twining her fingers in my hair. She used to sleep with it the way some babies sleep with a blanket or a teddy bear; every time she lay down for a nap I'd have to go with her. Eric thought it was a habit we should break; how else would she ever be able to go to sleep without me?

I had asked him, *Why should she ever have to?*

The Fasten Seat Belt sign dings, and I help Sophie into her seat and tighten the band around her waist. The plane pushes off from the jetway and rolls backward, heading onto the tarmac for takeoff. When the plane begins to accelerate and the nose rises up like a rocket, Sophie turns to me. 'Are we flying?'

My father and I used to have picnics at the airfield in Lebanon and watch the Cessnas and Pipers take off and land. We'd lie on our backs with the grass tickling our shoulders as the little planes vanished into colossal clouds, then reappeared like magic. When I asked him what kept a plane from falling out of the sky, he made me sit up and blow across the top of a paper napkin to see it rise like a flag in the wind. 'When the air moves faster on the top of the wings than the bottom,' he told me, 'the plane lifts.'

So I am ready when Sophie asks me this question. It's all about pressure. When it comes at you from all sides equally, nothing moves. But if one side exerts more than the other, you just might find yourself in flight.

I wonder if she has dimples, like me. If she can bend her thumbs all the way backward, double-jointed, like Sophie and I can. If she gave me my black hair or my fear of insects. If her labor was anything like mine.

I have spent so long sculpting her in my imagination, a combination of Marion Cunningham and Carol Brady and Ma Walton and Mrs. Cosby. She will cry when she sees me and hold me so tight that I can't breathe, and even then I will notice how seamlessly my body fits against hers. She will not be able to find words big enough to tell me how much she loves me.

But there is another voice in my head, one that knows things are different if my mother has, in fact, been alive all this time. Why didn't she try harder to find me?

All I ever really wanted in a mother is someone who could not be dragged from me, kicking and screaming, no matter how powerful the force of separation was. Someone who would give up her life if it meant I couldn't be a part of it.

Someone my father has always been.

When I fall asleep during the flight, I dream. He has just finished planting a lemon tree in my backyard. I want to make lemonade, but there isn't any fruit on the tree yet. It looks naked under that electric sky; all angles and switchbacks, skinny arms shivering.

His hands pat the dirt down at the bottom of the tree. He turns to me but the sun is in my eyes and I smile back without really seeing his face. In my lap is a striped cat; I feel for the missing stub of its tail and it bolts out of my clutches, between two barrel cacti that remind me of munchkins from The *Wizard of Oz*. 'What do you think, Beth?' he asks.

The dust stains his palms red, and when he wipes them on his jeans there are two upside-down five-fingered prints that become long-necked dinosaurs with their heads reaching toward each other. I think I want a dinosaur. I want a seal, too, to keep in the bathtub.

I tell him this, and he laughs. 'I know what you want, *grilla*,' he says, and then he swings me into his arms and so high that the sun kisses blisters onto the soles of my feet.

Arriving at Sky Harbor Airport is, I imagine, like landing on Mars – jagged mountains and blood-red soil as far as I can see. I step out of the double glass doors and walk into a solid wall of heat. I wonder how a place like this and a place like New Hampshire could possibly be part of the same country.

There is already a message on my cell phone from Eric – an address, actually. The lawyer sponsoring him to try a case in this state is an old classmate from law school, and someone – his secretary's cousin's friend, or something equally as complicated – has agreed to let us stay in her house while she moves in with her boyfriend.

I collect a skittish Greta from the oversized-baggage area, rent an SUV (*How long do you need it?* the clerk had asked, and I had stared at the woman blankly), and pile our luggage into the backseat and trunk around the collapsible dog cage. Going through the motions only reminds me of the thousand things I don't know: what the grocery store chains are out here; how to get to this house on Los Brazos Street; when I will see my father again. Sophie's backpack slips to her elbows, her hand rides on the taut pull of Greta's leash. She follows me, bouncing on the balls of her feet, trusting me to know where we're going.

Don't all children?

Didn't *I*?

We follow the Avis representative's directions, passing more stores and shopping malls than there are in all of New Hampshire. There seems to be a supplier for everything you might ever want or need – sushi, motorized scooters, bronze sculpture, paint-your-own ceramicware. I feel absolutely lost out here, and that, actually, is a relief. In Arizona I am not supposed to know anything; this is all naturally foreign. Unlike Wexton, here I have the right to wake up in the morning and not remember who or where I am.

The address Eric has given me is in Mesa, and must be a mistake. The only residences on Los Brazos are in a trailer park – not one filled with tidy rows of compact, immaculate homes with little gardens and window boxes, but something that resembles an enormous junk heap. There's a dusty parking lot encapsulating fifty motor homes, none numbered, all in various states of disrepair. Sophie kicks at the back of my seat. 'Mommy,' she asks, 'do we get to live in a bus?'

We drive past an old woman standing at the entrance of a trailer park, wrapped tight in a long raincoat in spite of the heat. Inside the fence, there doesn't seem to be a single living soul. I imagine how hot it must be to live inside a metal trailer, when the outdoor temperatures alone break a hundred degrees.

We'll stay in a hotel, I decide, but then I remember that we don't have enough money for that. Eric said that this might not be a matter of weeks, but months.

Some of the trailers have cacti planted next to their steps. Some have bronze garden ornaments stuck in the stones along their foundations. A young woman steps out of her door, and I immediately roll down my window. 'Excuse me!' I call out. 'I'm trying to find . . .' I look down at the number Eric left in his message.

'No habla inglés.' She hurries back inside her trailer, and pulls shut all the curtains so that we cannot peek inside.

I would drive to Eric, but he hasn't told me where he is. Before I know it, I've made a full circle through the motor home community, and I'm back on the driveway that leads out to the main road. The old woman is still standing there, and she smiles at me. She has the lined maple skin and moon face of a Native American; her short white hair is twisted into a red scarf on top of her head. Every one of her fingers is decorated with a silver ring, something I notice when she flashes us by pulling aside the lapels of her coat. Underneath, she is wearing a T-shirt that says DON'T WORRY, BE HOPI, and various items are anchored to plastic loops sewn into the satin lining of the jacket – rusted silverware, old 45s, and about ten Barbie dolls. 'Garage sale today,' she says. 'Extra cheap!'

Sophie's face lights up when she sees the dolls. 'Mommy—'

'Not today,' I say, and I smile tightly at the woman. 'Sorry.'

She shrugs and closes her coat.

I hesitate. 'Do you by any chance know which trailer is number 35677?'

'It's right over there.' Pointing, she indicates a decrepit building less than twenty feet away. 'Nobody lives in it, though. Girl moved out a week ago. The neighbor's got the key.'

The neighbor's trailer has all kinds of rainbow windcatchers suspended from the overhang of the doorway. A stool with a mosaic seat and plaster-sculpted human legs and feet supports a twisted cactus whose shoots look like the tangled map of the New York subway. Hundreds of brown feathers are tied with string and leather to the green branches of a paloverde tree in the front yard.

'Thanks,' I say, and telling Sophie to wait in the car, I leave the air-conditioning running and walk up to the door. I ring the bell, twice, but there's no answer.

'They're not home,' the old woman says, as if I haven't figured this out for myself. But before I can reply, I hear the approaching whine of a police siren. Immediately, I am back in Wexton, ten seconds before my entire life fell apart. I run for the car, for Sophie.

The police cruiser pulls in behind my rental, but when the officer gets out, he walks away from me and toward the old woman. 'Now, Ruthann,' he says, 'how many times do I have to tell you?'

She tightens the belt of her trench coat. '*Halíksa'i,* you can't tell me what I can't do.'

'This property isn't zoned commercial,' the policeman says.

'I don't see anyone selling anything.'

He flips up his sunglasses. 'What's under your coat?'

She turns to me. 'That's sexual harassment, don't you think?'

The officer seems to notice me for the first time. 'Who are you? A customer?'

'No, I'm just moving in.'

'Here?'

'I think so,' I explain. 'I was looking for my key.'

The policeman pinches the bridge of his nose. 'Ruthie, get yourself a table at one of those Indian flea markets, okay? Don't make me come back here.' He gets back into his car and zooms down the block again.

The old woman sighs and trudges up to the front door that I've been knocking on. 'Hold your horses,' she says, 'I'll get your key.'

'*You* live here?'

She doesn't answer, just unlocks the door and walks in. Even from this distance, the house smells like sugar burning. 'Well?' she calls after a minute. 'Come on.'

I get Sophie and Greta out of my car, and tell the dog to wait on the stoop. As Sophie and I step inside, Ruthann takes off her trench coat and spreads it over the back of a futon, the heads of the Barbies inside poking out like gophers. Nearly everywhere I look, there is some box of junk or a tin of beads and feathers; glue guns lay like discarded murder weapons on the floor. 'I know it's here somewhere,' she says, rummaging in a drawer full of twigs and pencils.

Behind me, Sophie slides one of the dolls out of its resting place in the coat. 'Mommy, look,' she whispers.

This Barbie doll has a miniature pint of chocolate ice cream in one arm and a *Sleepless in Seattle* video in the other. She wears sweatpants, fuzzy slippers, and has a gun strapped to her hip. A tag around her neck reads PMS Barbie.

It makes me laugh out loud. I reach into the trench coat and pull out another doll, Reality TV Barbie. She is wearing a jog bra and wedding veil and is holding a map of the Amazon. She has a half-eaten sheep's eye in her mouth, a fistful of dollars in her back pocket, and a Nike contract tucked into her athletic sock.

'These are very funny,' I say.

'I call them Black Market Barbies. Dolls for girls who don't want to stop playing yet.' The old woman crosses the room and holds out her hand. 'I'm Ruthann Masáwistiwa, owner and CEO of Second Wind, specializing in possession reincarnation.'

'What's that?'

'Finding homes for what other folks don't want. I'm one big portable Indian pawnshop.' She shrugs. 'Your old toaster might be someone else's in-box at work. Your cowboy boot could have a whole next life as a planter for geraniums.'

'What about the dolls?'

'Another rebirth,' she says proudly. 'I make them, down to every last accessory. Even the Prozac prescription bottle for Mid-Life Crisis Barbie. I wanted to carve katsina dolls, but only Hopi men can do that – women are supposed to carve with their wombs, if you get my drift. Then again, I don't like being told what *not* to do.'

I shake my head, trying to follow this conversation. 'Katsina . . . ?'

'They're spirits, to the Hopi. There are hundreds of different ones – male, female, plants, animals, insects – you name it. They used to visit in person, but now they come as clouds, or up through the earth, for ceremonies that bring rain and snow to the crops, and blessings. Katsina dolls are carved out of cottonwood, to give to children at these dances so they can learn the religion, but nowadays they're also a hot-ticket item for collectors.' Ruthann picks up one of her Barbies. 'Don't know if this'll have the same staying power, but I'm trying.' She reaches onto a shelf and pulls down a Kelly doll, Barbie's little sister, which she offers to Sophie. 'Bet you'd like this,' she says.

Sophie immediately sits down on the floor and begins to pull off Kelly's elastic clothes. 'I have a Kelly at home.'

'Ah. And where's that?'

'Next door,' I interrupt. I am not ready to tell this woman our story yet. I don't know that I'll ever be ready.

Ruthann squats down beside Sophie and pretends to pull out of her ear a long, red shoelace. It reminds me so much of my father, doing his magic tricks at the senior center, that tears line the column of my throat. 'Well,' Ruthann says. 'Will you look at that.'

At the end of the shoelace is a key. Ruthann cups her hands around Sophie's tiny face. 'You come play with my dolls whenever you want, Siwa.' Then she gets to her feet slowly and presses the key into my palm. 'Don't lose it,' she warns.

I nod. I think of all the ways I might interpret those words.

It takes two people to make a lie work: the person who tells it, and the one who believes it. The first lie my father must have told was to me – that my mother had died in a car crash. But why didn't I ask, when I was old enough, to visit her grave? Why didn't I question the fact that I had no maternal grandparents or uncles or cousins who ever visited? Why didn't I ever look for my mother's jewelry, her old clothes, her high school yearbook?

There were times when Eric was drinking that he'd come home, too careful in his movements to not be intoxicated. But instead of calling him on his bad judgment, I'd pretend everything was fine, just like he was doing. You can invent any fiction and call it a life; I thought that if I did it often enough, I might start to believe it.

Sometimes, when you don't ask questions, it's not because you are afraid that someone will lie to your face.

It's because you're afraid they'll tell you the truth.

★

There are bonuses to this trailer: you can walk the entire length of it, four times, in a single breath. You can stand in the kitchen and see into the bedroom. The kitchen table cleverly converts into an extra bed. To Sophie's delight, the entire interior is painted Pepto-Bismol pink, down to the toilet seat.

There's a phone book.

There are seventy-seven listings for 'Matthews' in the Greater Phoenix Region. Thirty-four live in Scottsdale. Just as the operator told me, there's no Elise Matthews, no E. Matthews, nothing that I could trace to my mother. It is entirely possible that she's become a different person, too.

The previous occupant, in a fit of mercy, has left behind an oscillating fan. I set it up in the bedroom, pointing directly at Sophie and Greta, who have curled up on top of the double mattress. Then I step outside and sit on the stoop. It is still blistering hot, although the sun has nearly set. The sky seems wider here, stretched like cellophane, and the stars are starting to come out. I am convinced they are a puzzle. If I stare at them hard enough, they'll move of their own accord; they will link their sharp arms and spell out all the answers.

We say it all the time – how we'd give up anything for someone we love – but I wonder, when push comes to shove, who'd truly step up to the line. Would Eric jump in front of a bullet to save me? Would I do it for Eric? What if it meant I'd die, or be paralyzed forever? What if it meant that I could never go back, that my existence would be divided from that point on into *before* and *after?*

The only person I can honestly say I'd save without a second thought is Sophie, simply because in the accounting scheme of my heart, her life means more than mine.

Had my father felt that way, too?

I take out my cell phone and dial Fitz, but his voice mail picks up. I dial Eric, and he answers. 'Where are you?' I ask.

'Looking at the most amazing view,' Eric says, as an unfamiliar car pulls in front of me. Eric leans out the window, still holding the phone to his ear. 'Want to hang up now?' he asks, and he smiles.

He gets out of the car, and I fall into his arms, the first place all day that feels familiar. 'How's Soph?' he asks.

'Sleeping already.' I follow him as he starts into the trailer to find her. 'Did you see him?'

Eric doesn't have to ask who I'm talking about. 'I tried. But the Madison Street Jail won't let me in without a Bar card.'

'What's that?'

'A little piece of paper that doesn't exist in New Hampshire, which says I'm in good standing with the state Bar association.' Eric stops dead in the entryway, staring at the pink couch and the cotton candy wallpaper. 'Jesus Christ, we're living inside a Hubba Bubba bubble.'

'I was thinking more like the Barbie Winnebago,' I say. 'What about me?'

'What *about* you?'

'Would they let me in to see him?'

On Eric's face, I see a play of responses: his reluctance to let go of me, now that we're both here; his fear of what I might find; his understanding that I need my father, right now, more than I need him. 'Yes,' he says. 'I think they would.'

I don't know why it's called 'getting lost.' Even when you turn down the wrong street, when you find yourself at the dead end of a chain-link fence or a road that turns to sand, you are *somewhere*. It just isn't where you expected to be.

Twice, I pass exits on the highway for Downtown Phoenix and have to turn around. Three times, I stop at a gas station to ask for directions. How hard can it be to find a jail?

When I finally arrive, I am surprised by how ordinary it is on the inside: the serviceable tile and banks of plastic chairs. This could be any state agency. I wonder if there are visiting hours I should have called for in advance. But there are other people in the lobby area – lanky black boys wearing baggy pants, Native women with tears still drying on their cheeks, an old man in a wheelchair with a toddler riding on his lap. I follow the lead of everyone else, taking a form from a stack on a table. They are simple questions, or would be for anyone not in my situation: name, address, DOB; relationship to the inmate; inmate's name. I take a pen out of my pocket and start to fill it out. *Delia Hopkins,* I write, and on second thought, cross it out. *Bethany Matthews.*

After I finish, I stand in line, trying to pretend it is any other familiar queue: the line at the grocery store; the line of parents waiting in their cars to pick up children after school; the wait to sit on the lap of a mall Santa Claus. When it is my turn, the officer looks at me. 'First time?'

I nod. Is it that obvious?

'I need your ID, too.' He does a double-take at my New Hampshire license, but enters the information into his computer. 'Well,' he says after a moment of watching the screen, 'you're clear.'

'Of what?'

'Outstanding warrants for arrest.' He hands me a visitation pass. 'You want to head to that door on the left.'

I am told to pick any free locker behind me and put all my personal belongings inside. Then comes a metal detector and an elevator ride, and when the doors open, I realize where they have been hiding this jail. It is large and gray, intimidating. There are echoes: steel striking steel; a man screaming; an intercom. An inmate holding a washcloth up to his eye walks by in the company of two officers, who step into the elevator we vacate. More officers sit inside a glass booth, monitoring our progress as we are led to the visiting room.

Inside are four booths, each divided by a line of reinforced glass, a telephone intercom on each side. Round metal stools are bolted to the floor, evenly spaced like the spruces at a Christmas tree farm. There are other people waiting here, too: a woman in a burka, a teenager with an angry scar across his cheek, and a Hispanic man whispering a rosary.

My father is the last prisoner to be brought in. He is wearing striped scrubs, just like you'd see in a cartoon, and for the first time this becomes real to me. He is not going to step forward and pull off the costume, tell me this has all been a bad dream; it is really happening; it is now my life. My hand comes up to my mouth, and I know he can't hear me draw in my breath like I'm drowning, but he touches the glass between us all the same, as if it might still be that simple to reach me.

He picks up the phone and mimes for me to do the same. 'Delia,' he says, his voice hammered thin. 'Delia, baby, I'm sorry.'

I've told myself that I won't cry, but before I know it, I'm doubled over on the tiny stool, sobbing so hard that my chest hurts. I want him to reach through the glass like the magician I used to think he was and tell me this is all just a misunderstanding. I want to believe whatever it is he has to say.

'Don't cry,' he begs.

I wipe my eyes. 'Why didn't you tell me?'

'You were too little, at first. And then, when you were older, I was too selfish.' He hesitates. 'You used to look at me like I was a hero. And I didn't think I could stand it if you stopped looking at me like that.'

I lean closer to the wall between us. 'Then tell me now,' I insist. 'Tell me the truth.'

Suddenly I remember being very small, and dumping all the pairs of tights I owned on my father's bed, a twisted ball of cabled blue and white snakes. *I hate wearing these,* I said to him. *They always wind up bunched at my knees, and make it so that at recess, I can't run.*

I thought he would protest, and tell me that I'd wear whatever was in my drawers and that was that. But instead he started to laugh. *You can't run? Well, we can't have that, can we?*

'We named you Bethany. You were so small when you were born – tinier even than a loaf of bread. I used a filing cabinet as a crib for you, when I took you to work with me.' He looks up at me. 'I used to be a pharmacist.'

A pharmacist? I scramble back over my memory, trying to find red flags I missed the first time around: my father's quick knowledge of the dosage of Baby Tylenol for Sophie's weight; his frustration when I couldn't understand high school chemistry. Why didn't he practice in New Hampshire, I wonder . . . and then I answer my own question: because he was licensed under another name, someone who disappeared off the face of the earth.

If you call yourself something different, does it change the person you are inside? 'Who were you?'

'Charles,' he says. 'Charles Edward Matthews.'

'Three first names.'

He startles. 'That's exactly what your mother said when we met.'

I draw in my breath when he mentions her. 'What was *her* real name?'

'Elise. I didn't lie to you about that.'

'No,' I say. 'Except instead of telling me you got divorced, you said she was dead.'

Let me tell you what happens when you cook down the syrup of loss over the open fire of sorrow: It solidifies into something else. Not grief, like you'd expect, or even regret. No, it gets thick as paste, black as ash; yet it isn't until you dip a finger in and feel that sharp taste dissolving on your tongue that you realize this is anger in its purest form, unrefined; a substance to be weighed and measured and spread.

I had come here, or so I thought, to make sure my father was all right, to show him that I was all right, too. I had come here to tell him that in spite of what the police had to say, in spite of what happened in court, I was not going to forget the childhood he'd given me. But suddenly, the scales don't balance, and those twenty-eight years I thought I knew are outweighed by the four I never had the chance to. 'Why?' I ask, the word clenched between my teeth. 'Why did you do it?'

My father shakes his head. 'I didn't want you to get hurt. Not then, Delia . . . and not now—'

'Don't call me that!' I am so loud that in the booth beside us, a woman turns around.

'I didn't have a choice.'

My heart is pounding, and I cannot stop. 'You had a choice. You had a thousand choices. To leave or not to leave. To take me with you, or not. To tell me the truth when I was five years old, or ten, or twenty. *I* was the one without the choice, Dad.'

I hurry out of the visiting room, so that he can feel what it's like to be the one left behind.

By the time I get back to the pink trailer, everyone's asleep. Sophie is on the couch, curled like a question mark around Greta, who opens one eye and thumps her tail at the sight of me. I kneel down and touch Sophie's brow; she's sweating.

A month after she was born, I bundled her up in her winter snowsuit in preparation for a trip to the grocery store, and buckled her into the infant carrier that snaps into a car seat. I left the carrier on top of the kitchen table while I put on my own coat and boots. I was halfway to the grocery store, driving on the highway, when my cell phone rang. It was my father calling. 'Missing something?' he asked. When I glanced in the rearview mirror, I realized that I'd never taken Sophie, in her infant carrier, out to the car. I'd left her on the kitchen table, strapped into the little half-moon seat.

I couldn't believe I'd left behind my own infant. I couldn't believe I hadn't felt off balance, as if I were missing an arm or a leg, since she was just as critical a part of me. Mortified, I told my father I'd come straight home. 'Just go to the store,' he'd said, laughing. 'She's safe with me.'

Broad hands slide under the front of my T-shirt, and I twist around to find Eric, still warm with sleep. He pulls me into the bedroom at the end of the trailer and closes the door. 'Did you see him?' he whispers.

I nod.

'So?'

'I had to talk to him through a glass booth . . . and he's wearing black-and-white stripes like some kind of . . . some kind of . . .'

'Criminal?' Eric says softly, and that's all it takes for me to start to cry again. He wraps his arms around me, lowering me onto the bed.

'He's in there because of me,' I say. 'And I don't even really know who that is anymore.'

Eric's body moves behind mine, one leg sliding warm between my own. He settles over me like fog, tracing the seam of me with his tongue. 'I do,' he says.

In my dream, I've been hiding. The kitchen floor glitters; it is covered with diamonds that I know are broken glass. There are shattered plates on the floor; the cabinets are wide open, with no mugs or dishes left inside.

There's yelling, almost as loud as the sound of glass breaking.

I can hear it, even after my hands are pressed tight over my ears. It sounds like the inside of a drum, like the dragon that's really my breathing, like the hard knot of tears in my throat that keeps me from swallowing.

I am aware, first, of the sun rising underneath the covers. Then comes the breath, heavy and wet as sand at the bottom of the sea. I sit up in an instant and throw back the sheet to find Sophie huddled in a small knot, raging with a fever.

I call for Eric, but he's gone; he has left me a note with the number of his friend's law offices. I can nearly hear my daughter's blood boiling. I ransack my luggage for a thermometer or aspirin or anything that might help, and when I come up empty-handed I carry her into the pink bathroom and stand in the tepid shower with her in my arms.

Sophie rolls her flushed face toward me, her eyes blind and blue. 'There's a monster in the potty,' she says.

I glance into the toilet, where a small dark feather is floating.

I flush it, twice. 'There,' I say. 'Gone.' But by now, Sophie's head lolls back; she is out cold.

In the bathroom there are no towels; I wrap Sophie in the shirt Eric discarded when he came home yesterday. Her teeth are chattering, her forehead blazes. She whimpers as I try to swaddle her tightly, and then hurry out the front door.

It is only eight in the morning, but I kick at Ruthann Masáwistiwa's door, still holding Sophie in my arms. 'Please,' I beg, when she opens it. 'I need to find a hospital.'

She takes one look at Sophie. 'Follow me,' she says, but instead of heading for my car, she walks into our trailer. She leans out the window that I opened last night for the fresh air, the one just over the couch where Sophie was sleeping. Ruthann's knotty hands run along the seam of the sash, searching the outside edges. 'Got it,' she says, and she plucks from the windowsill a brown feather that looks like the one I flushed down the toilet.

Ruthann holds the feather outside. When she lets go, it winnows up in a draft of wind and is carried away. '*Pahos,*' she says, and then she points to the paloverde bush in her front yard, a few feet away from the open window, where hundreds of feathers are still tied to the branches. 'They're prayer feathers. I make them to hold all the bad from last year. They're supposed to blow away in the winter, and the evil with them. I hang them up in the tree so that no one gets poisoned by coming close, but I guess one made its way to your little girl.'

I blink at her, incredulous. 'You expect me to believe my daughter's sick because of a . . . a *chicken feather?*'

'It's a turkey feather,' Ruthann says. 'And why would I expect you to believe anything?' She puts the flat of her hand against Sophie's forehead. Then she gestures for me to do the same.

Sophie's skin is cool to the touch; the fire in her cheeks has faded. She is sleeping evenly, one hand unfurled on my chest like a victory flag.

I swallow hard; place her gently on the bed. 'I'm still taking her to the doctor.'

'Of course you are,' Ruthann says.

You think you know the world you are living in. If you can feel it, and touch it, and smell it, and taste it, then it must be so. You tell yourself that you would bet your life on the simple fact that the sky is blue. And then one day someone comes along and informs you emphatically that you're wrong. *Blue,* you insist. *Blue as the ocean. Blue as a whale. Blue as my daughter's eyes.* But that person shakes his head, and everyone else backs him up. *You poor girl,* they say. *All of those things – the ocean, the whale, her eyes – they're* green. *You've gotten them mixed up. You've had it wrong all along.*

Two pediatricians, a neurologist, and three blood vials later Sophie is pronounced healthier than a mustang, whatever that means. One of the doctors, a woman with her hair pulled back so tight in a bun that it draws her eyes out at the edges, sits me down out of Sophie's range of hearing. 'Has there been any trouble at home?' she asks. 'Kids this age sometimes do things for attention.'

But this was no sore throat or stomachache; you cannot fake the kind of sick that comes from so deep inside. 'Sophie's not like that,' I explain, affronted. 'I think I know my own daughter.'

The doctor shrugs, as if she has heard all this before.

I drive toward our house gingerly, reversing Ruthann's directions. In the backseat, Sophie plays with the stickers a nurse has given her. The whole way I second-guess myself: Is this the correct turn? Can I make a right on red? Did I imagine this morning's episode? Maybe faulty judgment is contagious.

I realize, as I pull into the trailer park, that I am just about the same age my father was when he took me away.

I let Greta out for a while, and then take Sophie next door to Ruthann's. The old woman opens the door picking at her cuticles, which are covered with cauls of dried glue. 'Siwa,' she says to Sophie. 'You look much better.'

Sophie vines herself around my left leg.

'And shyer,' Ruthann adds. She frowns at Sophie's face. 'Open up,' she says, tapping her on the chin, and when Sophie does, Ruthann plucks a tiny pair of pink plastic sandals off her tongue, followed by strappy yellow heels, and finally a set of spa slippers. 'No wonder you were feeling sick,' she says, as Sophie's eyes go wide. 'Choking on all those old soles. Go on inside and see if you can find out which Barbies these belong to.'

When Sophie is gone, I look at Ruthann. 'You know, I don't believe in magic.'

'Me neither,' she admits. 'You never do, when you know how to do the tricks.'

I follow her into the trailer. 'What about this morning, then?'

She shrugs. 'A lucky guess. About five years back, there was a *pahána* – a white lady photographer – staying up near Shongopavi, and she got miserable stomach cramps all of a sudden. Indian Health Service docs couldn't figure it out, said there was nothing wrong with her. Turns out she'd taken some *pahos* that were lying around and tucked them in the brim of her straw hat. Soon as she brought the feathers back to where she'd found them, all the belly pain went away.'

I look over my shoulder, to the nearby tree where the other feathers still wait for the breeze. 'It could happen again.'

Ruthann glances up at the tree. 'Tomorrow the wind will blow a different way. Sooner or later, they'll all disappear anyway.'

I watch a light gust stir the feathers. 'Then what?'

'Then we do what we do best,' Ruthann says. 'Start over from scratch.'

Andrew

The intake area of the Madison Street Jail in Phoenix is called the Horseshoe, something I remember from the last time I was there. Not much has changed since 1976 – the cinder-block walls are still cold against my shoulder blades when I lean back against them; the mug shot area is tucked into a small alcove beside the pre-intake booth; the smell of industrial cleaner seeps through the air every time a detention officer opens the door to lead another man inside.

There's a line to get into jail. In the crowded pre-intake area two dozen local cops stand with their charges, rearranging themselves like some kind of cog puzzle every time a new entrant arrives. One man is bleeding from a cut above the eye; every now and then he lifts his cuffed hands to wipe it off on his wrist. Another is passed out in a chair. A prostitute standing at the mug shot background asks if she can turn the other way, because it's her better side.

I watch the freak show for about a half hour, and then I'm led behind a cubicle to the medical assistant. She's an overweight woman wearing scrubs printed with teddy bears, and she wraps a blood pressure cuff around my upper arm. The band tightens, and I imagine for a moment it is my neck, that at any moment the air will cut off and this will all be over.

'You on any medications?' she asks. 'When was the last time you saw a doctor? Have you had any alcohol in the past twenty-four hours? Are you feeling suicidal?'

Right now I don't feel much of anything. As if I have developed the thick, scaly skin that this desert environment requires.

As if you could prick me with a needle, a knife, a spear, and my body would not remember how to bleed.

I don't tell her this, though, and the nurse rips the blood pressure cuff off my arm. 'It's about time we got a quiet one,' she says to the deputy, and hands me back.

Other people are staring at me. Unlike them, arrested off the street and still wearing their sweatshirts and jeans and miniskirts, I came from a different jail. I'm wearing a jumpsuit the color of a hazard sign. I have no property in my pockets; it is already in a bag being carried by the deputy.

They are looking at me and thinking, *He has done something worse.*

The door opens, and a detention officer calls my name. He is wearing khaki cargo pants and a SWAT vest, as if he is in the middle of a war zone, which I suppose he is. The deputy drags me through the crowd. 'Have fun,' he says, turning me over to the custody of the county.

The Horseshoe reverberates with noise. There are DOs yelling to each other or into the mikes at their shoulders; doors ringing as they are slammed and locked; drunks crying out to friends they've hallucinated into existence. And then there is the bass line: the steady squelch of a working inmate's shoes on the floor as he mops; the hum of an air-exchange fan; the Christmas jingle of chains as a line of men are shuffled down the hallway. 'Congratulations,' the officer says to me. 'You're the two hundredth customer today.'

It is only one o'clock in the afternoon.

'That entitles you to a door prize. Instead of a pat down, you get a strip search.' He leads me into a room to the left of a metal plate that is bolted to the wall and tells me to undress. I turn my back, which is all the privacy I'm allowed. Through the window I see a female guard watching absently.

One of my seniors, a woman who died five years ago, had been a Holocaust survivor. She had seen her sister's head shot off in front of her face; she had seen boys from her own village join the SS and send girls they had once flirted with to the gas chambers. She had been pregnant when she arrived at Dachau, and had hid the truth from the officers and eventually aborted the fetus herself, because she knew she was too weak to carry to term. When Mrs. Weiss told me about burying her baby under rocks, her voice was flat and empty. I understood then that to add hate or pain or regret or any emotion at all was simply impossible. Under that strain, she would break.

So when the officer tells me to open my mouth, raise my arms, bend down and spread my legs wide, I go somewhere else. To the center of the sky, to the sinking clay bottom of a summer lake. When he asks me to stand up and lift up my scrotum, I do not even feel myself follow his instructions. These are someone else's hands, someone else's orders, someone else's pathetic life.

'All right,' he says. 'Get back into your clothes.' He opens a door farther down the hallway. Marked with a '3,' it is about half full. 'Hey, dude,' one of the men inside says to the DO. 'You gonna take care of this?' He points to a slick of vomit beneath the pay phone, and a man who's passed out face first in the puddle.

'Yeah, I'll get right on that,' the detention officer says, an inflection to his voice that suggests it is the lowest item on his list of priorities.

Men sit on a bench along one wall, men lie on the floor, and one kid is singing 'A Hundred Bottles of Beer on the Wall.' It's like fingernails on a chalkboard. 'Shut the fuck up,' says a black man, and he throws an orange at the boy.

There are phones. I look across the tiny tank, and wonder how we are supposed to use them, since all of our belongings and cash have been taken away. A Mexican teenager with a tear tattooed below his eye sees me looking. 'Don't think about it, Pops,' he says. 'It costs, like, five dollars a minute.'

'Thanks for the advice.' I step over the unconscious drunk. My shoe slips on the filth, and I have to grab onto the edge of the phone to right myself. There is a single word scratched into the metal receiver: 'WHY.' It seems as good a question as any.

I give the operator my home phone number for the collect call, but you don't answer.

The door to the tank opens again and a female DO screams a series of names: *'DEJESUS! ROBINET! VALENTE! HOPKINS!'* We file to the door, the lucky ones. Individually we are brought up to a counter to sign a release form cataloging all the possessions that used to be ours. I am asked to press a thumbprint onto the back of two colored cards. There is an empty space beside it; I realize that I will do the same on the day I leave. After three months or eight months or ten years in this system turn me into a different person, they will be sure they are releasing the right man.

A young girl whose hair smells like autumn is the one in charge of fingerprinting us. It is done on a machine and sent automatically to the FBI and the State of Arizona's main databank. There, it will magically connect to any other times you've been in trouble with the law.

Sophie's school recently had a Child Safety Day. They took pictures of the kids and mounted them on Safety Passports. They had the local police set up to roll the fingerprints of each boy and girl. This was all so that they would have a protocol in place if the child was ever abducted.

I helped out that day. I sat next to an officer of the Wexton PD and we made jokes about how the mothers were coming out in droves to the gymnasium at the elementary school not because they were concerned with safety, but because they had cabin fever after three days of steady snow. Child after child, I held those impossibly tiny fingers between my own, small and fleshy as peas, and rolled them across the ink pad. 'Jeez,' the officer had said, when I got good at it. 'Why haven't we hired you?'

Now, as I am standing in the Madison Street Jail rolling my own fingers across a blank screen, the technician seems surprised that I know how to do it myself. 'A pro,' she says, and I glance up at her. I wonder if she knows that the same treatment is given to the kidnappers as the kidnapped.

From Tank Six I can see the boy in the suicide chair. A young kid with hair that covers his face, he whispers rap lyrics to himself and curls his hands into fists to pull at the restraints every now and then.

The Mexican boy who advised me not to use the phone is here, too, now. He lifts up his hands when the door opens and the DO tosses a haul of plastic bags into the air, catching two of them before they land on the floor. 'Ladmo,' he says, sitting back down.

'Andrew Hopkins.'

This breaks up several of the men in the cell. 'It isn't my name,' the boy says. 'It's the lunch.'

I take the cellophane sack from his hand and look through the contents: six slices of white bread. Two pieces of cheese. Two rounds of questionable bologna. An orange. A cookie. A juice container. Just like what you and I pack Sophie for snack at school.

'Why does the lunch have a name?' I ask.

He shrugs. 'Used to be a TV program for kids, the *Wallace and Ladmo Show*. They gave out goodie packs called Ladmo Bags. Guess Sheriff Jack thought it was funny.'

Across the cell, a big man shakes his head. 'Ain't funny to make us pay a dollar a day for this shit.'

The Mexican sticks a long thumbnail in his orange and begins to peel it, one continuous stripe. 'That's something else Sheriff Jack thinks is funny,' he says. 'Once you're inside, you got to pay for your food.'

'Hey.' A Native American man who has been asleep in the corner rubs his eyes and crawls forward to snatch a Ladmo. 'What kind of animal has an asshole in the middle of its back?'

'Sheriff Jack's horse,' grumbles the big man. 'If you're gonna tell a joke, at least tell one we haven't all heard a thousand times.'

The Native American's eyes harden. 'Ain't my fault you pop in and out of here like some skinny dick in your mama.'

The big man stands up, his lunch tumbling to the floor. Ten square feet is a small space, but it shrinks even further when fear sucks out all the spare air. I press myself up against the wall as the big man grabs the Native American by the neck and hurls him forward in one smooth move, so that his head smashes through the plate glass.

By the time the DOs arrive, the Native American is lying in a crumpled heap on the bottom of the cell, with blood trickling down his collar, and the big man is eating his lunch. 'Well, shoot,' the officer says. 'That was one of the *stronger* windows.'

When the big man gets thrown across the hallway into one of the isolation cells, the boy in the suicide chair doesn't even react. The Native American is hauled off for medical attention. The Mexican leans down and grabs the two abandoned lunch sacks. 'The orange is mine,' he says.

We are told to shower, but no one does, and I am not about to stand out any more than I already do. Instead I follow the others as they strip down, each man putting his clothing into a plastic bag. In return, we are given orange flip-flops, black-and-white convict-striped shirts and pants, hot pink boxers, a hot pink thermal tee, and hot pink socks. Another of Sheriff Jack's policies, I am told; the pink keeps inmates from stealing the underwear when they're released. It is not until one of the other men turns his back that I see the writing: SHERIFF'S INMATE. UNSENTENCED.

It feels like pajamas. Loose and unstructured, an elastic around my waist. As if, at any given moment, I just might wake up.

We are the ones who have been remanded into the custody of the Maricopa County Sheriff's Office, the ones who have not been released on bail. There is a courtroom right in the curve of the Horseshoe, one that meets several times a day.

When it was my turn, I told the initial appearance judge

that I wanted to wait for my lawyer. 'That's nice, Mr. Hopkins,' he said. 'I'd like to wait for my pension, too, but we can't always get what we want.'

My hearing took less than thirty seconds.

T-3 is the cell where we wait to be given our placement in the jail system. The man beside me has taken off his sandals and sits in a lotus position, chanting. Now that we're dressed alike, we are all reduced to the same bottom line. There is nothing to differentiate the guy who shoplifted an electric razor from the one who slashed a gang member's throat with a straight edge. We cannot tell one another apart, and this is both a blessing and a curse.

Freedom smells of spores and ragweed and dust and heat and suntan oil and car exhaust. Of hot, buttered daffodils and worms hiding under the soil. Of everything that's outside, when you are in here.

Two detention officers escort me upstairs to the second floor of the Madison Street Jail, the maximum security pod. The elevator opens up into a central control area. I am strip-searched again, and then given a toothbrush the size of my pinky finger, toothpaste, toilet paper, golf pencils, erasers, a comb, and soap. I'm handed a towel, blanket, mattress, and sheet.

The house consists of four pods – cages, each with fifteen cells inside. A central guard booth looms in the middle of the space, communicating by intercom. In each cage, a handful of men sit downstairs at tables, playing cards or eating or watching TV.

After my paperwork is transferred, the officer on the floor opens the door to the cage. 'You're in the middle cell up there,' she says. Immediately I can feel everyone's attention settling on me like a rash.

'Fresh meat,' says one man, with a barbed-wire tattoo on his neck.

'Fish,' says another, and he purses his lips.

I walk past them, pretending I'm deaf. In my cell, I put my supplies on the top bunk. I can almost stretch out my arms and touch both walls.

I lie down on the mattress, which is wafer-thin and stained. Now that I'm alone, all the fear that's been building up inside me during the intake process – all the panic I've been pushing out of my mind and covering with utter silence – presses down on my chest so hard I cannot breathe. My heart is thundering: I am sixty years old and in jail. I am the easiest target.

When I took you, I knew this was always a possibility. But risk always looks different when you are beating the system than when you've been beaten.

A man walks into the cell. Tall and beefy, he has devil horns tattooed on his head and is carrying a Bible. 'Who the fuck are you?' he asks. 'I'm off at church and they stick someone in my cell? *Fuck* that.' He shoves the Bible under the mattress on the bottom bunk, then comes onto the landing and yells for the DO. 'What's with Grandpa?'

'There's nowhere else to put him, Sticks. Deal with it.'

The man smashes his fist against the steel door. 'Get out,' he orders.

I take a deep breath. 'I'm staying.'

Sticks – is that really a name? – comes toe to toe with me. 'What are you, a punk?'

A punk, as I remember it, is a guy who rolls cigarettes up in his T-shirt sleeve and tries to act like James Dean. 'Okay,' I say. 'Sure. Whatever. I'm a punk. You're a punk. We're all punks.'

When he looks at me, incredulous, and then turns on his heel and leaves, a sweet shock unravels inside me. Could it really be that easy? If I refuse to play the game, will I be left alone?

Hopkins.

My name is piped in through the intercom system, and I come to the front of the cell and peer at the DO who is speaking into the microphone in the central booth.

You've got a visitor.

★

I am expecting Eric, and instead, I find you.

I don't know how you've gotten to Arizona this fast. I don't know what you've done with Sophie while you're here. I don't know how you've made it past all these steel walls and locks and lies.

You're staring at me with every step, and at first I'm embarrassed – that you should see me like this, wearing convict stripes and stripped down to the very marrow of my faults. I'm too ashamed, at first, to even meet your gaze, but when I do, I'm even more ashamed. I bet you don't realize it, but there's still hope in your eyes. After all this, you still trust me to explain why your whole life has been upended. I am responsible for putting that trust there in the first place; I did not earn it as much as demand it by default.

How am I supposed to make you understand that in order to give you the life I thought you deserved to live, I had to take away the life you knew?

When you were little, and I had to count the minutes that I was allowed to see you, I wanted to give you the world. So I'd pick you up in my car and we'd drive across the desert with the windows rolled down. When we got far enough away, I'd turn to you and ask: *Where would you go, if you could go anywhere?* And you'd give me the answers of a little girl: *To the moon. To Candyland. To London Bridge.* I'd rev up the engine and nod, as if any of these destinations were possible. I think we both knew we'd never get there, but that hardly seemed to matter, as long as we were driving around looking for them. There were no car seats in those days; there were no seat belt laws, but you trusted me to keep you safe. You trusted me to take you somewhere wonderful.

You are on the other side of the glass booth, and you are sobbing. I pick up the phone, hoping you'll do the same. 'Delia, baby,' I say. 'Don't cry.'

You lift up the bottom of your shirt to wipe your eyes. 'Why didn't you tell me?'

Well. There are a thousand reasons for that, some of which

are truths I'm still not able to share with you, and never will be. But mostly, it was because I knew firsthand what it was like to love one person so hard that I'd staked my life on her, only to realize that somewhere along the line, she'd unraveled me. And I couldn't stand knowing that you might one day feel about me the way I had come to feel about your mother.

You ask me for your name, mine, my old profession. I hand these details to you like the bargaining chips a crisis negotiator would use to keep someone on the edge from jumping, except the life at stake here is the one we've carved out together. I watch your face for clues, but you do not look me in the eye.

When I forced myself to picture this moment in the origami folds of the night, I'd run through multiple scenarios: the police coming to the senior center; my credit card being denied at a gas station because it set off a red flag; Elise showing up on our doorstep. In each of them, I always pictured you holding fast to my hand, unable or unwilling to let anything come between us.

This is why, maybe, I'm caught off guard when you get angry. I don't know why I've always assumed that since I was the one to take you, I would also be the one who decided when to let go.

I didn't have a choice, I say, but my words curl under at the ends, like a beaten dog's tail.

'You had a choice,' you answer, but it's what you don't say that slices through me like a clean blade: *And you made the wrong one.*

For a long time, after we ran away, we both had nightmares. Mine involved you holding your mother's hand, stepping off the curb into a wall of oncoming traffic. I'd lurch forward to push you out of the way, only to discover that I'd been watching from behind a glass wall. I'd listen to the scream of brakes and your high cries, knowing I could not reach you.

When you leave the visiting area, I drop the phone and press my hands to the glass. I bang on it, but you can't hear me.

Your nightmares used to be about getting left behind. You'd rip the seam of sleep wide open and wake up, damp and sobbing. I'd rub your back until you fell asleep again. *Nightmares don't come true*, I'd soothe.

As it turns out, I was lying about that, too.

Instead of going back to my cell, I wander around the pod. There is a communal area where some of the inmates are playing cards or watching television. The toilet facilities are in the cells, but there is a room with showers off in the rear corner. It's empty now, and that's enough reason for me to duck inside.

In the aftermath of your visit, I am moving slowly, as if I'm swimming underwater. I had hoped to see you because I am selfish, but now I wish you hadn't come. It's only made me more sure of what I told Eric before I was extradited from New Hampshire: I am no longer a source of protection for you, but a source of pain. I heard as much, minutes ago, in the cramped breaths you took between sentences. For the first time in your life you wondered if you'd have been better off without me.

I gave up my life once trying to do what's best for you. Tomorrow, in front of a judge, I'll do it again.

I am leaning my forehead against the cool tile of the shower area when a shadow falls behind me. Sticks is there, surrounded by a brace of men as large as he is, their tattooed arms folded and their bodies blocking the exit.

'I'm no punk,' Sticks says.

The next thing I know I am splayed on the floor, my head ringing from a blow. There is an impossible weight on my legs, and I can feel my pants being ripped down. I try to curl up into a ball, but he starts hitting at my face and my gut. I try to yell for help. As his hands lock onto my legs I start kicking anywhere, anything, because I am not going to let this happen. I am not.

I start sewing together all the fury I've been gathering

together since the moment the police took me out of my kitchen in Wexton days ago. I let loose the panic I've stored for twenty-eight years, about being found out. So when his arm anchors me at the waist, when his hips are parenthetical to mine, I reach out for the bar of soap on the shower floor. I twist; shove it into his grinning mouth.

He lets go of me immediately and I roll to the side, dry heaving and grabbing at my clothes. I can't think of you in here; I can't think of anything but me. And I won't be left alone, not even if I try to fade into the background. Everyone else will just pick at me until they see what color I bleed.

That's all I can hold in my head, before everything goes black.

When I fall asleep in jail, it is never dark, and I am never tired. So I find myself imagining what got me in here in the first place, twisting it into a Mobius strip in my mind.

I don't count sheep; I count days.

I don't pray; I barter with God.

I make a list of the things I've taken for granted, because I always thought I would have access to them:

Meat that requires a knife. Pens. Caffeinated coffee.

A child's belly laugh. A butterfly's tango.

Paperwork.

Pitch dark. Snow clouds.

Utter quiet.

You.

I open one eye, the only one that works, and find myself staring at a short, muscular black man who is picking through a collection of food. It is nearly dark, and the door to the cell is locked. He takes an orange and slips it under his mattress.

I try to sit up, but feel like I've been beaten from head to heel. 'Who . . . are you?'

He turns, as if surprised to discover that I'm alive. 'Concise.'

'That's your *name?*'

'It's what the ladies call me. Because I may be short, but man am I sweet.' He takes a handful of carrots and eats them. 'Hope you weren't counting on dinner,' he says, pointing to what must have been my tray.

'What happened to . . .'

'Sticks?' Concise grins. 'The motherfucker got a D.'

'A *D?*'

'He in disciplinary segregation for a week.'

'Why didn't I get one?'

'Because even the DOs know: You get called a punk, and you either gotta fuck or fight.' He turns a sharp eye on me. 'Don't be gettin' comfortable. No way are you stayin' here for good. They didn't want to mix races at all, but I was all they got open.'

Right now it would not matter to me if Concise was African American, Hispanic, or Martian. He takes a postcard from the pocket of his striped shirt and sticks it through the bars at the front of the cell. On the door, he has fashioned a mailbox made of plastic spoons. There is even a little flag, colored in with red Magic Marker.

I wonder whether, if you rot here long enough, you grow a thicker skin. I wonder if prison is any different from this. Once I go to court and enter a guilty plea, that's where I will be headed – for years. Maybe one for each I stole from you.

I try to roll over and wince at the fire in my kidneys. 'Why are you here?' I ask.

'Because the damn Ritz was full up,' Concise says. 'What kind of fool question is that?'

'I mean, why are you in jail?'

'Six months for dealin'. Would have been three, but I already done time before. That's the thing about a habit. It's like a pet, man. It don't go away just because you're in here. It's waitin' to jump all over you the minute you walk back onto the street.'

From my vantage point on the bottom bunk, I look up and see the steel tray holding the upper mattress. I look at the tack welds and wonder how much weight they can support.

'Sticks, he one tough cracker, man. He thinks he own this pod.' Concise shakes his head. 'We all wonderin' who the hell you are.'

I close my eyes and think of all the people I have been in my lifetime: a boy who fell in love with a broken girl a thousand years ago; a father holding a newborn and thinking that nothing could ever make him let her go; a man starving for one more moment with his little girl; a fugitive on the run; a liar; a cheat; a felon. Maybe the habit that is always waiting to jump me on the other side of the fence is revival. Maybe I will do absolutely anything to wipe the slate clean, to start over.

'Call me Andrew,' I say.

Eric

The law offices of Hamilton, Hamilton and Hamilton-Thorpe are located in downtown Phoenix, in a mirrored building that scares the hell out of me when I walk up close and see that ghost of myself coming forward. Chris, the second Hamilton in the name lineup, went to law school with me in Vermont, knowing all along he had a nice cushy job waiting at his father's firm (the first Hamilton in the name lineup). The newest partner (the hyphenated one) is Chris's little sister, recently graduated from Harvard Law.

In order to try a case *pro hac vice* in a different state, you need a sponsoring local attorney. Actually, it's similar to AA, where someone older and wiser mentors you in the hopes that you do nothing to embarrass yourself. Chris is a former diver with the face of a choirboy who used to be able to charm professors into extensions without breaking a sweat. When I called and asked him to be my Arizona counsel, he didn't even hesitate before agreeing.

'I ought to tell you about the case,' I had said.

'Who cares?' Chris answered. 'It's an excuse to go out and have a few beers.'

I didn't tell him I no longer do that.

He was in court yesterday when I arrived at the law office in a mad rush, trying to contact the New Hampshire Bar Association. His sister, Serena, graciously ceded me the conference room at Hamilton, Hamilton and Hamilton-Thorpe; a vast expanse of paneled wood and barrister bookcases and brass-studded leather chairs.

No one is in the office this morning when I let myself in

with my newly minted key, but then, it is only 6:45 A.M. After yesterday's debacle with my nonexistent Bar card, I am determined to read up on Arizona case law before visiting hours begin at the jail.

I find myself staring at the legalese, all those blocks of type and tiny letters morphing into one another, until all I can make out on a page is the shape of a man holding out his hand, and a little girl reaching to grab it.

I was ten years old, and in serious training for the CIA. I had a walkie-talkie, a black-stocking balaclava, a flashlight, and a cheat sheet for Morse code. To practice, I was going to spy on my mother in the living room, although I was supposed to still be outside catching June bugs in old Jif peanut butter jars.

She was on the phone when I crept in on cat feet and flattened myself behind the couch with my tape recorder. 'He's a son of a bitch is all,' she said. 'Well, you know what? She can *have* him. She can have his pyramid schemes and his big promises and all his Casanova bullshit.'

I turned on the tape recorder and realized too late that I had hit play, and, worse, that the Halloween screams of a dozen humpback whales were filling the room. My mother jumped and peeked over the back of the couch, narrowing her eyes in a death laser. 'Andrea, I have to call you back,' she said.

A good CIA agent would unspool the tape and eat the evidence, I thought. *A good CIA agent would pull a cyanide pill from the folds of his suit and go down as a hero for his mission.*

My mother yanked me up by the ear. 'You liar,' she said, those long vowels a boozy breeze across my face. 'You're just like him.' She slapped me so hard across the head that I actually saw stars, and for a minute I was amazed that this could actually happen, that it wasn't just something you saw in a cartoon. I cowered, hating myself for that, hating her.

And then, just as suddenly, she was behind the couch with me, her octopus hands smoothing my hair and kissing my face and rocking me. 'Baby, I didn't mean to,' she said. 'You forgive me, don't you? You know I'd never hurt you. You and me, we're in this together, aren't we?'

I stood up and backed away from her. 'I got invited next door for dinner,' I said, and a red flare went off in my head. I *was* a liar.

'Well, you go then,' she replied, and she smiled her loose smile, the one that she used when she was embarrassed – not to be confused with the bright smile, the one she wore when she was completely lit; or the fake smile, the one that made my stomach feel like a cello strung too tight.

Outside, the neighborhood was painted like a hand-colored photo; nearly too dark to make out the reds of the peeling shutters or the snowflake blue of the hydrangeas. I headed for Delia's house but stopped as I came around the corner. Their kitchen window burned buttery as a candle, and inside I could see Delia and her father eating dinner. Fried chicken. Her father had both of the drumsticks in his hands, and he was making them do a can-can across the platter toward Delia.

I sat down on the lawn. I didn't really want to interrupt them, I realized. I just wanted to know that somewhere, in a household, this was going on.

'Eric, man, if you keep working this hard you're going to get me disinherited,' Chris laughs, and I jump awake with a start, my heart leaping like a fish pulled through six leagues of sea. I smooth my rumpled tie and rub my hand down my face. There is a crease in my cheek, the result of lying on top of an open book.

Chris does not look much different from how he did years ago in law school: the same relaxed posture; the same sandy blond hair; the same comfortable expression of a man who knows the world will always go his way. 'So, welcome to the family business,' he says. 'My sister said she got you settled yesterday. Sorry I couldn't be the one.'

'Serena was great,' I reply, clearing my throat. 'And the office is terrific.'

Chris sits down across the table from me. 'Must be a pain in the ass having to become fluent overnight in Arizona law.'

'I didn't think you *had* law down here. Isn't it still ten paces, turn, and draw your weapon?'

Chris laughs. 'Only half the time. You're forgetting the posses.' He takes a sip of coffee; just the smell of it makes me salivate. But I gave up caffeine with booze; the blood rush was too similar and I didn't want to tempt my body with the feel of a high. These days, I will not even take an aspirin for a garden-variety headache.

Chris lifts his mug toward me. 'There's more if you want some. Just brewed.'

'Thanks, but I don't drink coffee.'

'That's inhuman, you know.' He sits forward, his elbows on the table. 'So I suppose you should tell me about this case, if I have to be second chair. Must be a pretty important client, if he convinced you to haul your butt to Arizona to fight some charge.'

'He is pretty important,' I answer. 'He's my fiancée's father. He got indicted for kidnapping her during a custody visit in 1977.'

Chris's eyes widen. 'I am never going to complain about my in-laws again.'

I leave out the part about how Andrew as good as confessed to me at the Wexton PD. How he expressed the desire to plead guilty, and how I swore to Delia that I wouldn't let that happen. To try a case in another state, your professional conduct must be impeccable; I have already failed on two counts. 'Delia asked me to represent him. I haven't even seen Andrew since he was extradited. I spent the whole afternoon yesterday trying to convince the staff at the Madison Street Jail that I'm really a lawyer, and don't just play one on TV.'

The secretary sticks her head into the conference room. 'Oh, good, Mr. Talcott, you're awake,' she says, and a flush of embarrassment spreads over my collar. 'Your fiancée wants you to call her immediately, something about your daughter being sick.'

'Sophie?' I ask, but I am already reaching for the phone. Sick as in head cold, or sick as in bubonic plague? I dial Delia's cell number, and get her voice mail. 'Call me,' I say, and then I look up at Chris. 'Maybe I should swing by home, make sure she's all right . . .'

'This came for you, too,' the secretary says, and she passes me a fax.

It is a letter from the New Hampshire Bar Association, stating I am a member in good standing.

I ought to go check on Sophie, but I also need to talk to Andrew, in jail.

I have a feeling this isn't the last time I will be asked to choose between Delia's present life and her past.

Which came first: the addict or the drug?

You can't have an addiction unless there's something to crave; by the same token, a drug is nothing but a plant or a drink or a powder until someone wants it badly. The truth is, the addict and the drug came together. And therein lies the problem.

When you want something desperately, you shake with the need for it. You tell yourself you don't need more than one sip, because it's just the taste you crave, and once it's on your tongue you will be able to make it last a lifetime. You dream of it at night. You see a thousand mile-high obstacles between where you stand and what you want, and you convince yourself you have the power to hurdle them. You tell yourself this even when, leaping the first block, you wind up bruised and bloodied and flattened.

I have been fooling everyone for years. Sure, I've given up alcohol, but that was nothing compared to my other addiction. Love is the most dangerous craving of all, if you ask me. It turns us into people we aren't. It makes us feel like hell, and makes us walk on water. It ruins us for anything else.

I watch her doing the simplest things: brushing her hair into a ponytail, feeding the dog, tying Sophie's shoelaces, and I want to tell her what she means to me, but I never actually say the words. After all, to acknowledge Delia as a drug, I'd have to face the fact that one day I might have to go without her, and this I can't do.

Inside the lobby of the Madison Street Jail, a spot I became all too familiar with yesterday, are a bank of blue chairs and a wall-mounted television. Against one wall is a line of bank-teller windows, with signs posted above to separate VISITORS from ATTORNEYS ONLY. I approach that window, feeling like the first-class airline passenger bypassing the masses. The woman staffing the position remembers me from yesterday. 'You're back,' she says sourly.

I offer up my best smile. 'Good morning.' I push the letter from the New Hampshire Bar Association through the slit at the bottom of the Plexiglas window. 'See? I told you I was a genuine attorney.'

'Genuine attorney . . . that's one of those whatchamacallits. You know, like jumbo shrimp and working vacation and military intelligence.'

'Oxymoron.'

'Hey, you want to call yourself names, fine with me.' She picks up a pen. 'Which inmate did you want to see?'

While I wait for a detention officer to lead me into the jail, I sit in the bank of chairs and watch TV with some of the other visitors. Some have brought children who bounce on their laps like popcorn. The show currently airing is some sort of court TV – or so I think, until I read the sleeve badge of one of the bailiffs standing beside the judge's bench: Maricopa County Sheriff's Office. At that point I realize that this must be a closed-circuit film of some arraignment process that goes on inside the jail itself. 'La mirada!' the lady next to me says proudly, pointing at the television monitor so that her toddler will look. '¡No es Papá guapo!'

When my name is called, a beefy officer leads me to a metal detector, and then takes a cluster of keys from his belt to open a door that leads to an airlock about three feet square. From inside a control room, the inner door opens, admitting us into the jail.

We take an elevator up to the fourth-floor visiting area. Another detention officer holds court over a small assortment of inmates. Some speak to their attorneys in private rooms. A long central section features dozens of individual noncontact-visit booths. One inmate is chained to a stool, holding a phone in his hand. On the other side of a glass wall, a woman is crying.

'You can wait here,' the detention officer says. 'We'll go get your client.'

'Here' turns out to be a side room with a fluorescent light that hisses and spits like a wet cat. From this vantage point, I can't see the inmate anymore, but I can see the woman visiting him. She has leaned forward now, and is kissing the glass.

When I was eleven, I caught Delia making out with the bathroom mirror. I asked her what she was doing. 'Practicing,' she informed me, matter-of-fact. 'You might want to think about it, too.'

After a while I glance at my watch. Twenty minutes have gone by; I stand up and try to locate the detention officer. He is on the other side of the visiting room, bent over the *Arizona Republic*'s sports page. 'Excuse me,' I say. 'Has anyone found my client yet? Andrew Hopkins?'

The man gives me a blank stare, but he crosses the room and picks up a phone. He speaks into it for a few moments, and then returns to me. 'They thought someone came down to tell you. Your client's already been brought next door to court.'

I call Chris Hamilton on my cell phone as I'm flying up the steps of the East Courthouse. 'How fast can you be here?' I demand. As my sponsoring attorney, he has to be present in the courtroom even if my *pro hac vice* motion has been granted. I don't have time to call Delia, and I know she is going to kill me for that. But then, Andrew is about to face a judge without me – a judge to whom he plans to plead guilty.

The court building is ten times larger than any court in New Hampshire. A bailiff runs a metal detector just inside the entrance; a woman holds tight to a little boy's hand as she sets her purse on the conveyor belt. Attorneys crossing the lobby drift toward each other, making deals over cups of coffee. In the chairs, waiting, are sequestered witnesses in their itchy suits and welfare kids with coloring books and the personal recognizance returnees, their baggy pants riding low and their tooks pulled down past their eyebrows.

I try to find a clerk who can tell me on which of the nine floors, and in which of the twenty courtrooms, Andrew will be appearing, but no one seems to have that answer. So I run to the sheriff's office inside the court, the holding pen where inmates are kept waiting until they appear. The deputy at the desk has a Doc Holliday mustache and a Buddha belly. 'All's I know,' he says, 'is that if it's an arraignment, you're in the wrong damn courthouse.'

I am running over to the other courthouse – the *Central* Courthouse – when I see Chris hurrying toward the building. This one has thirteen stories with five courtrooms. One look at the line for the elevators, and I'm following him up a staircase. We reach the fifth floor, gasping. 'Not Guilty Arraignments,' he explains, and we burst into Courtroom 501 together like a comic book duo come to save the day.

I wish I could say I am filled with confidence when I walk into that courtroom, but if I'm going to be honest, I don't have a very good track record with success. It took me two attempts to pass the Bar. I started AA three times and then proceeded to once again drink myself into oblivion. I have no reason to believe that this latest challenge will be any different.

The judge is the most imposing justice I have ever seen. He easily weighs three hundred pounds, has flyaway gray hair, and fists the size of Easter hams. A placard on the bench announces him as The Honorable Caesar T. Noble. 'I can't believe you drew that judge,' Chris says under his breath. 'We call him No Bull.'

The inmate sitting alone at the defense bench gets to his feet, his ankle chains jingling. Standing, his profile is visible: It is Andrew.

'Mr. Hopkins, I see you don't have counsel present, so I'm going to ask you to enter a plea,' the judge says.

I start running down the center aisle. There is a saying sometimes chanted at AA meetings: Fake it until you make it. I've done it before. I can do it again.

The judge – hell, everyone in the room – looks to me. 'Excuse me,' Noble says, as I hurdle the bar and step up beside Andrew, squeezing his shoulder. 'Would you please identify yourself?'

'Eric Talcott, Your Honor. I'm an attorney licensed to practice in the state of New Hampshire, but I've filed a motion to appear before you *pro hac vice*. My sponsor for the State of Arizona is Christopher Hamilton . . . and, um, I'm certified to practice in this courtroom, provided the motion has been granted.'

The judge glances down at his file, and then back up at me. 'Sir, you are out of order. Not only don't I have this alleged *pro hac vice* motion, but I find it extremely disrespectful that you've come whooping into my courtroom and interfered with my proceedings.' He narrows his gaze until it nicks at my throat. 'Maybe that's the way y'all do things in New Hampshire, but here in Arizona, we don't.'

'Your Honor,' Chris says, smoothly stepping over the bar to stand next to me. 'If you please, I'm Chris Hamilton, and I'm responsible for that *pro hac vice* motion. We asked the clerk's office to bring the motion either to Your Honor or to another judge who might be in a position to sign it quickly . . . knowing as I do that Your Honor prefers, understandably, to have everything in order.'

Chris couldn't come any closer to kissing this guy's considerable ass.

Apparently, in Arizona, that actually works. The judge beckons to the clerk of the court. 'Call over and see if there's any kind of motion that's been filed and granted.'

The clerk picks up the phone and mouths words that don't carry any volume. I have never understood how they quite do that, but it's the same in every court. When he hangs up he turns to the judge. 'Your Honor, Judge Umatallo just granted the motion.'

'Mr. Talcott, this is your lucky day,' Noble says, without a trace of hospitality. 'How does your client plead?'

I make sure not to look at Andrew when I speak. 'Not guilty.'

Andrew stiffens, whispering, 'You told me—'

Under my breath, I cut him off. 'Not now.'

The judge flips through some of the pages in the file. 'I see that bail is set at million cash. I assume you want that continued, Ms. Wasserstein?' He glances toward the prosecutor, whom I haven't even considered until this moment. A woman with curly brown hair twisted into a severe knot at the back of her neck, she has a mouth that looks like it has no muscle memory of ever striking a smile.

'Yes, Your Honor,' she replies, and when she stands up I realize that she's pregnant. Not just pregnant, mind you, but in the full throes of really-any-day-now-I-could-drop-this-baby condition. Great. So the prosecutor I'm cursed with is an impending mother, one with natural sympathies toward a woman whose child was snatched.

'This is a kidnapping case of great importance to the State of Arizona,' she says, 'and given that the defendant is an extreme flight risk, we feel there shouldn't even be a question about whether or not bail should be continued.'

I clear my throat and rise. 'Your Honor, we'd really like you to rethink the bail question. My client has no criminal record whatsoever and—'

'I beg to differ, Your Honor.' The prosecutor lifts a computerized record on fanfold paper, then lets it unfold to the floor. From the length of the document, you'd think Andrew Hopkins was the criminal of the century.

'Would have been nice if you mentioned this,' I say through clenched teeth to Andrew. There is nothing worse for a defense attorney than having a prosecutor make a fool out of you. It makes your client look like a liar; it makes it seem as if you haven't done your job.

'The defendant has an assault conviction from December of 1976 . . . when he was known as Charles Edward Matthews.'

The judge bangs his gavel. 'I've heard enough of this. If one million was enough to hold the defendant in New Hampshire, then two million is enough to hold him in Arizona. *Cash.*'

The bailiffs haul Andrew away from me, his chains jangling. 'Where are you taking him?' I ask.

The judge purses his lips. 'It's certainly not *my* job to tell you how to do *yours,* Mr. Talcott. Who do they have running those law schools in New Hampshire, anyway?'

'I went to law school in Vermont,' I correct.

The judge snorts. 'Vermont's just like New Hampshire, except upside-down. Next case?'

I try to catch Andrew's eye as he's dragged off, but he doesn't turn around. Chris pats me on the shoulder; until this moment, I've forgotten he's even present. 'That's about as good as it gets here,' he commiserates.

As we walk through the gate I notice the prosecutor speaking to an older couple. 'What do you know about the county attorney?'

'Emma Wasserstein? That she'll probably eat her young. She's one tough lady. I haven't been up against her lately, but I doubt that pregnancy's softened her at all.'

I sigh. 'I was kind of hoping it was just some enormous tumor.'

Chris grins. 'At least it can't get any worse.'

But at that moment, Emma Wasserstein turns around, guiding the couple she is speaking with out of the courtroom. They are well-dressed, nervous; they have the cloudy confusion about them of people unfamiliar with the legal system. The man is about fifty-five, dark-skinned, hesitant. He has his arm around the woman, who stumbles into the aisle and bumps into me. 'Disculpeme,' she says.

The raven hair, the freckles she cannot quite hide with powder, the very bones of her face: I step back to make way for the woman who could only be Delia's mother.

Courthouses are full of sounds – the squeak of bailiff shoes, the quiet whisper of witnesses practicing testimony, the jangle of quarters, and the crank of the vending machines. But you rarely hear clapping, in spite of the fact that the best law is nothing more than a performance. So when I hear the applause, I find myself looking around to find its source. 'Not your finest showing,' Fitz says, walking toward me. 'But I'll give you an eight out of ten because you've got a jet-lag handicap.'

Just like that, I'm smiling from the inside out. 'God, it's good to see a friendly face.'

'After the showdown with Medea in there, I'm not surprised. Where's Delia?'

'I don't know,' I admit. 'She called me to say Sophie was sick, but I couldn't reach her.'

'You mean she doesn't know Andrew was arraigned?'

'*I* didn't even know until ten minutes ago,' I say.

Fitz blinks at me. 'She's going to murder you.'

I nod, and notice the memo pad sticking out of his pocket. Grabbing it, I flip through pages of notes from the arraignment. He's not here for the moral support; he's writing about this for the *Gazette*. 'Only after she murders *you*,' I reply dryly.

'Well,' Fitz says, ducking his head. 'Want to be my roommate in Hell?'

We start walking down the corridor. I have no idea where I'm headed; for all I know, this could be the hallway that leads back to the jail. 'You ought to go see her,' I suggest. 'We're living in a trailer in Mesa that's smaller than Greta's cage at home.'

'It's got to be better than the motel the *Gazette*'s springing for. It's conveniently located near Sky Harbor Airport. So near, in fact, that the toilet flushes every time a plane takes off.'

I take my pen from my breast pocket and reach for Fitz's hand, write the still-unfamiliar address down on his palm. 'Tell her I'll be home as soon as I can. Tell her to call me so I know how Sophie's doing. And if you can work it into the conversation, feel free to break the news about the arraignment.'

As I head down the hall, Fitz's laughter follows me. 'Coward,' he calls out.

I look over my shoulder and grin. 'Sucker,' I answer.

Thirty minutes later, I am right back where I started: in the visiting room of the Madison Street Jail. Again, I've had to argue with the same woman at the entrance about my Bar card. Again, I've been told to wait while my client is brought to me. This time, however, he actually shows up. Andrew lets the detention officer close the door to our tiny conference room before exploding. '*Not* guilty?' he accuses.

The job of a defense attorney is to act in the best interests of your client. But what if you think your client doesn't have his best interests in mind? And what if, to complicate matters, your client wants something that will bring great pain to a woman for whom you would lay down your life? 'For God's sake, Andrew. I'd think one night in jail would be enough to convince you that you don't want it as a permanent address.' His eyes flash, but he says nothing. 'And how do you think Delia would handle that?' I add. 'She was a mess after she saw you for just a half hour last night.'

'Not for the reason you think, Eric. She hates me. She hates what I did to her.'

Delia had been crying when she came home, but I hadn't asked her why. I'd assumed it was a normal reaction to seeing the father she loved in the confines of a jail. I hadn't asked; as her father's attorney, I wasn't supposed to . . . just as I am not supposed to reveal her thoughts about this trial to Andrew. 'She's the one who told me to plead you not guilty,' I confess. 'She insisted upon it.'

Andrew glances up at me. 'Before or after she saw me last night?'

I keep my eyes trained on his. 'After,' I lie.

Is there no end to this?

He sinks down into the chair across from me, and I register for the first time the bruises on his forehead and jaw, the parallel scrape of nails along his neck. At the arraignment I was so busy looking at the judge I never really focused my attention on my client. He is quiet for a long moment, so that the only sound in the room comes from the lamp overhead, which is in its death throes. 'There's a lot going on for her right now,' I say gently. 'You've known this outcome was a possibility for twenty-eight years; Delia's just discovered it. She needs a little time. And she needs to know that you're willing to give it to her.' I hesitate. 'You went to so much trouble to be with her, Andrew. Why would you want to stop now?'

I can see him thinking twice; that's all the opening I need. 'If I do what you want,' he says after a moment, 'what will happen to me?'

I shake my head. 'I don't know, Andrew. But I'm entirely sure of what will happen if you don't. And I think . . .' My attention is caught by an inmate walking past the conference room. Through the tiny window I make out his shoulder-length white hair, his stooped shoulders. This man must be seventy, eighty; this is what Andrew could become. 'I think everyone deserves a second chance,' I finish.

Andrew bows his head. 'Will you tell Delia what I tell you?'

He is asking me about the ethical tightrope beneath my feet. I can feel it, a cable of steel, something I'm used to balancing on as a lawyer. But then I look down, and remember that this man is more than just a client, that his daughter is more than just a material witness, and suddenly the ground moves a thousand miles farther away.

'What you say here, stays here,' I promise.

Andrew nods. 'All right,' he says, and the transaction takes place: a softening of his shoulders, an opening of his fist, a silent transfer of trust.

I clear my throat and impersonally extract a legal pad from my briefcase. 'Well,' I begin, all business. 'Tell me how you got her out.'

This is usually the point at which a client tells me, *I didn't do it.* Or, *I swear, I was just putting the car in a garage for someone, I didn't know it was stolen.* Or, *I was wearing my boyfriend's pants, how was I supposed to know he had a bag of pot in the back pocket?* But Andrew has already confessed, and there is a trail of evidence nearly thirty years long that proves he and his daughter lived under false names and pretenses.

His daughter. A woman who has three freckles on the base of her jaw that have always reminded me of Orion's belt, who knows all the words to the song 'The Wreck of the Edmund Fitzgerald,' who held my hand firmly under hers and pushed down against the hard knob swelling under the skin of her abdomen and said, 'I'm a hundred percent sure that's a foot. Unless it's a head.'

Andrew takes a deep breath. 'I had the whole weekend with her; it was part of the custody agreement. I told her we were going to take a trip. And you know how it is when you promise something like that to Sophie? You know how she starts—'

'Stop,' I interrupt. 'I can't have you comparing this to me and Sophie, all right?'

He starts again. 'You know how when you promise a kid that you're going to go somewhere special? Well, it's like holding out a handful of candy. Beth was thrilled about the prospect of a vacation.'

'Beth.'

'That's who she was . . . then.'

I nod, and write that name down on my legal pad. It doesn't suit her. I cross it off, heavy black lines.

'I stopped off at my apartment – I was living in a studio in Tempe after the divorce – and packed up as much stuff as I could into suitcases. The rest I left behind. We just started to drive.'

'You didn't have a plan?'

'I didn't even know I was going to go through with it, until I hit the highway,' Andrew says. 'I was just so angry—'

'Stop.' If he took Delia out of revenge or spite, I don't want to hear it. If I do, then I can't spin a defense for him without perjuring myself. 'So you got to the highway, and what did you do?'

'Headed east. I wasn't really thinking, like I said. We stayed at motels where you could pay in cash, and I registered under a different name every night. At some point I realized I was heading to New York. I mean, there were millions of people in the city. Who'd notice two more?'

Delia and I went to New York City when we were in college. She couldn't wait to go, back then. She said she'd never been there before.

'We stayed in some little hotel – I don't remember what it was called; it was close to Penn Station. I registered there as Richard Worth, and the desk clerk asked me if Mrs. Worth would be joining me. It just popped out: I said no, that my wife had recently died.' Andrew looks up at me. 'And then I realized Beth had heard every word.'

'What happened?'

'She started to cry. I had to get her out of the lobby before she went to pieces, so I told the desk clerk that my daughter was still very upset. I took her upstairs to the room and sat her down on the bed. I was going to tell her the truth, explain that it was all just a story I'd made up, but I couldn't. What if Beth blurted out to the same desk clerk that her father had been lying? Anyone in their right mind would have known there was something strange going on . . . and I couldn't take that chance.' He shakes his head, grimacing. 'I dug my own grave, by pretending Elise was dead in the first place. And if I'm going to be honest, the more I thought about it, the more it seemed like the safe thing to do. If Beth started talking about her mother out of the blue, or expected Elise to appear out of nowhere, or threw a tantrum, all I'd have to do is turn to whoever was watching or listening and explain that her mother had recently passed away. People would immediately give us the benefit of the doubt.'

Sympathy, as any defense attorney knows, can be bought with a good lie.

'What did you say to her, exactly?'

'She was four. She had no experience with death – my parents were both already gone when she was born, and Elise's mom and dad lived in Mexico. So I told Beth that something very bad had happened, that her mother had been in a car crash. I said that she'd been hurt, and that the doctors at the hospital tried to do everything they could to help her, but they couldn't, and so Mommy was up in heaven. I said that she'd never be able to see Elise again, but that I would take care of her forever.'

'How did she react?'

'She asked whether Elise would be better by the time we got home from our vacation.'

I look down at the legal pad, at my hands, at anything but Andrew.

'I tried to find things to do that would keep her busy. We went to the Empire State Building and the Museum of Natural History; we played on the Alice statue in Central Park. I bought her toys at FAO Schwarz. I took her on a Circle Line cruise. Then one night, I was in the bathroom at the hotel when Beth started screaming for her mother. I found her standing at the TV, her cheek right up against the screen. And sure enough, there was Elise on the six o'clock news, talking into a dozen microphones and holding up Beth's picture.'

Andrew gets up and starts pacing around the tiny room. 'I

knew I couldn't stay in a hotel forever,' he said. 'But I didn't know what I was going to do. To buy a house, you need an ID and a bank account, and I had neither of those anymore. Then one afternoon we were walking down Forty-second Street and Beth saw some flashing pinball lights at this place called Playland. She pulled me in, and I gave her some quarters for the arcade games. There was a group of teenagers in there, huddled around one girl's brand-new phony ID. They sold them at the arcade – looked like fake driver's licenses – and it got me thinking. I went up to the counter and asked the kid who was working there where I might go to get an ID. The kid shrugged and pointed to this Polaroid booth, where you could pull the curtain and get your picture taken. I took a twenty out of my wallet, and asked him the question again. He said he used to know a guy in Harlem, and for forty more bucks he managed to remember the name. When I called the number he gave me, I was told to go to a Harlem address after midnight.'

'Harlem?' I say. 'After *midnight?*'

'For twenty-five hundred dollars he gave me a driver's license, fake passports, and birth certificates for both of us. We got Social Security numbers, too. They were real identities, a father and a daughter who had died in a car accident. I almost backed out of the deal when I heard that, but then I saw the name he'd put on one of the passports: Cordelia Hopkins. Cordelia – that was the daughter in *King Lear* who stuck by her father, no matter what.' He looks up at me. 'I thought it was a good omen.'

I tap my fingers on the table. 'King Lear . . . Cordelia,' I say. 'You went to college, I assume.'

'Majored in chemistry. I went to graduate school, too. I was a pharmacist in Arizona.' He shrugs. 'I would have done it in New Hampshire, too, but I didn't have a license under my new name.'

'How did you wind up in Wexton?'

'Delia hated New York. We used to play a game . . . I'd

ask her if she could go anywhere, and see anything, what would it be?' Andrew looks up at me. 'That day she said snow.'

When you grow up in New Hampshire, you take winter for granted. But for a kid from Phoenix, this would be a mystery.

'I drove north,' Andrew says. 'The car ran out of gas a mile outside of Wexton, and we walked into town. I think I fell in love at first sight – the white church and the town green and even the benches with little brass plaques dedicated to old school principals. It all seemed like a movie set, like a place where there could be a happy ending. So Delia and I went into Wexton Savings and Loan and set up a bank account. We stayed at a bed and breakfast for a while, until I got a job as a janitor at the senior center – I'd worked with the elderly as a pharmacist, and thought it might be a good fit. They were so desperate they didn't even care about references. About a month later, a realtor found us a house we could afford.'

'The one next door to mine,' I murmur.

Andrew nods. 'Your mother came over with a casserole.'

Actually, I can remember her cooking it. She was sober, for once, and she made a vegetable lasagna that had won her first prize in a local recipe contest. It was her standard dish to offer congratulations on a birth, condolences on a death, or a neighborly welcome. She let me put the zucchini in one layer, in the shape of the letter E, which I had recently learned at preschool.

'Your mom introduced herself and then said, "Hopkins? You're not related to Eldred Hopkins over in Enfield, are you?"'

Andrew does not have to explain. You can reinvent yourself a million times, but the rules don't allow you to start in the center. Every life has a beginning, a middle, and an end; dissect *history* and you'll see the word that defines it as a tale, a narrative.

'I lied to her,' Andrew says matter-of-factly. 'And then to a thousand other people. I made it up as I went along. When I said we had come from Nashua, I had to create some job down there. I had to give a reason for my wife's death. I had to explain to the pediatrician why Delia didn't have any medical records. I thought I'd get caught, every single day. But eventually I told so many lies that I honestly started to believe them, because it was easier to play the game than to try to sort them all out in my head.' He turns to me, dry-eyed and resigned. 'You *can* fool yourself, you know. You'd think it's impossible, but it turns out it's the easiest thing of all.'

I'd sat on the kitchen counter while my mother mixed together the spinach and the ricotta and dribbled red sauce that made me think of blood. I'd watched through the window as she went up to the new neighbor's house and smiled at him, pretending she was always making casseroles for the neighborhood, as if she were some perfect sitcom mom. I was young, but even then I'd wondered how long it would take the new family next door to figure out this was all a ruse.

I meet Andrew's gaze. 'Yes,' I say. 'I know.'

Fitz

I drive to Mesa in a rental car, a Mercury whose radio is stuck on a Spanish-speaking station and whose air-conditioning doesn't work. When I unroll the window, wind and dust blow into my face. The temperature here is one you can reach by crawling into an oven. This is the kind of heat that changes the frontal lobes of the brain, that makes men kill each other for the smallest of infractions, that might lead a father to kidnap a child.

Eric's directions tell me to turn off at University Drive, and when I do, there is a man standing at the top of the exit ramp. He has a long gray ponytail, and wears a flannel shirt, in spite of the heat. He reminds me of some of the hardscrabble New Englanders who haunt convenience stores for refills of chewing tobacco and worship the late Dale Earnhardt. 'Hey, bro,' he says to me, and I remember with a start that my window is open. He lifts up a ragged piece of corrugated cardboard on which he's written: NEED HELP.

'Don't we all,' I say, and gun the engine as the light turns.

I pass a plethora of child-care centers – the hallmark of a town whose inhabitants have to pawn their kids off on someone else so they can be teachers and nannies and cops in upscale neighborhoods where they can't afford to live. There is shack after shack of Mexican fast-food places – Rosa's, Garcia's, Uncle Tedoro's. Many of the storefronts boast of sales in English and Spanish.

Just past a conversion van on the side of the road that's selling leopard-print dashboard covers, I see a trailer park – stubby silver Airstreams huddled like a crash of rhinos. As I

am wondering which of these Quonset huts might belong to
Delia, Sophie comes running out of a door. Her red sneakers
kick up dust as she races to another trailer, this one covered
with Christmas lights and feathers and windcatchers. If she's
sick, she sure doesn't look it.

'Sophie,' I yell, but she's already disappeared inside the
second home.

I park my car and walk up to the trailer. There is no doorbell, only the kind of triangle that ranch wives use to call
cowboys to dinner. I raise the wand and ting it, just a little.
The door opens, revealing a Native American woman with a
scarf wrapped around her head. 'I'm sorry,' I say, so surprised
to not see Delia that I cannot find any words for a moment.
'I must have the wrong address.'

But then Sophie pokes her head out of what must be a
closet. 'Fitz!' she yells, and comes at me with the force of a
natural disaster. 'If I stand on Ruthann's toilet I can touch all
the walls in the bathroom at once. Want to see?'

The Indian woman frowns at Sophie. 'I thought I hired you
to work for me, not to go stand on toilets.'

Sophie beams. 'Ruthann's paying me a dollar to glue the
sequins on One-Night Stand Barbie's miniskirt.'

'One-Night Stand Barbie?' I repeat.

'She's my featured item this month,' Ruthann says. 'Comes
shrink-wrapped with Rohypnol Ken. For you, only $29.99 for
the pair.' She gestures to the small foldout table in the center
of the tiny room, covered with beads and glitter and plastic
dismembered body parts stacked like a mass grave. Sliding
heavily into the bench seat, she pulls a pair of spectacles out
by a cord that snakes into her shirt and starts assembling arms
and legs and torsos into dolls. 'Nine ninety-nine?' she bargains.

I take a ten-dollar bill out of my pocket and slap it on the
table. Ruthann slips the money into her jeans and hands over
the dolls. 'She's not here, you know.'

'Who?'

She raises an eyebrow, and her fingers fly over a Barbie

head, braiding the hair. I let my gaze roam the trailer, which is packed to the gills with dusty old appliances, heaps of vintage magazines, smashed toys, and bald or filthy or amputee Barbies. 'I'm Fitz,' I say, a belated introduction.

'I'm busy,' Ruthann replies.

'Ruthann sells stuff that other people throw away,' Sophie says.

I have always wondered about the people who cruise the streets before the garbage trucks come, taking stained couches and broken bicycles from the rubbish piles. What some people cast off, I guess, other people would want to keep.

Ruthann shrugs. 'Some fools will buy anything made by an Indian. I could probably rearrange my own trash and say it's art, get myself a show at the Heard Museum.'

'I went to the hospital today,' Sophie says. 'I was sick when I woke up but Ruthann got rid of the feathers and now I'm better.'

I look at the old woman for explanation, but she just shakes her head.

Whatever was wrong with Sophie must have passed; she's perfectly fine now. 'Where's your mom, Soph?' I ask, but she shrugs. No one seems inclined to talk. I clear my throat, and fiddle with an arm. It looks like it belongs to Ken; it has a biceps muscle.

Ruthann tosses me a torso and a head. 'Knock yourself out.'

I start to put together a Ken, stopping only once to notice the lack of genitalia, and wondering why I never knew that Ken was a eunuch. Probably because the only girl I'd ever played with was Delia, and she wouldn't have been caught dead with a doll in her possession. When the body is assembled, I pick up a Sharpie marker and begin to draw dotted lines and symbols down the torso and over the extremities. I label spots: BAD LUCK. SEARING PAIN. SEXUAL DYSFUNCTION. MONETARY RUIN. Sophie cranes her chin over my arm. 'What are you making, Fitz?'

'Something for your mom. Voodoo Eric.'

Ruthann laughs, and when I look up I see her measuring me differently. 'You,' she decides, 'may turn out better than I thought.'

Just then the door opens, and I can see Delia tying Greta's leash to the arm of a large plaster garden gnome. 'Stay,' she instructs. When she walks inside and sees me, her face lights up. 'Thank God you're here.'

'Thank Southwest Airlines. They had more to do with it.'

'Ruthann,' Delia says, presenting me, 'this is my best friend in the world.'

'We've met.'

'Yes, Ruthann was kind enough to let me discover my inner artist.' I lift the doll and give it to Delia. 'It might come in handy. Listen, do you think we could go somewhere and . . . talk?'

I look around as I say this, but I can literally see the end of Ruthann's little trailer from where I'm standing. I can practically *touch* the end of Ruthann's little trailer from where I'm standing. 'Go on,' Ruthann says, waving us away. 'Sophie and me, we're busy.'

But Delia leans over and feels Sophie's forehead with her lips, an act I've never understood. Do all mothers automatically have some kind of thermometer gauge in their mouths? She turns to me. 'This morning—'

'I heard.'

'I couldn't even reach Eric to have him meet us at the hospital—'

'I know,' I reply. 'He told me he tried to call you on your cell.'

Delia looks at me sharply. 'You saw Eric already? You went to the law office?'

I shift uncomfortably. I think about the notes I have in my back pocket, about the arraignment. The ones I will write up and send in an e-mail to the *New Hampshire Gazette*. 'I ran into him in court. Your father was arraigned about an hour ago.'

Delia shakes her head. 'I don't understand. Eric would have called me.'

'I don't think Eric knew your father was going to be arraigned. He nearly missed the whole proceeding.'

She wanders outside the trailer and sits down beside Greta in the shade. 'I got mad at him last night.'

'Eric?'

'My father.' She draws up her knees, rests her cheek on them. 'I went to the jail to tell him I would testify or do whatever he needed me to do. I wanted to hear the truth, but when he started to tell it to me, all I could think about was how he lied. So I left.' Delia glances up, near tears. 'I walked out on him.'

I rest my hand on her shoulder. 'I'm sure he knows how hard this is for you.'

'What if he thinks that the reason I wasn't in court was because I hate him?'

'Do you?'

Delia shakes her head. 'It's like math that doesn't add up, you know? I mean, on the one hand, there's my mother, who's . . . out there, somewhere, which is *amazing* . . . and I can't ever get the time back with her that I lost. But on the other hand, I had the best childhood, even if it wasn't the one I started out with. My father literally gave up his life for me, and that's got to count pretty heavily.' She sighs. 'You can love a person and still hate the decisions they've made, can't you?'

I stare at her for a moment longer than I should. 'I guess,' I say.

'I still don't know why he did it,' Delia murmurs.

'Then maybe you ought to try asking someone else.'

She turns to me. 'I was going to ask you about that. I keep hitting dead ends. I didn't get a chance to ask my father for my mother's real maiden name when I was at the jail – I got too upset first. And I tried calling the City Hall records department and explaining, but they said that without it, they couldn't—'

'Give you this?' I reach into my back pocket and pull out a piece of paper.

I watch Dee read the unfamiliar address and phone number. 'The first class in Journalism School is How to Charm a Records Clerk,' I explain.

'Elise Vasquez?' she reads.

'She remarried.' I hand her my cell phone. 'Go ahead.'

Hope holds her frozen for a moment, and then Delia reaches for the phone. She punches in the Scottsdale area code before suddenly aborting the call. 'What's the matter?' I ask.

'Feel this,' she says, and she takes my hand and holds it just north of her heart.

It is racing, fluttering as fast as a hummingbird's flight, as fast as indecision, as fast as my own. 'You're nervous,' I tell her. 'Given the situation, that's pretty normal.'

'I'm not just nervous. Remember what it used to feel like, as a kid, the week before your birthday? Remember how all you could think about was the day of your party, and then when it was finally time, it wasn't nearly as amazing as you'd built it up to be?' Delia chews on her bottom lip. 'What if it turns out like that?'

'Dee, you've been wanting this moment your whole life. If there's any bright side to this whole nightmare, this is it.'

'But why didn't she want it, too?' Delia asks. 'How come she didn't try to find me sooner?'

'For all you know, she's been looking for twenty-eight years. She didn't know your name until two days ago.'

'Eric said that she might not have been the one pressing the authorities,' Dee points out. 'The state might have done that on its own. Maybe she has a new life, with new kids. Maybe she doesn't care whether or not I've been found.'

'And maybe when you get to see her, you'll realize it's an alias and she's really Martha Stewart.'

She smiles crookedly. 'Two felons as parents. What are the odds?' Hunching down, she buries her fist in the ruff of fur at Greta's neck. 'I want this to be perfect, Fitz. I want *her* to be perfect. But what if she's not? What if *I'm* not?'

I stare at the clear amber of her eyes, at the careful curve of her shoulder. 'But you are,' I say softly.

She throws her arms around me; I string this feeling beside the other hundred memories I have of her touching me. 'I don't know what I'd do without you,' Delia says.

I answer that rhetorical question silently. Without me, Delia would not have her family trauma splashed across the pages of the *New Hampshire Gazette*. Without me, she would not have any reason to believe I'm here for more than her moral support. Without me, she wouldn't have another heartache coming.

When she pulls away, her face is shining. 'What do you think I ought to wear?' she asks. 'I don't know if I should call first – no, I think I'll just go there. That way, I get to see her reaction . . . can you watch Sophie for me?'

Before I can answer, the door of the trailer slams behind Dee. Greta looks up at me and beats her tail against the ground. Like the bloodhound, I've already been forgotten.

I take my notes from the arraignment out of my pocket, rip them into bite-size pieces of confetti. I'll tell my editor that my flight was delayed, that I got lost en route to the court-house, that I was stricken by the stomach flu, whatever. I toss the handful, imagine them blowing into the desert.

Instead, though, they blow over the gate of the trailer park, onto the sidewalk. They hit a man standing on the street; a freak snowstorm of regret. I call out an apology, and realize it is the same vagrant from the highway exit. He's carrying his cardboard sign, holding it up to the cars that speed by: NEED HELP.

This time I walk right up to him. 'Good luck,' I say, and I hand him a twenty.

III

Nothing stands out so conspicuously, or remains so firmly fixed in the memory, as something which you have blundered.

– Cicero

Delia

If you think motherhood is an instinct, you'd be wrong.

In college, when I majored in zoology, I wrote my thesis on the way offspring can identify their mothers, and vice versa. Instinct, as it turns out, isn't defined as a trait you're born with, but one that develops as a parent and child bond. There's that famous Konrad Lorenz study – the scientist who had goslings trailing after him, because he allowed them to imprint on him when they hatched. I tracked hyenas and wild pigs and seals, all of whom used vocal clues and pheromones and physical resemblance to pick their mothers out of a crowd.

Attentive mothers tended to be the ones with the most helpless babies: humans and chicks and mice. On the other hand, fish, who could take care of themselves at birth, were left behind immediately by their mothers. In this sense, parenthood became solely about defense.

But every now and then I'd come across an anomaly: an instinct gone awry. Like the cuckoo, which would invade another bird's nest, throw out the real eggs, and leave its own behind to be reared by a surrogate parent. Or the seal pups that were abandoned when food went scarce. Or Neanderthals, who killed their young if the alternative was starvation. Sometimes, when conditions leave no other choice, parental instinct falls by the wayside.

Years later, I read that someone had found genetic components to good motherhood. The Mest and the Peg3 genes occur on chromosome 19, and, ironically, they only work if they're inherited from the father. Imprinting like this usually occurs in evolution because of a genetic battle of the sexes;

it's in the best interests of the female to have more litters, but it's in the best interests of the male to protect the child that's already been born.

The jury is still out on these findings, but I believe them. All I have to do is think of Sophie, and how there are certain details I wish I could freeze in amber: her munchkin voice or her iridescent pink fingernails or the xylophone of her laughter. It's no great stretch of imagination to assume that my father was the one who passed this feeling onto me, who made me conscious of the things we want to keep.

My mother's home is small and neat, afloat on a sea of white stones. There is a mailbox at the end of the driveway that says VASQUEZ. I stop in front of a saguaro that is at least eleven feet tall, and has an arm lifted in a friendly wave. Ruthann says it takes fifty years for a saguaro to sprout a single arm. She says that their flowers are so bright and beautiful they have been known to make sparrows weep.

I run my hand over my hair again. After pinning it back, and pulling it into a ponytail, I finally decided to leave it falling over my shoulders – surely she'd remember brushing it when I was little? I'm wearing the nicest outfit I threw into my suit-case in our hasty escape: a dark blue dress that I had planned on wearing to court. I smooth the skirt down, wishing I could will away the wrinkles. I take deep breaths.

How do you walk into someone's life again after twenty-eight years? How do you pick up, when you were too young to know where you left off?

For courage, I try to reverse the roles: What if it was Sophie coming to see me, after so long? I cannot imagine any circum-stance where I wouldn't immediately feel a connection to her; and I have shared roughly the same short amount of time in Sophie's life that my mother shared with me. I wouldn't care if she was pierced, bald, rich, poor, married, gay . . . *whatever* . . . just as long as she was back.

So why am I so worried about making a first impression?

I answer my own question: Because you only get to do it once. Every time after, you are only making up for what happened during that initial meeting.

I stand on the front step, wondering how I will ever get up the courage to knock, when the door swings open telekinetically.

The woman exits backward. She's wearing faded jeans and an embroidered peasant blouse, and looks much younger than I would have expected. 'Sí, bread and refried beans,' she calls out to someone still inside. 'I heard you the first time.' Then she steps out and plows right into me. 'Disculpeme, I didn't see—' Her hand comes up to cover her mouth.

Her face looks like a photo of me that has been crumpled and then, on second thought, smoothed again – my features, but worn soft by the finest lines. Her hair is one shade blacker than mine. However, it is her smile that renders me speechless. Two eyeteeth, twisted just a quarter turn – the reason I spent four years in braces and a retainer.

'Gracias a dios,' she murmurs. When she reaches out I let her touch me, my shoulder and neck and finally, cupping my cheek. I close my eyes and think of all the times I had stroked my own arm in the dark, pretending to be her; failing, because I couldn't surprise myself with comfort. 'Beth,' she says, and then she blushes. 'But that's not your name anymore, is it?'

In that moment it is not important at all what she calls me, but it is critical what I call her. My voice breaks. 'Are you my mother?'

I don't know which one of us reaches for the other, but suddenly I am in her arms, a place that I had to imagine my entire life. Her hands run over my hair and my back, as if she is trying to make sure I'm real. I try to narrow my mind to a sliver of recognition, but it's hard to know whether this feels familiar because I remember it, or because I so badly want it to.

She still smells like vanilla and apples.

'Look at you,' she says, holding me far enough away to stare at my face. 'Look at how beautiful you are.'

In the background, someone speaks: a low baritone with a hint of an accent. 'Elise? Who's there?' He steps forward, a lean man with white hair, coffee-colored skin, and a mustache. 'Ella podría ser su gemelo,' he whispers.

'Victor,' my mother says, her voice so full it spills over. 'You remember my daughter.'

I have no recollection of this man, but apparently he knew me. 'Hola,' Victor says. He starts to reach for me, and then on second thought, slides his arm around my mother's waist instead.

'I didn't know if it was all right to come here,' I admit. 'I didn't know if you wanted to see me.'

My mother squeezes my hand. 'I've been waiting to see you for almost thirty years,' she says. 'As soon as they told me who you were . . . now . . . I tried to call you, but no one answered.'

The relief her words send through me, the fact that she was *trying*, nearly buckles my knees. It wasn't that my mother hadn't called, it was that *I* hadn't *answered*. Because I was flying to Arizona, to be with my father while he stood trial.

We are both thinking this, and it reminds us that this is not just any reunion. Victor clears his throat. 'Why don't you two sit down inside?'

Her house is decorated with bright Talavera pottery and wrought iron. As we walk into the living room, I look for clues that will tell me more: toys that speak of other children or grandchildren; the titles of music CDs on the shelves; framed photos on the walls. One catches my eye – it is a snapshot of my mother and me, wearing matching embroidered dresses. I'd seen a similar photo, maybe taken the minute before, or after this one, in my father's secret stash.

'I'll get some iced tea,' Victor says, and he leaves my mother and me alone. You would think, when there is so much to say, that it comes easily. But instead we sit in an uncomfortable silence. 'I don't know where to start,' my mother says finally.

She looks down into her lap, suddenly shy. 'I don't even know what you do.'

'Search and rescue. I work with a bloodhound, and we look for missing people,' I say. 'It's crazy, given the circumstances.'

'Or maybe it's *because* of them,' my mother suggests. She folds her hands in her lap, and we look at each other for another moment. 'You live in New Hampshire . . . ?'

'Yes. My whole life – ' I say, before I realize that isn't true. 'Most of it, anyway.' I dig in my pocket for the photo I've brought along of Sophie, and pass it to her. 'This is your granddaughter.'

She takes the picture from me and pores over it. 'A granddaughter,' my mother repeats.

'Sophie.'

'She looks like you.'

'And Eric. My fiancé.'

I'd hoped that by seeing my mother some floodgate would open, and all the gaps in my mind would be filled with memory. I'd hoped that some reflex recollection would take over, so that when I heard her laugh or saw her smile or felt her touch, it would be familiar, instead of new. But after that initial embrace, we've gone back to what we really are: two people who have just met. We can't rebuild our past, because we haven't even leveled common ground.

For years, I'd sketched my mother out in my mind by stealing bits and pieces of other people's lives: a woman who stood in the town pool, coaxing her tiny daughter to jump off the side into her arms; a fairy-tale character who died tragically young; Meryl Streep in *Sophie's Choice*. Any of those women, I would have known in an instant; I would have been able to fall into easy conversation. Any of those women would have known what I have been doing all my life. In none of my imaginings was my mother Spanish-speaking, or remarried, or awkward. In none of my imaginings was she a total stranger.

When your mother is made out of dreams, anything real is bound to disappoint you.

'When is the wedding?' she asks politely.

'September.' At least, that was when it was supposed to be. I expected my father to give me away – before I learned he might be going to prison for not being able to do that in the first place.

'Victor and I are celebrating our silver anniversary this year,' my mother says.

'Did you have children?'

She shakes her head. 'I wasn't able to.' My mother looks down at her hands. 'Your father . . . did he remarry?'

'No.'

She lifts her gaze to mine. 'How is Charles?'

It is strange to hear him referred to by that other name. 'He's in jail,' I say bluntly.

'I never asked for that. I'm not going to lie – there was a time I was so angry at him for taking you I would have willingly sent him to prison for life – but it's been so long. The only thing I cared about, when the prosecutor called to tell me they'd found him, was you.'

I picture her standing in the driveway of this house, even though I know it isn't where I grew up. I imagine her expression at the moment she realizes I am not coming back. I see her face, but it has all of my own features.

My mother looks at me, hard. 'Do you . . . do you remember anything?' she asks. 'From before?'

'Sometimes I have dreams,' I say. 'There's one about a lemon tree. And one where I come into a kitchen with broken glass all over it.'

My mother nods. 'You were three,' she says. 'That wasn't a dream.'

It is the first time someone has been able to confirm a memory that I couldn't make sense of, and I feel my arms and legs go weak.

'Your father and I, we had a fight that night,' my mother says. 'We woke you up.'

'Was I the reason you got divorced?'

'You?' She seems surprised. 'You were the best part of our marriage.'

The question, now, is burning a path up my throat; the words come out like fire. 'Is that why he took me?'

Just then Victor enters the living room, carrying a tray. There is a pitcher of iced tea, and cookies the size of a baby's palm, covered in powdered sugar. Under his arm is a shoebox. 'I thought you might want this, too,' he says, and he hands it to her.

She is embarrassed by it. 'I thought it might not be the right time,' she tells him.

'Why don't you let Bethany decide that?'

'It's just some things I kept,' my mother explains, pulling the rubber band free. 'I knew that one day I'd find you. But somehow, I always expected you to still be four years old.'

There is a lacy christening cap, and the placard from the hospital bassinet with my name – my other name – written by a nurse in red ink, along with my weight: 6 lbs, 6 oz. A tiny china teacup with a chip in the handle. A square of paper with the carefully printed pencil letters of a child: I LV U.

Proof, that once I did.

The only other item in the box is a miniature patchwork quilt, made of triangles of red silk and orange shag and paisley print and sheer voile.

My mother shakes this out over her lap. 'I made this for you, when you were a baby, out of every bit of comfort I could find.' She touches the red silk. 'This came from a slip that once was my grandmother's. The orange was the throw rug from your father's dorm room. The paisley, a maternity dress of mine. And the voile, that came from my wedding veil. You ate with it and slept with it and I had to force you not to bathe with it. You used to hide underneath it when you were afraid . . . like you thought it might make you disappear.'

I had forgotten my blanket. I want to go home, I'd told him. We can't, he said, but he didn't tell me why.

'I remember,' I say softly.

I am four again: reaching up as she lifts me out of the bath; holding tight to cross a street; clutching this blanket with my fist. In a half hour my mother has managed to give me what my father couldn't: my past.

I reach across my mother's lap to touch the blanket, wishing it still had the same magic powers that it used to, that I might press it to my cheek and rub the corner of it against my eyelids and know that everything is going to be all right by the time the sun comes up. 'Mami,' I say, because that is what I used to call her.

I may not know my mother yet, but we have this much in common: Neither of us, it turns out, has been the only one who lost someone she loved.

It is strange, suddenly having a memory come back out of nowhere. You think you're going crazy; you wonder where this recollection has been hiding all your life. You try to push it away, because you think you've hammered out the whole timeline of your life, but then you see that one extra moment, and suddenly you are breaking apart what you thought was a solid segment, and seeing it for what it is: just a string of events, shoulder to shoulder, and a gap where there is room for one more.

There is so much I want to ask her; there are still so many questions.

When I get back to the trailer, Fitz is fanning himself with the phone book and Sophie is asleep on the couch. 'How did it go?' he asks.

I have been thinking about what I should tell him – and Eric, for that matter. It's not that I have anything to hide, but there's something about talking about the fragile bridge my mother and I just built that in some way would diminish it. 'She wasn't who I wanted her to be,' I say carefully, 'but that didn't turn out as bad as I expected.'

'What's she like?'

'She's younger than my father. And she's Mexican,' I tell him. 'She grew up there.'

Fitz laughs. 'And to think, you failed Spanish.'

'Shut up.'

'Was she happy to see you?'

'Yes.'

He smiles a little. 'And are you happy you saw her?'

'It's weird – not knowing anything about my own mother. But in a way, it's okay, because she doesn't really know anything about me. With my father, it was all imbalanced. He knew everything, and he kept it a secret.'

'Grandpa tells *me* his secrets,' Sophie says, and we both look over toward the couch. She's sitting up now, her face still rosy with sleep. 'Is he here yet?'

I sink down beside her and haul her onto my lap. There are so many times that I've been seized with a need to hold Sophie – after a particularly sappy movie, after a near-miss car accident in an ice storm, when I'm watching her sleep – what would it be like to have someone take that right away from me? 'What secrets does Grandpa tell you?' I ask.

'That he bought the cheap grapes at the supermarket, even though he told you they were the organic ones. And that he's the one who put your white shirt in the washing machine and turned it pink.' She turns to me. 'I don't know if Grandpa's going to fit in this house with the rest of us.'

I look at Fitz. 'Grandpa isn't going to be staying with us,' I tell Sophie. 'You know how the police came to the house the other day?'

'You said they were playing a game.'

'Well, it turns out that they weren't, Soph. Grandpa made a big mistake, one that hurt a lot of people. And because of that, he has to go . . . he's going to stay . . .' I try, but I cannot summon up the words.

Fitz kneels in front of us. 'You know how you got a Time Out when you threw the tennis ball in the living room and broke the window?' Sophie nods. 'Your grandfather has to live for a while in a place where grown-ups go when they get Time Outs.'

Sophie looks at me. 'Did he break a window?'

No, I think. *Just my heart.*

'He broke the law,' Fitz says. 'So for now, he has to stay in jail until a judge says he can leave.'

Sophie considers this. 'Bad guys go to jail. They wear handcuffs.'

'He's not wearing handcuffs and he's not a bad guy,' I tell her.

'What did he do?'

'He took a little girl away from home,' I say.

'Didn't her mother tell her not to talk to strangers?'

How do I tell Sophie that sometimes it's not strangers that prey on us; it's those we love who can do the most harm? 'It happened a long time ago,' I explain. 'And I was the little girl.'

'But he was still your daddy, right?' Sophie shakes her head. 'Daddies are allowed to take you places.'

'Not this time.' I feel my throat close like a fist. 'I didn't get to see my mother, not for lots of years – and I really missed her.'

'Why didn't you just tell him you wanted to go home?'

It is too complicated to explain it all to Sophie. That there were lies involved, and aliases. That people you love don't usually come back from the dead. That I couldn't tell my father I wanted to go home because I didn't know I was missing.

But now I do.

On the drive back to the Madison Street Jail, I wonder if Sophie will remember this trip to Phoenix when she gets older. I wonder if she'll be able to picture the short spikes of a prickly pear, like stubble on a woman's leg; if she'll know her grandmother; if she'll have any memory of her grandfather before he was imprisoned.

The truth is, she won't have to.

That is my job. What is a parent, really, but somebody who picks up the things a child leaves behind – a trail made of stripped-off clothing, orphaned shoes, tiny bright plastic game pieces, and nostalgia – and who hands back each of these when it's needed?

What is a parent but someone you trust to keep you safe, and to tell you the truth?

I am pacing the small cubicle when my father is brought in to see me. I can't look him in the eye, so I focus instead on the cut on his face, a fishhook that curves down the side of his cheek. I pick up the phone to talk to him. 'Who hurt you?' I ask, swallowing.

'It'll be all right.' He touches his face gingerly. 'I didn't think you'd be coming back so soon.'

'I didn't think I would, either,' I say. 'I'm sorry I missed your arraignment.'

My father shrugs. 'Plenty more where that came from,' he says. 'Is it true, what Eric said? That you wanted me to plead not guilty?'

'I love you,' I say, my eyes filling with tears. 'I want you to do whatever it takes to get out of there.'

He leans closer to the glass between us. 'That's exactly why I had to run away with you, Dee.'

'See, I could almost believe that. Except, I went to see my mother today.'

I watch his face go white. 'How is she?'

'Well, she's practically a stranger,' I say.

He splays his hand on the glass. 'Delia—'

'Don't you mean Bethany?'

Shock squeezes through the telephone connection between us, a static silence. 'Did you really have that bad a life?' my father asks tightly.

'*I don't know*. I have no idea what it would have been like if I'd been brought up by my mother.' When he doesn't answer, I keep talking. 'Did you know she saved my baby blanket? The one with all the patches? The one that I wanted to go back for the day we left, but you wouldn't let me? Did you know that she still celebrates my real birthday? *I* didn't even do that, growing up.'

My father sinks down heavily onto the stool in the booth.

'Maybe you can tell me what I'm missing,' I say, my voice too high and thin. 'Because the woman I spoke to was just as sorry as I was for having missed twenty-eight years.'

'I'll bet she's sorry,' my father says, so quietly that I think I've misheard him.

'What did she do to you?' I whisper. 'What did she do that made you so angry you had to get revenge by kidnapping me?'

'It wasn't what she did to me,' my father answers. 'It's what she did to *you.*' A vein starts to throb in his temple. 'We *did* go back for your blanket,' he says. 'We walked into the house, and you tripped over your mother, who was lying on the floor, passed out cold. And I can tell you exactly what your life would have been like, if she was the one who brought you up. You would have had to make yourself breakfast before kindergarten, because your mother was too hung over to do it for you. You would have had to check the toilet tank, to throw out the vodka bottle that was hidden inside. You would have wondered why she couldn't love you enough to want to stop. Your mother was a drunk, Delia. She couldn't take care of herself, much less a baby. That's the wonderful upbringing I took you away from. That's the truth I lied about. That's what I wanted you to miss.'

I stumble backward, the telephone line stretching like an umbilicus. I have learned this lesson over and over doing search-and-rescue work: If you choose to go looking for something, you'd better be ready for whatever it is you find. Because it may not be what you've been expecting.

'I gave you the mother you *didn't* get,' my father pleads. 'If I'd told you the truth – if I told you what she was *really* like – wouldn't that have been worse than the way you lost her the first time?'

For nearly a year after I was told about my mother's death, I would run to the door every time the doorbell rang. I was certain that my father had gotten it wrong. That any moment my mother was going to show up so that we could live happily ever after.

But she hadn't. Not because she was dead, as my father had told me, but because she had never existed.

I let the telephone receiver drop from my hand and turn around, away from the Plexiglas. I don't look back at my father, not even when he starts screaming both of my names and a guard comes to take him away.

I have never been a very good drunk. Even when I was a student at UNH, a few beers would make me sick and hard liquor only made me hyperaware, prone to wondering why the tables had been stained the color of hazelnuts and whether anyone ever bothered to clean the flies out of the ceiling fan in the ladies' bathroom.

I didn't know for a long time that Eric was an alcoholic. When Eric drank, he became only more engaging and funny and amusing. He did it so seamlessly, in fact, that it took me several years to understand that the reason Eric always seemed to be the same person, whether he had a beer in his hand or not, was not because he didn't get drunk, but because he was hardly ever sober.

The life of the party who can build geometric carbon models out of toothpicks and maraschino cherries and get a whole bar full of Japanese tourists to join in singing 'Yellow Submarine' becomes less charming when that same person forgets he is supposed to pick you up after work and lies about where he has been all night, and cannot hold a conversation in the morning unless he's had some hair of the dog that bit him. I've hesitated this long to accept his marriage proposal because I didn't want my child to grow up with a parent who is unreliable and selfish.

So how can I blame my own father for feeling the same way?

When I pull into my mother's driveway again, I am so upset that I am shaking. My mother comes to the door mixing something in a mortar and pestle; it smells like rosemary. Her face lights up when she sees me. 'Come on in.'

'Is it true?'

'Is what true?'

'That you're an alcoholic?'

The smile dries on my mother's face, paint peeling. She glances around the street to see who might have heard, and ushers me inside. There is a part of me dying to be told that this, like so many other things, is just another fabrication of my father's. This is another step in his scheme to make me hate my mother, too.

But she pushes her hair back from her face, tucks it behind her ears. 'Yes,' she says bravely. 'I am.' She folds her arms across her chest. 'And I haven't had a drink in twenty-six years.'

An honest confession can slice the hardest heart in two. 'Why didn't you tell me?'

'You didn't ask,' my mother says quietly.

But it is a lie, even if you don't say it. It is a lie when you force a connection, because you so desperately want there to be one. It is a lie when you tell yourself that you will have lunches together and pass down secret recipes and do all the hundred other things that I have fantasized daughters do with their mothers, as if that might actually make us any less foreign to each other. No one gets to start where they left off; it just doesn't work that way.

She reaches for me, and when I back away, her eyes fill with tears. 'You came here, and you were so happy to see me,' she says. 'I thought if I told you, I'd lose you all over again.'

'You let me think you were a victim,' I accuse.

'I was,' my mother says. 'I may not have been a perfect mother, but I *was* your mother, Beth. And I *loved* you.'

Past tense.

'That isn't my name,' I say tightly, and this time, it is my decision to leave.

Greta and I were once called during a blizzard to find a teenage girl who had left a suicide note and disappeared, leaving her single father in an absolute state of panic. It was down in Meredith, the Lakes Region. The local police had begun to search on a footprint trail, but the snow was falling so fast that her tracks vanished almost the moment they were located.

Locals had been warned off the roads that night; the only vehicles I passed on my way there were plows and sanding trucks. When I arrived, I was taken to the girl's father. He was rocking back and forth in an armchair, fist pressed to his mouth, as if he were afraid of the grief that might spill out. 'Mr. Damato,' I asked, 'does Maria have a special place? A spot she goes to when she wants to be alone?'

He shook his head. 'Nowhere I know.'

'Can you show me her room?'

He led me to the back of the house. The girl's room was typical – twin bed, milk-crate bookshelves, laptop, lava lamp. But unlike most teenagers' bedrooms, this one was spotless. The bed had been made, the papers cleared from the top of the desk. The clothes were all neatly hanging in the closet. The trash can had been dumped.

Because Maria Damato had already done her wash, too, I scented Greta off a pair of shoes I found in her closet. Outside, the snow whistled and spun around us. Greta started out west, toward the road, and then veered into the woods. At points she had to leap snowdrifts; at other times I fell on my hands and knees in them. Every time I opened my mouth, I tasted ice.

Two hours later Greta broke through the trees and began to tiptoe across the frozen flat of the lake. With all this snow, it did not look like a body of water, but instead a wide-open field. Snowflakes the size of quarters clotted on my lashes and lips, and gave Greta Groucho Marx eyebrows. The powder made the ice even more hazardous; we both went sprawling a few times. But finally Greta stopped and put her front paws on a mound that didn't sink. She turned a small circle; did it again.

I saw the girl's hair first, frozen into jagged spikes. I rolled her over and immediately began to do artificial respiration, but she came up scratching like a cat. 'Get off me, get off me!' she shrieked, and then she opened her eyes and started to sob.

The EMT workers who met us at the lake said that the snow had acted as an insulator, keeping Maria alive longer than she might have been otherwise. Her father, who had been called with the good news, was waiting at the front door when we returned. Holding my arm for support, Maria took a tentative step toward her father. Suddenly, Greta stepped between them and growled low in her throat.

'Greta,' I said, calling the dog off. But in that instant, I'd felt Maria relax. As if she'd been vindicated.

Believe me, I have seen it all: from delicate boys with the faces of sprites who run from the teasing of bullies; to teens who climb to the top of water towers, intent on dying closer to Heaven; to the willow-thin girls who hide in the night from their mother's boyfriends. My job, though, is to bring them home, not to judge the motives that made them run away. So that night, I returned Maria Damato to the custody of her grateful parent. I did what I was expected to do.

A month later the detective on the case called to tell me that Maria had shot her father and then killed herself. I gave Greta an extra serving of Dog Chow that day, for understanding more than any human had. It just goes to show you: Sometimes knowing what's right isn't a rational decision, or even what works on paper. Sometimes leaving is the best course of action after all.

When Sophie was two, Eric and I took her fishing. It was a lazy Sunday, and we were sitting on a dock on Goose Pond. Eric would thread a worm onto the hook and cast, then cup his hands around Sophie's on the fishing rod. She had just learned the word *fish*, and when we pulled a trout or a bass out of the water, she'd clap her hands and say it over and over.

To this day, I'm not sure how it happened. Eric had let go of Sophie to bait the hook, and I was pointing to the rainbow scales of the trout that we'd just released back into the cool, dark water. There was the tiniest splash, like a rock being skipped across the surface of the pond, and we both looked up to see that Sophie was gone.

She wasn't wearing a life jacket – she fought us like crazy when we tried to zip it up, and we'd rationalized with ourselves: With both of us watching her, what could go wrong? 'Sophie?' Eric yelled, the ragged edge of panic serrating her name.

I didn't think, just jumped into the water fully clothed and opened my eyes. It was cloudy and my shoes kicked up sand from the bottom, but there was a flash of something bright, and I lunged for it.

Sophie, who didn't know how to swim, had sunk like a stone, and was drifting underneath the dock. I grabbed her by her shirt, yanked her over my head, handed her to Eric. He laid her out on the rough weathered boards while she sput-tered and choked and I hauled myself out of the pond.

She was too frightened to cry, and although it felt like a lifetime, the whole episode had lasted less than two minutes. The bright spot I'd seen under the water was a necklace my father had given her for her birthday – a silver star, to wish on.

Sophie likes to hear the story of how we saved her life. She can repeat all the details, but they are trappings of a story we've seasoned to perfection over the years. She has no recol-lection of the incident firsthand, and Eric and I are both grateful for that. There are some things, I think, you're better off not remembering.

The back of the trailer park wedges wide into a dry, dusty vista, which is where Eric takes me to see the sunset: a fuchsia curtain being drawn down through the pleats of the moun-tains.

He's still dressed in a suit, but he's loosened his tie. We watch the sky turn every watercolor shade of orange and purple, a painting too lovely to be real, while a few feet away, Sophie throws a tennis ball for Greta to chase. 'I've been thinking that if law doesn't pan out for me, I'm going to audition as a Phoenix weatherman. Look, I've got it down: Monday, 104 and sunny. Tuesday, 104 and sunny. Wednesday, a cool 102 and—'

'Eric,' I say. 'Stop.'

He does, immediately. 'I was only trying to cheer you up, Dee. Fitz tells me you had a hell of a day.'

'You shouldn't have let me miss the arraignment,' I reply.

'It wasn't my fault. They never even told me it was scheduled.' He slides an arm around my waist. 'Tell me about your mother.'

I watch a hawk spiral overhead, his talons ripping the fabric of the sky to show a star or two. The sunset reaches its death throes, an explosion of ginger and pink and night. 'She's an alcoholic,' I say finally.

I can tell by the way he goes perfectly still that this is news for him. 'Back then, too?' he asks.

'Yeah.' I face him. 'Do you think that's why I fell in love with you?'

'God, I hope not,' Eric laughs.

'I'm serious. What if there was a part of me that couldn't fix her, so I had to fix you?'

Eric reaches for my shoulders. 'You couldn't even *remember* her, Dee.'

There is no denying this. But was it because I couldn't, or because I didn't want to? Memory isn't something that stays with you at all times. It's a quantity that gets *summoned* or *evoked* or *brought to mind*. It gets carried to an arena for our viewing pleasure. By definition, then, there are times it must go missing.

Or does it? When I used to complain about Eric's drinking, he told me I was being unreasonable. One beer, and I couldn't stand the smell on his breath. Now I wonder if this was some scent recollection, some unconscious understanding that a person who smelled of alcohol was bound to disappoint me.

'I went to the jail today, too,' I say.

'How'd that go?'

'On a scale of one to ten?' I look up at him. 'Minus four.'

'Well, maybe this day wasn't an entire wash. You might have found me an affirmative defense.'

'What do you mean?'

'If your father had a valid reason to take you – like that your mother's drinking put you at risk – and he tried to get legal recourse but couldn't, it might get him off the hook.'

'Do you think it'll work?'

'It's better than the defense I was planning on running,' Eric says.

'Which was?'

'You were actually abducted by Miss Scarlet, in the library, with the wrench.'

I shake my head, but he's managed to make me smile. When I think about my father, an ache rises like dough under my breastbone. I have not been fair to him; if anything, I'm guilty of the same offense: trying to keep the life we had from being ruined. Is it a crime when you love someone so much that you can't stand the thought of them changing? Is it a crime when you love someone so much that you can't see clearly?

Beside me, Eric throws Greta's tennis ball far over the scrub of the land. In the coming dark, his features are blurred. He could be anyone, and so could I.

Elise

You probably don't remember this, but I once told you the story of the minute my mother died. I was sixteen, and miles away at the time – she was visiting her sister in Texas – but I woke up with a start at midnight to find her sitting on the edge of my bed with her hand touching my face. 'Mami?' I whispered, and she disappeared, leaving behind a scent of tuberose so strong that in all the years since, I have never been able to scrub it from my own skin.

The next morning my aunt called to tearfully tell me about the car accident, which happened at the exact moment I had awakened the night before. When I told her about my mother's visit, it was no surprise to either of us. Ask any faithful Mexican and they will tell you what the *brujas* know: The dead come back to collect their footsteps.

Over the years, sometimes, I thought I could feel you standing behind me. I was certain that I could feel the paintbrush tickle of your hand on the canvas of my palm. I would start to run the water in the bathtub and hear you laughing from the other side of the door.

Each of these times I pretended it hadn't happened. I'd close my eyes more tightly or increase the flow of the faucet or turn up the radio. I didn't let myself admit that the only way I might see you, again, was in that last moment when you would be back to gather your footsteps like an armful of brilliant desert flowers, a consolation prize you would present to me in return for losing you forever.

On December 9, 1531, the Blessed Virgin Mary appeared to

an Indian named Juan Diego. A carpet of roses blossoming in the dead of winter and a Madonna with a coffee-colored face appearing on Juan Diego's robe were enough further evidence to convince the local bishop to erect a shrine to Our Lady of Guadalupe.

There are those who say Guadalupe is Tonantzin, an Aztec goddess who existed years before Juan Diego came along. The Spanish missionaries, knowing that she had quite a local following, baptized her into Christianity as Our Lady of Guadalupe. What they didn't realize was that Tonantzin was a goddess who could take away sins through secret rituals performed by her priestesses – the *brujería*. The missionaries, basically, made it perfectly fine for Catholic Indians to go to Mass, but also visit a witch.

My mother was a *bruja*, and I grew up watching her clients come for all sorts of spells – to guarantee healthy babies, to bless a new house, to keep a son from joining the armed forces. When she lit a red candle to Guadalupe and recited an Ave, Doña Tarano's liver tumor miraculously shrank. When she prayed to Saint Catalina de Alejandría, a family on the brink of debt came into a windfall. Of course, *brujas* are also specialists in justice when someone's wronged you. A curse from a *bruja* might punish a cheating husband, or unleash a rash on someone spreading gossip. People at the receiving end of a *bruja*'s curse understand that they have done something to deserve it; a hex only works on the guilty.

My mother taught me how to lay an altar and choose a *cuchillo;* how to learn what a reading of *los naipes* might say about my life, but when I was younger, I cast spells only for myself. I never expected to be a *bruja* here in Phoenix, but word travels fast among the Mexican community, and people have need of a good witch every now and then. I found, too, that when I was working magic, I had to focus so hard that for those few minutes I stopped blaming myself for losing you.

The day after you came to see me – one wonderful visit, then one awful one – I am having trouble concentrating on the client who is with me in my *santuario*. 'Doña Vasquez,' Josephina asks, 'did you hear what I just said?'

This is what I wish I'd told you yesterday: I'm not the person I was then, any more than you are. I have waited twenty-eight years to see you; I can wait a little while longer.

Please come back.

'The spell isn't working,' Josephina sighs.

I have been trying to silence her roommate, a college girl from ASU who spread so many lies about Josephina sleeping around that her boyfriend broke up with her. I suggested a case of *la lengua ardiente* – the burning tongue – to teach the roommate a lesson. 'Did you use the candle?'

I had given Josephina one the last time she visited, black wax molded in the shape of a woman. 'Yeah. I scratched her initials on the face, just like you told me, and I got that Ass-Kickin' Hot Sauce from Uncle Tio's Taco Palace, dipped the needle in it, and shoved it into the candle's mouth.'

'You lit it?'

Josephina nods. 'And I pictured her stupid horse face, like you said, and then blew the candle out. But she didn't come by the next day to say that she was sorry. And if that's not bad enough . . .' She lowers her voice. '*Then* I found a cobweb in the corner of my apartment, right after I cleaned.'

Well, that changes everything. Finding a spider web in an otherwise spotless space is a sure sign that someone is trying to hex you. 'Josephina, I think your roommate may just be a *diablera.*'

Just as there are good witches – *brujería* – there are evil witches. Their hexes, unfortunately, can land squarely on the shoulders of those who've done nothing to deserve them.

'Renee isn't even Mexican,' Josephina says. 'She's from New Jersey.'

'If she's a *diablera,* she may just be telling you that to keep you off guard.'

Josephina looks doubtful. 'But . . . she has big hair.'

I start to get up. 'If you don't want my help . . .'

'No! I do. Really.'

'All right. Take a tablespoon of graveyard dirt and a table-spoon of olive oil and mix the ingredients with the index finger of your left hand. Sprinkle this with black pepper. Then spread it on the picture of Renee in your college freshman face book and bury it in a cemetery.'

Josephina looks up at me, wide-eyed. 'What'll happen to her?'

'As the photo disintegrates, your roommate will feel more and more out of sorts. By the next full moon, she'll apologize for saying anything bad about you and she'll transfer to a college in a different state.'

A bright smile breaks over Josephina's face. She digs my fee – ten dollars – out of the front pocket of her jeans. 'Thank you, Doña,' she gushes, just as Victor pokes his head in.

He has never approved of my side career, no matter how many times I have tried to explain to him that this is not a job but a calling. After a while, I began to keep the practice hidden. It was not that I was trying to lie to my husband, it was simply easier for both of us to pretend that I wasn't doing this anymore, even if we both knew better.

'This is Josephina,' I say, introducing the girl to Victor. 'She volunteers with me at the Science Museum.'

Josephina thanks me again, and says she's going to be late for a class if she doesn't leave now. When Victor and I are alone, he puts his hands on my shoulders and kneads a bit. 'How are you doing today?'

After your second visit yesterday, when I cried for hours, he was the one who sat across from me, rationing Kleenex. It was partly for moral support, partly because he loves me, and partly to remind me that no matter what, I shouldn't swallow my sorrow down with alcohol. 'I'm okay,' I tell him. 'For now.'

'She'll come around, Elise,' Victor assures me.

You haven't been in my life for twenty-eight years; why, then, after only an hour in your company, do I feel the absence so much more acutely?

Victor strokes his hand over my hair. Sometimes I think that when I am hurt, he is the one who bears the pain. If you had grown up with me, this is one of the things I would have tried to teach you: Marry a man who loves you more than you love him. Because I have done both now, and when it is the other way around, there is no spell in the world that can even out the balance.

The very first time I met your father, he tried to rescue me. I was working in the middle of nowhere, at a bar frequented by bikers – not clean-cut college boys with axle grease on their hands who wandered in, dazed, after their cars broke down. He saw me pinned against a wall by two Hell's Angels while a third threw darts at me, and he launched himself at the big man.

As it turned out, I wasn't in trouble; the bikers were all regulars and we did this little dog-and-pony show every now and then. But I fell in love with Charlie at that moment. It wasn't his golden good looks, or his attempt at heroism that sent my head spinning; it was the fact that he believed I was worth saving.

I was one of the ghosthood of Mexican-Americans who lurked in the background of other people's lives – as chambermaids and busboys and gardeners. The only reason I was a bartender was because I could not sew a straight seam, so taking in piecework was not an option. Besides, I liked bartending. The yeasty smell of beer rising from the catch below the tap made me think of places where wheat grew, places I'd never been. Every time one of my customers got up and walked out the door, I let a little piece of me go with him. I thought that at this rate, sooner or later, I could vanish completely.

I gave your father a free drink, to thank him for trying to save me. I don't think he noticed that my hands were shaking, spilling beer all over the bar. Charlie pointed to my jeans, which were covered with couplets from poetry that I'd read.

I collected words the way some people collected shells or butterfly specimens. *'I'd rather learn from one bird how to sing,'* he read aloud, but the rest of the e.e. cummings phrase snaked under my thigh, hidden.

'Than teach ten thousand stars how not to dance,' I finished.

'Why is that written on your leg?'

'Because,' I said, 'I ran out of room on my jacket.'

'You must be an English major.'

'English majors smoke clove cigarettes and say things like *deconstruction* and *onomatopoeia* just to hear the sound of their voices.'

He started to laugh. 'You're right. I used to date an English major. She was always looking at things like laundry in a dryer, or toast, and trying to relate them to the subtext of *Paradise Lost.'*

I knew men. My mother had taught me how to read the sentences they did not say out loud, how to wear a red cord tied around my left wrist to keep away the ones who only saw you as a single step, rather than a destination. I could tell by the bitter almond smell that rose off a man's skin whether he had cheated on his partners in the past. But the men I had known were like me – boys who had grown up dreaming in Spanish, boys who believed you could light a red candle for a dose of luck, boys who knew that a man who spoke ill of his girlfriend might find his tongue stuck to the roof of his mouth when he awakened. Men like Charlie, on the other hand, went to universities and wrestled with mathematical theorems and combined chemicals to watch them rise in lovely clouds of invisible gas. Men like Charlie were not meant for girls like me.

'If you're not an English major,' he asked, 'then what *do* you do?'

I looked at him as if he were crazy – did he not see the four walls of this squat building around me? Did he think I was here because I liked the view? But I wanted him to know that there was more to me than just this job. I wanted him to think

I was mysterious and different and anyone except the person I really was: a Mexican girl who did not live in the same world as people like him. So I took my deck of cards out from beneath the counter. 'I read *los naipes*.'

'Tarot?' he said. 'I don't buy that stuff.'

'Then you have nothing to lose.' I opened the wooden box that held my deck and removed them, as usual, with my left hand. Then I said an Ave, and looked up at him. 'Don't you want to know if you'll get your wish?'

'What wish?'

'That,' I told him, 'is up to you.'

He smiled so slowly that I had to look down. 'All right then. Tell me my future.'

I had him cut the deck three times, for the Holy Trinity, and hand them back to me. Then I laid out nine cards: four in the shape of the Cross, five and six balanced below the arms of it, seven at the base, eight tipped on its side at the very bottom, and the last card smack in the center of them all. 'The first card,' I said, turning it over, 'shows your state of mind.' It was the Seven of Wands.

'God, I hope it means money. Especially if it's my engine that's dead.'

'It's a message,' I told him. 'It says that the truth can't stay hidden forever. These next three cards will tell you who's going to help you figure it out.'

I flipped them over. 'This is interesting. The Lovers, well, that's just what you'd think – a happy couple. Some sort of romantic relationship is going to be instrumental in helping you get what you want. The Strength card isn't as good as it sounds – it tells you not to take on more than you can handle. But I think that the Chariot cancels that out, because it's powerful, and means you're going to ultimately have good luck.'

I turned over cards five and six. 'The Eight of Wands is a warning against ugly actions that might destroy you . . . and this card, the Hanged Man . . . have you been committing any crimes lately? Because that's usually what this represents –

someone who better mend his ways, or God will get him even if the law doesn't.'

'I jaywalked yesterday,' Charlie said.

Cards seven and eight were the enemies plotting against him. 'These are both great cards,' I said. 'This is a child who's important to you, and who brings balance to your life.'

'I don't really know any kids.'

'A brother or sister?' I asked. 'No nieces, nephews?'

'Not even a cousin.'

I started scrubbing down the bar, although it was perfectly clean. 'Then maybe it's yours,' I said. 'Sometime.'

His hand crossed the wood, fingered the card. 'What's she going to look like?'

The suit was Cups. 'Light-skinned and dark-haired.'

'Like you,' he said.

I blushed, and busied myself by turning over the last card. 'This lets you know if your wish will come true, or if all those other things will get in the way.'

The card was the Seven of Cups – a wedding or alliance he would regret for the rest of his life. 'So?' Charlie asked, and his voice rang with the future. 'Do I get what I want?'

'Absolutely,' I lied, and then I leaned across the bar and kissed him over the map of our lives.

I never forgot you.

I have boxes, somewhere in the crawl space of the garage, full of the Christmas gifts and birthday presents you weren't here to open – stuffed animals and charm bracelets, sequined slippers and dress-up clothes that would have fit you way back when. Once Victor realized that I was still buying for you, he got upset – it wasn't healthy, he told me – and he made me promise I would stop. Not everyone understands how you can spin two lassos at the same time, one of hope and one of grief.

When the elementary school you might have attended held its fifth-grade send-off, I went to the auditorium and listened to everyone else's children dream of what they might grow up to be: a paleontologist, a recording star, the first astronaut to walk on Mars. I imagined you wearing braids, although that would have been too babyish a style for you by then. I celebrated your sweet sixteen at the Biltmore, where I made the penguin-breasted waiter serve tea for two, although you were not sitting across from me.

I never stopped hoping that you'd come home, but I did stop expecting it. Having your breath freeze up every time the doorbell chimes or the phone rings takes its toll on a person, and whether it is conscious or not, you eventually make the decision to divide your life in half – before and after – with loss being that tight bubble in the middle. You can move around in spite of it; you can laugh and smile and carry on with your life, but all it takes is one slow range of motion, a doubling over, to be fully aware of the empty space at your center.

When you love someone more than he loves you, you'll do anything to switch the scales. You dress the way you think he'd like you to dress. You pick up his favorite figures of expression. You tell yourself that if you re-create yourself in his image, then he will crave you the same way you crave him.

Maybe you understand what happened between me and Charlie better than anyone else would – when you are told you're someone you aren't, over and over, you begin to believe it. You live that life. But you are wearing a mask, one that might slip if you aren't careful. You wonder what he will do when he finds out. You know you are bound to disappoint him.

There was a moment, I admit, where I thought I had made him love me as much as I needed him to. When you were about eighteen months old, I got pregnant again. Charlie would sneak out of work during his lunch break and come home to me; he'd rest his head on my belly. *Matthew Matthews,* he'd say, trying names on for size to make me laugh. *Banjo. Sprocket. No, Cortisone. Cort for short.* He'd bring me little gifts from the pharmacy: chocolate candy bars, cocoa butter, butterfly hair clips.

I was twenty-one weeks along when my membranes ruptured. The baby was perfect – a little boy, the size of a human heart. I developed an infection; started bleeding. I was taken back to the OR, and given a hysterectomy. The doctors used words like uterine atony and artery ligation, disseminated intravascular coagulation, but all I heard was that I couldn't have any more children. I knew, even if no one was willing to say it to me, that this had been my fault, some fatal flaw in me. And when I came home from the hospital, I realized that Charlie knew this, too. He couldn't stand to look at me. He spent more and more time in the office. He took you with him.

I drank a lot before I met your father, but I honestly think it took that miscarriage to make me an alcoholic. I drank until I didn't see the regret in Charlie's eyes. I drank until even he could plainly see that I was a failure. I drank until I couldn't feel anything, most of all his touch. I think there was a part of me that knew if I drove him away, I would never have to say I'd been left behind.

But mostly I drank because that was when I could feel your baby brother, swimming through me like a silver fish. I didn't know until it was too late that trying to hold on to the baby I'd lost was going to cost me the child I already had.

I can't remember the moment I understood that I had to turn my life around, but I do know why. I was terrified that the detective assigned to your case would call me with news, and I'd be passed out. Or that – miracle – you'd show up at my door when I was out on a bender. What hurts the most, after all this time, is realizing that you had to disappear before I could find myself. Two years after you were gone, I was completely sober, and I've never strayed since.

The detective who was assigned to your kidnapping retired in 1990. He lives on a houseboat in Lake Powell. He sends Christmas cards, with pictures of himself and his wife. He was the one who called me to tell me you'd been found. But before the phone rang that morning, I had already opened a carton of eggs to find them all upended and cracked; I had seen a line of fire ants spell out your initials on my driveway. By the time Detective LeGrande called, I already knew what he was going to say.

There is one reading of *los naipas* that a person can do for herself: *El Evangelio*. It involves spreading fourteen cards in the outline of the Gospel and then five more in the shape of the Cross. The first time I ever did *El Evangelio*, I was learning to read the cards at my mother's side. For many years, I stopped doing it altogether, because too often the Fool card came up in places I did not want to see it. But after you disappeared, I spread the cards every Sunday night. And every time, the same two major Arcana would appear somewhere in the Cross. Number fourteen, Temperance, warned of rash actions I'd regret for the rest of my life; number fifteen, the Devil, said that someone had been lying to me.

After Detective LeGrande called, I took out *los naipas*. It was not a Sunday evening, and it was not in my *santuario,* just across the kitchen table. As always, the Devil and Temperance popped up in the Cross. But this time there were two other cards that I hadn't seen there before. The Star, which is the most potent card in the Tarot deck, and neutralizes the other cards around it. Set next to the Devil, like so, it meant that my old enemy was about to pay. From this day forth, your father would be powerless.

The other card was the Ace of Wands, which any novice *bruja* will tell you stands for chaos.

You have my hair, and my smile. You also have my stubbornness. It's a little like having your past self come calling, and wishing you could warn yourself about what will happen.

You told me what you remembered about your childhood, but you didn't ask me what I remember. If you had, I would have said *everything* – from the moment you arrived in this world and curled stiff as a snail against the overwashed cotton of my hospital gown, to the licorice twist of your braids beneath my fingers, to the way I went to kiss you before you left with Charlie for your weekend visitation, so sloppy and sure of myself that when I missed your cheek and landed on air I stupidly assumed I would have a thousand more chances to get it right.

After you vanished, I went to Mexico to visit a *bruja* with whom my mother had studied. She lived in a cottage with three blue iguanas who had the run of the house, and who were rumored to be former men who had treated her badly. I went on June 13, the feast of San Antonio de Padua. Her waiting room was packed with the needy, who shared their sad stories to pass the time: a woman who had left her grandmother's diamond ring in a public restroom; an elderly man who had misplaced the deed to his house; a child clutching a Perro Perdido flyer with a photo of a hot-eyed hound; a priest whose faith had gone off course. I waited silently, watching the red roosters peck at kernels of corn in her front yard. When it was my turn, I went into the *santuario* and handed the *bruja* the requisite small statue of San Antonio, along with my written description of what I had lost.

She whispered a prayer and wrapped the statue in the paper. She tied it with red string. 'A hundred pesos,' she said. I paid her, and then drove north, pulling over at the first body of water I could find. I threw the package as far as I could into the reservoir, and waited until I thought it might have sunk to the bottom.

San Antonio is the patron saint of things that have gone missing. Make an offering on his feast day, and what's lost will be back in your possession within a year. Unless, that is, it has been destroyed.

I went to that Mexican *bruja* every June until she died, and asked for the same spell each time. Year after year, when you were not returned to me, I never blamed her or San Antonio. I thought it was my fault; something I had left out or gotten wrong in the written description of you, which grew longer every year – from paragraph to epic poem to masterpiece. I would spend the following three hundred and sixty-four days crafting the note I would bring to the *bruja* the next time around, if you still hadn't turned up.

Although that *bruja* is long dead, I think I finally know what I should have written. Twenty-eight years is a long time to think about why I loved you, and it's not for the reasons I first assumed: because you swam in the space below my heart; or because you stanched the youth I was bleeding out daily; or because one day you might take care of me when I couldn't take care of myself. Love is not an equation, as your father once wanted me to believe. It's not a contract, and it's not a happy ending. It is the slate under the chalk and the ground buildings rise from and the oxygen in the air. It is the place I come back to, no matter where I've been headed. I loved you, Bethany, because you were the one relationship I never had to earn. You arrived in this world loving me more, even when I did not deserve it.

IV

Sometimes it is necessary
To reteach a thing its loveliness.
                    – Galway Kinnell,
              'St. Francis and the Sow'

Eric

When I was thirteen years old I met the perfect girl. She was nearly as tall as I was, with cornsilk hair and eyes the color of thunderstorms. Her name was Sondra. She smelled like lazy summer Sundays – mowed grass and sprinklers – and I found myself edging closer to her whenever I could, just to breathe in deeply.

I imagined things in Sondra's company that I'd never bothered to imagine before: what it would feel like to walk barefoot on a volcano; how to find the patience to count all the stars; whether it physically hurt to grow old. I wondered about kissing: which way to turn my head, if her lips would save the impression of mine, the way my pillow always knew how to come back to the curve of my head night after night.

I didn't talk to her, because this was all so much bigger than words.

I was walking beside Sondra when she suddenly turned into a rabbit and hopped away, disappearing underneath the hedge in the front of my house.

The next morning when I woke up from my dream, it didn't matter that this girl had never existed, that I had been unconscious when I had conjured her. I found myself crying when I took the milk out of the refrigerator for my cereal; it was all I could do to get from one minute to the next. I spent hours sitting on the lawn, trying to find a rabbit in our shrubbery.

Sometimes we don't know we're dreaming; we can't even fathom that we're asleep.

I still think of her, every now and then.

*

Our first week in Arizona passes slowly. I immerse myself in state case law; I wade through the prosecution's discovery. The environment seems to stir something up in Delia, who starts remembering more and more about her childhood – snippets that usually make her cry. She summons the courage to go visit her father a couple more times; she takes long walks with Sophie and Greta.

One morning I wake up to find Ruthann's trailer on fire. Smoke rolls over the roof in a thick gray cloud as I burst through the front door, yelling for my daughter, who spends more time over there than she does with us these days. But there are no flames inside, not even any smoke. And Sophie and Ruthann are nowhere to be found.

I run around to the yard behind the trailer. Ruthann sits on a stump; Sophie's at her feet. The plume of gray smoke I saw in the front of the house comes from a small campfire. Set in its center are two cinder blocks with a thin, flat stone balanced on top. A bead of water on the hot stone spits and dances. Ruthann does not look up at me, but takes a bowl filled with blue batter and ladles a spoonful onto the stone. She uses the flat of her hand to spread the batter as thin as it will go, pressing her palm down on the searing surface.

As the batter solidifies into a circle, Ruthann takes an onion-skin-thin tortilla from a plate beside her and settles it on top of the one still cooking on the stone. She folds in the sides and then rolls from the bottom up, making a hollow tube that she passes over to me. 'An Egg McMuffin it's not,' she says.

It looks, and tastes, like pale blue tracing paper. It sticks to the roof of my mouth. 'What's in it?'

'Blue corn, rabbit-ear sage, water. Oh, and ashes,' Ruthann adds. '*Piki* is an acquired taste.'

But my daughter – the one who will eat macaroni and cheese only if the noodles are straight, not curly, who insists that I cut the crusts off her peanut butter and jelly sandwiches and slice on the diagonal, instead of the half – is stuffing this *piki* in her mouth as if it's candy.

'Siwa helped me grind the cornmeal yesterday,' Ruthann says.

'*Siwa* means *Sophie*,' Sophie adds.

'It means *youngest sister*,' Ruthann corrects, 'but that's still you.' She spreads another circle of batter on the burning stone with her bare hand, lets it set, and flips it over in a seamless motion.

'Finish telling me the story, Ruthann.' Sophie looks over her shoulder at me. 'You *interrupted*.'

'Sorry.'

'It's about a rabbit who got too hot.'

Sondra, I think.

Ruthann folds up another piece of *piki* and rolls it in a paper towel, handing it to Sophie. 'Where did I leave off?'

'In the Great Heat,' Sophie says, settling down cross-legged in front of Ruthann. 'The animals were all droopy.'

'Yes, and Sikyátavo, Rabbit, was worst of all. His fur was matted with red dirt from the desert. His eyes were so dry they burned. He wanted to teach the sun a lesson.'

She folds another cone of *piki*. 'So Rabbit ran off to the edge of the world where every morning, Sun came up. He practiced with his bow and arrow the whole way. But when he got there, Sun had left the sky. Rabbit thought that was cowardly, but he decided to wait for Sun to return the next day. Sun, though, had seen Rabbit practicing and decided to have a little fun with him. Back in those days, you see, Sun didn't come up slowly like he does now. He'd burst into the sky with one leap. So the next day, Sun rolled far away from where he usually jumped into the sky and then leaped up. By the time Rabbit got his bow and arrow together, Sun was already so high he couldn't be touched. Rabbit stamped his foot and shouted, but Sun only laughed.

'One morning,' Ruthann continues, 'Sun got careless. He jumped more slowly than usual, and Rabbit's arrow plunged into his side. Rabbit was delighted! He'd shot the Sun! But when he looked up again he saw how flames bled from the wound. Suddenly the whole world seemed to be on fire.'

She stands up. 'Rabbit ran to a cottonwood, and a grease-wood tree, but neither one would hide him – they were too afraid of being burned to a crisp. Suddenly he heard a voice calling to him: "Sikyátavo! Under me! Hurry!" It was a small green bush with flowers like cotton. Rabbit ducked beneath it, just as the flames leaped over the bush. Everything crackled and hissed, and then went quiet.' Ruthann looks at Sophie. 'The earth all around was black and burnt, but the fire was gone. And the little bush that had saved Rabbit wasn't green anymore, but a deep yellow. Even today, that kind of bush grows green, and then turns yellow when it feels the sun.'

'What happened to Rabbit?' Sophie asks.

'He was never the same. He has brown spots on his fur, from where the fire burned him. And he's not so tough anymore, you know. He runs away and hides, instead of putting up a fight. Sun isn't the same, either,' Ruthann says. 'He makes himself so bright that no one can look at him long enough to shoot straight.'

Ruthann cracks her knuckles; silver and turquoise rings wink like fireflies. 'Let's clean up,' she says to Sophie, 'and then if your dad says it's okay, you can come with me to the garage sale around the corner and scope out inventory.'

Sophie runs into the house, leaving me alone with Ruthann. 'You don't have to keep her with you.'

'It's good to have a child to tell a story to.'

'Do you have any of your own?'

The lines of Ruth's face carve deeper. 'I had a daughter once.'

Maybe we can all be divided along this rift: Those who have been lucky enough to keep our children, and those who have had them taken away from us. Before I can find the appropriate response, Sophie comes out of the house, dragging a bucket of sand behind her. She pours it onto the fire, banking the embers, a small cloud of soot sighing up around her knees.

'Soph,' I say, 'if you can be a good girl, you can stay with Ruthann a little longer.'

'Of course she can be good,' Ruthann says. 'Where I come from, on Second Mesa, our grandmothers give us our names, and our grandfathers give us our manners. The ones who aren't good don't have grandfathers to tell them how to behave. And you have a grandfather, don't you, Siwa?' She hands Sophie the bowl of leftover batter. 'Kitchen sink,' she instructs.

The sun has risen high enough to gnaw on the back of my neck. I think of Rabbit, and his arrow. 'Thanks, Ruthann.'

She gives me a half smile. 'Watch your aim, Sikyátavo,' she warns, and she follows Sophie inside.

In 1977, in Arizona, a man could squirrel his daughter away to another part of the country and it was considered kidnapping. By 1978 the laws had changed, and that same man, for the same act, would be charged with custodial interference – a lesser felony. 'Jesus, Andrew,' I murmur, poring over the books in my borrowed conference room at Hamilton, Hamilton. 'Couldn't you have waited a few months?' Frustrated, I pick up one of the law books and whip it across the room, narrowly missing Chris as he walks in.

'What's the matter with you?' he asks.

'My client is an idiot.'

'Of course he is. If he wasn't, he wouldn't need a lawyer.' Chris sits down and leans back in the chair across from me. 'Boy, did you miss out last night, bud. Picture a natural redhead named Lotus, following me into the men's room at The Frantic Gecko to demonstrate how flexible a yoga instructor can actually be. *And* she had a friend who could lift her wineglass with her foot.' He smiles. 'I know, I know. You're practically married. But still. You got any Tylenol?'

I shake my head.

'Then I definitely need coffee. You take cream or sugar?'

'I don't drink—'

'Coming right up,' he says, and he leaves.

I break out in a sweat, imagining already what it will be like to have a cup sitting on the table a few inches from me, steaming and fragrant. What most people don't understand is the interstitial space between lifting that mug and emptying its contents in the sink. In that instant, which is only as long as a thought, need can grow to such enormous proportions that it muscles reason out of the way, and before you know it, I am lifting the drink to my mouth.

To drive my mind away from this, I start to flip through the pages of Arizona statutes to see if there's an affirmative defense for kidnapping, and finally find the paragraph I am looking for.

> *§13–417.* Necessity defense. *Conduct that would otherwise constitute an offense is justified if a reasonable person was compelled to engage in the proscribed conduct and the person had no reasonable alternative to avoid imminent public or private injury greater than the injury that might reasonably result from the person's own conduct.*

Or in other words: *I had to do it.*

Having an alcoholic wife isn't a reason to steal a child. However, if I can prove that Elise was an alcoholic, that she couldn't care for the child, that a call was made to protective services or the police, and that they didn't respond adequately; well, then Andrew has a shot at acquittal. A jury might be convinced that Andrew had exhausted all other possible options, that he had no choice but to take his daughter and run . . . provided, first, that Andrew can convince me.

Chris walks into the conference room. 'Here you go,' he says, sliding the mug across the table. 'The breakfast of champions. Now, if you'll excuse me, I'm going to find a physician to surgically remove my head.'

After he leaves, I walk toward the steaming mug. It has been years since I've taken a sip, and I can still taste the beautiful bitter of it. I inhale deeply. Then I dump the coffee – china mug and all – into the trash.

The detention officer manning the visiting area at the jail nods at me. 'Take any empty one,' he says. It's a quiet morning; the doors are all shut, and the lights are off. I open the first door on the right and turn on the light – only to find an inmate with his striped pants down around his ankles, screwing his attorney on top of the Formica conference table. 'Sonofabitch,' the guy says, his hand reaching to pull up his shorts. The woman blinks in the sudden light and tugs her pencil skirt down, knocking over a box full of files.

'Let me guess,' I say cheerfully to the lawyer. 'Pro boner work?'

With an apology, I settle myself into the next room to wait for Andrew. He comes in as I'm still picturing the attorney next door – a *pubic* defender, I guess you'd call her – and smiling. 'What's so funny?' Andrew asks.

It is the kind of story that, a week ago, I would have told him over dessert. But Andrew is dressed in the same stripes and pink thermals as the man next door, and that is sobering. 'Nothing.' I clear my throat. 'Look, we need to talk about your case.'

There is a right way and a wrong way to go about presenting an affirmative defense to a client. You basically explain where the escape hatch is and then say, 'Hmm, if you had a ladder to get up there, you'd be home free' – hoping like hell that your client will be bright enough to then volunteer that he does indeed have a ladder hidden away in his breast pocket. The fact that a ladder can't possibly fit in his breast pocket or that he never in his life owned a ladder is not nearly as important as the fact that he tells you, flat out, that he is in possession of one. As the attorney, all you need to do is hint to the jury about the ladder, you don't have to physically present it.

Sometimes the client gets what you're trying to do, some-times he doesn't. At best, you are leading your star witness; at worst, you are suggesting that he lie to you so that you have some semblance of a defense.

'Andrew,' I say carefully, 'I've been looking at the charges that were filed against you, and there *is* a defense that we might be able to use. Basically, it means saying that things were so bad in the household that you had no other alternative but to do what you did, which is take Delia away. The thing is, for this defense to apply . . . you also have to show that you had no alternative legal means of solving the problem.' I give Andrew a moment to let this all sink in. 'Delia told me that your ex-wife is an alcoholic. Maybe that impaired her ability to function as a good mother . . . ?'

Slowly, Andrew nods.

'Maybe you felt you deserved custody of Delia, because of this . . . ?'

'Well, wouldn't you have—'

I hold up a hand. 'Did you call the police? Or child protective services? A social worker? Did you try to get your custody agreement revisited in court?'

Andrew shifts in his seat. 'I thought about it, but then I realized it wasn't a good idea.'

My heart sinks. 'Why not?'

'You saw that assault conviction the prosecutor had—'

'What the hell was that all about, anyway?'

He shrugs. 'Nothing. A stupid bar fight. But I wound up in jail overnight because of it. Back then, the courts automatically gave custody to a mother even when the father had a spotless background. If you had a strike against you already, well, you might as well kiss your kid good-bye.' He looks up at me. 'I was scared that if I went to complain about Elise, they'd look up my record and decide I shouldn't even have visitation anymore, much less full custody.'

The necessity defense implies there was no legal alternative remaining, but this is not the scenario Andrew's painted. He didn't even try a legal route before exacting his own vigilante justice. But instead of telling him how damaging this is to his case, I just nod. The first rule of defense law is to keep your client believing that there is always a light at the end of the tunnel, a slim possibility for a better outcome.

When you get right down to it, the relationship between a

defendant and a lawyer is not all that different from the one between a child and an alcoholic parent.

'It's not like I didn't try,' Andrew says. 'I spent months following the rules. Even the day I left, I took her home first.'

My head snaps up; this is news to me. 'You what?'

'Beth had forgotten this blanket she used to take everywhere, and I knew she'd be miserable all weekend without it. So we went back. The place was a mess – the kitchen was piled high with dishes, and food was rotting on the counter; the refrigerator was empty.'

'Where was Elise?'

'In the living room, out cold.'

I have a sudden mental picture of the woman, lying facedown with her arm trailing off the couch and the sweet curl of bourbon soaking into the cushions where the bottle has spilled. But in my picture the woman doesn't have black hair, like Elise Vasquez did when I saw her in court. She is a blonde, and she is wearing a pair of orange Capri pants that were my mother's favorite.

All of the memories I have of my mother smell like alcohol – even the good ones, when she was bending down to kiss me good night, or straightening my tie before my high school graduation. Her disease was a perfume, one I used to lean into when I was a child and one I itched for when I was an adult. If you ask me for five concrete recollections from when I was a kid, chances are that three of them will involve some fiasco based on my mother's drinking: the time it was her turn to be Den Mother and the Boy Scout troop arrived to find her completely lit and dancing in her underwear; the track championship she slept through; the sting of her hand on my face when she actually wanted to punish herself.

These memories are the pillars I built my life on. But hiding behind them are the other memories, the ones that peek out only when I let down my guard: the hazy afternoon my mother and I sat with our heads bent over the sidewalk, watching ants construct a mobile city. Her voice, off-key, singing me awake in the morning. The summer days when she staked trash bags on the lawn and ran a hose, a makeshift Slip-N-Slide for the two of us. Her inconsistency, in a better light, became spontaneity. You cannot hate someone until you know what it might be like to love them.

Was having an occasional mother better than not having one at all?

Andrew has read my mind. 'You know what that's like for a kid, Eric. If it had been up to you, would you have wanted a household like the one you grew up in?'

No. I didn't want to grow up in a household like mine, but I did. And I hadn't wanted to turn out just like my mother, either, but I had. 'What did you do?' I ask.

'I took Delia, and left.'

'I meant before that. Did you bother to see whether your ex-wife was all right? Did you call anyone to take care of her?'

'She wasn't my responsibility anymore.'

'Why not? Because you had a piece of paper saying you'd gotten divorced?'

'Because I'd done it a thousand times before,' Andrew says. 'Are you defending me, or Elise? For God's sake, Delia was in the very same situation when she got pregnant, except you were the one lying drunk on the floor.'

'But she didn't run away from me,' I point out. 'She waited for me to get my head straight. So don't even begin to compare your situation to hers, Andrew, because Delia's a better person than you ever were.'

A muscle tics in Andrew's jaw. 'Yeah. I guess whoever raised her must have really known what he was doing.' He stands up and walks out of the conference room, beckoning to an officer to take him back to the safety of his cell.

Delia calls me on my cell phone while I am driving back to Hamilton, Hamilton. 'Guess what,' she says. 'I got a phone call from that prosecutor, Ellen . . .'

'Emma.'

'Whatever.' I can hear the smile in her voice. 'She asked to meet with me, and I told her I had a spot in my calendar between Hell Freezing Over and Not in This Lifetime. Where are you, anyway?'

'I'm on my way back from the jail.'

There is a silence. 'So how is he?'

'Great,' I say, adding a lift to my voice. 'We've totally got this under control.' My cell phone beeps, another incoming call. 'Hang on, Dee,' I tell her, and I switch over. 'Talcott.'

'It's Chris. Where are you?'

I look over my shoulder at the merging traffic. 'Headed onto Route Ten.'

'Well, get off it,' he says. 'You need to go back.'

The hair stands up on the back of my neck. 'What happened to Andrew?'

'Nothing that I know of. But you just got some mail from Emma Wasserstein. She's filed a motion to remove you as counsel.'

'On what grounds?'

'Witness tampering,' Chris says. 'She thinks you're feeding information to Delia.'

I slam down the phone, cursing, and it rings immediately; I've forgotten that Delia was on the other line. 'What else did you say to the prosecutor?' I ask.

'Nothing. She was trying to do the buddy thing, you know, but I wasn't falling for it. She said she wanted to meet with me, and I refused. She pumped me for information about my father.'

I swallow. 'What did you say?'

'That it wasn't any of her business, and that if she was fishing for information about him she'd have to talk to you, just like I do.'

Oh, shit.

'Who called?' Delia asks. 'Who was on the other line?'

'A courtesy call from Verizon,' I lie.

'You were on for a long time.'

'Well, they were being very courteous.'

'Eric,' Delia asks, 'did my father say anything else about me?'

Her question is clear as a bell; the cell phone reception is crystalline. But I hold the phone away from my ear. I make static noises. 'Dee, can you hear me? I'm going under some power lines. . . .'

'Eric?'

'I'm losing you,' I say, and I hang up while she is still talking.

In the motion filed by Emma Wasserstein, Delia is referred to as the victim. Every time I read the word, I think how much she would hate that. Chris, Emma, and I sit in Judge Noble's chambers, waiting for His Honor to speak. Massive and formidable, he is busy spreading peanut butter on a cheese sandwich. 'Do I look fat to you, Counselor?' the judge asks, although the question is directed at none of us in particular.

'Robust,' Emma answers.

'Healthy,' Chris adds.

Judge Noble pauses his knife and looks up at me. 'Generous,' I suggest.

'You wish, Mr. Talcott,' the judge says. 'I don't understand this whole good cholesterol, bad cholesterol thing. And I sure as hell don't understand why, if I'm going to eat a sandwich, I have to have a quarter of a teaspoon of peanut butter to go with it.' He takes a bite and grimaces. 'You know why I'm going to lose weight on the Zone diet? Because no one in their right mind would eat any of this crap.' He takes a deep, rumbling breath and shifts in his chair. 'I don't normally hold hearings during my lunch hour, but I'm going to suggest to my wife that perhaps I should. Because frankly, I find the subject of this motion so unpalatable that it has nearly ruined my appetite entirely. Why, if I got a dozen motions like this a day, my abs would look like Brad Pitt's.'

'Your Honor,' Chris says quickly, intercepting.

'Sit down, Mr. Hamilton. This isn't about you, and much

to my chagrin, Mr. Talcott apparently has a mind of his own.' The judge levels his gaze at me. 'Counselor, as I'm sure you're aware, witness tampering is one of the biggest ethical violations you can make as a defense attorney, one that will get your *pro hac vice* revoked and your ass kicked out of Arizona and most likely every other Bar association in this country.'

'Absolutely, Judge Noble,' I agree. 'But Ms. Wasserstein's allegations are false.'

The judge frowns. 'Are you or are you not engaged to your client's daughter?'

'I am, Your Honor.'

'Well, maybe in New Hampshire you've all intermarried so much that everyone's a cousin, and there aren't enough non-related attorneys to go around for your clients, but here in Arizona, we do things a little differently.'

'Your Honor, it's true that I have a personal relationship with Delia Hopkins. But it will not affect this case in any capacity, in spite of Ms. Wasserstein's specious allegations. Yes, Delia asks me about her father – but it's how he looks, and if he's being treated all right – questions that would be important on a personal level, and not a professional one.'

'We could ask Delia to corroborate that,' Emma says tartly, 'but she's probably already been coached in what to say.'

I turn to the judge. 'Your Honor, I'll give you my word, and if that's not good enough, I'll swear under oath that I'm not violating any ethical measures here. If anything, I have even *more* responsibility to my client, because I'm trying to keep his daughter's best interests a priority as well.'

Emma folds her arms above the shelf of her belly. 'You're too close to this case to do a decent job.'

'That's ridiculous,' I argue. 'That's like saying that you can't try a child kidnapping case because you're about to drop your own baby any second, and your emotions might keep you from being objective. But if I said that out loud, I'd be skating on pretty thin ice, wouldn't I? You'd accuse me of being prejudicial and sexist and outright anachronistic, wouldn't you?'

'All right, Mr. Talcott, shut your mouth before I wire your jaw closed for you,' Judge Noble orders. 'I'm making a finding on this right now. Your first obligation is to your client, not your fiancée. However, the State has to show me that you're actively engaging in witness tampering for me to actually remove you from this case, and Ms. Wasserstein has not proven that . . . yet. So you may remain Andrew Hopkins's attorney, Mr. Talcott, but make no mistake – every time you come into my courtroom, I'm going to be watching you. Every time you open your mouth, I'm going to be caressing my Rules of Professional Conduct. And if you make one wrong move, I'm going to refer you to the State Conduct Committee so fast you won't know what hit you.' He picks up his jar of peanut butter. 'Oh, hell,' Judge Noble says, and he sticks two fingers into the Jif and scoops out a dollop to eat. 'Adjourned.'

When Emma Wasserstein gets up and drops her papers all over the floor, I lean down to grab them for her. 'Watch your back, you hick,' she murmurs.

I straighten. *'Excuse* me?'

The judge watches us over the rim of his glasses. 'I said, *Nice comeback, Eric,'* Emma replies, and she smiles and waddles out of the room.

When I get home, Sophie is in the front yard, painting a prickly pear cactus pink. Her hands are small enough to weave the brush between the spines. I am sure that in this state, what she's doing is probably a felony, but frankly I am not in the mood to take any more family members onto my caseload. I pull the car up beside our elongated tin can and step out into the searing heat. Ruthann and Delia sit on nylon-woven folding chairs in the dust between our trailers, and Greta is sprawled in an exhausted puddle close to the paint can. 'Why is Sophie painting the cactus?'

Delia shrugs. 'Because it wanted to be pink.'

'Ah.' I squat down next to Sophie. 'Who told you that?'

'Duh,' Sophie says, with the kind of ennui that only four-year-olds can pull off. 'Magdelena.'

'Magdelena?'

'The *cactus.*' She points to a saguaro a few feet to the left. 'That's Rufus, and the little one with a white beard is Papa Joe.'

I turn to Ruthann. 'You name your cacti?'

'Of course not . . . their parents do.' She winks at me. 'There's cold tea inside, if you want some.'

I walk into her trailer and feel my way through the cabinets, past buttons and beads and rawhide-tied bundles of dried herbs, until I find a clean jelly jar. The pitcher of tea sweats on the counter; I fill my glass to the brim and am about to take a sip when the phone rings. After a moment I find the receiver under a stack of brown bananas. 'Hello?'

'Is Ruthann Masáwistiwa there?' a voice asks.

'Just a sec. Who's calling?'

'The Virginia Piper Cancer Center.'

Cancer Center? I step to the door of the trailer. 'Ruthann, it's for you.'

She is wielding the paintbrush for Sophie, trying to work color under the tight armpit of the cactus. 'Take a message, Sikyátavo. I'm busy with Picasso, here.'

'I think they really need to speak to you.'

She gives Sophie the paintbrush and steps into the trailer, letting the screen door slam behind her. I hold out the phone. 'It's the hospital,' I say quietly.

She looks at me for a long moment. 'Wrong number,' she barks into the receiver, and then punches the off button. I am quite certain that she doesn't realize she's folded her arm like a bird's wing, tucked over her left breast.

We all have our secrets, I suppose.

She keeps staring at me, until I incline my head just the tiniest bit, a promise to keep her confidence. When the phone rings again, she leans over and pulls the cord out of the wall. 'Wrong number,' she says.

'Yes,' I say quietly. 'It happens all the time to me.'

The McCormick Railroad Park is not crowded by the time we

get there, just before sunset. With its combination playground-carousel-miniature-steam-engine ride, the sprawling recreational area is a hot spot for the kindergarten set. Delia invites Fitz to come along; and I invite Ruthann, who pulls her junk-lined trench coat out of her cavernous purse and begins to solicit her resale wares to tired mothers.

I wait on the sidelines as Fitz and Delia take Sophie onto the carousel. She scrambles up onto a white horse with its neck straining forward. 'Come on,' Fitz yells to me. 'What have you got to lose?'

'My dignity?'

Fitz swings onto a powder pink pony. 'A guy who's secure in his manhood wouldn't be sitting out there like a loser.'

I laugh. 'Yeah, and do you want me to hold your purse while you're on the ride?'

Sophie fidgets on top of her horse as Delia tries to strap her in. 'Nobody else has to wear the seat belt,' she complains. Delia chooses a black stallion beside Fitz's. I listen as the music tinkles to life and the carousel begins to vibrate.

I won't admit this to any of them, but carousels scare the hell out of me. That calliope melody, and the way all the carved wooden horses seem to be in great pain – their eyes rolling wild, their yellow teeth bared, their bodies straining. As the carousel turns, the mirrored pillar in the center winks. Sophie comes into view and waves to me. Behind her, Delia and Fitz pretend to be jockeys, leaning forward on their horses.

The acne-pitted kid manning the controls flips the switch, and the carousel begins to wheeze to a stop. Sophie leans forward, caressing the plaster mane. Fitz and Delia appear again, standing up in the stirrups for a last stretch at the brass ring. They're batting at each other's hands and laughing. There's an S-curved steel bar at the top of the carousel that makes one of their horses rise as the other falls. It looks like they're moving separately, but they're not.

Two days later I land in the office of Sheriff Jack: head of the

Maricopa County Jail system and general media hound, with a personality so colorful he could give up his day job and become a disco strobe light. Everything I've heard about him is, regretfully, true, from the spittoon that he keeps on his desk (and uses liberally) to the framed photos of himself with every living Republican president to the bologna sandwich he himself eats for lunch, along with his prisoners. 'Let me get this straight,' he says, his amusement booming from beneath his bristled mustache, 'your client refuses to see you?'

'Yes, sir,' I say.

'But you wouldn't take no for an answer.'

I shift on my chair. 'I'm afraid not, sir.'

'And Sergeant Concannon says that you . . .' He looks down at a piece of paper in front of him. 'Sweet-talked her in an effort to get access to the inmate's pod.' He glances up. *'Sweet-talked?'*

'She's a very handsome woman,' I say, swallowing.

'She's a hell of a detention officer, but she's about as pretty as the business end of a donkey. A man less tolerant than myself might consider that sexual harassment.'

The last thing I need is to have Sheriff Jack calling Judge Noble and having a little chat. 'Well, sir,' I say, 'I find older women attractive. Especially those who are . . . diamonds in the rough.'

'Sergeant Concannon's so rough the carbons are still forming. Try again, boy.'

'Did I mention I have a friend who's a journalist from New Hampshire's largest paper, who'd like to write about you?' I will pay Fitz, if I have to. Hugely.

Sheriff Jack laughs out loud. 'I like you, Talcott.'

I smile politely. 'About my client, sir.'

'Sheriff Jack,' he corrects. 'What about him?'

'If I could just be brought up to his cell, even for five minutes, I think I could convince him that he ought to sit down with me for the sake of his own case.'

'We don't allow attorneys into the pods. Unless, of course,

they're criminals.' He thinks for a second. 'Maybe we *should* put the attorneys in the pods.'

'Sheriff.' I meet his gaze. 'I'd really like to have the opportunity to speak to Andrew Hopkins.'

There is a beat of silence. 'A journalist, you said?'

'Award-winning,' I lie.

He gets to his feet. 'Oh, hell. I need a good laugh.'

Sheriff Jack himself escorts me to the elevator, up to the second floor. This is different from the visitation room; here, a central control tower monitors four spider arms that house the inmates. There are locks everywhere.

Everyone knows who Sheriff Jack is – as we walk through the halls, detention officers greet him, but even more impressively, so do the inmates. 'Yo, yo, Sea Rag,' he says, as we pass a man who is being signed into his pod again.

''Sup, Dawg,' the man replies, grinning.

Sheriff Jack turns to me proudly. 'I speak it all. Ebonics, Spanish, you name it. I can say *Get your ass in line* in six different languages.'

He puts his hand on a doorknob that buzzes, and then opens. Another inmate, this one wearing a pink tank top, slouches on a chair with his nose buried in *The Fountainhead*. Up and down his arms words are tattooed: *Weiss Macht*. 'Put your shirt on,' Sheriff Jack orders.

We walk down a hallway that opens into a large, two-tiered room. Each side of the square holds an enclosed pod – barred cells on top, a common area on bottom. What it resembles – what a jail always resembles – is a human zoo. The animals are busy doing their own thing – sleeping, eating, socializing. Some of them notice me, some of them choose not to. It's really the only power they have left.

Sheriff Jack walks up into the control tower while I wait at the bottom of the stairs. A pair of black inmates start rapping, putting on a show for me.

> I'm the O.G. Mr. Wop
> On the trigga nonstop

Bust a cap on a cop
And watch his punk ass drop.
A 187 that's what it was
Greetin' all homies with the word of Cuzz
I was dressed in blue
Since the age of two
Down for my 'hood
'Cause it's the thing to do.

To their right, an old man with white hair cascading past his shoulders is making elaborate hand motions to catch the attention of one of the detention officers. Behind the glass, his frail arm movements look like a modern dance performance.

Suddenly the sheriff is standing next to me again. 'The good news is, your client isn't in there.'

'Where is he?'

Sheriff Jack smiles. 'Well, that's the bad news, boy. Disciplinary segregation.'

Disciplinary segregation is on level three, house two, in pods A and D. Andrew knows I am coming before he sees me; prisoners can sniff out lawyers at a distance, and my arrival has created a hum in the air. He stands with his back deliberately toward me as I am led to his cell. 'I don't want to speak to him, Sergeant Doucette,' he tells the detention officer.

She looks at me, bored. 'He doesn't want to speak to you.'

I stare at Andrew's back. 'Well, that's fine by me. Because God knows I don't feel like hearing what the hell landed you in lockdown.'

He turns around and stares at me for a long moment. 'Let him in.'

Sheriff Jack has said nothing about me being let into a cell; I can see the detention officer thinking the same thing. If Andrew and I are going to have a traditional attorney/client visit, it is supposed to be upstairs in one of the conference rooms. Finally, she shrugs – if one lawyer gets strangled by his own client, the detention officers would probably consider it a good start. When she opens the barred slider, it grates, like fingernails on a blackboard. I step into the tiny space, and Doucette rams the door home behind me.

Immediately, I jump. Even knowing I can leave at any time, it's uncomfortable; there is barely enough room for one man, much less two. Andrew sits down on the bunk, leaving me a small stool. 'What are you doing in here?' I ask quietly.

'Self-preservation.'

'I'm just trying to save you, too.'

'Are you sure about that?' Andrew says.

Time is elastic, in jail. It can stretch to the length of a highway; it can beat like a pulse. It can expand, a sponge, thick enough to make the few inches between two people feel like a continent. 'I shouldn't have gotten angry at you the other day,' I admit. 'This case isn't about me.'

'I think we both know that's a lie,' Andrew says.

He is right, on all counts. I am an alcoholic, representing a man who ran away from one. I am the child of an alcoholic, who didn't get to escape.

But I'm also a father who wonders what I'd do in the same situation. I'm a victim of my own mistakes, holding fast to a second chance.

I glance around the tiny Spartan room where Andrew has come for protection. We do all kinds of things to safeguard ourselves: lie to the people we love; split hairs to justify our actions; take punishment instead of waiting for it to be given to us. Andrew may be the one who's been charged, but we are both being tried.

I hold his gaze. 'Andrew,' I say soberly, 'let's start over.'

Andrew

In jail, a black inmate will call a white inmate peckerwood, cracker, honky, redneck. He'll call a Mexican a spic.

A white inmate will call a black inmate a nigger, a monkey, a spook, a toad. He'll call a Mexican a beaner.

A Mexican will call a black inmate *miyate*, which means big black bean; or *yanta*, tire; or *terron*, shark. He'll call a white inmate a gringo.

In jail, everyone comes with a label. It's up to you to peel it off.

The maximum security pod is made up of fifteen cells – five white, five Hispanic, four black, and the one that holds Concise and me. Considering themselves at a disadvantage, the blacks begin a campaign to get me traded for someone with the right color skin. They stand at the entrance to the dayroom, waiting for an officer to come in on his habitual twenty-five-minute walk, to plead their case.

I wander around the dayroom, not really fitting anywhere. The television is tuned to C-SPAN, one of the five channels we are allowed, and a reporter is discussing the good fortune of turkeys. 'Presidentially pardoned turkeys have reason to give thanks today,' the woman says. 'Animal welfare activists at PETA said on Monday that Frying Pan Park in Herndon, Virginia, has promised better treatment of Katie, the female pardoned by President Bush as part of last November's holiday tradition. The second turkey pardoned died last week, after living in substandard conditions.'

Elephant Mike, the Aryan Brotherhood probate in control

in Sticks's absence, turns up the volume. Enormous and muscular, with a shaved head and a spider tattooed onto the back of his scalp, he was one of the henchmen who came with Sticks to attack me in the bathroom. 'Hey, what's the address for PETA?' he says. 'Maybe they can get us better conditions.'

The reporter beams at the camera. 'Katie will be given a heated coop, more straw for bedding, extra vegetables and fruit, and some chickens in her pen for mental stimulation.'

Elephant Mike crosses his arms. 'Look at that. For stimulation, they get chicks, and we get spics.'

A Mexican stands up and walks past Elephant Mike, kicks his chair. 'Gringo,' he mutters. 'Chenga su madre.'

As I walk past Elephant Mike, he grabs my shirt. 'Sticks wanted me to give you a message.' I don't bother asking how Sticks, a whole floor away from us and in lockdown twenty-three hours out of the day, might be able to get word to Elephant Mike. There are ways to communicate in jail, from talking through the ventilation ducts in the bathrooms to slipping a note to someone at an AA meeting who will carry it elsewhere. 'In here, you stick with your own kind.'

'I thought I made it pretty clear that you aren't *my kind,*' I reply.

'I'm telling you this for your own protection.'

Without responding, I start to walk away. I take two steps, and then find myself flattened against the wall. 'At any minute, a fight might break out, and when that happens, you don't want to be beside a guy who may turn on you. All's I'm saying is, you're asking to get yourself in a wreck if you don't get it right, Grandpa.'

A voice comes over the intercom. 'Mike, what are you doing?' the detention officer asks.

'Dancing,' he says, letting go of me.

The officer sighs. 'Stick to the waltz.'

Elephant Mike shoves me and walks off.

I clench my fists so that no one will realize my hands are shaking. If this were any ordinary Thursday, I would have gotten to my office by eight-thirty. I would have called over to Wexton Farms – the assisted living community – to see if there was anything I needed to know about – recently hospitalized people, delays in the transit shuttle, dietary restrictions. I would have checked with the kitchen to see what was on the menu for the day and welcomed the day's entertainment – a lecturer from Dartmouth or a watercolor artist, sharing his or her passion with the seniors. I would have procrastinated by looking up news stories on the Internet about you and Greta and your rescues; I would have dusted off the picture of Sophie sitting on the corner of my desk. I would spend the day with people who valued whatever time they had left, instead of people who bitterly counted it down.

I head up the stairs to the cell. Concise is huddled on the floor around a cardboard box where he keeps his canteen possessions. At the sound of my footsteps he shoves what looks like a piece of bread underneath the bottom bunk. 'I'm busy in here. Step.'

It smells like oranges in the cell. 'What do you know about Elephant Mike?'

Concise glances at me. 'He think he's some tank boss but he's just doin' a mud check. You know, see if you stick up for yourself, or put grass under you.' He seems to remember that he is not supposed to be helping me, but rather doing his best to get me into another cell. 'If the dawgs find you in here, you gonna be hemmed up.'

I look down at my feet and pick up a Jolly Rancher wrapper, and begin to flatten it between my palms. 'Don't cap it tight,' I say.

When he turns around, I shrug. 'Moonshine. That's what you're making, isn't it?' Bread, oranges, hard candy – it wouldn't take a rocket scientist to figure out the chemical reaction Concise is aiming for.

'Do your own time, not mine,' Concise scowls, and he busies himself under the bunk again.

Taking my towel with me, I head toward the bathroom.

The shower stalls are empty at this time of day; Emeril is about to come on the Food Network and it is the one program that all races agree upon. I turn the corner and find Elephant Mike standing against the bathroom wall with his pants down around his knees, his eyes rolled toward the ceiling.

I recognize the boy kneeling in front of him, too. He calls himself Clutch and is barely old enough to grow a beard. No doubt, like me, he received Sticks's and Elephant Mike's warning, and was offered their protection, for a price. The currency of which I've interrupted.

A flush works its way up from my neck. 'Sorry,' I manage, and I leave the bathroom as fast as possible.

On the television, Emeril throws garlic into a sizzling pan. 'Bam!' he yells. I sit in the back of the dayroom and pretend to watch the TV, although I do not see a thing.

If you pay Sheriff Jack thirty dollars up front, you are allowed the privilege of using the canteen. Funds for these luxury items are deducted from your account. A dollar-fifty, for example, will buy you either a bottle of shampoo or a twenty-ounce soda. You can buy soap that is like lye and rubs your skin raw. You can buy antihistamine and poker cards and a Spanish-English dictionary. You can buy Moon Pies and Paydays and Pop-Tarts and trail mix. Tuna, toothbrushes, a thesaurus.

Sometimes I read the canteen order form, and think about who purchases what. I want to know who asks for Vicks VapoRub, if it reminds him of his childhood. I wonder who would order an eraser, rather than learn from his mistakes. Or, even worse, a mirror.

They sell artificial tears, too, but it's hard to conceive of an inmate who doesn't have enough of his own.

I share a toilet with a drug dealer. I have done business with a thrice-convicted rapist: three packages of cookies in return for a deck of cards. I have settled down to watch Thursday night TV beside a man who killed his wife and cut her into pieces with a Ginsu knife, stuffed the body parts into a truck tool box, and left it in the desert.

Just last year, I gave Sophie the stranger talk: don't take candy from someone unfamiliar; don't ever get into anyone's car except ours; don't talk to people you do not know. Sophie, who was born in a small New Hampshire town where folks knew her by name when she walked down the street, couldn't understand the warnings. 'How do you know who's a bad man?' she asked. 'Can you tell just by looking?'

What I should have told her at the time was: Yes, but you have to be watching at just the right moment. Because the same man who robs a general store at knifepoint might, at a traffic light, turn and smile. The guy who raped a thirteen-year-old girl might be singing hymns beside you at church. The father who kidnapped his daughter might be living right next door.

Bad is not an absolute, but a relative term. Ask the robber who used the cash he stole to feed his infant; the rapist who was sexually abused as a child; the kidnapper who truly believed he was saving a life. And just because you break the law doesn't mean you have intentionally crossed the line into evil. Sometimes the line creeps up on you, and before you know it, you're standing on the other side.

Off to the right, I hear someone taking a leak. It is underscored by the *scrip-scrip* sound of a weapon being honed on the cement floor – a toothbrush or a wheelchair spoke being sharpened into a shank. There's weeping, too, coming from Clutch, in the cell beside ours. He has cried every night since he's been here, into his pillow, pretending no one can hear. Even more amazing, the rest of us pretend that we don't.

'Concise,' I whisper quietly.

'Yo,' he says.

I realize that I don't really have a question to ask him. I just wanted to see if he is still awake, like me.

You come to visit me almost every day. We sit one pane of

glass apart from each other, reworking the clay of our relationship. You would think that the conversations at a jail visit are grave and furious, packed with the emotion that comes when you don't see someone for twenty-three hours a day, but in fact what we talk about are the details. I soak up the descriptions of Sophie, making breakfast for herself by putting the entire box of oatmeal into the microwave. I picture the trailer where you are living, the inside as pink as a mouth. I listen to an account of Greta having her first run-in with a common snake. You hold up pictures that Sophie's drawn, so I can see the stick-figure family and my crayoned place in it.

For you, too, it is all about the specifics of a world you can barely remember being a part of. Sometimes I tell you incidents that stand out in your childhood; sometimes you have precise questions. One afternoon you ask me about your real birthday. 'It's June 5,' I say. 'The silver lining is that you're almost a whole year younger than you think.'

'I can't remember my birthdays,' you muse. 'I thought all kids remembered their birthdays.'

'You had parties. Pretty standard stuff: movies, bowling, goody bags.'

'What about when I lived here?'

'Well,' I hedge. 'You were little. We didn't make a big deal about it.'

You frown, concentrating. 'I can picture a cake. It's on a tablecloth I don't remember us having in New Hampshire.' You look up at me, triumphant with recollection. 'It fell on the floor, and I cried because we didn't get to eat it.'

That is the version that I fed to you, when it happened. 'We had some of your nursery school friends over for your birthday,' I say carefully. 'Your mother had been drinking. She was singing and dancing and making a scene, and I told her to stop it. "It's a party," she said. "That's what people do at parties." I told her to go lie down, that I would take care of everything. She picked up the cake and threw it on the floor, and said that if she was leaving, then the party was over.'

You look at me, stricken; and immediately I'm sorry I brought this up.

'She didn't know what she was doing back then,' I say. 'She—'

'How can you defend her?' you interrupt. 'If Eric had ever . . . if he'd . . .' You fall silent, a puzzle coming together. Along with your chin and dimples, did I give you the tendency to fall for someone dysfunctional? Would this gene be passed along to Sophie, too?

'I don't want to talk about this anymore,' you whisper.

'Okay,' I say. 'Okay.'

I watch you sitting on the stool, bowed by the weight of what you're starting to remember, crushed by the episodes you don't. In this new place we've found, sometimes there aren't words, because the truth can be even more difficult than the lies. I lift my palm to the glass, pretending that it would be that easy to touch you. You lift yours, too, spread your fingers – a starfish. I picture the thousands of streets we have crossed, hand-in-hand. Of the high-fives we've exchanged after high school track meets and breathless father-daughter three-legged races. Sometimes I think my whole life has been about holding on to you.

A poem circulating around D-block:

> A boy was born with skin pure white,
> He loved to fuck and he loved to fight.
> He was raised in the right way,
> Stood up for his race day after day.

> When he grew up and became a man,
> He got sentenced to do life in the pen.
> During his sentencing he stood straight and tall,
> He told the judge, 'I'll do it all!'

So when he went down to hit the yard
Others tried him, and they tried him hard.
He never once lost a fight to another race,
When he walked by them, they gave him his space.

The off-brands didn't like this a bit,
So they all got together and put out a hit.
The following day five of them tried,
When the fighting was over, all five had died.

All the woods got together and decorated the yard
With bodies of off-brands and more than one guard.
The Warden tried to stop them, but peed down his leg,
All the fellas laughed and made the punk beg.

The Governor called in the National Guard,
The assholes came in to shoot woods on the yard.
They walked up to this man and saw how he was lying,
It was apparent to all that he wasn't done dying.

The strangest thing was, he was full of bullet holes
But not a drop of blood present from his head to his toes.
He looked up then and started to laugh,
He laughed at the soldiers and the prison staff.

'Why can't you see that I am a saint?
White's made by God, all others ain't.
The reason you don't see any blood on my hide
Is my heart pumps nothing but PURE WHITE PRIDE!'

On the rec yard, we sort by color; two or three men per group. The blacks play basketball; the whites stand at the far wall; the Mexicans huddle diagonally across from them. The yard isn't really a yard, more an enclosed paved square. The ceiling on top protects inmates from the fierce heat during the summer; the Swiss-cheese holes in the far wall let the fresh air and the sun stream in. Someone has hung an enormous flag from the ceiling of the jail; it blocks part of the light.

There is one guard for thirty men; he can't see everything. For this reason, the rec yard is one of the prime places for a deal to go down. Cigarettes are bought surreptitiously – both real stuff and makeshift: lettuce leaves or potato peels rolled up in pages of the Bible. The inmates who have a drug trade going make their pitches out here, too. Drugs are the only reason the colors have to interact; looking for speed is called 'chasing the dragon.' As I am watching, a white called Chromedome makes a sale to a Mexican. He takes a Sharpie marker out of his pocket and removes the tip of it, so that the buyer can inspect the goods. I'm close enough to smell the pungent vinegar scent of the black tar heroin he's got hidden inside.

Clutch, the kid, straggles at the edges of the whites like an unraveling thread. He is pale and skinny, with crooked buck teeth and freckles. His eyes are locked on the basketball game. From time to time his feet move in an imaginary play.

One of the blacks dives for a loose ball, but misses. It rolls against the wall by the DO's foot, and passes by in front of me. Clutch bends down and palms the basketball, spins it on one finger. He dribbles twice, the ball rising up to meet his hand magnetically.

'Fool, give us the ball,' says Blue Loc, one of the dominant blacks in the pod. Concise stands with his hands on his hips, sweating hard.

Clutch glances around, but he doesn't relinquish the ball. When Elephant Mike walks to the perimeter of the game, Blue Loc says, 'Tell your sister he betta act right foe he git smacked right.'

Mike stands toe-to-toe with Blue Loc. 'Since when do you tell me what to do?'

The detention officer approaches. 'Break it up,' he says.

'Man, we just flowin' . . .' Blue Loc replies.

Elephant Mike knocks the ball out of Clutch's hands. 'Go

wash up. You ain't touching me with those hands until you scrub off the spook that's all over you.'

The ball bounces toward Concise, but I intercept it. I toss it quickly at Clutch, who automatically catches it and goes for the three-point shot. When it swishes through the net, he grins, the first time I have seen the kid smile in three days.

'It's a game,' I say. 'Let him rotate in.'

Blue Loc comes forward. 'You talkin' to me?'

Concise turns to him. 'Yo, lay offa da pipe, cuzz. Jus' let's go.'

The play resumes, harder and faster. The detention officer goes back to his spot along the wall. When Elephant Mike walks away, Clutch looks at me. 'Why did you stick up for me?'

I shrug. 'Because you didn't do it yourself.'

Garnering respect is the same across races: Never break weak. Back the play of your brothers. Never let a woman in on the real deal. Stand strong in the face of adversity. Get one over on the system at every opportunity.

Have heart.

Keep your word, because it's the only thing you've got in here.

Concise is testing his hooch. As far as I can tell, he has several different bottles in various stages of fermentation; I suppose this way he can be sure of a steady income. 'Do you ever think about what's going on outside?' I ask.

He looks over his shoulder. 'I know what's goin' on outside. Bunch of fools watching ESPN and gettin' in each other's business.'

'I mean *outside* outside. In the real world.'

Concise sits down, his arms balanced on his knees. 'This *is* the real world, cuzz. Why you think we keep comin' back to it?'

Before I can answer, Clutch appears in the entry to our cell. He is holding a bottle of shampoo and quivering from head to toe. 'What's wrong?' I ask.

He looks like he is going to throw up. 'I can't,' he blurts out, and suddenly I see Elephant Mike standing behind him.

Mike grabs the bottle from Clutch and squeezes, so that human feces sprays all over me. 'You want to be a nigger so bad, rub this into your skin.'

It is in my hair, my mouth, my eyes. I gasp, trying to breathe around the awful smell of it, wiping it off me and then holding out my hands, covered with shit. Concise jumps Elephant Mike, as the detention officers rush into the cell. They pull Concise off Mike and throw him down into the mess on the floor. 'Stupid move, Concise,' the officer yells. 'You're one D away from being reclassified into close custody.'

Another detention officer grabs my arm and steers me out of the cell. 'You need to be decontaminated,' she says. 'I'll bring you stripes.' I turn around and see, over my shoulder, the first guard shove his knee into Concise's back to handcuff him.

They think Concise did this to me, I realize – a black guy trying to make his white cellie so unhappy that he'd beg to be transferred out. They assume that Elephant Mike, the same race as me, is there because he's come to my rescue.

'Wait,' I say, as the guard pulls me away. 'Mike did it!'

Concise, hauled to his feet, swings a heavy head toward me. His eyes are slitted; his jaw clenched.

'Ask Clutch,' I call out, and as I am shoved toward the shower, I see the boy's head turn at the sound of his name.

These are the words we use to refer to one another: Forty Ounce, Baby G, Buddha, C Bone. Half Dead, Deuce, Trigga, Tastee Freak. Preacher, Snowman, Floater, Alley Cat, Huero, Demon, Little Man, Tavo, Thumper. Bow Wow, Pinhead, Boo Boo, Ichabod. Chicago Bob, Pit Bull, Slim Jim, Die Hard.

In jail, everyone reinvents himself. You would never call a guy by any name except the one he gives you. Otherwise, you might remind him of the person he used to be.

★

Afterward, there is a pall cast over the pod. At lights out there is hardly any conversation. Concise lies on the top bunk. 'Mike's on the loaf for a week,' he says.

The loaf is a punishment, a severe form of disciplinary segregation. In addition to being separated and locked down and stripped of privileges, inmates are fed a brick of cuisine that has everything mashed into it – all food groups and a drink. It is the penalty for assaulting staff, for having a shank found on you, for throwing blood or bodily fluids.

'What happened?' I ask.

Concise rolls over. 'Clutch backed you up. I figure he's countin' down the seven days along with Mike. Because on Day Eight you can bet he be gettin' hammered.'

In this society, telling the truth is not rewarded, but lying to the right people is.

'The DO said that you could get reclassified,' I say after a minute.

Concise sighs. 'Yeah, well, whatever. They caught me cookin' up some stuff a couple times when they tossed my cell.'

To be moved into close custody is a bigger deal than he is letting on. Cellmates are housed alone and in lockdown for twenty-three hours a day, and worst of all, if you get convicted, the prison usually upholds whatever classification you had in jail.

'First thing in the mornin', you outta here,' Concise says. 'Clutch got an extra bunk in his cell, now. I don't need this grief.'

A few minutes later, Concise begins to snore. I close my eyes and try to listen to the sounds in the jail. It takes me a while to realize what's missing: For the first night since he's been here, Clutch isn't crying himself to sleep.

'Stripes!' Every morning we get a laundry call, the DO in charge swapping our towels and shorts or sheets or stripes for fresh replacements. As I walk down to the pod slider to make the exchange, I glance into Clutch's cell and see him still asleep, curled on his side in bed with the blanket pulled up to his face. 'Clutch,' I hear over the intercom. 'Clutch, rise and shine.'

When he doesn't come out, the officer goes to his cell. 'Clutch,' I hear the DO say, and then she calls for medical assistance.

There is a lockdown while the paramedics come. They cannot perform CPR; it is impossible to dislodge the sock that Clutch has stuck so far down his throat. He is pronounced dead by one of the jail shrinks.

They carry Clutch's body past our cell on a stretcher. 'What was his name?' I ask the EMTs, but they don't answer. 'What was his real name?' I yell. *'Doesn't anyone know his real name?'*

'Yo,' Concise says. 'Sissinit, cuzz.'

But I don't want to calm down. I cannot stand the fact that, under different circumstances, that might have been me. Is Fate getting what you deserve, or deserving what you get?

Concise glances at me. 'He better off like that, believe me.'

'It's my fault.' I turn to him, tears in my eyes. 'I told the DOs to talk to him.'

'If it wasn't you, it would have been someone else. Some*time* else.'

I shake my head. 'How old was he? Seventeen, eighteen?'

'I don't know.'

'Why not? Why didn't anyone ask him where he came from, or what he wanted to be when he grew up, or—'

'Because we all know how the story end. Wit' a sock down your throat or a bullet in your gut or a knife in your back.' Concise stares at me. 'Some stories, they the ones no one want to hear.'

I sink down on the bunk, because I know it is true.

'You wanna know what happened to Clutch?' Concise says bitterly. 'Once upon a time a baby boy was born in New York City. He didn't know his daddy, who was locked up in the pen. His mama was a crack whore who moved him and his two sisters to Phoenix when he was twelve, and then OD'd two months later. His sisters shacked up with their boyfriends' parents, and he hit the streets. The Park South Crips became his family. They fed him, clothed him, and one day when he was sixteen they let him in on the action when they sweet-talked a girl into having some fun, and they all took turns with her. Come to find out later she thirteen, and a retard.'

'That's how Clutch wound up here?'

'No,' Concise answers. 'It's how *I* did. Clutch's story, it's the same, the names are jus' different. Everyone in here got a story like that, except bling blings like you.'

'I'm not rich,' I say quietly.

'Yeah, well, you ain't from the streets neither. What you do to get in here?'

'I kidnapped my daughter when she was four years old, told her her mother was dead, and changed our identities.'

Concise shrugs. 'That ain't no crime, man.'

'The county attorney doesn't agree.'

'You didn't kill your daughter, did you?'

'God, no,' I say, horrified.

'You didn't hurt nobody. Jury'll let you go.'

'Well,' I say, 'maybe that's not the greatest thing.'

'You don't want out?'

I try to find the right way to explain to this man how I can never go back to the way things were. How, after a while, you believe the fiction you've told yourself so well that you cannot remember the fact upon which it was based. It has been nearly thirty years since Charles Matthews existed; I have no idea who he is anymore. 'I am afraid,' I admit, 'that it might be even harder than this.'

Concise looks at me for a long moment. 'When I got out the first time, I went to breakfast to celebrate. Found me a little diner and sat down and watched the waitress movin' in her short dress. She come to take my order, and I say I want eggs. "How you want them cooked?" she ask and I just stare at her like she speakin' Martian. For five years, there weren't no choice – if we had eggs, they be scrambled, period. I knew I didn't want them like that, but I didn't remember how else they could be. I'd lost all the words, just like that.'

Language, of course, vanishes like anything else in disuse. How much time before I cannot remember *mercy?* Before *forgiveness* is gone? How long will I have to be in here before I forget how *possibility* sits on the bridge of the tongue?

I am no less bound to circumstance than Concise, or Blue Loc, or Elephant Mike, or even Clutch. I would not have run with my child if I hadn't married Elise. I would not have married Elise if I'd been in a different bar that first night. I would not have been in that bar if my car hadn't broken down in Tempe, and I needed a phone to call for a tow. I would not have been in Tempe if I weren't taking a graduate course in pharmacology; padding my chances to get a better job with a bigger paycheck so that one day I could provide for a family I could not even yet envision.

Maybe Fate isn't the pond you swim in but the fisherman floating on top of it, letting you run the line wild until you are weary enough to be reeled back in.

When I look up, Concise is staring at me. 'I'll be damned,' he says softly. 'You one of us.'

Inker, the resident tattoo artist, melts down chess pieces for the monochrome green pigment he uses in his craft. His client already has sleeves – a run of tattoos covering his arms, from wrist to shoulder. It says White Pride down each of his triceps, and on his back is a Celtic knot. You can tell a lot about inmates by reading their skin. The swastikas and the twin lightning bolts tell you their racial affiliation. The spider webs and Constantine wire tell you they've been in prison. The clock faces have hands placed to show you how many years they did time.

I wonder where Inker plans on putting this new one. He will scrape the skin with a sharpened shank and rub the ink into it, to scar. He'll do it all in record time, between the detention officer's walk-throughs, meant to keep things like this from going on.

Behind the cover of a card game, Inker bends down over the bared left shoulder blade of his customer and begins to dig, blood welling up in the shape of a heart. 'Five-oh,' one of the card players says, a warning that an officer's coming. Inker slips his shank under his stripes, hides the tiny packet of ink in the ham of his hand.

But the guard that passes by doesn't even glance at Inker. He moves to the upper level, down the block of cells. I rise, running after him.

By the time I reach my cell, the detention officer has balled the bedding into a heap and tossed the mattresses off the bunks. He overturns my little cache of soap, toothbrush, postcards, pencils. Then he reaches under the bunk for Concise's cardboard box.

Concise isn't here; he's left the pod to attend church services. It is not that he's particularly religious, but going to church allows him the freedom to sell his bootleg alcohol to inmates he would not otherwise see. Of course, after having the cell tossed, he won't have any merchandise. And once he is moved to close custody, he won't have the means to make it at all anymore.

The detention officer opens up a tube of toothpaste, puts a taste on his finger and lifts it to his tongue. Then he reaches for the shampoo bottle full of hooch and unscrews the cap.

'It's mine,' I blurt out.

I would like to tell you that I'm being selfless when I say this, but it would be another lie. What I'm thinking is that Concise and I have a fragile trust; to start from scratch with a new roommate could be a disaster. What I'm thinking is that I have little to lose, and Concise has everything. What I'm thinking is that there might be a karmic balance to the acts one undertakes in life, that maybe keeping one person's existence as is can erase the time you changed someone else's.

★

Being in disciplinary segregation is like being a ghost, something at which I've actually had a fair amount of practice. The officers get right into your face, yet don't seem to really see you. For one hour each day, you are allowed into the dayroom by yourself, to shower and to haunt a greater space. You go for hours without using your voice. You live in the past, because the present stretches out so far it hurts to glimpse it.

Since there are an odd number of prisoners in the pod, I am in a cell by myself. At first, I consider this a blessing, then I begin to have my doubts. There is no one to talk to, to have to step around. Anything to break up my routine becomes a gift. So when I am told that my attorney has arrived for a visit, there's nothing I'd like more than to be taken down to the visiting room, if only for a diversion. But there is also nothing I'd like less. I know why you asked Eric to be my lawyer, but at the time, you didn't know the whole story . . . and neither did Eric. It is clear, from our last meeting, that Eric can't easily separate my story from his own. Would he have agreed to represent me if he'd known that he'd have to walk through the memories of his drinking all over again?

'Please tell my attorney,' I say, 'that I'd rather not.'

A half hour later, the inmates begin to stir. A few of them start hollering, others begin to pace like hamsters in a cage. I look back over my shoulder to see what's causing the stir, and find Sergeant Doucette leading Eric toward my cell.

I turn my back. 'I don't want to speak to him.'

'He doesn't want to speak to you,' she tells Eric.

Eric inhales sharply. 'Well, that's fine by me. Because God knows I don't feel like hearing what the hell landed you in lockdown.'

At that moment I remember when I first realized that Eric was going to be the one to take care of you after I let go. You were fourteen, and had just had four teeth pulled by the dentist; your whole face was numb with novocaine. Eric came to our house after school to visit, and I let him take you the chocolate milkshake you'd asked for. When the liquid dribbled down your chin, Eric wiped it with a napkin. Before he let go, though, he let his fingertips caress the side of your face, as if he was finding his way across a relief map. He did this even though, or maybe because, the dentist's shot kept you from feeling it.

'Let him in,' I tell the officer.

He is uncomfortable, holding on to the bars like a swimmer afraid to leave the side of the pool. 'What are you doing in here?' he asks.

'Self-preservation.'

'I'm just trying to save you, too.'

'Are you sure about that?' I say.

He looks away. 'This case isn't about me.'

When he asks me to start over, I have to think twice. It would be so easy to say no; to receive a court-appointed attorney and be convicted. I've given up my life before; I could do it again.

But there is another part of me that needs to see Eric succeed. He's my granddaughter's father, and you love him. I can still remember you sobbing against my shoulder after you drove him to rehab. If Eric loses this legal battle, will he start drinking and make you cry again? If he wins, will it make me believe what I couldn't when I looked into Elise's face: that someone who is given a second chance might actually make something worthwhile of it?

I rub my palms on the knees of my pants. 'I don't know what you want to hear, and what you don't.'

Eric takes a deep breath. 'Tell me how you met Elise.'

I close my eyes and I am a too-serious, overachieving grad student again. All my life I've gotten good grades; all my life I've done what my parents have asked . . . until now. It is their great shame that instead of becoming a doctor, I have chosen pharmacology; never mind the fact that I cannot stand the sight of blood.

I stand on the side of the road, kicking at the tires of my car as steam rolls out from the seam of the hood and spills onto the ground. I am going to miss my final in pharmacokinetics because of this.

Six miles later, dusty and sweaty, after figuring every sorry permutation of my ruined grad school grade point average and tanked career, I approach a mirage. It is a roadside bar; twenty monstrous Harleys are parked in front of it. I walk inside in time to hear the screaming. Two burly men have a stunning, black-haired girl pinned up against the wall; a third holds a fan of darts in his hand. The girl closes her eyes and yells as the first dart goes whizzing toward her shoulder. A second dart strikes inches from her ear. The biker has just lifted his hand to throw the third dart when I launch myself at him.

I have about as much effect as a mosquito; he bats me away and sends the third dart spinning to land between her knees, nailing her skirt to the wall.

The girl opens her eyes, grins, and glances down between her legs. 'No wonder you can't get a date, T-Bone, if that's the closest you can get.'

The other bikers all start laughing, and one of them extricates the girl from the darts. She walks toward me, and holds out her hand to help me to my feet. 'I'm sorry. I thought they were hurting you,' I say.

'Them?' She glances over her shoulder, at the bikers who have gone back to their arm-wrestling and their drinks. 'They're pussycats. Come on, then. Heroes drink on the house.' She ducks beneath the counter and pulls the tap, filling up a long glass of beer for me; I realize that she is the bartender.

She asks me what I'm doing here, and I tell her about my car. I say that I am missing my final. 'Ever wonder why it's called that?' she says. 'It's not like everything stops when you're done with it.'

I don't tell Eric how I found myself watching a shaft of sunlight play Elise's skin like the bow of a violin; how she could talk to one biker about basketball stats and make change for another and smile for me at the same time. I don't tell him how she made fun of me for nursing my beer, and then shared it with me. I don't tell him how she locked up early; how I drew the patterns of molecules for her on cocktail napkins, then between the stars, and finally on the flat of her bare back.

I don't tell Eric that until I met Elise, I had never stayed awake till dawn just to watch the sky burn a hole through the night, that I took my first go-kart ride on a track beside her. I don't tell him that she led me through graveyards to lay down flowers for people she had never known. I don't tell him how she would decorate the inside of my car with rose petals for me to find when I came out of class. That she would call me up to ask me what color I would be, if I were a color, because she was so completely purple and she wanted to know if we'd match. That she was like no one I'd ever met, that when I moved inside the kaleidoscope heart of her, I saw how dreary my life had been.

I don't tell Eric this, because it's all I have left of that girl.

'What happened?' he asks.

'She drove me home from the bar,' I say simply. 'A month later I found out she was pregnant.' She'd used words like *should* and *too soon* and *career* and *abortion*. I had looked right at her and asked her if she wanted to get married instead.

'What made you get divorced?'

There were a whole string of things, if I want to be honest about it. And yes, there was a trigger. But I should have known that someone who was such a child herself would not feel comfortable taking care of one. I should have been more supportive after our son was stillborn, instead of clutching Beth like a shield to ward off the grief. But most of all, I should have admitted to myself far earlier that the things I loved about Elise, the impulsiveness and the craziness and the spur-of-the-moment outlook, were not really part of her personality, but a product of the alcohol. That when she didn't drink, she was so insecure that nothing I said or did was enough to convince her that I loved her.

Eric nods; he has been there himself – on both ends of the equation. You cannot depend on an alcoholic, so you learn to live for the moments when they are present. You tell yourself you'll leave, but then they do something wonderful that reels you back: host a picnic on the living room floor in January; find the face of Jesus in a pancake; celebrate the cat's birthday by inviting all the other neighborhood cats for tuna. You use all the good times to paint over the bad, and pretend you can no longer see the grain of the wood that she's made of. You watch her wade through sobriety and secretly wish she would drink, because that is when she turns into the person you love; and then you cannot figure out who you hate more: yourself for thinking this, or her for reading your mind.

Eric stares at me, putting together everything I've said so far. 'You loved her. You *still* love her.'

'I never stopped,' I admit.

'Then you didn't take Delia because you hated Elise,' Eric says slowly.

'No,' I sigh. 'I took Dee so that *she* wouldn't.'

Broadway Gangsters, West Side City Crips, Duppa Villa, Wedgewood Chicanos, 40 Ounce Posse. Wetback Power Second Avenue, Eastside Phoeniquera, Hispanics Causing Panic, Hoover 59. Brown Pride, Vista King Trojans, Grape Street 103, Dope Man Association. Sex Jerks, Rollin' Sixties, Mini Park, Park South. Pico Nuevo, Dog Town, Golden Gate, Mountain Top Criminal. Chocolate City, Clavalito Park, Insane Born Gangster, Vista Bloods, Casa Trece. There are three hundred street gangs in the Phoenix area; these are just a few represented at Madison Street Jail.

Crips dominate the Phoenix area; Bloods rule Tucson. Crips wear blue and call Bloods 'slobs' as a sign of disrespect; they don't write the letters CK in succession, because that stands for 'crip killer,' and will spell a word *blacc* or *slicc* instead. A Blood wears red and calls Crips 'crabs'; he will cross out all *c*'s in his writing to show disrespect.

Members of two different Crip gangs who meet on the street will try to kill each other. In prison, they join in solidarity against the Bloods.

There is only one way to get a Crip and a Blood to stop fighting: Put them in front of an Aryan Brotherhood member and they will suddenly be on the same side.

Long before I get out of Disc Seg, there are rumors. About Sticks, returning to the maximum security pod and talking of retribution. About Blue Loc, who has become my staunch supporter. Watching me take the blame for something one of the blacks did has, apparently, set me squarely in their esteem.

When I am moved back down to maximum security, Concise is lying on his bunk, reading. 'Wuzz crackalackin'?' he says, a homeboy greeting that could mean anything. He doesn't really speak until the detention officer leaves. 'They treat you all right up on three?'

I start to make up my bed with sheets and a blanket. 'Yeah. I got the cell with the Jacuzzi and the wine cellar.'

'Damn, they always give that one to the white boys,' he jokes. 'Andrew,' he says, the first time he has ever used my name. 'What you did . . .'

I fold up my towel. 'It was nothing.'

He stands up, reaches out slowly, and clasps my hand. 'You took the fall for me. That was somethin'.'

Embarrassed, I break away. 'Well, it's over and done with.'

'No it ain't,' Concise says. 'Sticks is gonna beat a lesson into you in the rec yard. He been plannin' it for days now.'

I try not to let on how much this terrifies me. If Sticks nearly beat me to death as an afterthought on the first night I was in jail, what might he do with preparation?

'Can I ask you somethin'?' Concise says. 'Why'd you do it?'

Because looking out for yourself sometimes isn't about you at all. Because contrary to what inmates seem to think, situations are never black or white. But I just shake my head, unsure of how to put this into words.

Concise leans down and pulls out a box beneath the lower

bunk; it is filled with an arsenal of makeshift weapons. 'Yeah,' he says. 'I hear you.'

The morning of the fight, Concise shaves my head. All the inmates involved do, because it makes it harder for the DOs to sort out the participants afterward. The disposable razor leaves patches of hair, so I look like I have been attacked by a cat. I glance at Concise's smooth, dark skin. 'Well,' I say. 'I'm going out on a limb, here, but I think the guards might be able to tell me apart from the rest of the Crips.'

There will be thirty men in the rec yard at once: ten Mexicans, nine blacks, and ten whites, and me. For the past week, a steady stream of smuggling has enabled Concise to build up a weapon supply. We have stayed up late to fashion them: clubs, rolled out of *National Geographic*s and secured with the tape the kitchen uses to mark a special dietary meal; saps, a sock filled with two bars of soap or, in one case, a padlock nipped from an ankle chain, which can be swung at an enemy. We have broken out the single-edge razor blades we are given every morning, reset them in the pliant plastic of a melted toothbrush. We have fashioned shanks from the stainless-steel frames around the mirrors in our cell, from pieces of chain-link fence, from the metal stays in knee braces, even from a toilet-bowl brush, all filed to a deadly point along the cement floor at night. The handles are wrapped with strips ripped from bedsheets and towels, tied tight with the white cotton string from laundry bundles: You can grip the weapon more firmly, and you are less likely to be cut as your hand slips up the blade.

My own weapon has been specially made by Concise. Having pulled the metal tip off a number two pencil, he's inserted a sharpened staple to the eraser end, and placed a fan of cigarette batting in the other side. The dart, jammed into the hollow tube of a Bic pen, can be blown into the eye of an enemy at close range.

It is amazing to me, as we line up for rec, that the DOs do

not realize what is going on. Everyone has a weapon packed somewhere under their stripes. Once we get to the yard, we congregate in larger groups than normal – no one wants to be separated from his allies. No one touches the basketball.

'Stay cool,' Concise whispers to me. My heart is as thick as a sponge, and sweat breaks out behind my ears, in the cool crevice where my hair once was.

I do not see it coming, the sap that sings like a humming-bird and whacks me on my left temple. As I fall I am vaguely aware of the rush of bodies that push past me, the overgrown jungle of their feet. The officer's voice is high as a child's. *Multiple inmates involved in a fight on the rec yard. Backup needed immediately.*

The window of the multipurpose room, which overlooks the rec yard, is suddenly full of faces pressed to the glass. Guards stream through the adjacent door, trying to pull apart the blacks and browns and whites whose limbs are knotted together. Violence up close has a smell, like coppered blood and charcoal burning. I inch backward, shaking fiercely.

An opening in the wall of flesh spits a body into the space beside me. Sticks lifts his face and his eyes light up.

The strangest details register: the locker-room smell of the pavement underneath me; the cut on Sticks's shoulder that is shaped like Florida; the way he has lost one shoe. My legs tremble as I back away from him. My hand curls around the blow dart.

When he smiles at me, his teeth are covered in blood. 'Nigger-lover,' he says, and he holds up a zip gun in his left hand.

I know what it is, because Concise had wanted to make one, but couldn't get a bullet smuggled in in time. You grind off the top and bottom of an asthma inhaler, and then tear the thin metal open. Flatten it; roll it around a pencil to make a tube that fits a .22-caliber shell like a sheath. Wrap it in cloth, and enclose it in one hand; in your other, hold the firing pin – anything that can hit the rim of the bullet's casing when you smack one hand against the other. It is deadly accurate at a five-foot range.

I watch Sticks take a bent piece of metal – a handcuff key, I realize – and position it in his right hand. He spreads his fists apart.

In slow motion I lift the tube of the Bic pen and seal my mouth over one end. The blow dart flies at Sticks, the staple embedding deep in his right eye.

He rolls away, screaming; and with trembling hands I stuff the Bic pen tube down a drainage gate. The DOs begin to loose pepper spray that blinds me. When I hear something skitter by my ear, I try to look at it, but my eyes are the raw red of grief. I learn it by feel, the cool metal point of a miniature missile. Without hesitation, I grab the bullet Sticks has dropped.

'Easy, now,' a voice says behind me. A detention officer helps me to my feet. 'I saw you field the first blow. You all right?'

Somewhere between the moment I entered this rec yard, and the moment I will leave it, I have turned myself into a person I vaguely recognize. Somebody desperate. Somebody capable of acts I never imagined, until driven to commit them. Somebody I was twenty-eight years ago.

Another life in the day of a man.

I nod at the officer and bring my hand to my mouth, pretending to wipe off saliva. Then, untucking the bullet from the pouch of my cheek, I swallow.

V

The leaves of memory seemed to make
A mournful rustling in the dark.
      – Henry Wadsworth Longfellow,
         'The Fire of Drift-wood'

Delia

Ruthann tells Sophie that when she was a child, Hopi girls would wear their hair in whorls, intricately twisted buns above each ear. She parts Sophie's hair, ropes each side, and coils it tight. 'There,' she announces. 'You look just like a *kuwányauma.*'

'What's that?' Sophie asks.

'A butterfly, showing beautiful wings.' She wraps a shawl over Sophie's shoulders, and winds two Ace bandages up her legs: makeshift moccasins. 'Excellent,' she says. 'You're ready.'

Today she is taking us to the Heard Museum in Phoenix, where a festival is taking place. She has packed the car full of old board games and broken watches, pens that need refills, vases with chips and cracks. *If you have nothing to do,* she told us, *I could use some staff.*

An hour later, Sophie and I stand in the grassy bowl outside the museum, surrounded by a collection of Ruthann's junk while she wanders through the crowd in her Barbie trench coat, flashing potential customers. People sit in folding chairs and on blankets, drinking bottled water and eating fry bread that costs four dollars. At the bottom of the outdoor pavilion is a circle, where a small canopy shades a phalanx of men bent over an enormous drum. Their voices vine together and climb into the sky.

Many of the onlookers are white, but more are Native American. They wear everything from traditional costumes to jeans and American flag T-shirts. Some of the men wear their hair in braids and ponytails, and everyone seems to be smiling. Several other girls have hair wound to the sides like Sophie.

Suddenly a dancer steps into the center of the circle. 'Ladies and gentlemen,' the emcee announces, 'let's welcome Derek Deer, from Sipaulovi in Hopiland.'

The boy cannot be more than sixteen. When he walks, the bells on his costume jingle. He has a rainbow of fringe across his shoulder blades and down his arms, and he has tied a leather band around his forehead with a matching rainbow disk in the center. He wears biking shorts under his loincloth.

The boy sets five hoops on the ground, each about two feet wide. As the drummers start throbbing out their song, he begins to move. He taps forward twice with his right foot, then his left, and in the instant it takes to blink he kicks up the first hoop and holds it in his hand.

He does the same with the other five hoops, and then begins to make them extensions of his body. He steps through two and lines the remaining three up in a vertical line, then snaps the top ones open and shut in a massive jaw. Still moving his feet, he dances out of the hoops and fans all five across the breadth of his shoulders to turn himself into an eagle. He morphs from a rodeo horse to a serpent to a butterfly. Then he twists the hoops together, an Atlas building his burden, and spins this three-dimensional sphere out into the center of the performance ring. As the drummers cry, he dances a final circle and falls down to one knee.

It is like nothing I have ever seen. 'Ruthann,' I say, as she steps up beside me, clapping, 'that was amazing. That was—'

'Let's go see him.' She pecks her way between the people on the grass, until we are standing behind the drummer's pavilion. The boy is sweating profusely and eating a PowerBar. Up close I can see that the rainbow colors of his costume are hand-sewn ribbons. Ruthann boldly picks at the boy's sleeve. 'Look at these; one thread away from falling off,' she tsks. 'Your mother ought to learn how to sew.'

The boy looks up over his shoulder and grins. 'My aunt could probably fix them,' he says, 'but she's too busy being a businesswoman to pay attention to the likes of me.' He enfolds Ruthann in an embrace. 'Or maybe you brought your needle and thread?'

I wonder why she hasn't mentioned that the dancer is her nephew. Ruthann holds him at arm's length. 'You are turning into your father's double,' she pronounces, and this makes a smile split the boy's face. 'Derek, this is Sophie and Delia, *ikwaatsi.*'

I shake his hand. 'You were awfully good.'

Sophie bends down toward the hoop and tries to kick at it with her foot. It jumps a few inches, and Derek laughs. 'Wow, look, a groupie.'

'You could do worse,' Ruthann says.

'So, how are you doing, Auntie?' he asks. 'Mom said . . . she told me that you went to the Indian Health Service.'

Something shutters across Ruthann's face that is gone almost as quickly as I notice it. 'Why are we talking about me? Tell me whether I should bet on you winning.'

'I don't even know if I'll place this year,' Derek replies. 'I didn't have a lot of time to practice, what with everything that happened.'

Ruthann nudges his shoulder, and then points to the sky. In an otherwise perfectly clear blue day, a stunted rain cloud hovers. 'I think your father's come to make sure you finish well.'

Derek looks up at the cloud. 'Maybe so.'

He bends down to give Sophie a lesson on how to lift up a hoop with one's foot, while Ruthann explains that her brother-in-law, Derek's father, was one of the first casualties in the war with Iraq. In keeping with Hopi tradition, his body was to be sent back for burial by the fourth day. But the helicopter carrying his remains was shot down, and so he didn't arrive until six days after his death. The family did their best – yucca soap was used to wash his hair, his mouth was filled with food to keep him satisfied, his possessions were placed in the grave – but it was done two days too late, and they worried that he might not make it to his destination.

'We spent hours waiting,' Ruthann tells me. 'And then, just before it got dark, it rained. Not all over, but on my sister's house, and on her fields, and in front of the building where my brother-in-law had gone and enlisted. That's how we knew he'd made it to the next world.'

I look up at the cloud she believes is her brother-in-law. 'What about the ones who don't make it?'

'They stay lost in this world,' Ruthann says.

I hold up my palm. I try to convince myself that I feel a drop of rain.

'Ruthann,' I ask, as we drive back from the Heard, 'how come you live in Mesa?'

'Because the Phoenician just isn't swanky enough for me.'

'No, really.' I glance in the rearview mirror to make sure Sophie is still sleeping. 'I didn't realize you had family in the area.'

'Why does anyone move to a place like where we live?' she asks, shrugging. 'Because there's nowhere left to go.'

'Do you ever go back?'

Ruthann nods. 'When I need to remember where I came from, or where I'm headed.'

Maybe I should go, I think. 'You haven't asked me why I came to Arizona.'

'I figured if you wanted to tell me, you would,' Ruthann says.

I keep my eyes on the highway. 'My father kidnapped me when I was a baby. He told me my mother had died in a car accident, and he took me from Arizona to New Hampshire. He's in jail now, in Phoenix. I didn't know any of this until a week ago. I didn't know my mother's been alive the whole time. I didn't even know my real name.'

Ruthann looks over her shoulder, where Sophie is curled up like a mollusk against Greta's back. 'How did you come to call her Sophie?'

'I . . . I guess I just liked it.'

'On the morning of my daughter's naming, it was up to each of her aunties to suggest a name for her. Her father was *Póvolnyam*, Butterfly Clan, so each of the names had something to do with that: There was *Pólikwaptiwa*, which means Butterfly Sitting on Flower. And *Tuwahóima*, which means Butterflies Hatching. And *Talásveniuma*, Butterfly Carrying Pollen on Wings. But the one Grandmother picked was *Kuwányauma*, Butterfly Showing Beautiful Wings. She waited until dawn, and then took *Kuwányauma* and introduced her to the spirits for the first time.'

'You have a daughter?' I say, amazed.

'She was named for her father's clan, but she belonged to mine,' Ruthann says, and then she shrugs. 'When she got initiated, she got a new name. And in school, she was called Louise by the teachers. What I'm saying is that what you're called is hardly ever who you are.'

'What does your daughter do?' I ask. 'Where does she live?'

'She's been gone a long time. Louise never figured out that Hopi isn't a word to describe a person, but a destination.' Ruthann sighs. 'I miss her.'

I look through the windshield at the clouds, stretched across the horizon. I think about Ruthann's brother-in-law, raining on his family's fortune. 'I'm sorry,' I say. 'I didn't mean to get you upset.'

'I'm not upset,' she answers. 'If you want to know someone's story, they have to tell it out loud. But every time, the telling is a little bit different. It's new, even to me.'

As I listen to Ruthann, I start to think that maybe the math is not reciprocal; maybe depriving a mother of a child is greater than depriving the child of the mother. Maybe knowing where you belong is not equal to knowing who you are.

'Have you seen your mother since you've been here?' Ruthann asks me.

'It didn't go so well,' I say after a moment.

'How come?'

I am not ready to tell her about my mother's drinking. 'She's not what I expected her to be.'

Ruthann turns her head, looks out the window. 'No one ever is,' she says.

My favorite museum, as a child, was the New England Aquarium, and my favorite exhibit was the tide pool where you got to play God. There were sea stars, which could spit out their own stomachs and grow back limbs that were damaged. There were anemones, which might spend all their lives in one place. There were hermit crabs and limpets and algae. And there was a red button for me to push, which created a wave in the tank and spun all the sea life like the clothes inside a washing machine, before letting them settle again.

I loved being the agent of change, at the touch of a finger. I'd wait until it seemed the hermit crab had just settled, and then I would push the button again. It was amazing to think of a society where the status quo meant having no status quo at all.

There was a second exhibit at the aquarium that I liked, too. A strobe, spitting over the flow of an oversized faucet. I knew it was just an optical illusion, but I used to think that in this one corner of the world, water might be able to run backward.

Ruthann puts me to work, creating her butchered dolls. One day when we are sitting around her kitchen table making Divorced Barbie – she comes with Ken's boat, Ken's car, and the deed to Ken's house – she asks, 'What did you do in New Hampshire?'

I bend closer with the hot glue gun, trying to attach a button. Instead, I wind up affixing Barbie's purse to her forehead. 'Greta and I found people.'

Ruthann's brows lift. 'Like K-nine stuff?'

'Yeah, except we worked with a whole bunch of police stations.'

'So why aren't you doing it here?'

I look up at her. *Because my father is in jail. Because I am embarrassed to have done this for a living, without knowing that I was missing.* 'Greta isn't trained for desert work,' I say, the first excuse that comes to mind.

'So train her.'

'Ruthann,' I say, 'it's just not the right time for us.'

'You don't get to decide that.'

'Oh, really. And who does?'

'The *kiskuska*. The ones who are lost.' She bends down over her work again.

Is there a little girl, somewhere, being driven across a border right now? A man with a razor poised over his wrist? A child with one leg over the fence meant to keep him safe from the rest of the world? The desperate usually succeed because they have nothing to lose. But what if that isn't the case? If someone like me had worked in the Phoenix area twenty-eight years ago, would my father have gotten away with it?

'I suppose I could put out flyers,' I tell Ruthann.

She reaches for the hot glue gun. 'Good,' she says. 'Because you suck at dollmaking.'

On the way to the desert, Fitz tells me remarkable stories about a heart transplant patient who woke up with a love of the French Riviera, although he'd never left Kansas in his life; of a teetotaling kidney recipient who, postsurgery, began to drink the same martini her donor favored.

'By that logic,' I argue, 'then the memory of seeing you for the first time gets stored in my eyeballs.'

Fitz shrugs. 'Maybe it does.'

'That's the stupidest thing I've ever heard.'

'I'm just telling you what I read . . .'

'What about the guy in the 1900s who had a steel pike driven through his brain by accident?' I challenge. 'He woke up speaking Kyrgyzstani—'

'Well, I highly doubt that,' Fitz interrupts, 'since Kyrgyzstan wasn't a country until five years ago.'

'You're missing the point,' I say. 'What if memories get stored in the brain, and they aren't even necessarily ones we've had? What if we're hardwired with a whole iceberg of experiences, and our minds use only a tip of them?'

'That's a pretty cool thought . . . that you and I would have the same memories, just because it's how we're made.'

'You and I *do* have the same memories,' I point out.

'Yeah, but my seeing-Eric-naked recollection has a whole different causal effect on my system,' Fitz laughs.

'Maybe I'm not really remembering that stupid lemon tree. Maybe everyone has a lemon stuck in their mind.'

'Yes,' Fitz agrees. 'Mine, however, is a 'seventy-eight Pacer.'

'Very funny—'

'It wasn't, if you were the guy driving it. God, do you remember the time it broke down on the way to the senior prom?'

'I remember the oil on your date's dress. What was her name? Carly . . . ?'

'Casey Bosworth. And she wasn't my date by the time we got there.'

I pull off the road, into a vista of pebbles and red earth, and then hand Fitz a bottle of water and a roll of toilet paper. 'You remember the drill, right?'

He will lay a trail for Greta and me to follow, just like he's done for years in New Hampshire. But because this terrain is unfamiliar to me, Fitz will leave bits of toilet paper on trees and cacti as he goes, to let me know that Greta is on the right trail. He gets out of the car and leans down into the window. 'I don't think we covered coyote protection in the training manual.'

'I wouldn't worry about the coyotes,' I say sweetly. 'I'd be far more panicked about the snakes.'

'Funny,' Fitz replies, and he starts walking, a massive redhead who is going to be a hectic shade of sunburned pink in no time at all. 'If Greta screws up, drive south. I'll be hanging out with the border patrol drinking tequila.'

'Greta won't screw up. Hey, Fitz,' I call out, and wait until he turns, shading his eyes. 'I actually wasn't kidding about the snakes.'

As I drive off, I watch Fitz in the rearview mirror, staring down nervously at his feet. It makes me laugh out loud. Memories aren't stored in the heart or the head or even the soul, if you ask me, but in the spaces between any given two people.

According to the Hopi, sometimes we no longer fit the world we've been given.

In the beginning, there was only darkness and Taiowa the sun spirit. He created the First World and filled it with creatures that lived in a cave deep in the earth. But they fought among themselves, so he sent Spider Grandmother down to prepare them for a change.

As Spider Grandmother led the creatures into the Second World, Taiowa changed them. They were no longer insects, but animals with fur, and webbed fingers, and tails. They were happy to have the space to roam free, but they didn't understand life any better than before.

Taiowa sent Spider Grandmother back to lead the way into the Third World. By now, the animals had transformed into people. They made villages, and planted corn. But it was cold in the Third World, and mostly dark. Spider Grandmother taught them to weave blankets to keep warm; she told the women to make clay pots to store water and food. But in the cold, the pots couldn't be baked. The corn wouldn't grow.

One day a hummingbird came to the people in the fields. He had been sent by Masauwu, Ruler of the Upper World, and Caretaker of the Place of the Dead. He brought with him fire, and he taught the people its secret.

With this new discovery, the people could harden their pots and warm their fields and cook their food. For a while, they lived in peace. But sorcerers emerged, with medicine to hurt those they didn't like. Men gambled, instead of farming.

Women grew wild, forgetting their babies, so that the fathers had to care for the children. People began to brag that there was no god, that they had created themselves.

Spider Grandmother returned. She told the people that those of good heart would leave this place, and the evil ones, behind. They did not know where to go, but they had heard footsteps overhead in the sky. So the chiefs and the medicine men took clay and shaped a swallow out of it, wrapped it in a bride's robe, and sang it to life.

The swallow flew toward the opening in the sky, but he was not strong enough to make it through. The medicine men decided to make a stronger bird, and they sang forth a dove. It flew through the opening and returned, saying, 'On the other side, there is a land that spreads in all directions. But there is nothing alive up there.'

Still, the chiefs and the medicine men had heard footsteps. They fashioned a catbird this time, and asked him to ask the One Who Made the Footsteps for permission to enter his land.

The catbird flew past the point where all the other birds had gone. He found sand, and mesas. He found ripe squash and blue corn and splitting melons. He found a single stone house, and its master, Masauwu. When he returned, he told the chiefs and the medicine men that Masauwu would allow them to come. They looked up, wondering how they would ever reach the hole in the sky.

They went off to find Chipmunk, the planter. Chipmunk planted a sunflower seed in the ground, and by the power of singing, the people made it grow. But it bent over with its own weight, and could not reach the hole.

Chipmunk planted a spruce, and then a pine, but neither grew tall enough. Finally, he planted a bamboo, and the people began to sing. Every time they stopped to catch their breath, the bamboo stopped growing and a notch formed. Finally the bamboo passed through the hole in the sky.

Only the pure people were allowed into this Fourth World. Spider Grandmother went up the bamboo first, with her two warrior grandsons. As the people emerged, a mockingbird sorted them into Hopi and Navajo, Zuni and Pima, Ute and Supai, Sioux and Comanche and whites. The warrior grandsons took their buckskin ball and played their way across the earth, creating mountains and mesas. Spider Grandmother made a sun and a moon. Coyote tossed the leftover materials into the sky, to make the stars.

The Hopi will tell you that evil managed to sneak in up the bamboo, anyway. That the time of this Fourth World is almost done. Any day now, they say, we might find ourselves in a new one.

Tracking with a bloodhound takes away from the romance of scent. The smell that makes you want to bury your face in the neck of your lover, the trace of perfume that turns men's heads when a beautiful woman walks by – these are merely skin cells decomposing. For Greta and me, scent is a matter of serious business.

After buckling on her leash, I walk Greta over to the baseball cap Fitz has left behind. Lifting it up, I watch her breathe in so deeply the fabric sucks into her nostrils. 'Find him,' I instruct, and Greta leaps over the bent fence and heads off, nose to the ground.

This is a world populated by birds with unlikely names: the Common Flicker, the Harris Hawk, the Mexican Jay. We see agave plants, and chain-fruit cholla, rose mallow, paintbrush, tackstem. We walk by flora that I have only seen in books – brittlebush and cheeseweed, filaree, jojoba. We pass cacti that are mutations, their arms growing inward instead of out; their heads twisted like the folds of a human brain.

Greta moves across the flat of the land slowly. I keep my eyes on the plump arms of the saguaros and the Modigliani necks of the ocotillo, where every now and then Fitz has left me a piece of toilet paper to let me know that Greta's heading in the right direction.

She stops at the dried-out husk of a saguaro, and sits down.

Suddenly she plants all four feet firmly on the ground and bares her teeth. The hair on the line of her spine stands on end; she growls.

The javelina is about four feet long, with a bristled gray hide. Its yellowed tusks turn down at the ends; it has a mane that runs the length of its back. It looks up from its meal of prickly pear and grunts.

I can never remember if you are supposed to run from a bear or stay perfectly still; I have absolutely no clue if there is safety etiquette for a javelina. The pig takes a cocky step toward Greta, who skitters sideways. I pull on her leash just in time to keep her from crashing into a stubby Medusa of a cactus.

Suddenly Greta yelps, and falls to the ground, clawing at her nose. The cactus she didn't brush into has somehow managed to hook itself into her snout. Spines cover her muzzle, a few have worked their way into the gummy black gasket of her lips.

Greta's mournful howl sends a flock of cactus wrens to the skies. The javelina, startled, thunders off. Without a second thought I kneel down and haul Greta over my shoulders in a fireman's carry. I don't feel her seventy-five pounds as I start running. 'Fitz,' I yell as loud as I can, and I try to find him with the clues he's left us.

We are bent over Greta in the back of the Explorer. I'm lying over her, to keep her from moving, and stroking her head and her ears. Fitz leans close to her snout, pulling the spines free with a pair of needlenose pliers I carry in my emergency kit. 'I think they call it teddy bear cholla,' he says. 'Nasty stuff . . . it jumps at you.' When he opens Greta's mouth, gently, she snaps at him. 'Almost finished, sweetheart,' Fitz soothes, and he pulls the last spines out of her gums. Then he leans forward to make sure he hasn't missed any. 'That's it. You may want to double check my veterinary skills with a professional, but I think she's going to be okay.'

I take one look at Greta, and then at Fitz, and burst into tears. 'I hate it here,' I say. 'I hate how hot it is and that there are snakes and that nothing's green. I hate the smell of that stupid jail. I want to go home.'

Fitz looks at me. 'Then go,' he says.

His easy answer is enough to bring me up short. 'Why aren't you talking me out of it?'

'Why should I?' Fitz says. 'Your father isn't going anywhere anytime soon, and he'd be the first one to tell you to get on with your life. Sophie would do better back in New Hampshire, in an environment she's used to. It's not like you have to stick around to get to know your mother—'

'What's that supposed to mean?'

'True or false: You don't care whether or not you see her again.'

True, I want to say. Except, I can't.

'I thought I'd come here, and it would all make sense,' I say, wiping my eyes with the hem of my T-shirt. 'I just wish I could remember it all.'

'Why?'

No one has asked me that question yet.

'Well, because I don't know who I used to be,' I say.

'I do. Eric does. Christ, Delia, you have a hundred witnesses to help you with that. If you really want something to worry about, try figuring out who you're *going* to be from now on.' He bends his knees and rolls onto his side. 'You want to know what I think?'

'Would you stop if I said no?'

'I think you're angry at your mother for losing you in the first place.'

Grudgingly, I nod.

'And you're angry at your father for taking you.'

'Well . . .'

'But most of all, I think you're angry at yourself for not being smart enough to figure this all out on your own,' Fitz says. 'So what if you lived in New Hampshire, instead of

Arizona? What's important is where you'll be living five years from now. So what if you had some lemon tree growing in your backyard? I'd rather know if you want to plant one in your garden now. So what if you have some crazy fear of spiders? That's what hypnosis is for.' He reaches out and pulls on one of my braids. 'If you don't want someone to change your life for you again, Dee, you've got to change it yourself.'

At that moment, everything comes clear. It's like having someone walk up to a chalky window that you've been trying to see through for days, and wiping it clean. Some people have a detailed history, others don't. There are plenty of adopted children who grow up without knowing an ounce of information about their birth parents; there are criminals who walk out of jail and become pillars of the community. At any moment, a person can start over. And that's not half a life, but simply a real one.

It is also a terrifying prospect: that the relationships we use as the cornerstones of our personalities are not given by default but are a choice; that it's all right to feel closer to a friend than we do to a parent; that someone who's betrayed us in the past might be the same person with whom we build a future. I lean back against the wall of the car, dizzy. 'You make it sound so easy.'

'And you make it more complicated than it has to be,' Fitz counters. 'Bottom line: Do you love your father?'

'Yes,' I say quickly.

'Do you love your mother?'

'He wouldn't let me.'

Fitz shakes his head. 'Delia,' he corrects. 'He couldn't *stop* you.'

I watch Greta's breathing even out in sleep. 'Maybe I'll stay a little longer,' I say.

Fitz

It takes only a week in Arizona to turn me into a professional liar. When my editor calls, asking me for something about the Hopkins trial, I let my voice mail pick up until my mailbox is full. When she finally wises up and calls me in the middle of the night on my hotel phone to say that I have six hours to produce a story or lose my assignment, I tell her that I'll have it on her desk. Then I e-mail her and say that motions were filed in the case that kept me in court all day, and beg an extension. When a second week goes by and I have produced absolutely nothing, Marge tells me to come back home to New Hampshire and earn my paycheck. She assigns me a piece about army engineers who have discovered a composite compound to prevent frost heaves, a topic that lets me clearly know I have been demoted in her mind. I tell her I'll be on the first flight out.

I don't leave Phoenix.

Instead, I sit down and fabricate a piece about the Army Corps of Engineers, and asphalt and spring thaw and water tables. I decide that since it will be buried in the middle of the paper, fudging it a bit – okay, completely – isn't awful.

Before I know it, this lying jag of mine has spread like maple syrup into all other venues of my life, sticky and somehow impossible to clean up. I call the owners of the pizza place I live above and say there has been a death in my family, would they be kind enough to give an extension on my rent check? I phone the office and explain that I can't make the Monday meeting because I have a respiratory virus – something SARS-like and highly contagious. I let Sophie weave me a crown of

Indian paintbrush, and when she asks when we are going home, I tell her *soon*.

When Delia leans on me, I tell myself I'd do the same for any old friend.

That's the crazy thing about lies. You start to fall for them, yourself.

Every journalist wants a 'death row' exclusive. You want to be the voice of truth that is heard; you want to be the megaphone through which the penitent's words are carried. You want the reader to listen to the inmate and think, Maybe we are not all that different. But not every journalist knows that his exposé will break the heart of the woman he loves.

When Andrew walks in – thinner than I remember him being, and with a badly shaved head – everything stops for me. Seeing him in his stripes is a little embarrassing, like catching your grandfather in his boxer shorts, a vision that you wish, the very moment you see it, that you never had. He seems so completely different from the man I used to know, as if this is a distant cousin, with similar features arranged in an entirely new way. I wonder which came first: this Andrew, or the other?

I am surprised that he's agreed to see me, if you want to know the truth. In spite of the fact that I practically grew up in his living room, Andrew knows that I write for the *Gazette*.

He picks up the handset, I do the same. What I want to ask Andrew, as he stares at me through this sheer wall, is why he did it. What I say instead is, 'I hope you didn't have to pay a lot for the haircut.'

When he starts to laugh, I can see it for just a glimmer of a second – the man I used to know.

My defining memory of Andrew involves communicating. Delia and Eric and I had been poking around an old dump site in the woods for pottery shards and Indian arrowheads and elixir bottles when we stumbled upon an ancient suitcase. Opening it, we discovered what seemed to be spy equipment

– headphones and a switchboard and a frequency meter – with the wires torn out of the back and the speakers falling off the seams. It was too big for us to carry home, but we desperately wanted it, and a fast vote decided that of all of our parents, the only one who seemed remotely likely to help us with it was Andrew. 'That's a ham radio,' he told us, when he cracked open the suitcase. 'Let's see if we can get it to work.'

Andrew asked around at the senior center – some of the old-timers remembered that particular brand, and what knobs and buttons controlled volume and frequency. He took us with him to the library to get electronics books, to the hardware store to get wire and clamps, and to the basement while he tinkered.

One day, with the three of us clustered beside him, he turned on the radio. A high, dizzy whine came out of the speakers while he fiddled and spoke into the microphone. He had to repeat his message twice, but then, to our shock and delight, someone answered. Someone in England. The thing about a ham radio, he told us, is that you could always find someone to talk to. But you had to be careful, he warned, about giving away too much information about yourself. People were not always who they seemed to be.

'Andrew,' I say to him now, 'did you really think you'd get away with it?'

He rubs his palms over the knees of his pants. 'Is this on or off the record?'

'You tell me,' I say.

Andrew bows his head. 'Fitz,' he confesses, 'I wasn't thinking at all.'

While I am trapped in the desert, waiting for Delia and her wonderdog to find me underneath a paloverde tree, I look at the parched throat of this cracked earth and imagine all the ways a man might die.

Naturally, the first one to come to mind is thirst. Having finished my token bottle of water an hour ago, and finding

myself in the beating heat of this dry desert, I imagine de-
hydrating to the point of delirium. The tongue would swell
like cotton batting, the lids of the eyes would stick. More
preferable – now, anyway – would be drowning. Must be a
nasty fight at first, all that fluid going where it shouldn't. But
at present, the thought of water – extra water – is really just
too enticing. I wonder what it would be like at the end; if
mermaids come to string your neck with shells and give you
openmouthed kisses. If you just lie down on the sand and
watch the sun shimmy a million leagues away.

Suffocation, hanging, a gunshot wound – all of these are
too damn painful. But cold . . . I've heard that's sort of a nice
way to go. To lie down in snow and go numb, at this moment,
would be nothing short of a miracle. And then, of course, there
is martyrdom, which I'm approaching at a damn fast rate. I'm
burning, after all, even if it's not for my convictions. Does
flesh charring off at the bone hurt less when you know you
are right, even though everyone thinks you are wrong?

That line of reasoning leads me right to Andrew.

And then it's a fast beeline to thinking of Delia.

I don't think anyone has ever died of unrequited love. I
wonder if I'll be the first.

After we ring the doorbell, I squeeze Delia's hand. 'Are you
sure you're ready for this?' I ask.

'No,' she says. Delia smooths Sophie's hair and adjusts the
collar on her shirt until she twists around, shrugging off her
mother's touch. 'Does this lady have kids?' Sophie asks.

Delia hesitates. 'No,' she says.

Elise Vasquez opens the door and drinks in Delia, there's
really no other way to describe it. I have a sudden recollection of Delia in the hospital bed after she delivered Sophie,
when the world had shrunk small enough to only hold the two
of them. I guess it is like this for every mother and child.

Someone who doesn't know Delia as well as I do would not
notice the little flicky thing she is doing with her left hand, a

nervous habit. 'Hi,' she says. 'I thought maybe we could try this again.'

But Elise is staring at Sophie as if she's seen a ghost – and of course, that's exactly what Sophie is: a little girl who looks considerably like the one Elise Vasquez lost. 'This is Sophie,' Delia introduces. 'And Soph, this is . . .' When she gets to the spot where she should fill in the blank, her cheeks burn and she says nothing at all.

'Call me Elise,' Delia's mother says, and she squats down to smile into her granddaughter's eyes.

Elise has shiny dark hair twisted into a knot at the base of her neck, and a fine graph of lines at the corners of her eyes and mouth. She is wearing a peasant shirt embroidered with colorful birds, and jeans covered with Sharpie-marker lines of text. My eyes focus on one: *Oh daughter of ashes and mother of blood.*

'Sandburg,' I murmur.

Elise looks up at me, impressed. 'Not many people read poetry these days.'

'Fitz is a writer,' Delia says.

'Actually, I'm a hack for a second-rate paper.'

Elise traces the phrase on her jeans. 'I always thought it would be wonderful to be a writer,' she says. 'To know, just like *that,* how to put the right words together.'

I smile politely. The truth is, if I do miraculously manage to put the right words together, it's by default, because I've already used up all the wrong ones. And when you get right down to it, what I don't say is probably more important than what I do.

Then again, maybe Elise Vasquez already knows this.

She stares out the sliding glass door into the backyard, where Victor has taken Sophie to see a bird's nest, where the eggs are hatching. He lifts her up so she can get a closer look, and then they disappear behind a wall of cacti.

'Thank you,' Elise says, 'for bringing her.'

Delia turns to her. 'I won't keep you from seeing Sophie.'

Elise glances at me uncomfortably.

'He's my best friend,' Delia says. 'He knows about all of it.'

Just then Sophie comes running back inside. 'It's so cool . . . they have teeth on their beaks,' she says breathlessly. 'Can we stay until they're out?'

Sophie tugs on Delia's hand, until she stands up. In the doorway, Victor chuckles. 'I tried to explain that it might take a while,' he says.

Delia answers him, but she is looking at her mother. 'That's all right,' she says. 'I don't mind waiting.' She lets Sophie pull her outside, toward the tree.

Elise Vasquez and I stand shoulder to shoulder, watching the woman we both feel we lost, and maybe never really had.

On the way home, we stop for coffee. Sophie squats on the sidewalk at the café, drawing a crime-scene outline around Greta with colored chalk. Delia drums her fingers on the edge of her cup but doesn't seem to be inclined to drink anything from it. 'Can you picture them together?' she asks finally, when the wheels of her mind have stopped turning.

'Elise and Victor?'

'No,' Delia says. 'Elise and my father.'

'Dee, no one can ever imagine their parents doing it.'

Take mine, for example. The sad fact is, my parents *didn't* do it. They managed to have me, of course, but most of the time I was growing up, my salesman father was off screwing a flight attendant in another city, and my mother was furiously busy pretending he wasn't.

But my father was not Andrew Hopkins. In all the years I've known Delia, I can't remember him dating anyone seriously, so I can't even fathom what he'd look for in a woman. If you asked me, though, I'd never have imagined him falling for someone like Elise. She reminds me of an orchid, exotic and fragile. Andrew is more like ragweed: stealthy, resilient, stronger than you think.

I look at the comma curve of Delia's neck, at the bony points of her shoulder blades, a terrain that has been mapped by Eric. 'Some people aren't meant to be together,' I say.

Suddenly a ragged man wearing a hairnet and flip-flops walks toward us, holding a stack of pamphlets. Sophie, scared, hides behind her mother's chair. 'My brother,' the vagrant asks me, 'have you found the Lord Jesus Christ?'

'I didn't know he was looking for me.'

'Is He your personal savior?'

'You know,' I say, 'I'm still kind of hoping to rescue myself.'

The man shakes his head, dreadlocks like snakes. 'None of us are strong enough for that,' he replies, and moves on.

'I think that's illegal,' I mutter to Delia. 'Or at least it should be. Nobody should have to swallow religion with their coffee.'

When I look up, she's staring at me. 'How come you don't believe in God?' Delia asks.

'How come you do?'

She looks down at Sophie, and her whole face softens. 'I guess it's because some things are too incredible for people to take all the credit.'

Or the blame, I think.

Two tables over, the zealot approaches an elderly couple. 'Believe in the Father,' he preaches.

Delia turns in his direction. 'It's never that simple,' she says.

When Delia was pregnant with Sophie, I was the labor coach. I sort of fell into it by default, when Eric, who had promised that he wouldn't fuck up this time, wound up drying out just about the time Lamaze classes started. I found myself sitting in a circle of married couples, trying not to let my heart race as the nurse instructed me to settle Delia between my legs and trace my hands over the swell of her belly.

Delia went into labor in the middle of the frozen foods aisle at Shaw's market, and she phoned me from the manager's office. By the time we got to the hospital, I had worked myself into a near panic about how I would be able to do whatever it was that I was supposed to do as a labor coach, without having to look between her legs. Maybe I could request a position at her shoulders. Maybe I could pull the doctor aside and explain the logistics of the situation.

As it happened, I didn't have to worry about that at all. The minute the anesthesiologist rolled Delia onto her hip to insert the epidural, I took one look at the needle, passed out, and wound up with sixty stitches at my hairline.

I awakened on a cot next to her. 'Hey, Cowboy,' she said, smiling over the tiny peach of a head that poked out from the blanket in her arms. 'Thanks for all the help.'

'Don't mention it,' I said, wincing as my scalp throbbed.

'Sixty stitches,' Delia explained, and then she added, 'I only had ten.'

I found myself looking at her head. 'Not there,' she said, giving me a moment to figure it out. 'You're not going to pass out again, are you?'

I didn't. Instead, I managed to lurch to the edge of Delia's hospital bed, so that I could take a look at the baby. I remember looking into the fuzzy blue of Sophie's eyes and marveling at the fact that there was now one other person in this world who understood what it was like to be completely surrounded by Delia, who'd already learned that it couldn't stay that way.

I had Sophie in my arms when Eric came in. He went straight to Delia and kissed her on the mouth, then bent his forehead against hers for a moment, as if whatever he was thinking might be transferred by osmosis. Then Eric turned, his eyes locking on his daughter. 'You can hold her,' Delia prompted.

But Eric didn't make any move to take Sophie from me. I took a step toward him, and saw what Delia must have overlooked – Eric's hands were shaking so hard that he had buried them in his coat pockets.

I pushed the baby against his chest, so that he'd have no choice but to grab hold. 'It's okay,' I said under my breath – To Eric? To Sophie? To myself? – and as I transferred this tiny prize to Eric's arms, I held on longer than I had to. I made damn sure he was steady, before I let go.

I have seventeen messages, all from my editor. The first starts by asking me to call her back. By the third, Marge is demanding it. Message eleven reminds me that if monkeys can be sent into space, they can certainly be trained to write for the *New Hampshire Gazette*.

In the last voice mail, Marge tells me that if I don't have something on her desk by nine A.M., she is going to fill my page space with the Xeroxes of my ass that I took at the office Christmas party.

So I pull down the shades in the motel. I turn up the TV, to drown out the moans of a couple one thin wall away from me. I crank up the air-conditioning. *Andrew Hopkins,* I type, *is not what you expect when you walk through the corridors of the Madison Street Jail.*

I shake my head and hit the delete button, erasing the paragraph.

Like any father, all Andrew Hopkins wants to talk about is his daughter.

That sentence, I backspace into oblivion.

Andrew Hopkins has ghosts in his eyes, I write, and then think: We all do.

I pace around the island of the bed. Who wouldn't jump at the chance to change something about his life? Two hundred more points on an SAT, a Pulitzer, a Heisman, a Nobel. A more handsome face, a thinner body. A few more years with the babies that grew up when you had forgotten to pay attention. Five more minutes with a loved one who has died.

The moment I would do over is the one I've never been brave enough to have. I'd tell Delia how much I love her, and she would look at me the way she has always looked at Eric.

What I want to write – what I *need* to write – is not what the *New Hampshire Gazette* is paying me for. Sitting down at my laptop, I erase what I've written. I start fresh.

VI

Why is there then
No more to tell? We turned to other things.
I haven't any memory – have you? –
Of ever coming to the place again.
             – Robert Frost, 'The Exposed Nest'

Eric

Chris Hamilton's paralegal spends three days trying to trace the current whereabouts of the neighbors who used to live next door to Elise and Andrew twenty-eight years ago. She sticks her head in the door of the conference room shortly after lunchtime. 'Want the good news or bad news?'

I look up over the stack of papers I'm wading through. 'There's actually good news?'

'Well, no. But I thought I'd make you feel better.'

'What's the bad news?'

'Alice Young,' she says. 'I found her.'

Alice Young was a teenager who lived with her parents next door to Elise and Andrew; at one point she had babysat for Delia. 'And?'

'She's in Vienna.'

'Good,' I say. 'Subpoena her.'

'Might want to rethink that. She lives with the sisters of the Order of the Bloody Cross.'

'She's a *nun?*'

'She's a nun who took a vow of silence ten years ago,' the paralegal says.

'For Christ's sake . . .'

'Exactly. However, I did manage to find the other neighbor, Elizabeth Peshman. She's at some place called Sunset Acres; I assume it's a retirement community.'

I take the information. 'Did you call?'

'No one answers,' she says.

It's a Sun City, Arizona, address; it can't be that far away. 'I'll go find her.'

It takes me two hours to reach the town, and there are so many retirement communities I wonder how I'll ever find the right one. However, the clerk who sells me gas and a Snickers bar knows the name right away. 'Two lights, and then a left. You'll see the sign,' she says, as she rings me up.

From the looks of things, Sunset Acres is not a bad place to finish up one's life. It is a turn off the main drag, a long drive lined with saguaros and desert rock gardens. I have to stop at a stucco guard booth – apparently these seniors value their privacy. The man inside is stooped and age-spotted, and looks like he could be a resident himself. 'Hi,' I say. 'I'm trying to find Elizabeth Peshman. I tried to call—'

'Line's down,' the guard says. He points to a small parking lot. 'No cars allowed. I'll take you up.'

As I walk beside the guard, I wonder what sort of facility wouldn't allow cars up to the main building. It seems like quite an inconvenience, given the fact that some of the residents have to be arthritic or even disabled. As soon as we crest the hill, the guard points. 'Third from the left,' he says.

There are acres of crosses and stars and rose quartz obelisks. OUR DEAR MOTHER, reads one tombstone. NEVER FORGOTTEN. DOTING HUSBAND.

Elizabeth Peshman is dead. I have no witness to corroborate the fact that thirty years ago, Elise Matthews was the drunk that Andrew says she was. 'Guess you're not talking either,' I say out loud.

Although it is beastly hot, there are fresh flowers wilting in pots beside Elizabeth's tombstone. 'She's real popular,' the guard says. 'There are some folks here who never get visitors. But this one, she gets calls from a bunch of old students.'

'She was a teacher?' I ask, and my mind catches on the word. A *teacher*.

'You get what you need?' the guard asks.

'I think so,' I say, and I hurry back to my car.

Abigail Nguyen is mixing paste when I arrive. A slight woman with two knots of hair at the top of her head, like the ears of a bear, she looks up and gives me a smile. 'You must be Mr. Talcott,' she says. 'Come on in.'

When the preschool where Delia went closed down in the mid-eighties, Abigail started her own Montessori classes in the basement of a church. She was the third school listed in the Yellow Pages, and she had answered the phone herself.

We sit down, giants on miniature chairs. 'Ms. Nguyen, I'm an attorney, and I'm working on behalf of a girl you taught in the late 1970s . . . Bethany Matthews.'

'The one who was kidnapped.'

I shift a little. 'Well, that hasn't been determined yet. I'm representing her father.'

'I've been following it all in the papers, and on the local news.'

As has the rest of Phoenix. 'I wonder, Mrs. Nguyen, if you might be able to tell me about Bethany back then.'

'She was a good child. Quiet. Tended to work by herself, instead of with her peers.'

'Did you get a chance to know her parents?'

The teacher glances away for a moment. 'Sometimes Bethany came to school disheveled, or wearing dirty clothes . . . it raised a red flag for us. I think I even called the mother . . . what was her name again?'

'Elise Matthews.'

'Yes, that's right.'

'What did Elise say when you called?'

'I can't remember,' Mrs. Nguyen says.

'Do you recall anything else about Elise Matthews?'

The teacher nods. 'I assume you mean the fact that she smelled like a distillery.'

I feel my blood flow faster. 'Did you report her to child protective services?'

The teacher stiffens. 'There weren't any signs of abuse.'

'You said she came to school disheveled.'

'There's a big difference between a child not being bathed

every night, and parental neglect, Mr. Talcott. It's not our job to police what happens at home. Take it from me – I've seen children burned on the soles of their feet by their parents' cigarettes, and I've seen children come to school with broken bones and welts on their backs. I've seen children who hide in the supply closet at pickup time because they don't want to go home. Mrs. Matthews might have liked her afternoon cocktail, but she deeply loved her little girl, and Bethany clearly knew that.'

You'd be surprised, I think.

'Mrs. Nguyen, thank you for your time.' I hand her my card, with Chris Hamilton's office number penciled in. 'If you think of anything else, please call me.'

I have just started my car in the parking lot when there is a knock on the window. Mrs. Nguyen stands with her arms folded. 'There was one incident,' she says, when I roll down the window. 'Mrs. Matthews was late to pick up. We called the house, and kept calling, and there was no answer. I let Bethany stay for the afternoon session of school, and then I drove her home. The mother was passed out on the couch when we got there . . . so I took her home with me and let her stay the night. The next day, Mrs. Matthews apologized profusely.'

'Why didn't you call Bethany's father?'

A breeze blows a strand of Mrs. Nguyen's hair from her bun. 'The parents were going through a divorce. A week before, the mother had specifically asked us not to allow her husband to have any contact with the child.'

'How come?'

'Some threat he'd made, if I remember right,' Mrs. Nguyen says. 'She had reason to believe that he might take Bethany and run.'

Andrew looks thinner; although that might just be the baggy prison uniform. 'How's Delia?' he asks, like always. But this time, I don't answer. My patience is wound too tight.

I stand with my hands in my pockets. 'You told me that the kidnapping of your child was a spur of the moment thing, a knee-jerk reaction to a bad situation. You told me that when you went home to get Delia's blanket, you saw your ex-wife passed out and knew it was time to take matters into your own hands. Did I get that right?'

Andrew nods.

'Then how do you explain the fact that you threatened to take your daughter away from your wife before you actually did it?' Frustrated, I kick a chair so that it spins across the tiny conference room. 'What else aren't you telling me, Andrew?'

Muscles tighten along the column of Andrew's throat, but he doesn't answer.

'I can't do this alone,' I say, and I walk out of the room without look- ing back.

Thirty days before Andrew's trial, the State notices up its witnesses. I respond like I always do – by requesting the criminal records of everyone the prosecutor plans to call to the stand. This is basic defense law, for those who have no defense: Do what you can to shoot holes in anything and everything the State throws your way.

I get the records in the mail as I am running out the door to the courthouse for a 404B hearing that Emma Wasserstein's scheduled. Waiting for the judge to receive me in chambers, I open the envelope. Delia doesn't have a record, of course, so there are only two criminal record printouts. It's not much of a surprise to find a clean report for Detective LeGrande, the retired policeman who had once been in charge of the kidnapping case. It's the second report that interests me, anyway – the one for Elise Vasquez. Delia's mother was busted on a DWI charge after a car accident in 1972.

It's a felony. It happened when she was pregnant with Dee. It's not going to be easy, but I'm sure as hell going to try to impeach Elise with that conviction on the witness stand. It's a credibility argument: If someone's been drinking chronically, his or her memory recall is even more suspect.

I ought to know.

Emma Wasserstein turns the corner and comes to a halt when she sees me outside the judge's chambers. 'He's not ready yet?'

I glance at her prodigious belly. 'Unlike you,' I say, 'apparently not.'

She rolls her eyes. 'Maybe you didn't get the memo, but we aren't in seventh grade anymore.'

The door opens, and Judge Noble's assistant lets us into chambers. 'Very cranky,' she warns under her breath. 'Someone hasn't had his protein today.'

We retreat to our seats and wait for Judge Noble to let us know it's all right to speak. 'Ms. Wasserstein,' he sighs, 'what is it this time?'

'Your Honor, I'd like to have a prior bad act admitted as evidence. Namely, the assault conviction of Charles Matthews in December of 1976. It goes to motive.'

'Judge, that's completely prejudicial,' I say. 'We're talking about a scuffle years ago, one which is completely irrelevant to the charge at hand.'

'Irrelevant?' Emma stares at me. 'Did you happen to notice whom your client was beating up at the time?' She hands me a copy of the old assault charge – the same one I skimmed when I got it during discovery, figuring it had nothing to do with this case. My eyes hone in on the victim's name: Victor Vasquez.

Six months *before* Andrew absconded with his daughter, and three months *before* his divorce, he beat up the man who would later marry his ex-wife.

Which, actually, does go toward motive . . . namely revenge, if your wife is screwing around with a guy before you're even out the door.

The judge gathers the papers on his desk into their file. 'I'm going to allow it,' he says. 'Is there anything else, Counselor?'

Emma nods. 'Your Honor, I think it's clear to all of us that Mr. Talcott hasn't noticed up a formal necessity defense. That leads me to believe that he's going to run this trial as an all-out slander of Elise Vasquez.'

It's exactly what I'm planning to do.

'I'd like to say on the record that I truly hope this doesn't turn into a smear campaign of the victim, just because counsel doesn't have anything redeeming to say about his own client.'

The judge fixes his gaze on me. 'Mr. Talcott, I don't know if they allow character assassination in the courtrooms of New Hampshire, but you can be assured that we certainly don't allow it here in Arizona.'

'Regular assassination, though, would be a different story,' I murmur under my breath.

'What was that?' the judge asks.

'Nothing, Your Honor.' Andrew is guilty as hell of kidnapping, but there must be ways around that. It's the way defense law works: You always plead *not guilty*, when what you really mean is *guilty, but with good reason*. Then you talk to your client and he gives you details from his sorry life that will win the sympathy of the jury.

Assuming, that is, that those details from your client's sorry life don't thwart you at every turn. I think back to what the nursery school teacher said about Andrew threatening to take his daughter; to Emma's smug expression when she handed me Andrew's old assault charge. What else hasn't he told me that might screw this case up even more?

'You've got thirty days to pull a rabbit out of a hat, Counselor,' Judge Noble says. 'Why are you still standing here?'

When Andrew walks into our private conference room at the jail, I glance up. 'Let's add this to the list of things you ought to mention to your attorney, who is trying his best to get you acquitted: that your prior conviction for a bar fight just happened to involve your wife's future husband.'

He glances up, surprised. 'I thought you knew. It was right there on the record at the arraignment.'

'You feel like enlightening me any further?'

He stares at me for a long moment. 'I saw him,' he confesses, his voice cracking. 'I watched him touching her.'

'Elise?'

Slowly, Andrew nods.

'How did you find out there was something going on?'

'Delia had drawn a crayon picture for me on a piece of scrap paper. I was hanging it up in my office at the pharmacy when I happened to notice there was writing on the back. I thought it might be something important, so I turned it over . . . it was a letter Elise had been writing to someone named Victor. I was still married to her. I *loved* her.' He swallows. 'When I asked Dee where she got the paper from, she said the drawer next to Mommy's bed. And when I asked her if she knew anyone named Victor, she said he was the man who came over to take a nap with Mommy.'

Andrew gets up and walks toward the door, with its tiny streaked window. 'She was in the house. She was only a baby.' He stands with his hands on his hips. 'I came home early from work one day, on purpose, and caught them together.'

'And you messed him up so bad he needed sixty-five stitches,' I say. 'Emma Wasserstein is going to use that whole episode to explain why you turned around and kidnapped your daughter six months later. She's going to say it was a premeditated act of payback.'

'Maybe it was,' Andrew murmurs.

'Do *not* say that on the stand, for God's sake.'

He rounds on me. 'Then *you* make up the story, Eric. Give me a goddamned script and I'll say whatever you want.'

It would be enough, I realize, for any defense attorney: a client willing to do whatever I say. But it's different this time, because no matter what facade I build over the truth, we'll both know there's something hiding underneath. Andrew doesn't want to tell me more, and, suddenly, I don't want to hear it. So I pick three words from the quicksand between us. 'Andrew,' I say heavily, 'I quit.'

Fitz is trying to make fire. He's put his glasses down on the dusty ground, and has positioned them in direct line with the sun, to see if they'll ignite the crumpled ball of paper underneath the rims. 'What are you doing?' I ask, unraveling my tie as I approach the trailer.

'Exploring pyromania,' he says.

'Why?'

'Because I can.' He squints up at the sun, then moves the glasses a fraction to the left.

'I told Andrew I quit,' I announce.

Fitz rocks back on his heels. 'Why'd you do that?'

Glancing down at his combustion experiment, I say, 'Because I can.'

'No you can't,' he argues. 'You can't do that to Delia.'

'I don't think it's healthy to have a spouse who looks at you and thinks, "Oh, right, he's the guy who got my father locked away for ten years."'

'Don't you think it's going to hurt her more when she finds this out?'

'I don't know, Fitz,' I say pointedly, thinking that this is the pot calling the kettle black. 'Maybe she'll find out what you're doing first.'

'Find out what?' Delia says, coming out of the trailer. She looks from me to Fitz. 'What are you doing?'

'Trying to talk your fiancé out of being an asshole.'

I scowl at him. 'Just mind your own business, Fitz.'

'Aren't you going to tell her?' he challenges.

'Sure,' I say. 'Fitz is writing about the trial for his paper.' Immediately I feel like a jerk.

Delia steps back. 'Really?' she says, wounded.

Fitz is red-faced, furious. 'Why don't you ask Eric what *he* did today?'

I've had it. First the hearing in chambers, then the argument with Andrew, and now this. I tackle Fitz to the ground, knocking his glasses to the side as we scuffle on the dirt. Fitz has gotten stronger since the last time we've done this, which must have been ages ago. He grinds my face into the pebbles, his hand locked on the back of my neck. With a jab of my elbow in his gut, I manage to get the upper hand, and then my cell phone begins to ring.

It reminds me that, in spite of how I'm acting, I'm not some stupid adolescent anymore.

I frown at the unfamiliar number. 'Talcott,' I answer.

'This is Emma Wasserstein. I wanted to let you know that I'll be adding a witness to my list. The man's name is Rubio Greengate. He's the guy who sold your client two identities back in 1977.'

I walk around to the back of the trailer, so that Delia won't hear. 'You can't spring this on me now,' I say, incredulous. 'I'll object when you file the motion.'

'I'm not springing anything on you. You've got two weeks. I'll have the police reports of the interview we've done with him on your desk by tomor- row morning.'

This means that the prosecution has established a witness to tie Andrew to the abduction – and for reasons I've never understood, juries hang on the words of witnesses, even when their accounts aren't accurate. I open my mouth to tell Emma that I could actually care less, that I'm excusing myself from this case starting immediately, but instead I only hang up the phone and walk back to where Delia is now standing alone.

She looks like she has been stung, like she is still smarting. And why shouldn't she? It's not every day you find out that someone you trust has been lying behind your back; for Delia, this is becoming commonplace. 'I told Fitz to go to hell,' she says quietly. 'I said he could quote me on that in twenty-point type.' She turns to me. 'I should have realized that if he came all the way out here, it was because he had an agenda.'

'For what it's worth,' I say, 'I don't think he wanted to write this story any more than you want to see it written.'

'I told him things I haven't even told *you* . . . God, Eric, I took him *with* me the last time I went to see my mother.' She pushes her hair off her face. 'What else is wrong?'

'What do you mean?'

'Fitz said you had something to tell me. Is there something wrong with my father's case?'

She is staring at me with those beautiful brown eyes, the same ones I remember from a thousand moments in my life: the summer Sunday when I showed off by jumping off the high dive at the town pool; the February vacation when I broke my leg skiing; the night I made love to her for the first time.

To the left of her foot, the paper that had been beside Fitz's glasses bursts into flame.

'There's nothing wrong with his case,' I lie, and I don't tell her that I'm giving up, either.

Nighttime in Arizona is an embarrassment of riches. Sophie and I sit on the roof of the trailer, wrapped in a blanket. I show Sophie the Big Dipper, and Orion's Belt, and a winking red star. She is more interested, though, in locating the alphabet. Just this morning I found one of my depositions on the kitchen table, covered with multiple streams of the letter *B*. 'Daddy,' she says, pointing. 'I see a *W*.'

'Good for you.'

'There's another *W*, too.'

The moon is full tonight, and when Sophie points at the stars I can clearly see the trio: W-O-W. To my surprise, when I spell out the letters, she tells me what the word is. 'Ruthann taught me,' Sophie says. 'I know *wow* and *cat* and *dog* and *yes*.'

As she settles back in the *V* of my legs, I realize that if someone stole Sophie away from me, even if that person was Delia, I would search for her forever. I would turn over every single star, if that's what it took to find her. But by the same token, if I knew that someone was going to steal her away from me, I guarantee you that I'd take her first and run.

Suddenly Sophie stands up and bends over, so that her head is between her legs. She looks up at the sky from this vantage point while I panic about her falling off the top of the trailer. 'Did you know,' she says, 'that WOW, upside down, is MOM?'

'I guess I never noticed.'

Sophie leans against my heart. 'I think it's like that on purpose,' she says.

Sometime after midnight Delia climbs up to the roof of the trailer and sits down cross-legged behind me. 'My father's going to go to jail, isn't he,' she says.

I gently lay Sophie down on a bed of blankets; she's fallen asleep against me. 'You can't ever tell in a jury trial—'

'Eric.'

I duck my head. 'There's a good chance.'

She closes her eyes. 'For how long?'

'A maximum of ten years.'

'In Arizona?'

I slip my arm around her. 'Let's deal with that when and if it happens.'

With the moon watching like a hawk, I run my hands over the river of her hair and the landscape of her shoulders. We slip into my sleeping bag together – a tight fit – and she slides over me, her legs pressed the length of mine and her skin slick. We are attentive to silence – Sophie is asleep a few feet away – and that changes the tenor of the act. Without words, the other sensations expand. Sex becomes desperate, secret, precise as a ballet.

We move, while coyotes pace the desert and snakes write in code across the sand. We move, while the stars rain down on us like sparks. We move, and her body blooms.

Then we turn onto our sides, still linked, too close for anything to come between us. 'I love you,' I whisper against her skin. My words fall into the tiny divot at the base of her throat, the pockmark left behind after a sledding accident.

But Delia has had that mark ever since I met her, at age

four. The sledding accident would have occurred beforehand, when she was living in Phoenix.

Where it doesn't snow.

'Dee,' I say urgently, but she is already asleep.

That night I dream of running on the surface of the moon, where everything weighs less, even doubt.

Andrew enters the private attorney-client conference room. 'I thought you quit.'

'That was yesterday,' I reply. 'Listen, that scar, on Delia's neck . . . it didn't come from a sledding accident, did it.'

'No. It was a scorpion sting.'

'She was stung by a scorpion on her *throat?*'

'She got stung on the shoulder, but by the time Elise found her, she was already in bad shape. At the hospital, they tried to intubate her, but couldn't do it the regular way, so they cut a hole in her windpipe and put her on a ventilator for three days until she could breathe on her own again.'

'What hospital did you bring her to?'

'Scottsdale Baptist,' Andrew says.

If Delia had been brought into a hospital in 1976 for a scorpion bite, there will be records: written proof that in her mother's solitary care, this child had been harmed. If it happened once, there was every chance it would happen again. And that might be enough justification for a jury to understand why a protective father might run off with his little girl.

I gather up my papers and tell Andrew I'll be in touch. Then I race into the parking lot behind the jail, where I turn the air-conditioning on full blast and call Delia on my cell phone. 'Guess what,' I say when she answers. 'I think I know why you're afraid of bugs.'

Scottsdale Baptist Hospital is now Scottsdale Osborn. An administrative assistant who has been following the kidnapping on local news channels has given Delia her old hospital records in return for an autograph. We sit down together in an archive closet, surrounded by walls of files with the colorful confetti of routing tabs. Delia opens the folder, and the musty scent of the past rises up from the small stack of paperwork. I watch her scan the pages, and wonder if she realizes she's fingering the dime-size hollow at the base of her throat.

'You read it,' she says a moment later, shoving the folder at me.

BETHANY MATTHEWS. Date of Visit: 11/24/76.

History: 3 y/o WF brought in by mother following questionable scorpion sting to L shoulder approximately 1 h PTA. Pt c/o pain to L shoulder as well as difficulty breathing, nausea, and double vision. Mother reports patient has had intermittent 'jerking' of her arms as well as two episodes of non-bloody, non-bilious emesis. No LOC, no chest pain, no bleeding.

PMH: None

Allergies: NKDA

Tetanus: UTD

PE: 128/88 177 34 99.8 98% on RA 20 kg. Anxious, agitated 3 y/o °+ in moderate distress.

HEENT: Horizontal nystagmus, PERRLA, copious salivation, OP clear

Neck: Supple, non-tender, no LAD, no thyromegaly

Lungs: Slight rhonchi bilaterally, slight incr. WOB, no retractions

CV: Regular, tachy, no m,r,g

Abd: s/nt/nd/+bs

EXT: 2x3 area of erythema on posterior left shoulder, no ecchymoses, no bleeding. 2+ distal pulses x 4

Neuro: Alert, anxious, horizontal nystagmus to L side, dysconjugate gaze, facial droop on L side, gag reflex not intact. 5/5 strength x 4 extremities, sensitive to light touch except at area around envenomation, occasional opisthonos

Laboratory data: WBC 11/6 Hct-36 Plt 240 Na 136 K 3.9 Cl 100 HCO3 24 BUN 18 Cr 1.0 gluc 110 Ca 9.0 INR 1.2

PTT 33.0; Urinalysis Sp Gr 1.020, 25–50 WBC, 5–10
RBC, 3+ BAC 1+ SqEpi, +nitrite, +LE

ED decision-making: Pt presented to ED with s/s consistent
with severe envenomation. After receiving 2 mg versed i.v.
the patient was initially improved, but became agitated
when Dr. Young attempted to remove the patient's clothing
in order to fully assess her. Antivenin was unavailable.
Additional doses of versed were ineffective, and the decision was made to sedate and paralyze the patient for intubation. Because of the copious secretions, orotracheal
intubation was impossible, and a needle cricothyrotomy
was performed successfully. The patient was then admitted
to the PICU and underwent a subsequent tracheostomy
by peds general surgery. Pt ventilated for 3 days. Urinalysis
also revealed a urinary tract infection, and the PICU team
has been notified of this finding.

'I don't understand what it says,' Delia murmurs.

'You couldn't breathe,' I say, skimming the notes. 'So the
doctors made a surgical opening in your throat and hooked
you up to machines that breathed for you.' I read further down
the page:

ED social worker was requested because mother
presented as intoxicated; father notified.

Here is proof, in black and white, that medical professionals
thought Elise Hopkins was so drunk she was unable to take
care of her child.

Delia turns to me. 'I can't believe I don't remember this.'

'You were young,' I justify.

'Shouldn't I have at least some sense of being in a hospital
for a few nights? Of breathing with a ventilator? Or of fighting
the doctor? I mean, look at what it says, Eric. I had to be
sedated.'

She gets up suddenly and walks out of the closet, asking

the administrative assistant where the pediatric ICU ward is. Determined, she gets into the elevator and heads upstairs.

It looks different, surely, than it used to. There are bright murals of aquariums and Disney princesses on the walls and rainbows painted on the windows. Children tethered to IV poles navigate the halls with their parents; babies cry behind closed doors.

A candy striper gets off another elevator and pushes past us, her face hidden by a bouquet of balloons. She brings them into the room opposite us; the patient is a little girl. 'Can we tie them to the bed,' she asks, 'and see if I float?'

'I didn't have balloons,' Delia murmurs. 'They weren't allowed in the ICU.' She crosses in front of me, but she might as well be a thousand miles away. 'He brought me candy instead . . . a lollipop shaped like a scorpion. He told me to bite it back.'

'Your dad?'

'I don't think so. This is crazy, but it was someone who looked like Victor. The guy my mother's married to now.' She shakes her head, bewildered. 'He told me not to tell anyone he came to visit.'

I scuff my shoe on the linoleum. 'Huh,' I say.

'If I got bitten in 1976, my parents were still married.' Delia looks up at me. 'What if . . . what if my mother was having an affair, Eric?'

I don't answer.

'Eric,' Delia says, 'did you hear me?'

'She was.'

'What?'

'Your father told me.'

'And you didn't tell me?'

'I couldn't tell you, Delia.'

'What else are you holding back?'

A hundred answers run through my mind, from details of conversations I have had with Andrew in jail to the deposition I took from Delia's former nursery school teacher, things that she is better off not hearing, although she would never believe me if I told her so. '*You're* the one who wanted me to represent your father,' I argue. 'If I tell you the things he tells me, I get tossed off the case, or disbarred. So, you pick, Delia. Do you want me to put *you* first . . . or *him?*'

Too late I realize I never should have asked that question. She shoves past me without saying a word, and strides down the hallway.

'Delia, wait,' I say, as she steps into the elevator. I put my hand between the doors to keep it from closing. 'Stop. I promise; I'll tell you everything I know.'

The last thing I see before the doors close are her eyes: the soft, bruised brown of disappointment. 'Why start now,' she says.

The taxi drops me off at Hamilton, Hamilton, but instead of going into the office building I take a left and start walking the streets of Phoenix. I walk far enough that the tony stucco storefronts disappear and I find myself in places where kids in low-riding pants hang out on the corner, watching traffic without flicking their yellow eyes. I pass a boarded-up drugstore, a wig shop, and a kiosk that reads CHECKS CASHED in multiple languages.

Delia is right. If I managed to figure out a way to keep her from knowing what her father told me, surely I would have been able to figure out a way to keep the Bar Association from knowing what I might have told her. It doesn't matter that, in terms of legal ethics, I shouldn't have disclosed to her any information about her father's case, or her own absent history. It doesn't matter that I promised as much to Judge Noble, and to Chris Hamilton, my sponsor in this state. The bottom line is that ethics are a lofty standard, but affection ranks higher. What is the point of being an exemplary attorney in the long run? You never see that on anyone's tombstone. You see who loved them; you see who they loved back.

I duck into the next store and let the air-conditioning wash over me. There is the unmistakable yeasty smell of cardboard cartons; the ching of a cash register. One wall is covered with the emerald green bottles of foreign wines; the entire back shelf is a transparent panorama of gins and vodka and vermouth. The full-bellied brandies sit side by side like Buddhas.

I head to the corner of whiskeys. The cashier puts the Maker's Mark into a brown bag for me and hands me back my change. When I leave the store I twist off the cap of the whiskey bottle. I lift the bottle to my lips and tilt back my head and savor that first, blessed, anesthetic mouthful.

And, like I expect, that's all I need for the fog in my head to clear, leaving one honest admission: Even if I had been free to tell Delia anything and everything, I still wouldn't have done it. As Andrew has been trying to explain for weeks: It was easier to hide the truth than to hurt her.

So does that make me guilty . . . or admirable?

What is right, in the end, is not always what it seems to be, and some rules are better broken. But what about when those rules happen to be laws?

Tipping the whiskey bottle, I spill the entire contents down a sewer grate.

It is a longshot, but I think I've just found a way out for Andrew Hopkins.

Delia

By the time I reach my mother's house, my emotions are hanging by a thread. I've been lied to by Fitz and by Eric; I've been lied to by my father. I have come here because, ironically, my mother is my last resort. I need someone to tell me the things I want to hear: that she loved my father; that I have jumped to the wrong conclusion; that the truth is not always what you think it is.

When my mother doesn't answer the doorbell, I let myself into her unlocked house. I follow her voice down a hallway. 'How does that feel?' she asks.

'*Much* better,' a man answers.

I peer through a doorway to find my mother gently tying a knot in a silk cord around a younger man's neck. Seeing me, he startles, nearly falling off his stool.

'Delia!' she says.

The man's face turns bright red; he seems incredibly embarrassed to have been caught, even fully clothed, with my mother. 'Stay,' she says. 'Henry and I are finishing up.'

He digs in his pants for his wallet. 'Gracias, Doña Elise,' he mutters, shoving a ten-dollar bill into her hands.

He's *paying* her?

'You have to keep wearing your red socks, and your red underwear for me. Understand?'

'Yes, ma'am,' he replies, and he backs out of the room in a hurry.

I stare at her, speechless for a moment. 'Does Victor know?'

'I try to keep it a secret.' My mother blushes. 'To be honest, I wasn't sure how you'd react, either.' Her eyes suddenly brighten. 'If you're interested, though, I'd love to teach you.'

It is then that I notice the rows of jars behind her, filled with leaves and roots and buds and soil, and I realize we are talking about very different things. 'What . . . is all this?'

'It's part of the business,' she says. 'I'm a *curandera,* a healer. Sort of a doctor for the people doctors can't help. Henry, for example, has been here three times already.'

'You're not sleeping with him?'

She looks at me as if I'm crazy. 'Henry? Of course not. He's been hospitalized twice because his throat keeps swelling shut, but no medical professional can find anything wrong with him. The minute he walked in here, I knew it was one of his neighbors hexing him – and I'm working with him to break the spell.'

My own business involves things that cannot be seen, but it's rooted in the basics of science: human cells, attacked by bacteria, which create vapor trails. Once again, I look at this woman and think she is an utter stranger. 'Do you honestly believe that?'

'What I believe doesn't matter. It's what *he* believes. People come to me because they get to help with their cure. The client knots the special cord, or buries the sealed matchbox, or rubs the candle. Who doesn't want to have a hand in controlling their own future?'

It was what I had thought I wanted. But now that I am starting to remember, I am not so sure. I touch my hand to the scar at my throat; the discovery that brought me here. 'If you're a healer, why couldn't you save me?'

Her eyes fall to the small hollow. 'Because back then,' she admits, 'I couldn't even save myself.'

Suddenly this is all too hard. I am tired of putting up walls. I want someone with the strength – and the honesty – to break them down.

'Then do it now,' I demand. 'Pretend I'm some client.'

'There's nothing wrong with you.'

'Yes, there is,' I say. 'I hurt. I hurt all the time.' Tears pierce the back of my throat. 'You've got to have some magic that makes things disappear. Some potion or spell or cord I can tie around my wrist that'll make me forget how you drank . . . and how you cheated on my father.'

She steps back, as if she's been slapped.

'What could you give me,' I ask, my voice shaking, 'to make me forget . . . that you forgot about me?'

My mother hesitates for a moment, and then walks stiffly to her shelves. She pulls down three containers and a glass mixing bowl. She opens the seals. I smell nutmeg, summer-time, a distillation of hope.

But she does not mix me a poultice or make a roux for me to swallow. She doesn't wrap my wrists with green silk or tell me to blow out three squat candles. Instead, she comes hesi-tantly around her workbench. She folds me into her arms, even as I try to break free. She refuses to let go, the whole time that I cry.

It seems as if we have been driving forever. Ruthann and I take turns during the night, while Sophie and Greta sleep in the backseat. We head north on Interstate 17, passing places with names like Bloody Basin Road and Horsethief Basin, Jackass Acres, Little Squaw Creek. We pass the skeletons of saguaros, inside which birds have made their homes; and the smashed amber glass from beer bottles, which line the side of the road like glitter.

Gradually, the cacti vanish, and deciduous trees begin to pepper the foothills. The altitude makes the temperature drop, to a point where the air is so cool I have to roll up the window. Walls of striated red rock rise in the distance, set on fire by the rising sun.

I'm not running away, not really. I just sort of invited myself to accompany Ruthann on a trip to visit her family on Second Mesa. She wasn't too keen on the idea, but I pulled out all the stops: I told her that I thought it was important for Sophie to learn about the world; I told her that I wanted to see more in Arizona than the jail system; I told her that I needed to talk to someone, and that I wanted it to be her.

As we drive, I tell Ruthann about Fitz's story for the *Gazette*. I tell her about the scorpion sting, and what I remembered about Victor, and what Eric already knew. I don't tell her about my mother. Right now, I want to keep that moment to myself, a silver dollar tucked into the hem of my mind to take out in an emergency.

'So you *really* begged to come to Second Mesa because you're angry at Eric,' Ruthann says.

'I didn't beg,' I say, and she just raises a brow. 'Well, maybe just a little.'

Ruthann is quiet for a few seconds. 'Let's say Eric had told you that your mother had been having an affair when he first found out. Would it have kept your parents from splitting up? No. Would it have kept your father from running away with you? No. Would it have meant that your father wouldn't have been arrested? Nope. Far as I can tell, the only purpose served by telling you would be to get you even more upset, kind of like you are now.'

'Eric knows how hard this is for me,' I say. 'It's like doing a jigsaw puzzle and going crazy because I can't find the last piece, and then realizing that Eric's had it stashed in his back pocket.'

'Maybe he's got a reason for not wanting you to finish that puzzle,' Ruthann says. 'I'm not saying what Eric did was right. I'm just saying it might not be wrong, either.'

We drive on in silence to Flagstaff, and then veer right onto a different road. I follow Ruthann's directions to a turnoff for Walnut Canyon. We park in a lot next to a ranger's truck, but the gates aren't open yet. 'Come on,' Ruthann says. 'There's something I want you to see.'

'We have to wait,' I point out.

But Ruthann just gets out of the car and reaches into the backseat for Sophie. 'No we don't,' she says. 'This is where I'm from.'

We climb over the gates and hike down a trail into a canyon that opens up like a seam between the scarlet rocks. Prickly pear and pinyons grow along the track like markers. The path winds tightly, a sheer four-hundred-foot drop on one side and a wall of rock on the other. Ruthann moves quickly, stepping over the narrowest of passes and crawling around spires and through crevices. The deeper we get, the more remote it seems to be. 'Do you know where you're going?' I ask.

'Sure. My worst nightmare used to be getting lost in here with a bunch of *pahanas.*' Turning, she flashes a smile. 'The Donner party ate the Indians first, you know.'

We descend into the canyon, the gap between our path and the facing mass of rock growing narrower and narrower, until we have somehow crossed onto the other side. Sophie is the one who spots it first. 'Ruthann,' she says, 'there's a hole in this mountain.'

'Not a hole, Siwa,' she says. 'A *home.*'

As we get closer I can see it: Carved into the limestone are hundreds of small rooms, stacked on top of one another like natural apartment buildings. The walkway spirals around the mountain, until we reach the mouth of one of the cliff dwellings.

Sophie and Greta, delighted by this carved cave, run from the cedar tree twisted into the mouth of the doorway to the back of the hollowed room. The rear wall is charred; the space smells of brittle heat and fierce wind. 'Who lived here?' I ask.

'My ancestors . . . the *hisatsinom.* They came here when Sunset Crater erupted in 1065, and covered their pit houses and the farms in the meadows.'

Sophie chases Greta around a small square of rocks that must have been a fire pit. It is easy to imagine a family huddled around that, telling stories into the night, knowing that dozens of other families were doing the same thing in the small spaces surrounding them. There is a reason the word *belonging* has a synonym for *want* at its center; it is the human condition.

I turn to her. 'Why did they leave?'

'No one can stay in one place forever. Even the ones who

don't budge, well, the world changes around them. Some people think there might have been a drought here. The Hopi say the *hisatsinom* were fulfilling a prophecy – to wander for hundreds of years before returning to the spirit world again.'

Across the way, on the trail we've come in on, the day's first tourists crawl like fire ants. 'Did you ever think that maybe you've got it upside down?' Ruthann says.

'What do you mean?'

'What if the whole kidnapping experience isn't the story of Delia?' she asks. 'What if disappearing wasn't the most cataclysmic event of your life?'

'What else would be?'

Ruthann lifts her face to the sun. 'Coming back,' she says.

The Hopi reservation is a tiny bubble inside the much larger Navajo reservation, spread across three long-fingered mesas that rise 6,500 feet above sea level. From a distance, they look like the stacked teeth of a giant; closer, like batter being poured.

Almost twelve thousand Hopi live in small clusters of villages, and one of those, Sipaulovi, sits on Second Mesa. We park at a landing and hike up a hill, over shards of pottery and bones – an old habit, Ruthann tells me, from when families would bury food in the ash of their housing foundations to keep from going hungry. We reach a small, dusty plaza at the crest of the mesa, a square surrounded by one-story houses. There aren't any adults outside when we arrive, but a trio of little children, not much older than Sophie, dart in and out of the shade between the buildings, appearing and disappearing like ghosts. Two dogs chase each other's tails. On the roof of one building is an eagle, with brightly painted wooden toys and bowls at its feet.

Through the windows of the houses I can hear music – recorded native chants, cartoons, commercial jingles. There is electricity at Sipaulovi, but not at some of the other villages; Ruthann says that at Old Oraibi, for example, the elders felt that if they took something from the *pahanas*, the *pahanas* would demand something in return. Running water is a new thing, she says, dating back to the 1980s. Before that, you had to carry water in a bucket from a natural spring at the top of the mesa. Sometimes when it rains, there are still fish in the puddles.

Ruthann corrals me, slipping her arm through mine. 'Come on,' she says, 'my sister's waiting.'

Wilma is the mother of Derek, the boy we watched doing the Hoop Dance a few weeks earlier. I follow Ruthann to one house on the edge of the plaza, a small stone building with one facing window. She opens the door without knocking, releasing the rich smell of stew and cornmeal. 'Wilma,' she says, 'is that *noqkwivi* burning?'

Wilma is younger than I expected – maybe five or six years older than me. She is in the process of trying to brush a little girl's hair, in spite of the fact that the little girl refuses to sit still. When she sees Ruthann, a smile splits her face. 'What would a skinny old lady like you know about cooking?' she says.

The house is full of other women, too, wearing a rainbow of colorful housecoats. Many of them look like Wilma and Ruthann – sisters, aunts, I suppose. Hanging on the white walls are carved katsina dolls, like the ones that Ruthann told me about weeks ago. In the corner of the room is a television, crowned by a doily and a vase of tissue paper flowers.

'You almost missed it,' Wilma says, shaking her head.

'You know me better than that,' Ruthann answers. 'I told you I'd be back before the katsinas left.'

From here the conversation slides into the streaming flow of Hopi that I can't follow. I wait for Ruthann to introduce me, but she doesn't, and even stranger, no one seems to think this is odd.

The little girl who is having her hair brushed is finally freed from her chair, and walks up to Sophie. She speaks in perfect English. 'Want to draw?'

Sophie slowly peels herself away from me and nods,

following the girl into the kitchen, where a cup of broken crayons sits in the center. They begin to draw on brown paper, squares cut from grocery bags. I sit down next to an old woman weaving a flat plate from yucca leaves. When I smile at her, she grunts.

The house is the strangest combination of past and present. There are stone bowls with blue corn being hand-ground into meal. There are prayer feathers, like the ones tied to Ruthann's paloverde tree and the ones left in Walnut Canyon. But there are also linoleum floors, Styrofoam cups, and plastic table-cloths. There's a Rubbermaid laundry basket and a teenage girl painting her toenails scarlet. There are two worlds rubbing right up against each other, and not a single person in this room seems to have trouble straddling them.

Ruthann and Wilma are having an argument; I know this only because of the tone and volume of their words, and the way Ruthann throws up her hands and backs away from her sister. Suddenly there is a trilling cry – the low hoot of an owl, something I recognize from walking in the woods in New Hampshire. Immediately, the women begin to whisper and peer out the windows. Wilma says something that I would swear is Hopi for *I told you so.*

'Come on,' Ruthann says to me. 'I'll show you around.'

Sophie seems happy coloring; so I follow Ruthann outside to the plaza again. 'What's going on?' I ask.

'There's a ceremony tomorrow, *Niman.* It means the Home Dance. It's the last one, before all the katsinas go back to the spirit world.'

'I meant with Wilma. I guess I shouldn't have come, after all.'

'She's not angry because you're here,' Ruthann says. 'It's the owl. No one likes to hear them; it's bad luck.' We have walked down a narrow footpath that leads away from the plaza, and are standing in front of a small home made of cinder block. A tongue of smoke licks its way out the chimney. Ruthann shields her eyes and stares up at it. 'This is where I used to live when I was married.'

I think about my own wedding ceremony, fallen by the wayside in the wake of my father's trial. 'I wonder if Eric and I will ever get around to that.'

'The Hopi way takes years. You do the church thing, to get that out of the way, and you find a place to live, but it takes years for your groom's uncles to weave your *tuvola,* your bridal robes. Wilma had already had Derek by the time her Hopi wedding came. He was three years old, and walked with his mother during the ceremony.'

'What's it like?'

'A lot of work. You have to pay the groom's family back for the robes, with plaques that you weave and food you prepare.' Ruthann grins. 'Four days before my wedding, I went to live with my mother-in-law. I fasted, but I had to cook for her and her family – a test, you know, to see if you're worthy of her son, even though I'd been married to him by law for three years already. There's a tradition that the groom's paternal aunts come over and throw mud at the groom's maternal aunts, while each side complains about the bride and the groom, but it's all a big joke, like those crazy bachelor parties *pahanas* have. And then, on the day of, I put on one of the white robes Eldin's uncles had made me. It was beautiful – there were tassels hanging down, each one smaller than the next, like the canes I would use as I got older, getting closer and closer to the earth until my forehead touched it.'

'What's the second robe for?'

'You wear it the day you die. You stand on the edge of the Grand Canyon, spread out the robe, step onto it, and rise into the sky as a cloud.' Ruthann looks down at her left hand, on which she still wears a gold band. 'You *pahanas* have all these rehearsals for your wedding day . . . to us, the wedding day is the rehearsal for the rest of our lives.'

'When did Eldin die?' I ask.

'In the middle of a drought, in 1989.' Ruthann shakes her head. 'I think the spirits picked him on purpose, someone larger than life, because they knew he'd be able to bring us rain. On the night he came back, I stood outside this very house,' she says. 'I tilted back my head and I opened my mouth and I tried to swallow as much of him as I could.'

I stare at the smoke, curling out of the chimney of the house. 'Do you know who lives here now?' I ask.

'Not us,' she says, and she turns and starts walking slowly up the path.

Greta and I sit at the edge of Second Mesa as the sun goes down. *Dear Mami,* I write on the back of a grocery bag.

Do you know that when you are in elementary school, every teacher celebrates Mother's Day? And because they all felt bad for me, I didn't have to make the bath salts or the woven paper basket or the card.

Do you know that the first time I went to buy a bra, I waited in the lingerie department until I saw a woman walk in with a little girl, and I asked her to help me?

Do you know that when I was ten, I tried to be Catholic, so I could light a candle to you that you'd see from Heaven?

Do you know that I used to wish I'd die, so I could meet you?

I glance up, staring out at the pancake landscape in the distance. *For someone who can't remember very much, there seems to be a lot I can't forget.*

I know you're sorry, I write. *I just don't know if that's good enough.*

When I put down the pencil, it rolls over the edge of the cliff. Even in this utter quiet, I can hear my mother apologizing for her actions; I can hear my father justifying his. You would think it would be simpler, having them both in close proximity, but instead it makes it easier for them to tear me apart. They are both pleading for my vote; so loud that I can hardly make up my own mind.

Again.

I love my father, and I know that he was right to take me. But I am a mother, and I can't imagine having my child stolen away. The problem is that this isn't a case of either/or.

My mother and father are both right.

And at the same time, they were both wrong.

When Ruthann walks up behind me, I nearly jump out of my skin. 'You scared me,' I say.

She looks tired, and lowers herself slowly to the ground. 'I used to come here a lot,' she says. 'When I needed to think.'

I draw up my knees. 'What are you thinking about now?'

'What it feels like to come home,' Ruthann says, turning to the San Francisco peaks in the distance. 'I'm glad you bullied me into bringing you.'

I grin. 'Thanks. I think.'

She shields her eyes against the red glare of the sunset. 'What are you thinking about?' she asks.

I stand up and tear the paper into pieces. 'The same thing,' I say, and together we watch the wind take them away.

Before dawn the next morning, the plaza is already crowded with people. Some sit on metal folding chairs, others crouch on the roofs of the houses. Ruthann follows Wilma to a spot at the edge of the square, under the overhang of a building. There is no sun yet, but this dance will go on all day; and by then, it will be scorching.

Sophie is quiet. Perched on my hip, she rubs her eyes. She looks at the golden eagle still tethered to one roof, which beats its wings every few minutes, and sometimes cries.

When the sun is a fist on the horizon, the katsinas arrive in a single file, up from the kivas where they have been preparing. They carry armloads of gifts, which they pile in the plaza. Because it didn't rain last night, they have not been allowed to drink this morning, and they will not, no matter how hot it gets.

There are almost fifty of them – *Hoote* katsinas, I am told – all dressed alike. They wear white skirts with red sashes, and loincloths with different patterns. Their arms are decorated with cuffs, their chests are bare. On their left ankles are bells; on the right, rattles. They hold rattles in their right hands, and juniper – *womapi* – in the left. A necklace with a shell hangs down between each set of shoulder blades; a foxtail swishes between every pair of legs. Their bodies are covered with red ochre paint and a dusting of cornmeal, but the most imposing part of their costumes are the masks – a crown of feathers spiking up from the back of an enormous black wooden head, dog's snout, bared teeth, bug-eyes.

Sophie buries her face in my neck, as they begin to chant. The song is deep, guttural, building to a crescendo. The katsinas turn to the beat of the music in pairs as an old man weaves between them, sprinkling cornmeal and urging them to dance harder.

Ruthann pats Sophie on the back. 'Ssh, Siwa,' she says. 'They're not here to hurt you. They keep you safe.'

When they stop dancing an hour or so later, they jangle toward the heaps of gifts they've carried up from the kivas. They toss baked loaves of bread to the people sitting on the roofs. They pass out watermelons and grapes, popcorn balls, peaches. They hand out bowls of fruit, squash, corn, Little Debbie cakes. Wilma, a recent widow, is given one of the biggest baskets.

Finally, they pass out presents to the children. For the boys, there are bows and arrows wrapped with cattails and corn-stalks. For the girls, katsina dolls tied with boughs of juniper. One dancer, perspiration pouring down his arms and sides, sweeps across the plaza to the spot where we are sitting. He holds two katsina dolls, their painted faces glazed by the sun. He hands one to Wilma's daughter, and then kneels in front of Sophie. She shrinks away, cowed by the vivid flecks of his mask and the clean sharp smell of his sweat. He shakes his carved head, and after a moment her fingers close around the doll.

The agility with which this particular katsina moves, and the long lines of his body, are familiar. I marvel at his foot-work and wonder if, underneath the mask, this might not be Derek, the hoop dancer we met in Phoenix, Ruthann's nephew.

'Isn't that—'

'No, it's not,' Ruthann says. 'Not today.'

The katsinas, ready for a short break, split into two lines that fold back upon each other and march out of the plaza, down the mesa in a long, undulating line toward the kiva. The clouds seem to follow them.

Ruthann reaches for Sophie, who is holding her new doll tight. She rests her cheek to the crown of my daughter's head and watches the katsinas go. 'Good-bye,' she says.

The next morning when I wake up, Ruthann is gone and Sophie is still fast asleep beside Greta. I tiptoe outside in time to see a man climb to the roof where the golden eagle is tied, watching the ceremonies. The bird beats its wings, but a tether around its foot keeps it from flying away. The man talks softly to the bird as he moves closer, finally wrapping the eagle in a blanket.

When a woman comes out of the house beside me, I turn to her, alarmed. 'Is he trying to steal the bird?' I ask. 'Should we do something?'

She shakes her head. 'That eagle, Talátawi, he's been watching us since May, to see that we've done all the ceremonies well. Now it's time for him to go.' She tells me that her son was the one who captured Talátawi, as his father lowered him by rope down a cliff to an eagle's nest. That the eagle's name means Song to the Rising Sun; and that since they've named it, the bird is a member of their family.

I wait for her husband to untie the bird, to see it fly off. But as I watch, the man wraps the blanket more tightly around the eagle. He holds it while the bird fights to breathe, and finally it goes limp. 'He's killing it?'

The woman wipes her eyes. The eagle, she tells me, is smothered in cornmeal. All of his feathers will be removed except for a few, to be used in *pahos* and ceremonial objects that will bless the people of Sipaulovi. Talátawi's body will be buried with gifts from the katsinas, and will journey to tell the spirits

that the Hopi deserve rain. 'It's all for good,' she says, her
voice shaking, 'but that doesn't make it any easier to let go.'

Suddenly, Wilma slams out of the screen door. 'Have you
seen her?' she asks.

'Who?'

'Ruthann. She's gone missing.'

Knowing Ruthann, she's gone to raid the junk piles that
dot the reservation. Yesterday, as we were hiking up toward
Sipaulovi, she told me that the Hopi believe when something's
wrecked or used up, it has to be given back to the earth, which
is why trash is left on the ground and garbage in a heap.
Eventually, after you die, you'll get back whatever it is that
was broken.

At the time, I'd wondered if this held true for hearts.

'I'm sure she's fine,' I tell Wilma. 'She'll be back before you
know it.'

But Wilma wrings her hands. 'What if she walked too far,
and couldn't make it home? I don't know how much strength
she's got.'

'Ruthann? She could probably win an Ironman competition.'

'But that was before the chemotherapy.'

'The *what?*'

Wilma tells me that when Ruthann found out, she went to
see a native healer. But it had spread too far too fast, and she
turned to traditional medicine. She told Wilma that I've been
driving her to the hospital for her appointments. But I have
never taken Ruthann to any doctor; she has never even
mentioned having cancer.

On the roof behind us, the man sings a prayer that's striped
with grief, and rocks the body of Talátawi in his arms like an
infant.

'Wilma,' I say, 'I want you to call the police.'

I don't want anyone coming with me – namely, a tribal police
escort – so I surreptitiously scent Greta off a shirt in Ruthann's

suitcase. The bloodhound immediately begins to strain at her leash, even before I give the command. With Wilma talking to the cops and Derek babysitting for Sophie and his own little sister, Greta and I sneak away unnoticed.

We move across yellowed ground split by deep fissures; we step gingerly over slabs of stone that have tumbled from the crests of the mesas. In some places it is easier than others – in the soft layer of dust that coats the earth, there will be a footprint; some of the vegetation has been kicked aside, or crushed. In other places, the only trace left behind of Ruthann is a thread of her scent.

There are any number of dangers that might befall Ruthann out here – dehydration, sunstroke, snakes, desperation. It is terrifying to think that her recovery might sit squarely in my hands, and at the same time, there is a part of me that's almost relieved to be doing this sort of work again. If I'm actively looking for someone, it must mean that I'm no longer the one who is lost.

Suddenly Greta stops hard and alerts. She lopes off at a run, as I try to dodge boulders and juniper bushes in an effort to keep up. She turns onto a rutted road made for four-wheel-drive vehicles, and leads me into the bowl of a small canyon.

We are ringed by sheer rock walls on three sides. Greta edges closer to the cliffs, pushing her nose along the cracked earth. My boots kick over shards of corrugated pottery and broken arrowheads and owl pellets. On the facings of the rock are markings: spirals, sunbursts, snakes, full moons, concentric circles. I trail my fingers over figures with spears and bighorn sheep; over boys holding what looks like a flower over their heads and girls trying to snatch them away; over twins connected by a wavy umbilicus. One entire wall is like a newspaper – hundreds of drawings densely packed into the space. It is amazing how much of the story I can understand, although these must have been hammered into place a thousand years ago.

I am distracted by one symbol: a stick figure that could only be a parent, holding the hand of what could only be a child.

'Ruthann!' I call out, and I think I hear an answer.

Greta sits at the edge of a narrow crevice, whining as her paws scrabble for purchase. 'Stay,' I command, and I take hold of the edges and hoist myself up to the thin ledge six feet off the ground. From here, I can see another foothold; I start to climb.

It is when I've worked myself deep into the split of the rock, too far in and too high up to see Greta anymore, that I notice the petroglyph. This artist went to great pains to show this was a woman – she has breasts, and loose hair. She is pointed upside down, and her head is separated from her body by a long, wavy line. On the facing rock are a series of notches, precisely cut. I realize it is a calendar; meant for a solstice. On a particular day, the sun will hit this just right; and a line of light will slice the neck of the falling woman.

A sacrifice.

A rain of pebbles from overhead makes me glance up in time to see Ruthann step onto the lip of the cliff, another fifteen feet above me. Her body is wrapped tight in a pure white robe.

'Ruthann!' I shout, my voice caroming off the rock walls, an obscenity.

She looks down at me. Across the distance, our eyes meet.

'Ruthann, don't,' I whisper, but she shakes her head.

I'm sorry.

In that half-second, I think about Wilma and Derek and me, all the people who do not want to be left behind, who think we know what is best for her. I think about the doctors and the medicines Ruthann lied about taking. I think about how I could talk her down from that ledge like I have talked down a dozen potential suicide victims. Yet the right thing to do, here, is subjective. Ruthann's family, who wants her alive, will not be the one to lose hair from drugs, to have surgery to remove her breast, to die by degrees. It is easy to say that Ruthann should come down from that cliff, unless you are Ruthann.

I know better than anyone what it feels like to have someone else make choices for you, when you deserve to be making them yourself.

I look at Ruthann, and very slowly, I nod.

She smiles at me, and so I am her witness – as she unwraps the wedding robe from her narrow shoulders and holds it across her back like the wide wings of a hawk. As she steps off the edge of the cliff and rises to the Spirit World. As the owls bear her body to the broken ground.

As soon as I can get a satellite signal, I call the tribal police and tell them where they can find Ruthann's body. I let Greta off her leash and toss her the stuffed moose, her reward for making a find.

I won't tell anyone what I saw. I won't tell them that I had a chance to stop her. Instead, I will say that this is how Greta and I found Ruthann. I will tell the police that I must have been minutes too late.

In fact, I got there just in time.

I pick up my cell phone again, and dial another number. 'Please come get me,' I say, when he answers, and it takes me a while to find the rest of the words I need – where I am, where he is, how long it will take to reach me.

Yesterday morning, before the Home Dance, when the golden eagle was still on the roof waiting for the katsinas, another eagle arrived. The two birds spent the afternoon in quiet company. Ruthann said sometimes that will happen: the eagle's mother visits. And at the end of the day, she flies off, leaving her son behind to do what he has to do.

I wonder if the mother eagle will come back to the village now, and see that her offspring is missing. I think maybe she won't. I think maybe she knows to look for him in better places.

Louise Masáwistiwa arrives at Sipaulovi that evening. Dressed in a business suit, with her thick black hair chopped into a trendy bob, she could not look more different from her mother if she tried.

She is bent over Wilma's kitchen table, her hands wrapped around a mug of tea, when I meet her. Her eyes are red; her features are Ruthann's. 'You must be the one who found her at Tawaki,' she says.

I have since learned that Ruthann committed suicide at a special site, one with petroglyphs dating back to 750 B.C. No one is allowed there without an archaeological permit, and if you walk along the basin opposite the cliffs, you will eventually wind up in Walnut Canyon, and the cliff dwellings. 'I'm so sorry,' I tell Louise.

'She never wanted to get treatment. She only said she would because I argued with her about it. I argued with her about everything.'

Louise reaches for a paper napkin from a holder in the center of the table and wipes her eyes, blows her nose. 'They found a lump in her breast four months ago. They did surgery that same week. It was a pretty aggressive tumor, but the doctors thought that maybe with some chemo and radiation, they'd be able to keep it under control. I probably could have told them right then and there that no one could ever keep my mother under control.'

'I think,' I say carefully, 'that Ruthann knew what she wanted.'

Louise stares down at the checkered plastic tablecloth. A handful of pennies are scattered on the red squares, like a makeshift checkerboard. She picks a few up, curls her fist around them. 'My mother taught me how to count coins,' she says quietly. 'I couldn't get it right for the longest time. I thought a dime was a penny, because it was smaller. But my mother wouldn't give up. She told me that if I was going to understand anything in this world, it ought to be change.' Louise wipes at her eyes. 'I'm sorry. It's just . . . it's crazy, isn't it, the way we always say that children belong to their parents, when it's really the other way around?'

I suddenly remember being very little and being embraced by my father. I would try to put my arms around my father's waist, hug him back. I could never reach the whole way around the equator of his body; although I'd squeeze hard, he was that much larger than life. Then one day, I could do it. I held him, instead of him holding me, and all I wanted at that moment was to have it back the other way.

Louise opens her hand so that the coins fall like rain. 'Wouldn't you know it,' she says, her mouth curving into a smile. 'Now I work at a bank.'

Sophie and I stand on the edge of Second Mesa, underneath the shadow of a circling hawk. 'What it means,' I explain, 'is that Ruthann isn't here anymore.'

She looks up at me. 'Is she where Grandpa is?'

'No. Grandpa's going to come back,' I say, although I don't know if this is true. 'When you die, it means you go away, forever.'

'I don't want Ruthann to go away.'

'Me neither, Soph.'

Because I need to, I reach down and haul her into my arms. She wraps herself around me, her lips pressed to my ear. 'Mommy,' she says, 'I want to go wherever you do.'

Had I said that once, to my mother?

At the sound of footsteps behind us, I turn around. Fitz walks forward slowly, not sure whether it's all right to interrupt. 'Thank you for coming,' I say, and the words come out too stiff.

'I owed you one,' Fitz answers.

I look down at the ground. He doesn't ask me what happened; he doesn't ask me why I've called him and not Eric. He knows, without me saying so, that I can't talk about that either yet. 'I know I told you to go to hell,' I say, 'but I'm glad you ignored me.'

'Delia, that newspaper story—'

'You know what?' I say, trying to keep my voice from

breaking. 'Right now, I don't need a journalist. But I sure could use a friend.'

He hunches his shoulders. 'I have references.'

I offer up the smallest smile, a bridge between us. 'Actually,' I confess, 'you're the only one who applied.'

We have just gotten into the car to drive back to Phoenix when the snow begins to fall, a freak act of nature. It starts as a few stray flurries, and then sticks to the ground. Dogs leap around, skidding trails with their paws; children come out of the houses edging the plaza to catch snowflakes on their tongues. Derek and Wilma, in the middle of the funeral preparations for Ruthann, stop what they are doing to look up at the sky. They will tell each other, and the people of Sipaulovi, that this is proof Ruthann has made it to the Spirit World.

But I think this sign might also be for me. Because as Fitz drives away from Second Mesa toward Phoenix, the snow falls harder, blanketing the hood and the windshield and the mesas and the highway until the land is as white as the robe of a Hopi bride, as white as winter mornings in New Hampshire. As a child, I would stand at my window to see the folds of snow draped over my house and Eric's and Fitz's, like a sorcerer's scarf. It was easy to pretend that underneath, everything had disappeared – shrubs and brick paths and soccer balls, hedges and fences and property lines. It was easy to pretend that when the magician pulled away his kerchief, the world would start over from scratch.

I don't think Fitz is at all surprised when I ask him to make a detour on our way home. He waits in the parking lot with Sophie and Greta, who are asleep in the backseat of the car. 'Take your time,' he says, as I walk into the jail.

There is only one other inmate with a visitor. My father sits down on the other side of that wall of Plexiglas and picks up the phone. 'Is everything all right?'

I look at him in his stripes, with a bandage wrapped around his left hand and a healing cut on his temple, with a nervous tremor that makes him keep glancing to the side, to see if someone is coming up behind him, and I cannot believe that *he* is asking *me* that question.

'Oh, Daddy,' I say, all the tears coming at once.

He balls his hand into a fist and then, from the core of it, pulls a plume of a Kleenex – sleight of hand. But then he remembers that he can't get the tissue to me through the barrier of the wall, or over the telephone connection. He smiles faintly. 'Guess I haven't learned that trick yet.'

When we did our magic show for the seniors, my father had had to convince me to do the vanishing act. He explained the reality to me – *out of sight is out of mind* – but I still believed that once the black curtain came down, I'd be gone for good. I was so nervous that he cut the tiniest of holes in the curtain for me. If I could keep an eye on him, he said, then surely I wouldn't really disappear.

I had forgotten about that hole until just now. It makes me wonder if I had remembered, even unconsciously, the way we had run away from home. If even at six years old, I had to learn to trust him to bring me back.

Maybe if it hadn't been such an awful day, I would have noticed that on the ride home from the jail, Fitz has gotten quieter and quieter. But I've been thinking of Ruthann, and my father. It isn't until we pull up to the trailer and I see Eric's car outside that I panic. Two days ago, which feels more like two hundred, I had left him behind in the hospital, angry at him for doing the job I had asked him to do. 'Come in,' I beg Fitz, turning to him like I always do for support. 'Be a buffer.'

'I can't.'

'Pretty please,' I say. I glance into the backseat, where Sophie is still snoring in little puffs beside the dog. 'You can carry her in.'

Fitz looks at me, his face expressionless. 'No. I'm busy.'

'Doing what?'

When he rounds on me, angry, it is so unlike the Fitz I

know that I find myself shrinking back against the passenger seat. 'For God's sake, Delia, I just drove six hundred miles for you, and you weren't even technically speaking to me.'

Heat rises to my cheeks. 'I'm sorry. I thought . . .'

'What? That I have nothing better to do? That I don't have a life? That I might not spend all that time with you wishing I was doing this?' His hands lock on each side of my face and he pulls me forward, like gravity. When his mouth seals over mine it is brutal, bitter. The stubble of beard on his face leaves a mark on my skin, raw and shaped like regret.

He isn't Eric, and so our lips don't move in a familiar rhythm. He isn't Eric, and so our teeth grit against each other. He holds the back of my head, as if he is afraid I will break away. My heart beats so hard I begin to feel it in forgotten places: behind my eyes, at the base of my throat, between my legs.

'*Mommy?*'

Fitz immediately releases me, and we both turn around to see Sophie watching us curiously from her car seat. 'Oh, Jesus,' he murmurs.

'Sophie, honey,' I say quickly, 'you're having a dream.' I fumble for the door latch and step out of the car, then reach into the back and haul my daughter into my arms. 'Isn't it funny, the things we think we see when we're sleeping?'

She sinks into my shoulder, boneless, as Greta bounds out of the car. By now, Fitz is standing outside, too. 'Delia—'

A light goes on in the trailer, and the door opens. Eric, bare-chested and wearing boxers, comes down the aluminum stairs. He takes Sophie out of my arms, a transaction of commerce.

Before we can say anything to each other, the sound of Fitz's car engine slices the night in half. He peels away, leaving a cloud of dust and grit in his wake.

'Ruthann's sister called to see if you got home,' Eric says quietly, so that he doesn't wake Sophie. 'She told me what happened.' I follow him up the steps, wait to answer until he has laid Sophie down in our bed and pulled up the covers. He closes the door to the tiny bedroom and then puts his hands on my shoulders. 'You all right?'

I would like to tell him about the Hopi reservation, where the very ground you are standing on might crumble beneath your feet. I'd like to tell him that an owl can spell out the future. I'd like to explain what it looks like to watch someone fall twenty stories and to see, at the same time, a storm in the shape of her body begin to climb into the sky.

I'd like to apologize.

But instead I find myself going to pieces. Eric sits down on the floor of the trailer with me in his arms. He lets me keep all my words to myself.

'Dee,' he says after a while, 'will you promise me something?'

I draw away, wondering if he, like Sophie, saw what had happened in the car. 'What?'

He swallows hard. 'That I won't wind up like your mother.'

My heart cinches. 'You won't start drinking again, Eric.'

'I wasn't talking about alcoholism,' he says. 'I was talking about losing you.'

Eric kisses me so tenderly that it unravels me. I kiss him back, trying to find the same depth of faith. I kiss him back, although I can still taste Fitz, like a stolen candy tucked high against my cheek, sweet when I least expect it.

VII

'I have done it,' says my memory.
'I cannot have done it,' says my pride,
refusing to budge. In the end – my
memory yields.
– Friedrich Nietzsche, *Beyond Good and Evil*,
'Fourth Part: Maxims and Interludes'

Andrew

'**D**rink this,' Concise says, and he holds up a bottle of shampoo.

I look at him as if he is crazy. 'No way. It'll make me sick.'

'Well, sure it will, fool. Everyone wants to know where that bullet went. You ain't gonna wait for it to come out the other end.'

In the wake of the fight in the rec yard, Sticks has been sent to the hospital for ophthalmological surgery, the blow dart embedded deep in his eye. He'll be sequestered for a disciplinary stint, but eventually he'll be back, and we will pick up where we left off.

Taking the shampoo bottle out of Concise's hand, I swallow half the contents. A moment later I charge for the toilet in the cell, bracing my hands on the bowl.

'No, it'll go down the sewer!' Concise grabs my shoulders and pivots me so that I vomit into the stainless-steel bowl of the sink. The bullet hits the drain with a ping.

'That,' Concise says, grinning, 'is fuh sheezy.' He reaches under the bunks and tosses me a towel.

It is when I turn around to catch it that I notice Fetch lurking outside our cell. A gangly stickbug of a kid, with White Pride tattoos curled around his biceps like asps, he's one of Sticks's posse. And he's been watching every move we've made.

'Yo, cracker,' Concise calls out. 'You want to squeal to Sticks, we got a message for him.' He points his finger at Fetch, a makeshift gun. '*Bang,*' he says.

In this jail, the whites control the inflow of hard drugs, and in

our pod, the contact for goods is Sticks. Concise and his hooch
are small-time runners by comparison. The drugs get smuggled in off the streets. They're offered to the members of the
Aryan Brotherhood upstairs in close custody first, then whites
in general populations, and finally to other races. Money is
exchanged by acquaintances on the outside – any massive
transfer of funds in jail accounts would immediately trigger
suspicion from the DOs.

Sticks, now wearing a patch over his left eye, has just come
in from an AA meeting, a prime place to make deals. It has
been two weeks since the incident in the rec yard, but that
might as well be yesterday in jail. He walks toward my stool
and kicks it. 'You're in my way,' he says.

'I'm not in your way.'

Sticks shoves me three feet forward. 'You're in my way,'
he repeats.

Concise and Blue Loc are a sudden, implacable wall. They
stand with their arms crossed, their muscles dark and flexed.
Outnumbered, Sticks backs off.

Concise and I walk up the stairs side by side. We don't
speak until we have turned the corner on the landing. 'What
he say to you?' Concise asks.

'Nothing.'

We both stop dead in the entryway to our cell. The entire
space has been tossed – towels flung into the toilet, food stores
emptied, bottles of Concise's hooch opened and spilled in
puddles across the floor. One of our mattresses has been
ripped in half, small tumbleweeds of yellowed foam are all
over the floor.

'Sticks and his peckerwood buddies did this,' Concise says.
'You know what they were lookin' for,' he adds, and it isn't a
question.

For the first time that day, I stop doubting Concise – who
has insisted that the bullet cannot be left hidden in our cell,
who would not listen to my protests when I told him I absolutely, positively, was not going to do what he suggested I do.

For the first time that day I am fully aware of the small metal missile I pushed deep inside of me that morning, a suppository full of vengeance.

To become a member of a prison gang, you might as well start in jail. Prospective members of the Aryan Brotherhood, the Mau Mau, and the Mexican Mafia – or EME, as they call themselves – are recommended by made members. A yes vote, taken among other members, lets you in on probation. Probates are subject to a background check – no crimes against children, no being a source for anyone in law enforcement – and you are given a sponsor, a member who takes you under his wing.

For the Aryan Brotherhood, a probate has to prove himself for two years. You will be expected to keep weapons hidden with you. You will be asked to fight. You will be expected to ferry drugs from one place to another. If you have drug connections, you will be expected to supply the members. If you make money from any of this, you have to share it with everyone.

At the end of two years, you will be assigned a hit – a murder sanctioned by the governing force of your gang. For the Aryan Brotherhood, that's three particular inmates in the Special Management Unit of the Arizona State Prison.

You will be given a weapon and told how to commit the murder. Your sponsor will come with you, when it's time. After all, if there is an eyewitness to a murder you've committed, you most likely won't squeal . . . and since there was an eyewitness to a murder *he* committed, he isn't squealing, either. It is one big pyramid scheme.

Once you've done your job, you will be allowed to put on a wet patch – a tattoo. Gothic letters – AB – scraped into the skin of your arm or chest or neck or back. You must be in prison to be inked, so some time may pass between your hit and when you officially become a gang member.

If a made member has the chance to take care of a sanctioned hit and misses the opportunity, it's a mistake punishable by death at the hands of his own kind.

A few days later, we are in the pod watching the news when a local update comes on. At these, everyone perks up – if there's a report of crime, there's an excellent chance someone in the pod knows who committed it. Today, there is word of a raging fire in the Phoenix area.

The reporter is a tiny woman with hair the same color as the flames. 'Police say a meth lab may be to blame for this morning's fatal fire, which destroyed a home in the North Phoenix area on Deer Valley Road last night. Firefighters were called in after an explosion took the life of Wilton Reynolds. At this hour . . .'

There is a mighty roar behind me, and the sound of a garbage can being overturned. When I look over my shoulder, I see Concise standing over the mess. The DOs immediately rise to attention, so I turn to the control booth. 'It was an accident,' I say, righting the can. I grab Concise by the arm and pull him upstairs to our cell. 'What are you *doing?*'

He sits down. 'Sinbad's my brother.'

'Sinbad?'

'That homey they were talking about on the news.'

It takes me a moment to understand that Concise is referring to the victim in the fire. 'You mean the meth cook?'

'He told me he knew what he was doin',' Concise mutters.

'You said you had two sisters.'

'He's my *brother,*' Concise repeats, stressing the metaphor. 'I grew up with him on the streets. This was gonna be our big thing.'

'*You* were in business making meth? Do you have any idea what that drug does to people?'

'We weren't givin' it away,' Concise snaps. 'If someone was fool enough to mess himself up, that was his problem.'

I shake my head, disgusted. 'If you build it, they will come.'

'If you build it,' Concise says, 'you cover your rent. If you build it, you pay off the loan sharks. If you build it, you put shoes on your kid's feet and food in his belly and maybe even show up every now and then with a toy that every other goddamn kid in the school already has.' He looks up at me. 'If you build it, maybe your son don't have to, when he grow up.'

It is amazing – the secrets you can keep, even when you are living in close quarters. 'You didn't tell me.'

Concise gets up and braces his hands against the upper bunk. 'His mama OD'd. He lives with her sister, who can't always be bothered to take care of him. I try to send money so that I know he's eatin' breakfast and gettin' school lunch tickets. I got a little bank account for him, too. Jus' in case he don't want to be part of a street gang, you know? Jus' in case he want to be an astronaut or a football player or somethin'.' He digs out a small notebook from his bunk. 'I'm writin' him. A diary, like. So he know who his daddy is, by the time he learn to read.'

It is always easier to judge someone than to figure out what might have pushed him to the point where he might do something illegal or morally reprehensible, because he honestly believes he'll be better off. The police will dismiss Wilton Reynolds as a drug dealer and celebrate one more criminal permanently removed from society. A middle-class father who meets Concise on the street, with his tough talk and his shaved head, will steer clear of him, never guessing that he, too, has a little boy waiting for him at home. The people who read about me in the paper, stealing my daughter during a custody visit, will assume I am the worst sort of nightmare.

I run my hands over my scalp – fuzzy, now that the hair is growing in again. 'It's the phosgene gas,' I tell him.

'What?'

'That's what killed your friend. The chemical reaction necessary to make meth produces a lethal gas. If you disconnect your tubes the wrong way, you die.'

Concise blinks at me. '*You* a meth cook, too?'

'No. But I've got advanced degrees in chemistry.' I sit down and motion for the notebook Concise is still holding. I rip a page out of the back and then rummage underneath my pillow for a pencil – sharp enough, it makes a good weapon to sleep with in your hand.

It takes me a few minutes and several corrections, but when I have the reactions down right, I hand the recipe to Concise. 'Find another friend. This'll work.'

'No way. You ain't gettin' involved. This ain't who you are.' He crumples up the paper and tosses it on the floor of the cell.

Who I am, and what I am capable of doing, has always managed to surprise me. I think about the day I ran away with you; how I took you to a diner and let you order every single dessert on the menu, so that you would think the best of me before you could begin to think the worst.

I reach for the paper. 'Your son,' I say. 'What's his name?'

The first thing you need to make meth is a lot of friends, because drugstores limit the number of cold tablets a single person can buy at once. They come in boxes of twenty-four, and you need thousands to get the right amount of pseudo-ephedrine. You also need rubber tubing and faucet coupling, acetone, and alcohol. Muriatic acid, cat litter, and duct tape. Iodine crystals and flasks and beakers. Red phosphorus – the stuff on the heads of matches, but in far greater supply. You'll need coffee filters and funnels and lye and cleaning gloves. You'll need a Pyrex pie plate and canning jars with lids.

Grind the pills into powder in a blender. Put this into a canning jar. Fill with alcohol, cover, and shake until it settles. Filter this through more alcohol, several times. Pour the liquid into pie plates and microwave until the liquid evaporates. Crush the powder as fine as you can, rinse with acetone, and set the residue into another plate. Break it apart and let it dry.

In the meantime, set up your glassware.

★

I have been in jail for twenty-five days when I am given a nickname by the blacks: The Chemist. I learn a new vocabulary: Glass is meth that's been washed in acetone and has very few impurities, therefore costing more. A teener is a sixteenth of an ounce. An eight ball is an eighth of an ounce. A quarter – of a gram, that is – is the usual injected dose and goes for $25 on the streets. A dime bag is ten dollars' worth. Tweaking is being high on meth. To be spun is to be tweaking for too long. Sketching is the state between these two.

I try not to think about the actual drug transactions, about the strangers I am harming. But there is a part of me that knows they are the price I'm paying for my safety in this jail, and the protection of the blacks. There is a part of me that whispers, *I told you so. You ruined one life, what made you think you wouldn't ruin a hundred more?*

An army of spies on the outside become the arms and legs of the operation. They buy the supplies, make the meth, and set up bank accounts for Concise and me. I didn't want any profits, but Concise was adamant – if I was taking the risk, I was taking the rewards, too – and so I conceded. I imagine using the funds to keep kids like Concise's son off the streets – a senior center, maybe, but for the younger, more desperate set.

It brings me right back to the question I've been circling since I got here: Once you make a mistake, can any amount of compensation erase it?

Concise locates diabetics in different pods who can steal syringes from the outpatient clinic where they go for their insulin shots. Most users prefer to shoot up, which is why the needles are in high demand, but meth can also be smoked, snorted, or mixed with coffee or juice.

He has a full list of customers before the first batch is even ready.

On the day that jury selection begins for my trial, I am given a suit and blue shirt. I don't recognize it, and I find myself stroking the fabric and wondering if you picked it out on my behalf. I am so overwhelmed by the thought of putting on something, anything, other than stripes that I don't realize at first how upset Concise is. 'Chicken Neck Mike ain't gonna be in place for the drop-off,' he says.

He hands me a letter from an inmate in a different pod. Since prisoners aren't allowed to communicate with one another, it's been kited: Someone on the outside has received the note from Mike, and mailed it back to Concise. According to the note, Mike is supposed to smuggle in the first shipment of meth today when he goes to the courthouse for sentencing, but his attorney rescheduled the date, and therefore Chicken Neck Mike will miss the transfer.

'Well,' I say after a moment. *'I'm* going to be there.'

Inmates are shackled together for the transfer to the court-house. We carry our alter egos under our arms – jeans and muscle tees, button-down shirts, a suit. At the courthouse the chains are unlocked, and we are allowed to change. Eric has forgotten to bring me socks; so I slide my bare feet into my loafers.

We are led en masse to the courtroom and seated in the jury box together; one by one we will be called to a table beside our attorneys. Eric isn't here yet, and I'm grateful: I would not want him to see what I am about to do.

There is no difference, of course, between providing the recipe that launches thousands of grams of methamphetamine or being the physical link that transports it back to the jail – you are implicated by your actions either way – but in some corner of my mind, being an active participant in smuggling drugs is more shameful.

Concise has told me that Blue Loc's girlfriend will pass me what I need to bring back. 'You jus' sit there,' Concise said to me, 'and let the stuff come to you.'

For nearly a half hour, I wait in the jury box; watching lawyers filter into the courtroom and talk to one another, or read through their motions. The judge is nowhere in sight. I admire the soaring ceiling, the span between walls – architecture that I've forgotten.

A young woman hurries down the center aisle and corrals a deputy. She is wearing a pinstriped suit that clings to the curves of her waist and hips, and sensible black heels. Her cornrowed hair has been twisted into a neat knot, and her skin is the color of maple syrup. 'Yes, I'm a paralegal for Eric Talcott,' I hear her say, and she points right at me. 'He needs his client to review a motion for today's appearance. If I could just . . .' She smiles into his eyes.

A moment later, she comes toward me. 'Mr. Talcott wanted you to take a look at this,' she says, and she leans over the divider of the jury box with a manila folder.

There is absolutely nothing written on the papers in the file. She points to them and whispers, *'Nod.'* I do, and a tiny knotted balloon slides out of the crease of the folder to drop softly between my feet.

She snaps her folder shut and makes her way out of the courtroom. I try to imagine her with Blue Loc when he is not Blue Loc, but just some guy living with a girl downtown. Then I bend down and tuck the balloon into my fist. Slip it into the waistband of my pants.

Eric arrives a few minutes later and asks the deputy's permission to approach me, too. By now, I'm sweating so hard there are stains beneath my arms. I feel like I'm on the verge of passing out. 'You okay?' he asks.

'Great. Fine.'

He gives me a funny look. 'What the hell was that deputy talking about? Some paralegal wanted to see you?'

'It was a mistake. She was looking for a different guy named Hopkins.'

Eric shrugs. 'Whatever. Look, what's going to happen today—'

'Eric,' I interrupt. 'Is there any chance you can get me out to use the bathroom?'

He glances at me, then at the deputy. 'Let me see.'
Apparently, I am enough of a physical wreck to merit a special
break, because a different deputy is summoned to escort me
to the restroom. He stands outside the stall and whistles while
I drop my pants. From behind my ear I take the dollop of
ointment Concise gave me that morning for this purpose – a
'keep on person' medication for skin lesions. Grimacing, I wipe
the salve over the little white balloon, until it is lubricated
enough to be pushed into my rectum.

Ten minutes later, I take my seat at the defense table
beside Eric. I keep my eyes on the parade of potential jurors
who walk through the courtroom doors. I scrutinize the
woman with acne, the man who keeps checking his watch,
the freckled girl who looks just as frightened to be here as I
am. They take the jury surveys that Eric hands out. Some
of them glance at me with narrowed eyes, others purposely
keep their expressions blank. I wish I could speak to them.
I would tell them that they couldn't possibly judge me any
more harshly than I've judged myself. I would tell them that
when you look at a person, you never know what they're
hiding.

Wear gloves. Run water through your Alyn condenser. Very
quickly add your red phosphorus, using a coat hanger to
unclog it if you have to. It's the exothermic reaction you're
looking for, and it will be immediate. Quickly plug the top that
leads to your vinyl tubing, and tape the connection.

When yellow fumes rise from the mixture, shake the
condenser. If the pressure gets too high, put the flask into an
ice bath until it slows down. Eventually, the mixture will swell
up, like a mousse, and then recede.

At some point the cat litter in the milk jug at the other end
of your setup will turn hot and purple. Disconnect the rubber
tubing from the Alyn condenser. Cut the vinyl tubing off as
close to the milk jug as you can. Cover immediately with duct
tape.

Be careful. Do not untape. Inside is the phosgene gas that killed your friend.

Twitch is a twenty-two-year-old who looks fifty. He hangs out in the corners of the rec yard, peeling scabs that fester between his fingers and toes and sniffing at the blood that wells up and still reeks of the meth that runs through his system. When he smiles at you, which isn't often, you can see the black holes where he's lost teeth, and the plush white carpet of his tongue.

Most of the time he is spun out – too high on meth to sleep – and subject to hallucinations. He's not a violent addict, but a paranoid one, and recently he's become certain that the DOs are bodysnatchers. He plucks at my shirt as I walk by him. 'How much longer,' he whispers. He is talking about our supply.

That initial balloon I smuggled in from the court was given to the Mau Mau upstairs in close custody – the black prison gang members. Having given his tithe, Concise has opened the proverbial door for business.

Our first in-house batch arrived in a Bible. The same girl who'd played paralegal at court for me brought a leather-bound edition to the minister who leads the Baptist services here. She cried as she explained how her boyfriend – Concise, this particular day – had found Jesus, and how she'd inscribed a Bible specially for him, only to be told by the detention officers that inmates were only allowed books arriving directly from Amazon.com. Was there any possible way that the minister might be able to get this gift to her boyfriend?

What self-respecting minister would ever turn down a request like that?

When Concise received the Bible during his next appearance at services, he thanked the minister profusely, and then came back to the cell and thanked God. Hidden in the spine, under carefully reglued leather, was an ounce of meth to be sold. That ounce, which would net $1,000 on the streets, was worth $400 a gram in prison – or, as Concise figured, $11,200.

Twitch grabs my sleeve again, and I shake him off. 'I told

you, I'm not the one who makes the deals.' I turn away just in time to witness a transaction going down between Concise and Flaco, one of the Mexican Nationals.

'It's a hundred fifty,' Concise says.

Flaco's eyes darken. 'You sold Tastee Freak the same quarter gram for a C-note.'

Concise shrugs. 'Tastee Freak ain't no spic.'

Flaco agrees to the price and leaves; he will be given his prize after Concise receives word of a money transfer from his friends outside. 'You taxed him,' I say, walking up to Concise. 'Isn't that . . . isn't it . . .'

I am about to say 'wrong,' but realize what a stupid distinction it is.

'Why?' I ask. 'Because he's Mexican?'

'Now, that would be jus' plain racist of me,' Concise says, and he grins. 'It's because he ain't black.'

From a rec yard rap:

> Sittin' in a four-corner cellblock
> My weapon is a shank, not a Glock.
> Early in the mornin' the cells pop
> Off to the chow hall is our next stop
> Eatin' cold-ass eggs, that's what it was
> See my homeboy Coast, what up, cuzz?
> Mobbin' the yard, our car is deep
> We always strapped and ready to creep.
> Hit the iron pile, gettin' swoll to the hub
> Ready to war with any scrub
> My big bro Snoop gave us word
> Shit is gonna jump is what he heard
> So post up and get ready to stick
> Any mutha fucca that tries somethin' slick
> The handball court was the spot
> To run steel in a fool was my plot
> Me and this fool on the killin' field

I shanked him in the necc, it got real.
When his punk-ass gasped, I hit him again
Ran my shank right under his chin.
I left the punk dead in his traccs
187 tat on my bacc
In this cell I'm left to rot
Doin' life on a murder plot
I don't care, I'll do it again
Doin' twenty-five to life in the state pen.

The diabetic who has been providing Concise with needles also gets him an asthma inhaler, traded from an emphysemic inmate. At night, after lights out, he scrapes the head and foot off the thin tin canister, fashioning a hollow tube. He carefully pries the cylinder open by applying pressure with a toothbrush until it is a flat piece of metal, ready for shaping.

It will become a zip gun, a deadly chamber for the bullet we're still hiding.

When I am out of the cell, I make sure Concise will be present to stand guard over our treasure. If he's going to be gone, too, one of us hides it on our bodies. We treat this tiny missile of gunpowder with the care and reverence a new parent would give an infant.

Tonight, Concise is working on his weapon harder than usual. 'Do you ever think about what you'll do, on the outside?' I ask quietly.

'No.'

His flat denial surprises me. 'There's got to be something you'd like to do.'

'The world ain't no Hallmark commercial, Chemist,' Concise says. 'Most of us are just doin' life on the installment plan.'

'You could move away with your son. Find a job some-where.'

'Doin' what?' Concise asks. 'You think people go out of their way to hire brothers with a prison record?' He shakes his head. 'Whether or not you get inked in here, you leave with a tattoo.'

I'd like to think that we can be a hundred different people in one lifetime. But maybe Concise is on to something; maybe once you change, there's a piece that stays that way forever. Until, eventually, you cannot remember who you were in the first place.

Concise rubs the edge of the zip gun more furiously along the cement. 'What's the rush?' I ask.

Rumors about an upcoming race riot spread like smoke; usually they are so thick in the cells you can barely breathe for all the guarded anticipation. But I have heard nothing. In fact, Sticks spent most of the afternoon in his cell, brooding.

'The white boys jus' lost their supplier,' Concise says. 'He got beat to death on the outside. Sticks gotta find himself some drugs, or he ain't gonna get his patch.'

For all that Sticks controls the whites in our pod, he is still taking orders from someone upstairs in close custody, someone who will expect him to find a new source.

'He's going to come to us?' If Concise taxes the Mexicans, I can only imagine what fine he'll impose on the whites.

'He gonna come,' Concise confirms. 'But that don' mean we got to sell it to him.'

Once you have filtered out your solids, add naphtha to the jar. When the mixture separates, add lye. Stir, so that it doesn't boil over.

Pour the contents into a coffeemaker pot. When the mixture separates again, pour the top layer into the liter bottle with a sports top. Shake hard for five minutes.

When the liquid settles, invert the bottle, and pour the bottom layer onto a pie plate. A pH strip dipped into the contents should turn red.

Microwave the pie plate until the water evaporates off. The crystals left behind are the finished product.

★

There are certain corners of hallways in this jail where the surveillance cameras don't spy. One stretch is where church and AA meetings are held, another is leading out to the infirmary. These are the spots for a well-placed elbow to the kidney, or a slip of a shank. Whether or not you intend to do so, you speed up as you round the turns.

I am just returning from the GED course meeting – my Ph.D. in chemistry seems insignificant when compared to an entire hour outside bars – when I feel a hand grab me and push me against the wall. A toothbrush, its handle scraped sharp as a knife, is held to the skin of my throat.

I assume it is Sticks. So when I hear, instead, a Mexican accent, I am almost relieved. 'Tell the *miyate* we don't want to pay extra,' Flaco says.

I can smell the sour stink of urine, and I realize it's mine. He lets go of me; I fall onto my hands and knees. 'And if you don't listen, gringo,' he threatens, 'I know a nice detention officer who will.'

When I get back to the cell, Concise is going through his mail. A packet from his lawyer's return address – a forgery – contains a legal pad full of notes. Concise has pulled back the gummy red fixative at the top of the pad to reveal a tiny square cut through the layers of pages, making a little pocket for contraband. Inside is a tiny plastic bag no bigger than a tooth, filled with our second batch of meth. As I enter the cell, he sniffs and makes a face. 'What happened to you?'

'Flaco would like you to reconsider taxing Mexicans.' I turn away from him, strip. Pull on my spare pair of stripes and wad the soiled ones into a ball.

'Flaco's a fool. He's on the fence with the Chicanos, anyway – he screwed up his first assigned hit for the EMEs.'

I sink down onto the lower bunk. 'Concise, he's threatening to tell the DOs.'

Concise walks toward me and reaches out one finger. He touches it to the spot on my neck where Flaco had held his shank. I brush my fingers across the skin and they come away bloody.

'It's nothing.'

Concise's nostrils flare, a bellows. 'It ain't nothin'.' He flattens his palms across the globe of his shaved head; palpable thought. 'You're out.'

'Out of what?'

'The game. The business. The whole thing.'

Astounded, I just stare at him for a second.

'You a liability, man. You got too many enemies in here, because you white but you don' act white. I can't take that kind of risk.' He begins to reseal the razor pocket in the legal pad. 'I'll buy you out, fair and square.'

When you are in jail, trust becomes a commodity more rare than gold. How can you believe someone who has built a life out of lying? How can you close your eyes at night, knowing your cellmate has been arrested for murder? The answer is: Because you have to. The alternative – being a loner – is not really an alternative at all. You have to mesh into a group to survive, even if you are surrounded by people who have cheated and stolen their way into position beside you. You have to find someone worthy of watching your back, even if making that pact means admitting that you are just as flawed as everyone else here.

Having Concise, and the African Americans in the pod, standing up for me has afforded me a freedom from Sticks and his cronies. But more than that, it's given me something I haven't had for years: a sense of belonging. When you spend your life running by design, you may get far, but you rarely let yourself get close to anyone. I've had you, all I've ever wanted, but it has come at a price. I left the only woman I've ever loved; I never whiled away the hours with a fishing buddy; I kept chatty coworkers at a careful distance. When you let people into the inner sanctum of your life, you risk having them see the heart of you, and I couldn't chance that. In an odd, amazing way, Concise is the first friend I've had in nearly thirty years. It doesn't matter that he's a drug dealer; it doesn't matter that he is black; it doesn't matter that he's offering me an honorable discharge from an operation I never felt comfortable with in the first place. All I know is that a minute ago, it was us against them . . . and now it is not.

'You can't do this,' I say, my whole body starting to shake.

'I do whatever I want,' Concise snaps over his shoulder. 'Go on, get lost. You supposed to be good at that.'

I am off the bunk and on top of him before he can even finish his sentence. He is, in that instant, Sticks and Flaco and Elephant Mike and every faceless man and woman out there in the world who has passed judgment on me without hearing all the facts. He's younger and stronger, but I've come from behind to surprise him. I am able to knock him to the ground and pin him with my weight.

'You fool. You know what happen if the DOs find out you sellin'?' Concise grunts. 'It's a criminal investigation. It's time on top of the time you already gonna do.'

That is when I understand: Concise doesn't want to end this alliance between us; he wants to protect it. He is trying to save me before I can be implicated along with him.

At the altercation, a small crowd has gathered around the front of our cell – Blue Loc, poised to jump in and pull me off Concise, a small knot of White Pride boys who are cheering me on, and Sticks, who stands with his arms crossed, an inscrutable expression on his face.

One of the detention officers pushes through. 'What's going on?'

I relax my hold on Concise. 'We're good.'

The DO's eyes hone in on the cut on my neck, still bleeding.

'Cut myself shaving,' I say.

The guard doesn't buy a word of it. But the spark that could ignite this pod has dissipated; he's done all he needs to. As he pushes at the other inmates, getting them to disperse, Concise gets to his feet and shakes his clothes straight.

'I helped get you into this,' I tell him. 'I'm not leaving now.'

★

The next day is my last day for jury selection, and Concise's first day of trial. We are both headed over to the courthouse at the same time. 'Bet you got yourself a Brooks Brothers button-down shirt,' Concise says.

As a matter of fact, I do. 'What about it?'

He grins. 'Chemist, Brooks wasn't no brother.'

'I suppose you think I ought to go to court wearing pinstripes and spats.'

'Only if you're Al Capone.' Our conversation is interrupted as Twitch flings himself into our cell. 'I ain't conducting business now,' Concise says tersely.

The addict's eyes dart wildly. 'I'm doin' you a favor, man,' he says. 'Thought maybe you'd do me one, too.'

What he means is that in return for whatever information he thinks he can provide, we might give him a free teener. Concise folds his arms. 'I'm listenin'.'

'I heard one of the DOs talking when I was up in the infirmary this morning – they're using the Boss Chair,' Twitch says.

'Why should I believe you?'

Twitch shrugs. 'I'm not the one with a bullet up my ass.'

'If I come back from court and what you said is true,' Concise says, 'I'll give you what you want.'

At the promise of another hit, Twitch nearly floats out of the cell. Concise turns to me. 'We got to hide the bullet in here.'

I look at him like he's crazy. If we're both leaving the cell, and there's no one to watch over the prize possession, then our modus operandi is to take it with us. 'If Twitch ain't bullshittin', then today we ain't just gonna get strip searched. They gonna sit us down on a metal detector chair, too.'

Concise wriggles under the bottom bunk and starts to scrape the cement between the bricks. A few minutes of digging creates a hole deep enough to house the .22. He backs out from under the bed and starts rummaging through his personal items for toothpaste, and Metamucil. He mixes these together in the sink; scoops it into his palm. 'Keep an eye out,' he says; and he creeps under the bunk again, this time to grout.

Concise and I are handcuffed together for the trip back from the courthouse to the jail. He is quieter than usual, almost haunted. The sad fact about being in jail is that no matter how bad you think it is there, the reality of what you face in court is worse. I am only beginning to taste that bitter future; Concise has swallowed it whole today. 'So,' I say, trying to lift his spirits, 'you going to pull an OJ?'

He glances over his shoulder. 'Oh, yeah. I got them eatin' out of my hand, man.'

'But can you get a bloody glove over it?'

Concise laughs. We are buzzed in through the level slider, and strip searched once again before being allowed back into our pod. I follow him upstairs to our cell and fall onto the lower bunk. Distantly, I am aware of one of the DOs beginning his security walk. Late afternoon, the general noise level is at a high hum – guys hollering to one another across the common room or slamming a hand of cards down on a metal tabletop when they get gin, televisions blaring, toilets flushing, showers running.

Concise sinks down onto the stool, his hands between his knees. 'My lawyer says I'm looking at ten years,' he says after a moment. 'By the time I get out, my boy's gonna be as old as I was when I got jumped into the Crips.'

There's nothing to say; we both know that no matter how we try to convince ourselves we'll outrun our past, it always crosses the finish line first.

'Hey,' he says. 'Do us a favor and check the goddamn bricks.'

I get down on my hands and knees and start to crawl under the lower bunk. But I can smell it before I can even see the telltale hole: the pungent mint, the ground powder that dusts the cement floor.

Then there is a shot.

★

It is louder than you think. It echoes against the walls, and leaves me deaf. I shimmy out from underneath the bunk and catch Concise as he falls off the stool. His eyes roll back; his blood soaks me. 'Who did this?' I scream into the crowd that has already gathered. I try to find the shooter, but all I see are stripes.

Concise falls on top of me in a heavy tangle of limbs and desperation. *What is black and white and red all over*, I think, a joke Sophie once told me. I cannot remember her punch line, but I know a different one: *a black man dying in jail; a white one watching him go.*

I hear the crackle of a radio, and the jail comes alive with a web of response: *Officer needs assistance in three-two B pod. Man down. All officers on levels two and three respond to three-two B pod. David two, did you copy?*

David two copies: Ten-seventeen.

Inmates in B pod, lockdown.

Steel scrapes as the cell doors are shut.

I am dragged away from Concise. Someone is asking me if I'm hurt and looking at my arms and chest – places where I am covered in Concise's blood. I am handcuffed behind my back and led to the ghost town of the East Dayroom.

In the middle of all this, no one has bothered to turn off the television. Emeril's bursts of instruction are interrupted by the RN shouting to call 911; by a deep voice saying, 'More pressure'; by the jangling arrival of the Phoenix Fire Department paramedics.

'This is hot hot hot,' Emeril says.

They will take Concise to Good Samaritan Hospital, the closest trauma center. 'Hey,' I yell out, as he is carried past on a stretcher. 'Is he going to be okay?'

'He's dead,' a voice replies. 'But then, you already knew that, didn't you?'

When I look up, I see a tall, well-dressed black man with a detective's badge clipped to his belt. He stares at my uniform, covered with Concise's blood, and I realize that, like every other black man in the Madison Street Jail, he believes I am a killer.

The Homicide Division Offices at the General Investigation Division are near Thirty-fifth and Durango. I am kept waiting while the detectives systematically interrogate everyone else in the pod – from the officers and the blacks who say that just days ago Concise and I were fighting, to Fetch, the young white boy who watched me vomit out the bullet after the rec yard fight.

Whoever did this knows that no one will believe a white man and a black man in jail might forge a friendship. Whoever did this knows that the blacks will assume I was the one who killed Concise – after all, everyone knows it is my bullet that went into him. The whites, for once, will agree with them.

Whoever did this was trying to punish both of us.

Detective Rydell has hooked me up to a CVSA – a voice stress analyzer. It's like a polygraph, only more accurate: It doesn't measure physiological reactions due to stress, but instead microtremors in a voice frequency range that the human ear can't hear. Microtremors are present only when a person isn't telling the truth, or so the detective tells me.

'I took a shower that morning,' I say. 'I knew I was going to court.'

'What time was that?'

'I don't know. Maybe eight o'clock.' I do not tell him about Twitch, and the Boss Chair, and about the way Concise and I carved a hole in the brickwork for our bullet. 'Then I read until it was time to leave the pod.'

'What did you read?'

'A novel, something from the jail library. Baldacci.'

Rydell folds his arms. 'You did nothing between approximately eight-fifteen A.M. and eleven?'

'I might have gone to the bathroom.'

He stares me down. 'Piss or shit?'

I rub a hand down my face. 'Can you tell me why the

answer to that is going to help you figure out who killed Concise?'

Rydell exhales heavily. 'Look, Andrew. You got to see this from my point of view. You're an educated man, thirty years the victim's senior. You aren't a career criminal. Yet you're telling me that you bonded with this guy. That you actually found something you had in common.'

I think about Concise, talking about his little boy. 'Yes.'

There is a moment of silence. 'Andrew,' Rydell says, 'help me to help you. How can we prove you didn't kill this guy?'

There is a knock on the door of the interview room, and the detective excuses himself to go speak with another investigator. After he lets himself out, I look down at my shirt. The blood has started to dry, stiff, against my chest. I wonder if someone has called Concise's son. I wonder if they'd even know how to find him.

The door opens again, and Rydell approaches with a face as blank as glass. 'We just found a zip gun in your buddy's locker. Care to comment?'

I can see it, buried under the stash of medications and food items that Concise had gotten from the canteen: the zip gun that he had been dutifully crafting to prevent a moment like this. I had assumed that it, too, had been stolen. But apparently, someone else had been making one, too.

I find myself fighting for breath, for logic. 'It wasn't used.'

Rydell doesn't even blink. 'There's no ballistics testing for a zip gun,' the detective says. 'But I bet you know that, being educated and all.'

I swallow hard. 'I'd like to speak to my attorney.'

I am given a telephone with a long cord, and Rydell stands over my left shoulder while I dial Eric's cell phone. I try three times, and am told over and over by a tinny voice that the person I am trying to reach is not available.

I am beginning to think that single sentence is the story of my life.

★

I am kept alone in a cell, since the detectives can't interrogate me until I reach Eric. In spite of the isolation, however, the rumors reach me. Flaco has been bragging to the *carnales*, the patch-holding New Mexican Mafia members. The white boys, he says, are too wimpy to pull off a stunt like this. Chicanos are the ones with the big *juevos*. The detectives ought to be speaking to the *real* man who killed that nigger.

Forty-eight hours after Concise's death – forty-eight hours during which I am unable to reach my attorney – the detectives take Flaco up on his offer to talk. During the interview, Flaco whips out a zip gun he's hidden beneath his testicles during the pat-down search prior to transfer to GID, and presents it to Detective Rydell.

There is only one inconsistency, one that anyone in B pod would realize and that the detectives don't: In jail you know exactly who has what weapon. Concise had been making a zip gun, one that has already been found in our cell, where he'd left it. Only one other zip gun existed in our pod, the one Sticks had tried to use on me during the rec yard fight.

The only weapon Flaco was known to have was the shank he'd made out of that toothbrush.

I think of what Concise told me once, of Flaco screwing up his first assigned hit. Killing Concise would help him save face and prove he's macho enough to be a soldier in the Mexican Mafia. If Flaco knew he was headed for a long prison sentence anyway, maybe he'd rather do it with the respect of the *carnales*.

But how had he gotten Sticks's zip gun?

The next day, I am brought back to GID to speak with Detective Rydell. 'Barium,' I say, the moment he comes into the room. 'And antimony compounds. Even if you can't match a bullet to a zip gun with ballistics, you can test for gunshot residue.'

'You can also test it for blood, since the most accurate way to use one is to press it up against the victim's head.' He leans forward. 'I've got two zip guns. One of them had blood residue on the edge. Coincidentally, that same gun tested positive for the chemical compounds you get when you fire a .22 round, which happens to be what was in your cellie's brain. The other zip gun,' he says, 'was the one we found in your cell.'

I fall back against the chair. I cannot find the strength to answer the detective when he tells me I am no longer a suspect.

I am relocated to general population again, this time on Level 2, and placed in a cell with a man nicknamed Hazelnut who has a habit of pulling his hair out in small tufts and weaving them with threads from the blanket into macramé. This, though, is better than the alternative – even if Flaco's in custody, I cannot expect the blacks to protect me anymore, and my status with the whites will not have changed. I wonder how long a body can last without any sleep; how many nights it will take me to make a shank.

I stop speaking, because I can't trust ordinary language anymore. Words, in spite of what you think, don't always stay fixed. Take 'emancipation': it might be reconfigured into a *maniac night op* or an *inanimate cop* or *maintain, cope.* 'Madison Street Jail' becomes *rationalism jested* or *slanted majorities.* 'Delia Hopkins,' by another name, could be *diaphone silk, akin polished, oedipal knish.* And 'Andrew Hopkins'? Shake it up a bit and you find *dank ownership. Orphans winked. Kidnaper shown.*

Only twenty-four hours into my residency on Level 2, I'm moved. Another inmate has requested a switch because he's been threatened by his cellie – a white boy named Hayseed. Hayseed specifically asked the DOs if he could cell with me instead, saying we are old friends.

We aren't friends. I don't even know him. My best guess is that he knows about the meth; maybe he thinks I have some on me. I enter the cell and take his measure: Hayseed is still a kid – all yellow hair and buck teeth. 'I hope you don't mind, man, about the switch. That other guy, he *reeked.* I don't think he showered in, like, three months. And I knew you were stuck with the Human Hairball; so I figured you might not mind a change of scenery.'

Hayseed likes to talk. He segues from the merits of Kabuta tractors over John Deere, to the fact that Nebraska is where Spam is made, to the barrettes he stole from the girls he raped and hid in the rotten core of a Ponderosa pine tree. I spend a lot of time staring at the upper bunk. *Hayseed: ash eyed, ye hades.* I count the number of coughs that ripple through the quiet after lights out. I do what it takes to stay awake, and think I've succeeded until the middle of the night, when I wake up to find that my nostrils and mouth are blocked, Hayseed's hand pressed tight against my flesh. I thrash out with my arms and legs; I try to reach for his wrists, but he is standing behind me and there are already stars at the corners of my vision.

'Wake up, Nigger-lover,' Hayseed whispers. 'Your spook shouldn't have refused to sell to the Brotherhood. It was enough to make the boys upstairs give the green light for the hit.' His palm grinds down against my jaw, my teeth. 'My brother said the nigger never even saw it coming.'

His *brother* killed Concise? What about Flaco?

'It was almost too easy, the way the spic volunteered to hide the gun after it was done. But Flaco didn't tell no one he was gonna say he'd made the hit, just so he could get his wet patch with the Mexican Mafia. *You* were supposed to go down for doing the deed.'

Hayseed leans close. 'My brother also wants me to give you something,' he says, and he parts his fingers wide enough for me to gulp for air. He kisses me full on the mouth. Without missing a beat, he backhands me across the cheek, so hard that I start bleeding.

'I don't know your brother,' I choke out, terrified.

'Guess he never did get a chance to tell you where he got his nickname,' Hayseed says. 'But then, a smart guy like you already knows that Nebraska's out in the *Sticks.'*

★

When Eric arrives the sun is just coming up. I still have cotton wadded into my broken nose, courtesy of the infirmary. One of my eyes has swelled shut. My throat is raw from the yelling I did to call the detention officers to the cell.

Eric stands up when I open the door to the conference room. 'I know I've been sort of . . . unreachable . . . for the past couple of days. I've been going through a rough – holy shit, Andrew!' When he sees the condition of my face, he goes pale. 'They didn't tell me—'

'I can't stay here,' I say wildly. 'You have to get me out.'

'Andrew, your trial starts in two—'

'I won't go back to that cell, Eric!'

He nods tightly. 'All right. I won't leave here until they put you in administrative segregation.' The words are a balm; all I've needed to hear. I find myself sinking to my knees, bowing to the floor like a supplicant.

I do not think I've ever cried in front of Eric; I don't think I've ever cried in front of anyone until two days ago. You make yourself strong because it's expected of you. You become confident because someone beside you is unsure. You turn into the person others need you to be.

'Andrew,' Eric says, and I can hear how he is embarrassed for me. But I know how much lower there is for me to sink – that's the difference between us.

'I can't do this,' I say.

'I know. I'm going to talk to—'

'I mean in the long run, Eric. I can't go to prison.' I meet his gaze, my eyes still damp. 'If I do, they'll kill me, too.'

Eric clasps my hand. 'I swear to you,' he vows. 'I'll get you acquitted.'

Like anyone else who finds himself adrift at sea, I reach for this lifeline. I believe him, and just like that, I remember how to float.

Fitz

If it had been easy for Romeo to get Juliet, nobody would have cared. Same goes for Cyrano and Don Quixote and Gatsby and their respective paramours. What captures the imagination is watching men throw themselves at a brick wall over and over again, and wondering if this is the time that they won't be able to get back up. For everyone who adores a happy ending, there's someone else who cannot help but rubberneck at the accident on the side of the road.

You wonder, though, what would have happened if Juliet's best friend started flirting with Romeo. If Gatsby got drunk one night and told Daisy how he really felt. If any of those poor romantic fools would have driven hours north to the Hopi reservation and doubled back, the word *sucker* fizzing like acid in their bellies as they sneaked glances across the car at the woman they loved, knowing she was going home to another man.

You wonder if any of them would have been as stupid as I was, and kissed her.

'Listen,' I say. 'It was an accident.'

One look and I can tell she isn't buying it.

'I promise it won't happen again.'

But Sophie narrows her eyes. 'Liar.'

I have taken her out for ice cream, mainly because the thought of staying away from Delia, after yesterday, was both what I wanted more than anything and equally impossible; and mostly because once I arrived on her doorstep we were both so mortified that I grabbed the first excuse I could, Sophie, and ran.

'Liar?' I repeat. 'Excuse me?'

'You kiss her all the time,' Sophie says. 'You hug her, too. When you come back from trips.'

Well, maybe. But they are the sideways pecks and careful embraces of a friend; one that keeps three inches of space between our bodies, so that we meet at the shoulders and then grow progressively farther away.

'She smells good, doesn't she?' Sophie asks.

'She smells great,' I agree.

'It's okay to kiss people when you love them.'

'I don't love your mother,' I tell her. 'Not like *that*, anyway.'

'You give her all your french fries, even when she won't give you back onion rings,' Sophie says. 'And when you say her name it sounds different.'

'How?'

Sophie thinks. 'Like it's covered with blankets.'

'I do not say your mother's name like it's covered in blankets. And I don't always give her my french fries, because you're right, she doesn't share.'

'But you still don't yell at her when she's not being fair,' Sophie points out. 'Because you don't want to hurt her feelings.' She slips her hand into mine and repeats, 'You love her.'

She runs toward the playground without me. It has been so long since I was Sophie's age that I've forgotten there are building blocks of love, and that the very bottom layer is comfort. When I was little, who was I most myself with? Who could I trust with my mistakes, my dreams, my history? My parents, my nursery school teacher. Delia, Eric. These were the first people I fell for.

Could it still really be that simple? Could romantic love and platonic love and parental love all be different facets of the same diamond – brilliant, no matter which face is turned up to the sun?

No, because I am not Sophie's age. No, because I know what it is to hear a woman sigh off the cloak of this world the moment she drifts asleep; no, because I have fallen into the meadow of her body. No, because puzzling through my sixth-grade math homework one day I realized that what Delia felt for Eric was not what Delia felt for me, and that this equation was not an *equal* sign, but a *greater than*.

I wonder if maybe Sophie knows me better than I know myself. I *do* hold the word *Delia* balanced lightly on my tongue, as if it is made up of butterflies. I *would* give her every last one of my french fries. I *have* kissed her, whenever the opportunity was socially acceptable. And even though it isn't fair, I·haven't blamed her for not loving me. But here's where Sophie is wrong: It's not because I don't want to hurt Delia's feelings.

It's because when she is bruised, I'm the one who aches.

I'm dragging my proverbial feet, or at least the brake of the rental car, the whole way back to Delia's trailer. It is ridiculous to think I can avoid her forever. Maybe she'll want to pretend that kiss never happened. Maybe I can just apologize and we can go on making believe.

But when I pull up, her car is missing. Sophie gets out of the backseat and hurries up the steps to the trailer. I hesitate for a moment, but before I can make a clean getaway, Eric walks outside and holds up a hand in greeting.

He looks like hell. His eyes are ringed with dark circles; his clothes appear to have been slept in. 'Listen, Fitz,' he says, 'about the other day . . .'

I stand, poleaxed. Did Delia tell him?

He sighs. 'It wasn't my place to tell Delia you were writing a newspaper story about her father's trial.'

By comparison, that transgression seems a thousand light-years away, and far less damning. 'I'm sorry, too,' I say, speaking of a different mistake. I fumble with the latch of the car door.

'Do you forgive me for being a dick?'

'Already have.'

'Then why are you running out of here faster than Jesse Helms at a Gay Pride parade?'

'It isn't you,' I admit.

'Ah.' Eric walks toward the car. 'Then it must have something to do with the way Delia ran out of here with Greta.'

'Faster than Jesse Helms?'

'Faster than Trent Lott at an *Ebony* magazine get-together.' Eric grins. 'What are you two fighting about?'

You, I think. When you think about the way the three of us have woven our lives together, Eric is the knot at the center. I'm terrified to work it free; I just might discover I've unraveled everything else.

I can still see him looking down at me from the crest of the oak in his backyard, crowing because he'd made it to the top first. I can hear his voice over the matchstick strike of rain on the roof of our clubhouse, swearing that the homeless guy who lived in the culvert near the Wilder Dam turned into the Devil at night. I can feel the strength of him, clapping me on the back the first time we saw each other on break from college. I can see the way his eyes shine, when Delia's face is what's reflected back in them.

I would never ask Delia to choose between Eric and me, because I could never choose between the two of them.

'I'm just tired,' I say finally. 'Headache.'

Eric heads back to the trailer. 'Come on in. I'll find you some aspirin.'

Sighing, I follow him into the trailer. Sophie is in the bedroom, playing ventriloquist for a batch of Barbies and Kens. The small table in the kitchen is piled high with paperwork. 'I don't know how I'm going to be ready in time for tomorrow morning,' Eric murmurs. 'Some Wexton Farms seniors are flying in today, they're character witnesses. I'm supposed to pick them up at the airport.' He looks at me. 'Rock, paper, scissors?'

With a sigh, I nod, and ball my hand into a fist. 'Rock, paper, scissors, shoot,' we say simultaneously, and I throw paper while Eric throws scissors.

'You always throw scissors,' I complain.

'Then why the hell do you always throw paper?' He offers a grateful smile. 'It's USAir, and it lands at three. And you're going to need six wheelchairs.'

'You owe me,' I say.

'Yeah, what's my tally up to . . . seventy-five billion and six?'

'Give or take.' I walk around the table, trailing my hand over the paperwork. Words jump out at me: *hostile witness, assailant, provocation.* Two definitions are scrawled in marker across a legal pad: *Lie: to deceive. Lie: to be in a helpless or defenseless state.*

'Andrew's in pretty bad shape,' Eric confides.

I glance up. 'So's Delia.'

'Yeah.' He meets my gaze. 'Did she tell you why she left for the Hopi reservation in the first place?'

I draw in a breath. 'It didn't come up.'

'She got angry, because I hadn't told her something her father told me in confidence. And the thing is, Fitz, it's just going to get worse during the trial. I'm going to have to do stuff and say things that she's not going to want to hear.'

'She'll forgive you, when it's all over,' I say woodenly.

'*If* Andrew's acquitted,' Eric qualifies. 'I've spent my whole life thinking that one of these days, my luck is going to run out. That one of these days Delia is going to open her eyes and realize that I'm not the guy she thinks, but just some loser who can't get his act together. What if today's that day?'

I try to draw an answer out of the heart of me, but can't. 'I'm going to look for that aspirin,' I manage, and I walk into the bathroom.

I close the door behind me and sit down on the lid of the toilet. If I didn't have a headache to begin with, I'm certainly developing one now. I stand up and rummage through the medicine cabinet, which is a whole different kind of pain: Here are Delia's antiperspirant, her toothbrush, her birth control pills. Here is a layer of intimacy I haven't been granted.

There are no bottles of aspirin, so I find myself kneeling

down under the sink and tearing apart the cabinet beneath it. Shampoo, Sophie's rubber duck, witch hazel. Pine Sol and Vaseline and suntan lotion. A soft stacked fortress of toilet paper rolls.

That's when I see the whiskey. I reach deep into the cabinet and pull out the half-empty bottle that has been wedged into the corner. I carry it out of the bathroom in the crook of my elbow. Eric sits at the table, his back to me. 'You find it?'

'Yeah,' I say. 'I did.' I lean over his shoulder and set the bottle down on top of a file folder.

Eric freezes. 'It's not what you think.'

I sit down across from him. 'No? Then what's it for? Lighting the barbecue? Stripping wallpaper?'

He gets up and closes the bedroom door, where Sophie is playing. 'You have no idea what trying this case is like. And when Delia left . . . I just couldn't handle it anymore. I'm terrified of screwing up, Fitz.' He spears the fingers of one hand through his hair. 'Andrew nearly got killed while I was off on my little bender,' he says. 'Believe me, that was enough to sober me up fast. It was just a taste, honest. And I haven't touched it since then.'

'Just a taste?' I take the bottle off the table and walk to the sink, unscrew the cap, and pour the contents down the drain.

As Eric watches me, his features change. It's regret, and I know, because I've seen it every single morning on my own face.

I remember how we all loved Eric when he'd downed a few, how he was always the most charming, the smoothest, the funniest. I remember, too, what it was like when he could overturn a kitchen in three minutes flat; when Delia would show up on my doorstep, sobbing, because he'd locked himself in a room and it had been four days.

'Been there, seen it, got the T-shirt,' I say to Eric, and I throw the empty bottle at him so that he catches it. 'Does she know?'

Eric shakes his head. 'Are you going to tell her?'

I would like to, more than anything. But I have become a master at not telling Delia the things I should have.

Without responding, I walk out the door of the trailer and then turn around. The mesh of the screen cuts Eric into a mosaic, a piecemeal Humpty Dumpty who cannot remember who he was before the fall. 'You're right,' I say. 'You don't deserve her.'

As I drive, I pick up my cell phone. I'm going to call Delia. I'm going to get this over with, once and for all.

I punch in her cell number and get a recording, stating that my number is not recognized by the cellular service.

I wait a few moments, thinking maybe I need to get to a part of the city covered by another set of towers, but five miles later and then ten, I receive the same message. I pull onto the side of the road and call the customer service hotline for the cellular company.

'Fitzwilliam MacMurray,' the rep says, as she looks up my number.

'That's me. What's the problem?'

'According to my records, your service was turned off two days ago. Oh, but there's a note in your records. It's a message from a Marge Geraghy.'

My editor. 'And?'

The rep hesitates. 'It says that next time, you should remember that your cell phone bills go directly to the company. And that you're fired.' There is a beat on the line. 'Is there anything else I can help you with?'

'Thanks,' I say. 'I think that's plenty.'

Shortly after midnight there is a knock on the door of my motel room. With the way my day has been going, I fully expect it to be the manager, telling me that my credit card has been revoked, too. But when I open it, Delia is standing on the other side. 'Buy me a drink,' she says, and my heart leaps.

I stare at her for a moment, and then dig into the front

pocket of my jeans and hand her three quarters. 'The soda machine's at the end of the hall.'

'I was hoping for something with proof.' She tilts her head. 'How come it's called that, anyway?'

'Because moonshine used to be used for barter. If you could mix equal parts of the liquid with gunpowder and light it on fire, there was evidence it was at least fifty percent alcohol.'

Her mouth drops open. '*Why* do you know that?'

'I wrote a story about it once.' This would be the perfect opportunity for me to mention that Eric might be a more willing drinking buddy, that in fact he might have a bottle hidden right under their bed she could borrow. But instead I say, 'You don't like to drink.'

'I know. But it works for everyone else when they want to escape.'

I lean against the doorjamb. 'What are you escaping from?'

'I can't sleep,' she admits. 'I'm too worried about tomorrow.'

'What about Eric?'

'He *can* sleep.' She pushes her way into my room and sits down in the middle of the bed, whose covers haven't been disturbed.

The conversation comes so easily, I begin to wonder if I am the only one who was present during that devastating, magnificent kiss last night. Then I realize that Delia has come to give me a way out. Maybe if we both pretend it never happened, it will be true. There are plenty of people – rape victims and Holocaust survivors, widows and, *God*, kidnapping victims – whose worlds crack and splinter, who still manage to look back at the level horizon of their lives without seeing the break.

But there's another part of me that knows no matter how Delia and I go forward from this point, it won't be the same. Because when she smiles, I will look away before it is contagious. When we sit beside each other, I will make sure that our shoulders do not brush. When we speak, there will be spaces between our words just the shape and size of that damn kiss.

I step away from her – one giant, mother-may-I step – toward the plastic expanse of the motel desk. It is covered with stacks of paper, a Bic pen that has exploded like the Red Sea, a chain of gum wrappers. Tonight's dinner: a half-eaten Ring Ding. 'Actually, I'm busy,' I say. 'I was working.'

'Oh,' she says, deflated. 'Your *Gazette* piece.'

'The *Gazette* fired me.'

She turns. 'You said you were writing a piece on my father's trial.'

'No,' I correct, 'I said I was *supposed* to.'

Delia crawls off the bed and walks toward the desk. She lets her fingers trail over the pages I have written all these weeks when I could not write anything else; pages that amassed in such quantity I never realized what I was producing. 'Then what's this?'

I take a deep breath. 'The story of you.'

She picks up the manuscript. *'I was six years old the first time I disappeared,'* she reads, the words coming alive for the first time. 'Is that me, talking?'

I nod. 'That's the way I heard you, in my head.'

Delia leafs through the first few pages, and then pushes it into my arms. 'Read it to me,' she demands.

So I clear my throat. *'I was six years old the first time I disappeared,'* I repeat. *'My father was working on a magic act.'* I read as Delia, as Eric, as Andrew, as myself. I read for hours. I read until my voice goes raw. I read until Delia falls asleep and I wake up in one of her dreams. I read until she takes over. And just as the sky starts blushing, she runs out of words.

'Why didn't you tell me?' she whispers.

'You had someone else.'

'The person you fall for when you're twelve might not be the same one you fall for when you're thirty-two.'

'Then again,' I say, 'sometimes it is.'

We are curled in concentric circles, the polyester cover of the queen bed pooled around us. It reminds me of the divot a whale leaves on the smooth surface of the water after it breaches. A footprint, that's what it's called, because every one is different.

Delia would say it's just another piece of useless information I'm storing. Maybe, but I also know that she reads the last page of a book before she decides to read the first. I know that she likes the smell of new crayons. That she can whistle through her fingers and detests curry and has never had a cavity. Life is not a plot; it's in the details.

I reach out to touch Delia's face. 'We're not going to talk about what happened yesterday, are we,' I ask softly.

She shakes her head. 'We're not going to talk about this either,' she says, and she leans forward by degrees, giving me the chance to back away before the kiss settles.

When we break apart, I feel like I'm on a window ledge, dizzy and certain that every move I make will be the wrong one. I can't find a single word that won't feel like glass in my mouth. 'You have to go,' I tell her.

Just before Delia reaches the door, she turns. In her arms she still clutches the last batch of pages I've written. 'I want to know how it ends,' she says.

VIII

A liar should have a good memory.
– Quintilian, *Institutions Oratoriae, iv.* 2, 91

Delia

I remember walking the gray halls of Wexton High: Eric and I pretzeled with our hands in each other's back jean pockets, Fitz spouting off beside us about everything from what words had been admitted to the *Webster's Dictionary* to why even a blue lobster, if you boil it, turns red. I would nod at all the right places but I didn't really listen to Fitz; I was more concerned with the notes Eric would slide through the breathing holes of my locker and what it felt like when his fingers slipped underneath the hem of my T-shirt to ride on the knots of my spine. And yet it turns out that I actually remember most of what Fitz said. I was paying attention even when I told myself I wasn't. If his voice hasn't been the melody of my life, it's been the bass line, so subtle you don't notice it until it's missing.

I park in front of the trailer and let myself inside quietly. It is barely six in the morning; Eric and Sophie will still be asleep. I reach into the cabinet above the sink and take out the coffee grounds, start a fresh pot, and suddenly feel hands on my shoulders and a kiss on my cheek.

A kiss.

'You're up early,' Eric says.

He is dressed to the nines in a dark gray suit and a crimson tie, so striking with his dark hair and light eyes that it takes my breath away. 'I was . . . having trouble sleeping,' I say. 'I went out.' Is it lying if I do not tell him I've been gone the whole night, and he doesn't ask?

He sits down at the table, and I bring him some orange juice. But instead of taking a sip of it, he traces the yawning mouth of the glass. 'Delia,' he says. 'I'm going to do the best I can today.'

'I know that.'

'But I also wanted to say I'm sorry.'

My mind swirls with sentences I read last night in Fitz's writing. 'For what?'

Eric looks at me with so much unsaid that I expect the moment to crystallize, fall to the table like a marble. But he lifts his glass, breaking the spell. 'Just in case,' he says.

Eric understands that the world is rarely the way it is supposed to be. And he knows that, given the chance, we don't have to wait for someone to make messes of our lives. We do a good enough job, ourselves.

Sophie thumps down the hallway, dragging one of her stuffed animals by its arm. 'You woke me up,' she accuses, but she crawls into Eric's lap, trusting one of the very people she's just blamed. She rubs her nose with the sleeve of her nightgown and leans against his lapel, still half-asleep.

We make messes of our lives, but every now and then, we manage to do something that's exactly right.

The challenge is figuring out which is which.

There is a playroom staffed by volunteers at the courthouse, a place where Sophie can crawl through tunnels and twist pipe cleaners while, upstairs, her grandfather stands trial for kidnapping. I drop her off with a promise to come back soon, and then head into the courtroom to take my seat.

I am waylaid by reporters, who corner me with their microphones: *Have you reconciled with your mother, Delia? Have you maintained contact with your father?* I shove past the hooks and claws of their questions and duck into the courtroom. Eric is already at the defense table, organizing files with Chris Hamilton, his second chair. There are more reporters queuing in the rear, artists with sketch pads. And leaning against the far wall is Fitz, his eyes locked on me.

A side door opens and two bailiffs escort my father inside.

He is wearing a suit again, but his face is pillowed and bruised, as if he has recently been in a fight. He is freshly shaved.

I used to love to watch my father shave. I had no mother to show me the wonders of blush and mascara; to me the mystery was watching the cream rise like a meringue in my father's palm, and then using it to paint the curve of his jaw. I'd make him put it on my cheeks, too. I'd pretend to shave beside him with a toothbrush. Then we would lean into the mirror together – my father checking for spots he had missed; and me, glancing from his eyes and jaw and lips to mine, trying to find all the matches.

As a child, all I ever wanted was to grow up to be just like him.

It's really hard to hate a pregnant woman. Emma Wasserstein stands up and walks heavily toward the jury box, bellying up to the polished railing. 'Imagine that you are four years old, ladies and gentlemen, living in Scottsdale with your mother. You have a pink bedspread and a swing set in your backyard and you go to nursery school. You see your father on week-ends, like you have ever since your parents divorced. And you are happy.

'But then one day, your father tells you you aren't Bethany anymore. You don't understand this, not any more than you've understood the fast flight from town, the motels, the new clothes, the dyed hair. When he introduces you to strangers, he calls you "Delia." You say you want to go back home, and he tells you you can't. He says that your mother is dead.'

She begins to walk back to the prosecutor's table. 'Because he's your father, because you love him and trust him, you believe him. You believe your mother really is gone. You believe you aren't Bethany anymore – you believe you never *have* been.

'You move to New Hampshire and watch your father, now calling himself Andrew Hopkins, being hailed as a model citizen. You live the story he creates for you. And you forget, for twenty-eight years, that you were ever once a victim.'

She faces the jury again. 'But there was a second victim here, who never forgot. Elise Matthews woke up every morning wondering if this was the day her baby would be returned to her. Elise Matthews spent a quarter of a century not knowing if Bethany was still alive, not knowing where she might be, not even knowing what she might look like anymore.'

Emma folds her hands around her prodigious belly. 'The relationship between an adult and a child is not an equal one. We are bigger and stronger and wiser, and because of that, we enter into an unwritten contract that grants us the responsibility to put a child's interests before our own. Charles Matthews, ladies and gentlemen, violated that contract. He took a little girl with no regard for her emotional well-being and forced her into an unfamiliar, frightening life, three thousand miles away from her real home. He'll try to tell you he was being a hero. He'll try to get you to buy his lies, too. But here is the truth, ladies and gentlemen: Charles Matthews decided he was not happy with the custody arrangement worked out between himself and his ex-wife, Elise, and so he took what he wanted and ran.'

She turns to the jury again. 'Two thousand children vanish every single day in this country. The most recent report of the National Incident Studies of Missing, Abducted, Runaway, and Thrownaway Children Report found that 797,500 children went missing in 1999. Of those, only 58,200 were nonfamily abductions. Which means that every day in the United States, thousands of parents kidnap their own children, just like Charles Matthews did – *because they can*. But sooner or later, if we're lucky, we catch up to them.' Turning, Emma points to my father. 'For twenty-eight years, that man got away with breaking a mother's heart. For twenty-eight years, he got away with breaking his daughter's trust. For twenty-eight years, he got away with breaking the law. Don't let him get away with it for another minute.'

Eric stands. 'What Ms. Wasserstein hasn't told you, ladies and gentlemen,' he says, 'is that Elise Matthews was damaged long before that broken heart. An alcoholic, lying in her own vomit, unconscious – that was the mother Bethany Matthews inherited. That was the woman entrusted to care for her, the woman who was too drunk to even realize that her daughter was there. Did Andrew Hopkins take his daughter? Absolutely. But it wasn't an act of vengeance, it was an act of mercy.'

Walking around behind my father, Eric puts his hand on one shoulder. 'Mrs. Wasserstein would like you to believe that this man plotted and planned, intending to ruin his daughter's life during a routine custody visit, but that's not the case. The truth is, Andrew did bring his child home that day. And he found the television blaring, the house wrecked . . . and Elise Matthews passed out and reeking of alcohol. Maybe at that moment, Andrew Hopkins remembered the image of his daughter, lying still in an ICU bed just months before, after her mother's neglect led to a near-fatal scorpion sting. Maybe he even tried to keep his child from having to witness her mother in that state. Only one thing is certain: He knew, unequivocally, that he couldn't bring his child back to that. Not then, and not for another second.

'Why didn't he go to the authorities then? Because, ladies and gentlemen, the courts were biased against Andrew already, for reasons you'll learn. Because in our legal system in the late seventies, custody almost always went to the mother following a divorce, even a mother who wasn't capable even of caring for herself, much less a child.'

Eric heads back to his seat, hesitating midway. 'You all know what you would have wanted to do, if you'd come home to find your ex-spouse too drunk – *again* – to safely care for your child. Andrew Hopkins is guilty of one thing, ladies and gentlemen: loving his daughter enough to keep her safe.' He faces the jury. 'Can you honestly blame him for that?'

My mother is wearing a conservative blouse and skirt, but her hair is wild around her face and her hands are covered with turquoise and garnet rings. She looks nervously over the head of the prosecutor to where Victor sits, encouraging her with a smile.

The judge, a heavy man shaped like a wedding cake, signals Emma Wasserstein to begin. 'Can you state your name for the record?'

'Elise,' my mother says. She clears her throat. 'Elise Vasquez.'

'Thank you, Ms. Vasquez. Are you remarried?'

'Yes, to Victor Vasquez.'

Emma nods. 'Would you please tell the jury where you live?'

'Scottsdale, Arizona.'

'How long have you lived there?' Emma asks.

'Since I was two.'

'And how old are you now, Mrs. Vasquez?'

'I'm forty-seven.'

'How many children do you have?'

'One.'

'What's her name?'

My mother's eyes find mine. 'It used to be Bethany,' she says. 'Now it's Delia.'

'Did you know Bethany when she became Delia?'

'No, I didn't,' my mother murmurs. 'Because her father stole her from me.'

This wakes up the jury, interest passing through them like lightning. 'Can you explain what you mean by that?' Emma asks.

'We were divorced, and we had joint custody of Bethany. Charles – that used to be his name – was supposed to bring her back on a Sunday, after spending the weekend with her. He never did.'

'Do you see your ex-husband in the room today?'

My mother nods, and points at my father. 'That's him.'

'Let the record reflect that Mrs. Vasquez has identified the defendant,' Emma says. 'What did you do when he never returned with your child?'

'I called and left messages at his apartment, but there was no answer and he didn't call me back. I gave him the benefit of the doubt. I thought maybe the car had broken down, or he'd taken her somewhere for the weekend and they'd gotten hung up, you know. I waited until the next day, and when no one contacted me, I drove to his apartment. I convinced the superintendent to unlock the door and that's when I realized something was wrong.'

'What do you mean by that?'

'All his clothes were gone. Not just enough for an overnight, but the entire closet. And the things that were important to him – like his research books and a photo of his parents before they died and this baseball he'd caught at a Dodgers game as a kid – they were all missing, too.' She looks at Emma. 'So I called the police.'

'What did they do?'

'Set up roadblocks and went to the Mexican border and put Bethany's picture on the news. They asked me to give a press conference, to get public support. There were hotlines set up, and posters and flyers.'

'Did you get any responses?'

'Hundreds,' my mother says. 'But none of them led to my baby.'

Emma Wasserstein turns toward my mother again. 'Mrs. Vasquez, when was the last time you saw your daughter, prior to her kidnapping?'

'The morning of June 18. Charlie was supposed to bring her back on June 19. Father's Day.'

'And how long did you have to wait to see your daughter again?'

My mother's eyes find mine, unerringly fast. 'Twenty-eight years,' she says.

'How did you feel during that time?'

'I was devastated. There was a part of me that never gave up hope that she'd come back.' My mother hesitates. 'But there was a part of me that wondered if I was being punished.'

'Punished? Why?'

Her voice becomes a broken road. 'Beautiful little girls should have mothers who don't forget to send them to school with a toilet paper roll for Craft Day. Or who know all the hand signs for Itsy Bitsy Spider. Beautiful little girls should have mothers who are waiting with a Band-Aid even before they fall off the tricycle. But instead, Bethany got me.' She takes a ragged breath. 'I was young, and I . . . would forget things . . . and get angry at myself – so I'd have a drink or two to feel less guilty. But that drink turned into six or seven or a whole bottle, and then I'd miss the Christmas concert or fall asleep when I was supposed to be making dinner . . . and I'd feel so awful about it that I'd have to have another drink just to forget how I'd screwed up again.'

'You drank when your daughter was present, in the house?'

My mother nods. 'I drank when I was upset. I drank when I wasn't upset, to keep myself from getting that way. I drank because I thought it was the one thing I had control of. I didn't, of course. But when you pass out, distinctions like that stop mattering.'

'Did your drinking affect your relationship with your daughter?'

'I'd like to think that she knew how much I loved her. In all the memories I've got of her, she's happy.'

'Mrs. Vasquez, are you an alcoholic?'

'Yes.' My mother looks up at the jury. 'I always will be. But I've been sober for twenty-five years now.'

Sometimes Eric's mother would go away, for weeks. He told us that she was visiting her sister; years later, I learned she didn't have one. Once when we were kids, he admitted to me that it was easier when she was gone. I thought he was crazy: As someone who believed her mother was dead, I would gladly have taken one with faults over none at all.

And just like that, I remember that before I left my mother, she left me.

★

There is a commotion in the aisle of the gallery, and I realize that Fitz is standing at the edge of my row, heatedly whispering with the man beside me in an effort to have him give up his seat. Fitz pulls a twenty-dollar bill from his wallet and the man gets up so that Fitz can slide into place beside me. 'Stop thinking,' he commands, and he squeezes my hand.

Eric gets up for the cross-examination and approaches my mother. I wonder what he sees when he looks at her. Me, maybe. Or his own mother.

'Mrs. Vasquez,' he says, 'you said that in all the memories you have of Delia, she's happy.'

He is calling me Delia, I realize, to remind everyone of who I really am.

'Yes.'

'But you don't have a lot of those memories, do you?'

'Not enough,' my mother says. 'I didn't get to watch her grow up.'

'You didn't seem to watch her much when she was a baby, either,' Eric counters. 'Isn't it true that in 1972 you received a felony conviction for driving under the influence of alcohol?'

'Objection, Your Honor!' Emma calls out. She and Eric approach the bench, talking in whispers that are picked up by the judge's microphone. 'Your Honor, that conviction is so old it's got wrinkles. It happened before Bethany Matthews was even born, and has absolutely no relevance.'

'Under Article 609 of the Rules of Evidence, I'm impeaching the witness's credibility with a prior conviction. And technically, Judge, Bethany Matthews was present at the time of the crime. She was a two-month-old fetus.'

'Mr. Talcott, you certainly couldn't be planning to start a debate about the rights of the preborn,' Judge Noble warns. 'The objection's sustained.' He turns to the jury. 'Ladies and gentlemen, I'd like you to disregard what you just heard.'

But once you throw a stone, there are ripples in the pond, even if you remove the rock. Were there other times I was in the car when my mother was drunk; times she hadn't gotten caught?

'Mrs. Vasquez,' Eric says, 'your daughter was stung by a scorpion once while you were home alone with her, wasn't she?'

'Yes.'

'Can you tell us how that happened?'

'She was about three years old, and she put her hand in the mailbox. The scorpion was inside it.'

'You asked a three-year-old to get the mail?'

'I didn't ask her; she chose to go out there herself,' my mother clarifies.

'Maybe you didn't ask her because you were unconscious at the time. Drunk.'

'I really don't remember if that was the case.'

'No?' Eric says. 'This might refresh your memory. May I approach the witness?' He hands my mother a manila folder marked Defendant's Exhibit A. 'Do you recognize this document, Mrs. Vasquez?'

'It's a medical record from Scottsdale Osborn Hospital.'

Eric points to the bottom of the page. 'Would you read this sentence to the jury, please?'

She purses her lips together. 'Mother presented as intoxicated.'

'Medical professionals write these records,' Eric says. 'Wouldn't you say they're trained to judge whether someone is intoxicated or not?'

'Nobody examined me that night,' my mother replies. 'They were there to take care of Bethany.'

'How fortunate, given that she was brought in not breathing.'

'She had a reaction to the scorpion venom that was very severe.'

'So severe, in fact, that she was treated in the emergency room for four and a half hours?'

'Yes.'

'So severe that she needed a tracheostomy – a hole cut into her windpipe – to assist her breathing?'

'Yes.'

'So severe that she was kept for three days following that in the pediatric ICU; three days that doctors told you repeatedly that she might not live?'

My mother's head is bowed toward her lap. 'Yes.'

'On the night that Delia was due to come home from her weekend visit with her father, had you been drinking?'

'Yes.'

'What time of day did you start?'

She shakes her head. 'I'm not sure.'

'Was Victor living with you, then?'

'Yes, but he wasn't there,' she says. 'I think he was at work.'

'What time was he expected home?'

'It was a long time ago,' my mother says.

'Do you remember if he was supposed to come back before or after your daughter was dropped home?'

'After,' she says. 'He worked a second shift.'

'Did you continue to drink through the entire afternoon?'

'I . . . suppose I did.'

'Did you pass out?'

'Mr. Talcott,' my mother says evenly, 'I know what you're trying to do. And I'm the first to admit that I have not been a saint. But can you honestly tell me that you've never in your life made a mistake?'

Eric stiffens. 'I get to ask the questions, Mrs. Vasquez.'

'Maybe I wasn't the most competent mother in the world, but I loved my child. And maybe I wasn't a responsible adult, but I learned from my mistakes. I shouldn't have been punished for twenty-eight years. No one deserves that.'

Eric wheels around so quickly that my mother rears back in her chair. 'You want to talk about *deserving?* What about a childhood of coming home from school and wondering what you're going to see when you open the door?' he asks. 'Or hiding the invitations to open school night in the hope that your mother won't show up, drunk, and embarrass you? Or being the only third grader who knows how to do his own laundry and go food shopping because nobody else was doing it for me?'

The courtroom goes so silent that the walls seem to have a pulse. Judge Noble frowns. 'Counselor?'

'For *her*,' Eric corrects, his face flushed. He sinks into his chair. 'Nothing further.'

'I'm fine,' Eric assures me minutes later, when we have adjourned for a recess. 'I just forgot where I was for a moment.' In the conference room where we've sequestered ourselves, he raises a Styrofoam cup, his hand still trembling. Some water splashes onto his shirt and tie. 'It might even have worked in our favor.'

I do not know what to say. As it is, I am shaken myself: I knew what to expect in terms of testimony, but I never considered the cost of what memories it was going to jog.

'I'll get some paper towels,' I manage, and I head toward the ladies' room.

Standing in front of the sink, I burst into tears.

I lean down and splash my face with cold water, until the collar of my blouse is damp. 'Here,' says a voice, and I am handed a paper towel.

When I look up, my mother is standing next to me.

'I'm sorry you had to listen to that,' she says quietly. 'I'm sorry I had to say it.'

I press the towel against my face, so that she won't see that I'm crying. She rummages in her purse and then opens a small ceramic pillbox. 'Take this. It'll help.'

I look at the caplets in my hand skeptically, picturing her witch's workbench.

'It's Tylenol,' she says dryly.

I swallow them and wipe my mouth with the back of my hand. 'Where did you go?' I ask.

She shakes her head. 'When?'

'You left us, once. You went away, maybe for a week.'

My mother leans against the wall. 'You were so little. I can't believe you even remember.'

'Yeah,' I say. 'Go figure. Were you getting drunk? Or were you getting dry?'

She sighs. 'Your father gave me an ultimatum.'

I hadn't been told where she'd gone. I had wondered if I'd done something wrong, that made her vanish. I had spent that week being extra careful: picking up my toys after I was done playing, looking both ways before I stepped off the curb, brushing my teeth for two whole minutes each time.

I'd wondered if she'd come back.

I'd wondered if I wanted her to.

I never said these things to my father, keeping my fear from him the same way he kept his from me.

'Did it work?' I ask.

'For a while. And then . . . like everything else . . . it didn't.' My mother looks up at me. 'Your father and I never should have gotten married, Delia. It all happened very fast – we hardly knew each other, and then I got pregnant.'

I swallow hard. 'Didn't you love him?'

She rubs at an invisible mark on the sink counter. 'There are two kinds of love, *mija*. In the safe kind, you look for someone who's exactly like you. It's what most folks settle for. But then there's the other kind of love. Everyone's born with a ragged edge, and some folks crave the piece that's a perfect fit. You'll search for it forever, if you have to. And if you're lucky enough to find it, it looks so *right,* you start to tear at your own seams, thinking, *maybe I could look just as perfect.* But then, of course, when you try to get close to their other half, you don't fit anymore.' She looks up at me. 'That kind of love . . . you come out of it a different person than you were when you started.'

She takes a deep breath. 'I was a high school dropout who worked in a biker bar. Your father was the sort of person who had already planned out his life. He actually thought I was capable of being a mother, of taking care of a family – and God, I wanted to believe him. I wanted to be the person he saw when he looked at me . . . it was so much more than I ever imagined of myself.' She smiles faintly. 'Like you,' my mother says. 'I desperately wanted to be someone who didn't really exist, because that was who he loved.'

She leans toward me and fixes the collar of my shirt. It is such a maternal, intimate thing to do that it takes me by surprise. Then she reaches into her pocket, and slips something into my hand.

It is a small red cloth bag, sewn shut, and it burns against my skin. Suddenly, I can smell the rotten flesh of mangoes and sun-spotted tomatoes in a Mexican mercado; I can taste the bitter blood of a hundred babies being born. I can see vendors shoulder to shoulder, calling out, *¿Qué le damos?* I can see an old woman kneeling on a quilt beside a statue of an owl, a red candle growing from its beak. I notice iguanas the length of my legs and packs of Tarot cards wrapped in plastic and keychains made of the neckbones of rattlesnakes. I smell urine and roasted corn and the smiling raw mouth of a watermelon. It is my mother's world, I realize, in the palm of my hand.

I stare down at it. 'I don't want your help,' I say.

My mother folds my fingers over the tiny purse. 'No. But your father might.'

Former detective Orwell LeGrande has spent the past fifteen years of his retirement from the Scottsdale PD on a houseboat in the middle of Lake Powell. His skin is the crusty brown of cowboy leather; his hands are leopard-dotted with sunspots. 'In 1977,' he replies to the prosecutor, 'I was with the violent crimes unit.'

'Did you ever have any contact with Elise Matthews?'

'I was on duty on June 20 when she called to report her daughter missing. I responded with several officers. When we got to the defendant's apartment, Ms. Matthews was a wreck. Her child had been due back the previous evening, at five P.M., after a custody visit with the defendant, but she never came home.'

'What did you do?' Emma asks.

'I called the local hospitals to see if the child and her father had been admitted. But there was no record of their names, or of any John or Jane Doe with the same characteristics. Then I checked the registry of motor vehicles, to see if the car had been reported stolen or in an accident. A search of the apartment led me to believe we might have an abduction on our hands.'

'What happened next?'

'I had dispatch put out a message to local officers, so they could alert us if the car or the subjects were found.'

'Detective, what other measures did you take to try to find the defendant?'

'We got his credit card records, but he was smart enough to not use plastic on the road. And we got access to his bank account.'

'What did that reveal?'

'It had been closed out on June 17 at 9:32 A.M., with a withdrawal of $10,000.'

Emma pauses. 'Do you remember what day of the week that was?'

LeGrande nods. 'Friday.'

'Let me get this straight,' Emma says. 'The defendant withdrew $10,000 from his bank account on the Friday *before* his scheduled custody visit?'

'That's correct.'

'As an experienced detective, did you consider that to be an important detail?'

'Absolutely,' LeGrande says. 'It was the first piece of proof I had that Charles Matthews had deliberately planned to kidnap his daughter.'

Rubio Greengate has a head full of snakes. Cornrowed in crazy stripes and patterns, they end in long ropes that fall to his waist. With his two front teeth made of solid gold, and his baggy black pants and vest, he is a modern-day pirate. He slouches on the witness stand as Emma Wasserstein paces in front of him. 'Mr. Greengate,' she says.

'Call me Rubio, sugar.'

'Maybe not,' the prosecutor replies. 'How did you get involved in this case?'

'I saw it on the news, and I said, *I know that guy.*'

'What exactly is your line of business, Mr. Greengate?'

He flashes a smile. 'I'm in the market of reinvention, sugar.'

'Please tell the jury what you mean by that,' Emma says.

He leans back in the witness chair. 'For a fee, I can get you a new identity.'

'How do you get these identities?'

He shrugs. 'Read the obits. Go to records departments – you know, I'm a relative of someone who died; or I've lost my mother's death certificate. You can always make up something that gets the authorities to turn over what you need.'

'Once you have these documents, what do you do?'

'People know how to find me. If they need to disappear, I make it happen. I got my own laminating machine, a printing press, a photo shop, and more engraving plates than the Federal Mint.'

'When did you meet the defendant?'

'Long time ago. Twenty-eight years, to be exact. Back then, I didn't have quite the operation I do now. I was keepin' a low profile, and working out of the attic of a crack house in Harlem. One night, this guy showed up, askin' for me.'

'It's been, as you said, quite a while. How do you know for sure it was the defendant you met that night?'

'Because he had a kid with him. A little girl. I ain't got many clients with kids.'

'What time of day was it?'

'After midnight; that's when I opened up shop.'

'How would he have to get to your shop?'

'He'd come up the stairs, and ask someone for directions.'

'What was going on on the stairs?' Emma asks.

'It's a crack house, what you think was going on? Couple

of folks lying around shootin' up, smokin', some fellas fightin', you name it.'

'So, he took his young daughter through this scene, and then what?'

'He told me he needed to become someone else.'

'Did you ask why?' Emma says.

'I respect my clients' privacy. But I had the perfect set of IDs for him – a thirty-year-old father with a four-year-old girl. I gave him the Social Security numbers and some doctored birth certificates and even a driver's license.'

'How much did you charge for the new identity?'

'Fifteen hundred. I cut him a break and only took a thousand for the kid.'

'How long did the whole exchange take?'

'About an hour.'

'How were you paid?'

'Cash,' Greengate says.

'Do you remember anything in particular about the little girl?'

'She was cryin'. I figured it was past her bedtime and all.'

'What did her father do?'

He grins. 'It was actually pretty cool, man. He did magic tricks. Pulled a quarter out of her ear and shit.'

'Did the little girl say anything?'

He thinks for a minute. 'After we signed everything, and the money changed hands, he told the kid they were playin' a game, and everyone had a new name. He said she was gonna be Delia now. And she asked what they were gonna call Mommy.'

As Emma lets this sink in, I try to see the girl I used to be, the one I never got to know. I try to imagine the words Rubio Greengate has tossed into the courtroom, sitting on my own tongue. But I might as well be any member of the jury: These aren't recollections to me, they're brand-new pictures.

Why do some memories bleed out of nowhere and others stay locked behind doors?

'Mr. Greengate, you've had some previous felony convictions. Several theft charges are on your record, and you've been arrested for manufacturing identities.'

He spreads his palms. 'Professional hazard.'

'Were you serving time in jail or prison twenty-eight years ago, when Bethany Matthews disappeared?'

'No. I was workin'.'

'Right now, Mr. Greengate, you've been charged with petty identity theft in New York.'

'Yeah.'

'Were you in custody in that state, before you came to us with this information?'

'Yeah.'

'Are you receiving some benefit for your testimony here today?'

He smiles. 'The DA say if I testify here, I get a reduced sentence there.'

'In light of that, Mr. Greengate, can you give us a reason to believe you actually are telling the truth?'

'I know something about those dead folks that never came out in the obits,' he says. 'I had to doctor up the copies of the birth certificate when the guy paid for them.'

'Mr. Greengate,' the prosecutor says, walking toward him with a piece of paper, 'do you recognize this?'

Greengate looks it over. 'It's a copy of the original birth certificate. The one I fixed for the girl.'

'Can you read the part that's highlighted?'

He nods. 'Cordelia Lynn Hopkins,' he says, 'Race: African American.'

During the lunch recess, I tell Eric that I need to go let Greta out. Instead of driving home, though, I leave the car in the lot and start walking east. I hold my breath every time I cross an intersection, like she told me to. I close my eyes when a shadow crosses my path.

The first body of water is one of the canals that run through

Phoenix, the reservoir of water tapped from the Colorado River. I remember Ruthann saying the Pueblo Indians had designed the canals in the city, the ones still being used years later. This, to me, seems like good fortune, so I take off my shoes and sit on the bank.

The tiny *mojo* bag is pinched between my fingers. Inside is a pinch of white pepper, a little sage. A sprinkling of powdered garlic and some cayenne. A spot of tobacco, a thorn from a cactus, a tiger's eye stone. My mother says that for the past four nights, she has slept with this underneath her pillow, but that it will take both of us to make this work.

Muddy water moves through the sieve of my toes. I turn to the north, then the east, then the south, then the west. *If you are up there, Ruthann,* I think, *I could use your help right now.*

'Sanctified Santa Marta,' I say, feeling foolish. 'Slay the dragon of his misfortune.'

I pick at the stitches that hold the charm bag shut. The contents float on the air, then settle on the surface of the water. The stone sinks right away; the rest of the powder is harder to track.

But I watch until I cannot see a speck anymore, like she instructed. I fold the red fabric and tuck it inside my bra, where I will keep it until the moon asks for it back.

When I'm finished with the *mojo,* I step out of the canal and put on my shoes. I walk back to the courthouse. It's not that I believe, exactly. It's just that, as with most acts of faith, I can't afford not to.

After court is adjourned, Eric goes back to the law offices to prepare for tomorrow's testimony. Fitz comes with me to pick Sophie up from the day-care center, and suggests we all go get something to eat, but I am afraid to be alone with him, I don't know how I'm supposed to feel. 'Rain check?' I say, trying to sound breezy and comfortable. I hurry Sophie outside the court before Fitz can plead his case, only to run into a gauntlet of reporters. The lights on their cameras blind me, and send Sophie burrowing into my arms; it's enough to make me understand that all I really want to do is crawl into our pink trailer and hide.

I make peanut butter and jelly sandwiches for dinner, and then as I'm watching Sophie draw pictures of blue whales and mermaids and other creatures that live in the bottom of the sea, I fall asleep.

In my dreams I'm wearing a collar, and Greta is holding my leash. She wants me to find something, but I have no idea what I am supposed to be looking for.

When I wake up, the first thing I think about is not my father's trial. The sun has bitten halfway through the horizon, and the whole trailer is flooded in an eerie orange light, as if Sophie's colored it completely while I've been sleeping. I glance down at the floor and see a scattering of pictures, but she's not drawing anymore.

'Soph?' I call, sitting up. I walk into the bathroom, but she's not there. I check in the bedroom. 'Sophie?'

I check under the bed, in the hamper, under the kitchen cabinets, in the refrigerator, anywhere a child might play hide and seek. Outside the trailer, the only thing I hear are the distant rumble of cars and an occasional dog barking. 'Sophie Isabel Talcott,' I say, as my heart starts to race. 'Come out right now.'

I glance across at Ruthann's dark trailer, where Sophie had spent so much time this past month.

Greta wriggles out from the spot beneath the trailer steps where she's been lying in the shade. She looks up at me and whines. 'Do you know where she is?'

I start banging on the doors of neighbors I have never bothered to meet, asking for Sophie. I check every nook and cranny of the pink trailer. I stand in the front yard again, and call out her name at the top of my lungs.

How hard would it be to take a little girl when no one is watching?

I suddenly hear my mother's voice, from the witness stand: *Can you honestly tell me that you've never in your life made a mistake?*

I fumble in my purse for my cell phone and call Eric. 'Is Sophie with you?'

He is distracted by something else; I can tell by his voice. 'Why would she be at the office?'

'Then she's missing,' I tell him, choking back tears.

There is a beat of utter disbelief. 'What do you mean she's missing?'

'I fell asleep. And when I woke up . . . she's not here.'

'Call the police,' Eric orders. 'I'm coming home.'

The police want to know how tall Sophie is, how much she weighs. If she was wearing a blue shirt or a yellow one. If I remember the brand of her sneakers.

Their questions rope me like a noose; I don't have any of the right answers. I can't be sure if she was wearing a blue T-shirt today, or if that was last week. I haven't measured her lately. I know she has pink sneakers, but I cannot tell them the brand name.

The details I can give them are not the ones that will help find a missing child, but they're indelibly inked on my heart: the dimple Sophie has in only one cheek; the space of the gap between her front teeth; the beauty mark that sits square on her back. The sound of her voice when she calls for me in the middle of the night; the rock she has in her pocket that glitters like gold in the sun. I can tell them that she is just tall enough to touch the door frame when she is on my shoulders. I can estimate her weight, by judging what's missing in my arms.

Eric sits on the trailer steps, answering their questions. He has taken off his tie, but he is still sporting the suit he wore in court. I am aware of the other neighbors, watching us from their porches and trailer windows. I wonder if they know who we are; if they are aware of the irony.

The detective speaking to Eric puts his notepad away. 'Sit tight, Mr. Talcott,' he says. 'We'll put out an Amber alert immediately. The best thing you can do is stay right here, just in case Sophie finds her way back.'

I watch him radio in the information we have given him, I hear distant sirens. Was this how my mother felt, when she realized I was missing? As if the entire core of her had been removed; as if this planet suddenly seemed much larger than it had ever been before?

I can't trust the police to find my child. I can't trust anyone.

I wait until the detective has gone to speak to the neighbors; and then I whistle for Greta. 'You ready to work, girl?' I croon, and I rub her between the ears.

Eric stands up. 'Delia,' he says. 'What do you think you're doing?'

Instead of answering him, I slip on Greta's harness. I don't care about stepping on the toes of a police administration I do not know; I don't care about the detective's instructions to stay put. All I know is that I was the one who screwed up, by falling asleep. This is the seminal difference between my own mother and myself: I will search for my daughter longer, and harder, than anyone else.

At the promise of a search, Greta's whole body starts to quiver. 'I'm her mother,' I say to Eric, because in any perfect world, that ought to be explanation enough.

If Sophie was taken away in a car, I am not going to get very far. A scent will only carry if, by chance, the window was rolled down. But when I find Sophie's pillow and scent Greta off it, she takes off immediately. She circles around the front yard, where Sophie has played for a month. She sniffs the cacti Sophie painted under Ruthann's direction. She casts in widening circles, and then she finds a path that takes us out of the trailer park.

As Greta works, her nose pressed to the pavement, I think about everything that might go wrong: the desert wind, scattering the scent cones; the spongy, scorching asphalt that might mask Sophie's smell with its own bitter black one; the onrushing cars and exhaust that might interrupt Greta's careful track. The dog is heading toward the highway, the same way we came home from court today, and although I am trying hard not to think about it, I'm wondering if Greta is picking up that old scent instead.

I try to remember all the statistics: how many kids disappear every day in America; how, exponentially, the chance of finding a missing child decreases after a certain amount of time missing; how long a person can survive in the desert without water.

Greta and I have been searching for only a half hour when she cuts behind a shopping center and then doubles back. She takes off at a run, and I race after her. 'Sophie?' I start yelling at the top of my lungs. *'Sophie!?'*

And then I hear it: 'Mommy?'

In utter disbelief, I let go of Greta's leash. She rounds the concrete corner of the building and jumps up, her front paws nearly reaching Sophie's shoulders.

I fall to my knees before Sophie, sobbing, grabbing for every inch of her that I can. She is holding an ice cream cone in her left hand, and she doesn't seem to understand why I have been reduced to a puddle in front of her. 'I thought you were lost,' I gasp into the sweet skin of her neck. 'I didn't know where you'd gone.'

'But we left you a note,' Sophie says, and that's when I realize she is not alone.

In front of the ice cream parlor stand Eric, the detective, and Victor Vasquez. 'I would have called you,' Eric says, 'but you left so fast you didn't take your phone.'

Victor steps forward, an embarrassed flush covering his face. 'You were sleeping, and after all that happened today, I didn't want to wake you up. So Sophie and me, we left you a message.'

The detective holds it up – crayoned, on one of the pieces

of paper Sophie had been using for her pictures. TOOK SOPHIE FOR AN ICE CREAM – BACK IN 1/2 HOUR! – VICTOR. 'It was caught behind the couch,' the detective says. 'The fan must have blown it off the table.'

Mortified, I take it from his hand. 'I'm so, so sorry,' I murmur. 'I guess I overreacted . . .'

The detective shakes his head. 'That's what we're here for,' he says. 'And believe me, we love it when it works out like this.'

As Eric thanks the detective, Sophie slides her hand into mine. 'You told me I can't go anywhere with strangers,' she says, 'but I already met Victor.'

Victor turns to me. 'I should have realized—'

'No,' I say. 'Really. It's my fault.'

'Look at what Victor brought me!' Sophie tugs me toward one of the wrought-iron tables outside the ice cream parlor, on which sits a bird's nest. Inside are the remains of several speckled eggs. 'He said that the babies aren't living there anymore, so I could have it.'

Victor puts his hand on the crown of Sophie's head. 'I thought, with everything that's going on right now, she might need an extra friend.'

I nod at him, trying to smile in gratitude. I can feel the heat of Eric's gaze on me, wondering why I wasn't more thorough, wondering, like me, if this trial is taking a toll on me in ways I hadn't even expected. To avoid that discussion, I turn my attention to Sophie's prize. I listen to her chatter about the hatchlings, and where they've flown off to by now. When she carefully places an eggshell in my hand, I feign excitement, even though all I can see is something that's been broken.

A hostile witness is someone who is going to be unsympathetic to a lawyer, or the lawyer's client. In my father's case, the prosecution is going to have to be the one to call me to the stand, presumably to show the jury the damage that was done to me. But I'm more likely to stand up for my father than incriminate him, which means that it's in the prosecutor's best interests to ask me leading questions, something she normally wouldn't be allowed to do with a witness she's called to the stand. To that end, she's asked the judge to consider me hostile.

It makes me wonder if I am. Has this whole fiasco made me unreceptive? Aggressive? Angry? Will I come out of this trial more changed than I was, even, by my father's actions?

Eric has given me a pep talk this morning, reminding me that no matter what Emma Wasserstein does, she cannot put words in my mouth. In the wake of Sophie's disappearance last night, I am focused and centered – so intent on thinking before I act or speak that I can't imagine this prosecutor getting the best of me.

'Good morning,' she says.

A cool wall of cross-purpose separates us. I am careful not to look her in the eye. 'Hello.'

'You're not very happy about being here today, are you, Ms. Hopkins.'

'No,' I admit.

'You realize you're under oath.'

'Yes.'

'And you realize your father does stand accused of kidnapping you.'

Eric stands. 'Objection, Your Honor. It's not for her to make the legal conclusion.'

'Sustained,' Judge Noble says.

Emma doesn't flinch. 'You must have a very strong bond with your father, after all those years.'

I hold my answer between my teeth, sure this is a trap I am walking into. 'Yes. He was the only parent I knew.'

'You're a parent, too, aren't you?' Emma asks.

Inside, I freeze: Could she have found out already about Sophie's disappearance last night? Is she going to discredit me with my own mistakes? 'I have a daughter. Sophie.'

'How old is she?'

'Five.'

'What do you like to do with Sophie?'

Immediately, an image of her rises in my mind, like the sweetest cream. *We go looking for bugs – caterpillars and snails – and then build them houses out of grass and twigs. We tattoo each other with Magic Markers. We do puppet shows with the extra socks in the laundry basket.* Just thinking these things is reassuring, makes me remember that sooner or later, I get to leave this witness stand and go home with her.

'Do you tuck her in every night?' Emma asks.

'When I'm not working.'

'And in the morning?'

'She wakes me,' I say.

'Would it be fair to say that Sophie relies on the fact that you'll be there in the morning, when she comes looking for you?'

Emma Wasserstein has looped this noose so slyly that I haven't even felt the rope being placed around my neck. 'Sophie is lucky enough to have two very responsible parents she can depend on,' I answer coolly.

'You've never been married to Sophie's father, have you.'

I steadfastly refuse to glance at Eric. 'No. We're engaged.'

'Why don't you tell the jury who Sophie's father is?'

Eric is out of his seat like a shot. 'Objection. Irrelevant.'

The judge folds his arms. 'You're the one who said you could handle this case, no matter how close to home it got, Mr. Talcott. Overruled.'

'Who is Sophie's father, Ms. Hopkins?' Emma repeats.

'Eric Talcott,' I say.

'The attorney in this courtroom right now? The one defending your father?'

At her words, the jury stops staring at me, and scrutinizes Eric. 'That would be the one,' I reply.

'Does Mr. Talcott ever go out with Sophie alone, just father-daughter?'

I think back to last night; how I'd immediately assumed,

hoped, that it had been Eric who'd taken Sophie somewhere. 'Yes.'

'So you've been in a position before where you've been waiting for them to come home.'

'Yes.'

'Have they ever been late?'

I press my lips together in a firm line.

'Ms. Hopkins,' the judge says, 'you have to answer her.'

'Once or twice.'

'When they were late, did you call the police?'

I wouldn't have called the police, if I knew Eric was with her. I wouldn't have called the police if I'd known that Victor was with her, either. It was when I thought Sophie was alone, or with a stranger, that I'd panicked. 'No, I didn't.'

'Because you trusted Mr. Talcott to bring her back, isn't that right?'

'Yes.'

'Just like your mother did, the day you were taken by *your* father?'

'Objection,' Eric calls, but Emma is already speaking again.

'You don't remember anything specific about your mother's drinking, isn't that true?'

I look up at the prosecutor. 'Actually, I do,' I say. Eric is surprised; I haven't had a chance to tell him any of this. 'She left home once. Back then, I didn't know where she was going. I just assumed it was my fault. I spent a lot of time trying to keep out of her way, and I figured she finally found a way to get around me.'

'Did your father ever tell you where she went?'

'No,' I say. 'But she did. Rehab.'

Emma smiles, delighted. 'Your one memory of your mother, then, is of when she was actively trying to get help with her drinking?'

And your father still *took you?* I shake my head to clear the words she hasn't said, and maybe that is what dislodges it – another memory, with its pin already pulled and its smoke billowing history. Something is blinding – a mirror, maybe, that keeps catching the sun. My mother is holding it. *Come on, Beth, this was your idea,* she says, but it's taking me longer to walk up the hill. She sits down on it – not a mirror, but a silver tray. I crawl between her legs and her arms fold around me tight. *Who needs snow?* she says, and then we are bouncing down the rocky red slope with our matching hair flying out behind us.

In the gallery, I find my mother's face. I wish I could explain the feeling when a piece of you suddenly reattaches, a piece you weren't even aware was gone. You are afraid to speak, because you don't know what might come out of your own mouth. You begin to question whether you're making this up, whether everything you've thought to this point is just a lie.

You want more, and you're terrified to have it.

Was she drunk, when we went sledding on the sand? Was I so glad to have her with me, holding on tight, that it didn't even matter?

'Is it true, Ms. Hopkins, that your father told you your mother was dead?' Emma asks.

'He said she had died in a car accident.'

'And you believed him?'

'I had no reason not to,' I say.

'When you found out your mother was alive, you were very curious to meet her, weren't you.'

I can feel the prick of my mother's eyes on me. 'Yes.'

'You wanted to see if she was at all like the mother you'd imagined all those years.'

'Yes.'

'But then your father told you that, in fact, this mother, the one you'd built to mythic proportions in your mind, was an alcoholic. That she had put you in danger, as a child, and that's why he'd abducted you.'

I nod.

'You didn't want to believe your father, did you?'

'No,' I admit.

'But you had to,' Emma insists. 'Because if you didn't, then you were right back where you started: with your father lying.'

'That's not the way—'

'You can't deny, Ms. Hopkins, that your father is a liar. Why, by your own testimony—'

'*Yes!*' I interrupt. 'He's a liar. He lied to me for twenty-eight years, is that what you want me to admit? But the alternative was the truth, and no one ever wants to hear that. I can tell you for a fact that I didn't want to. It was much easier to think my mother was dead, believe me, than to find out she was an alcoholic who couldn't take care of me.' I turn to the jury. 'Just like it's much easier to think that someone who breaks the law deserves to be punished—'

'Your Honor!' Emma says.

'—especially when it's what you hear from the prosecutor and on television and every time you open up a newspaper, even when you know, deep down, he was right to do it.'

'Judge, I'd like the court to strike the surplus testimony as nonresponsive,' Emma insists.

'You're the one who led her there,' the judge replies, shrugging.

Eric catches my eye and winks at me, proud.

I have managed to rattle the prosecutor, and that makes me sit a little taller. 'Ms. Hopkins,' Emma says, smoothly changing her line of questioning, 'you do search and rescue for a living, is that correct?'

'Yes.'

'Can you explain what that is, for the jury?'

'My bloodhound, Greta, and I work with law enforcement agencies, cooperating with them to help find missing people.'

'How do you find a child who's wandered off?' Emma asks.

'I give my bloodhound, Greta, a scent article – something uncontaminated, that last touched the child. Usually it's a pillowcase or pajamas or sheets, something that was as close to the skin as you can get. But if I don't even have that, a footprint is enough. I'll get Greta to sniff it, and then I follow her lead.'

'You've met parents whose children are lost, right?'

'Yes,' I say.

'How do they act?'

'Most of them are frantic,' I say. Like me. Last night.

'Have you ever had to tell anyone that you can't locate the child?'

'Yes,' I admit. 'Sometimes the trail just ends. Sometimes the weather conditions affect the search.'

'Have you ever had to stop looking?'

I can feel my mother's eyes on me. 'You try not to,' I say, 'but sometimes you don't have a choice.'

'Ms. Hopkins, have you ever been sent after a runaway . . . or a suicidal person?'

'Yes.'

'They don't always want to come back with you, I imagine.'

I am thinking of a cliff on a mesa; a woman who stepped off the edge of the world. 'No.'

'When you find these particular people, you bring them back, even though they're reluctant, don't you,' Emma says.

I had wondered, in the days since Ruthann's death, why she hadn't protested harder when I told her I wanted to come to Shipaulovi. She must have known what she was planning to do there; having Sophie and me tagging along must have weighed heavily on her conscience. Unless . . . she had wanted someone there to bear witness. And she'd wanted that someone to be me.

Maybe she believed that because of what I'd been through, I knew that what was expected and what was right are rarely the same set of footsteps. Because of what I'd been through, I understood that sometimes you lie because you *have* to.

'Yes,' I say to Emma. 'I bring them back.'

Emma Wasserstein's eyes light in triumph. 'Because you know you should,' she clarifies.

But I shake my head. 'No,' I say. 'Although I know I shouldn't.'

★

Maybe every couple should have a judgment day like this: a witness stand, a wooden chair. A stack of invisible questions set between them like fruit that they will peel raw and feed to each other, each hoping the other will admit what brought them to this point. As Eric comes toward me to begin the cross-examination, the room falls away from us, and we might as well be nine again: lying on our backs in a field of black-eyed Susans; pretending we had landed on an orange planet, that we were the only inhabitants.

'So,' he says simply. 'How're you doing?'

It makes me smile. 'I'm holding up.'

'Delia, I haven't discussed this case with you, have I?'

We have rehearsed these questions; I know what he is going to say, and what I am supposed to. 'No.'

'You weren't too thrilled with me because of that, were you?'

I think about the fight we had, after the visit to the hospital. Of my flight to Hopiland. 'No. I thought you were hiding information from me that I deserved to have.'

'But you didn't hire me to represent your father because you thought I'd discuss the case with you, did you?'

'No. I hired you because I know you love my father as much as I do.'

Eric passes by me, stands in front of the jury. 'What does your father do for a living?'

'He runs a senior center in Wexton, New Hampshire.'

'Did he make enough money to provide for you as a child?'

'We didn't live in luxury or anything,' I admit, 'but we certainly had enough.'

'Your father provided for you emotionally, too, didn't he?'

Is there a right answer to this question? Can you quantify love? 'He was always there for me. No matter what I needed to talk about.'

'Did you talk about your mother with him?'

'He knew I missed her. But I knew it hurt him to talk about her, and I didn't really bring it up all that often. Nobody likes to talk about the things they've lost.'

'As it turns out, though, he'd never really lost your mother, had he?'

I can still hear her voice in the restroom, telling me that she really did love my father. 'She never died in a car crash,' I say slowly, 'but he lost her long before that, I think.'

Eric clasps his hands behind his back. 'Delia,' he asks after a moment, 'why aren't we married?'

I blink at him; this is not from our script. The question surprises the prosecutor as much as it surprises me; she objects.

'Your Honor,' Eric says, 'I'd like a little leeway. It's not irrelevant.'

The judge frowns. 'You can answer the question, Ms. Hopkins.'

Suddenly I understand what Eric is trying to do, and what he wants me to say. I wait for him to face me, so that I can tell him, silently, that I am not willing to let him sacrifice himself to save my father.

Eric takes a step closer and places his hand on the rail of the witness box. 'It's okay,' he whispers. 'Tell them.'

So I swallow hard. 'We aren't married . . . because you are an alcoholic.'

The words are hinged, rusty; I have worked so hard to not say them out loud. You might tell yourself that candor is the foundation of a relationship, but even that would be untrue. You are far more likely to lie to yourself, or your loved one, if you think it will keep the pain at bay.

This is something my father understood, too.

'When I drank, I was pretty awful, wasn't I?' Eric asks.

I bow my head.

'Isn't it true that I'd disappoint you, tell you I was going to be somewhere, and then completely forget to meet you; tell you I was going to run an errand for you and then not go?'

'Yes,' I say softly.

'Isn't it true that I would drink until I passed out, and you'd have to drag me to bed?'

'Yes.'

'Isn't it true that I would go off on rampages, get angry over the stupidest things, and then blame you for what went wrong?'

'Yes,' I murmur.

'Isn't it true that I could never finish something I started? And that I'd make promises that we both knew I'd never keep? Isn't it true that I'd drink to perk up, to calm down, to celebrate, to commiserate? Isn't it true that I'd drink to be sociable, or to have a private moment?'

The first tear is always the hottest. I wipe it away, and still it sears my skin.

'Isn't it true,' Eric continues, 'you were afraid to be with me, because you never really knew what I would be like? You'd make excuses for me, and clean up my messes, and tell me that next time, you'd help make sure this didn't happen?'

Yes.

'You enabled my drinking, by making it easier for me to get drunk without consequence . . . no pain, no shame. No matter how bad I got, you were there for me, right?'

I wipe my eyes. 'I guess so.'

'But then . . . you found out that we were going to have a baby . . . and you did something pretty remarkable. What was that?'

'I left,' I whisper.

'You didn't do it to punish me, did you.'

By now, I am crying hard. 'I did it because I didn't want my child to see her father like that. I did it because if she grew up knowing you that way she would have hated you, too.'

'You hated me?' Eric repeats, taken aback.

I nod. 'Almost as much as I loved you.'

The jury is so focused on our exchange that all the air in the room goes still, but I notice only Eric. He offers me a Kleenex; then smooths my hair away from my face, his hand lingering on my cheek. 'I don't drink anymore, do I, Dee?'

'You've been sober for more than five years. Since before Sophie was born.'

'What if I fell off the wagon tomorrow?' he asks.

'Don't say that. You wouldn't, Eric—'

'What if you knew I was drinking again, and I had Sophie with me? What if I was taking care of her?'

I close my eyes and try to forget that he has even thrown these words into the open, where they might breed and multiply and become fact.

'Would you enable me again, Dee?' Eric asks. 'Would you get Sophie in on the act, so that she could make excuses for her alcoholic parent?'

'I'd take her away from you. I'd take her, and I'd run.'

'Because you love me?' Eric asks, hoarse.

'No.' I stare at him. 'Because I love *her.*'

Eric turns to the judge. 'Nothing further,' he says.

I start to rise from the witness stand, my legs unsteady, but Emma Wasserstein is already approaching me. 'I don't understand, Ms. Hopkins,' she says. 'What is it about an alcoholic's behavior that might make you worry about your daughter's safety?'

I look at her as if she's crazy. 'Alcoholics are unreliable. You can't trust them. They hurt other people without even thinking about what they're doing.'

'Sounds kind of like a kidnapper, huh?' Emma turns to the judge. 'The prosecution rests,' she says, and she sits back down.

On the last good day, my father got up before me. He was downstairs making pancakes for Sophie's breakfast by the time I came downstairs. On the last good day, we ran out of coffee and my father wrote it on a list we kept stuck to the fridge. I did a wash.

On the last good day, I yelled at my father because he forgot to feed Greta. I folded his clean socks. I laughed at a joke he told me, something about an asparagus that went into a bar, which I no longer remember.

On the last good day he went to work for three hours and then came home and put on the History Channel. The program was about the Airstream RV. When it first came out, no one quite knew what to make of the silver bullet, so the company sent a caravan of them on a promotional tour across Africa and Egypt. The native tribes came up to the RVs and poked at them with spears. They prayed for the beasts to leave.

On the last good day, my father didn't fall asleep while he was watching this show. He turned to me and said words that at the time were only words, not the life lessons they've since exploded into. 'It just goes to show you,' my father told me, on the last good day, 'the world's only as big as what you know.'

Andrew

During the long drive east, the states all bled into one another and leagues of insects committed suicide against the front grille of the car. We would stop at gas stations and load up on Hostess cherry pies and Coca-Cola. We'd listen to the blur of words on the Spanish-speaking radio stations.

Every now and then, I would reach behind me blindly into the backseat where you were sitting, just to let you know I was there. 'High-five,' I'd say. But you never slapped my palm in response. Instead, you'd slip your fine-boned, fairy hand into mine; as if you were trying to say *Yes, I accept your invitation to this dance.*

It takes Irving Baumschnagel seven minutes to walk from the front row of the gallery to the witness stand, mostly because he is too stubborn to accept the help of a bailiff to steady him. Eric leans toward me, watching his unsteady progress. 'You're sure he can do this for us?'

Irving is one of the seniors from Wexton Farms that Eric's putting on the stand as a character witness. 'He's much sharper than he looks.'

Eric sighs. 'Mr. Baumschnagel,' he says, rising to his feet. 'How long have you known Mr. Hopkins?'

'Almost thirty years,' Irving says proudly. 'We were on the planning committee together in Wexton. He got the senior center up and running just about the time I was ready to start using it.'

'How does he contribute to the community?'

'He always puts other people first. He sticks up for causes that most people would rather forget,' Irving says. 'Like old people. Or poor families – we have our share in Wexton. Where most folks in town would prefer to pretend they don't exist, Andrew will run food and clothing drives.'

'Do you know Delia Hopkins?' Eric asks.

'Sure.'

'In your opinion, what lessons did Delia learn from her father?'

'Well, that's easy,' Irving says. 'Just look at what she chose to do for a living: search and rescue. I doubt she would have picked that if she hadn't seen her father putting other people first his whole life.'

'Thank you, Mr. Baumschnagel,' Eric says, and he sits back down beside me.

Rising, the prosecutor crosses her arms. 'You said that the defendant spent his life putting other people first?'

'That's right.'

'Would it be fair to say that he considered other people's feelings?'

'Absolutely,' says Irving.

'That he was capable of figuring out who needed help?'

'Yes.'

'Who needed a break?'

'Sure.'

'Who needed an opportunity to change his or her life?'

'He'd *find* that opportunity for you, if you needed it,' Irving insists.

'Would it be fair to say, Mr. Baumschnagel, that the defendant was willing to give a person a second chance?'

'No question about it.'

'Well then,' the prosecutor muses. 'I guess he really *had* become a different man.'

Daddy, you would say, look at my braids. Look at the worst bug bite ever. Look at my handstand, my eggroll dive, my finger painting. Look at my splinter, my spelling list, my somersault, the toad I found. Look at the present I made you, the grade I got, the acceptance letter. Look at the diploma, the ultrasound, your granddaughter.

I couldn't possibly remember all the things you've asked me to look at. I just remember that you asked.

The amazing thing about Abigail Nguyen is that she doesn't look more than a few years older than she did when Bethany was part of her nursery school class. She is tiny and composed, and sits on the witness stand with her hands folded neatly in her lap as she answers Eric's questions. 'She was a bright, sweet kid. But after her parents separated, there were times she'd come in and I just knew she hadn't had breakfast. She'd wear the same clothes to school three days in a row. Or her hair would be in knots, because no one had bothered to brush it.'

'Did you talk to Bethany about this?'

'Yes,' she says. 'She usually told me that Mommy was sleeping, so she made herself breakfast or did her own hair.'

'How did Bethany get to school?'

'Her mother drove her.'

'Did anything about Elise Matthews ever strike you as disturbing?'

'Sometimes she looked . . . a little worse for the wear. And often she smelled like she'd been drinking.'

'Mrs. Nguyen,' Eric says, 'did you speak to Bethany's father about this?'

'Yes. I distinctly remember one occasion when Elise Matthews didn't come to pick Bethany up after school – we let her stay for the afternoon session, too, and then we called her father at work.'

'What was his reaction?'

She glances at me. 'He was extremely upset and angry with his wife's behavior. He said he'd take care of it.'

'What happened after that?' Eric asks.

'Bethany attended class for three more months. And then one day,' the teacher says, 'she disappeared.'

I would carry you on my shoulders so you could see better. I used to think to myself, I will do whatever it takes to be able to carry you forever. I will join a gym. I will lift weights. I will never let on that you've grown too big for this, that you've gotten too heavy.

It never occurred to me that one day you might ask to walk on your own.

'So,' the prosecutor says. 'She just up and vanished?'

'Yes,' Mrs. Nguyen says.

'It's not in the child's best interests to have their education interrupted, is it?'

'No.'

'Now, Mrs. Nguyen, you said you saw a three-year-old child come to school with unbrushed hair, is that right?'

'Yes.'

'You testified that she was sometimes hungry.'

'Yes.'

'You said that she'd wear the same clothes to school three days in a row.'

'Yes.'

The prosecutor shrugs. 'Doesn't that describe just about any four-year-old child, at some point?'

'Yes, but this wasn't a onetime occurrence.'

'As a teacher, have you ever been in contact with the Department of Children Protective Services?'

'Unfortunately, yes. We're required by law to report abuse. The minute we believe a child is in extreme danger, we make the call.'

'And yet you didn't report Elise Matthews, did you?' Emma points out. 'Nothing further.'

Your favorite toys, as a child, were animals. Stuffed and

beanbag, enormous and minuscule – it didn't matter, as long as you could arrange them around the house in some sort of complicated scenario. You weren't the kind of kid who wanted to play 'vet.' Instead, you'd pretend that you were a rescue worker intent on making your way up Everest to rescue a stranded mountain lion, but halfway up one of your sled dogs would break its leg, and it was up to you to do field surgery before continuing on to save the wildcat. You would steal bandages from the first-aid kit at the senior center and erect . a triage center under the dining room table; the mountain lion was a stuffed cat hiding under the couch in the den; in the bathroom you had tweezers and toothpicks in your surgical suite. I used to watch you. I used to wonder if you were just a natural expert at reinventing the world, or if I'd somehow made you that way.

The whole way back to jail I feel the elements of my body resisting; a magnetic pole that has become so similar to the one it's approaching it cannot help but be repelled. But almost immediately, a detention officer comes to tell me I've got a visitor. I expect Eric, coming to practice tomorrow's testimony with me until it runs like a well-oiled machine, but instead of being escorted to a conference room for attorneys and their clients, I'm led to a central booth. It isn't until I am nearly face-to-face with her that I realize Elise has come to see me.

Her dark hair is a waterfall. She has writing on the inside of her palm and up her left arm. 'Some things never change,' I say softly, and point.

She glances down. 'Oh. Well. I needed a cheat sheet on the stand.' When she smiles at me, the little cubicle I am trapped in swells with heat. 'It's good to see you. I just wish it was under different circumstances.'

'I'd settle for a different venue,' I say.

She bows her head, and when she looks up, her face is flushed. 'It sounds like you've had a very good life in Wexton. All those senior citizens . . . they adore you.'

'A poor substitute,' I joke, but it falls flat. I look from the crooked part of her hair to the eyetooth that's twisted the tiniest bit – the little flaws that made her more striking instead of less so. Why had she never been able to understand that?

'You're still so goddamned beautiful,' I murmur. 'In twenty-eight years, you know, I still haven't met anyone else who talks back to characters in the middle of a movie. Or who stops using punctuation because it's cramping the style of the alphabet.'

'Well, I learned a little from you, too, Charlie,' Elise says. 'A very wise pharmacist once told me that there are certain elements you can't mix together, because even though it seems like they'd be perfect together, they're lethal. Bleach and ammonia, for example. Or you and me.'

'Elise—'

'I loved you so much,' she whispers.

'I know,' I say quietly. 'I just wished you'd loved yourself a little more.'

'Do you ever think about him?' Elise asks. 'The baby?'

I nod slowly. 'I wonder how much would have been different, if he'd—'

'Don't say it.' There are tears in her eyes. 'Let's do it this way, Charlie, all right? Let's pick just one sentence out of all of the ones we should have said – the best, most important sentence – and let's say just that.'

This is my old Elise – whimsical, loopy – the one I couldn't help but fall for. And because I know she is sinking in the quicksand of regret, just like me, I nod. 'Okay. But I go first.' I try to remember what it was like to be loved by someone who did not know limits, and had not yet been ruined by that. 'I forgive you,' I whisper; a gift.

'Oh, Charlie,' Elise says, and she gives me one right back. 'She turned out absolutely perfect.'

In the blue light of the cell, I make a mental list of the best moments of my life. They aren't the milestones you'd imagine;

they are the tiniest seconds, the flashes of time. You writing a note for the tooth fairy, asking if you had to go to college to be one. Waking up to find you curled up in bed beside me. You asking if I'd made the pancakes from scrap. You fishing, and then refusing to touch whatever you caught. You reaching into my pocket for quarters to feed the downtown meter. You doing cartwheels on the front lawn, looking like a long-legged spider. You spinning cotton candy and getting the sugar all over your hair. Pulling back the curtain of the magic box so you could step inside in your tiny sequined suit. Drawing it aside, so we could all see you reappear.

The amazing thing is, I could sit here for hours and still not run out of the best moments of my life. There are twenty-eight years' worth of them.

From up here, it's different. There's a flimsy railing between me and the rest of the courtroom – this witness stand – but that doesn't keep their eyes from striking me like hammers. 'It was the Saturday before Father's Day,' I say, looking right at Eric. 'Beth was excited, because she'd made me some card with a tie on it at nursery school. When I picked her up, she practically flew out to the car. We had a barbecue and went to the zoo. But then she remembered that she'd forgotten her blanket, the one she slept with. I told her we'd swing by the house and pick it up.'

'When you got there, what did you see?'

'There was no answer when I knocked. I went around to the side windows and saw Elise passed out in a puddle of her own vomit in the entryway. Dog feces and urine were all over the floor. And broken glass.'

I see Emma Wasserstein lean back as Elise taps her on the shoulder. The two women whisper for a moment.

'What did you do next?' Eric asks, bringing me back to focus.

'I thought about going in, and cleaning her up, like I'd done a thousand times before. And like a thousand times before,

Beth would watch me do it. And one day, she'd be the one taking care of her mother.' I shook my head. 'I just couldn't do it anymore.'

'There had to have been an alternative,' Eric says, playing Devil's Advocate.

'I'd already given her an ultimatum. After our second baby was stillborn, she started drinking so heavily that I couldn't make excuses for her anymore, and I got her to enroll in a treatment program. She dried out, for a month's time, and then she was drinking more than ever. Eventually I filed for divorce, but that only took *me* out of the situation. Not my daughter.'

'Why didn't you contact the authorities?'

'Back then no one believed a father could do as good a job raising a kid as a mother . . . even an alcoholic one. I was afraid if I asked the court for more time with Beth, I'd lose *all* visitation rights with her.' I look down at the ground. 'They weren't too sympathetic to fathers who had prior convictions; as it was, the only reason I'd gotten as much time with Beth as I had was because Elise hadn't contested it.'

'What was the prior conviction for?' Eric asks.

'I had spent a night in jail after a fight, once.'

'Who was the person you assaulted?'

'Victor Vasquez,' I say. 'The man Elise wound up marrying.'

'Can you tell the court why you fought with Victor?'

I run my thumbnail into a groove of the wood. Now that this moment is here, it's harder than I thought to make the words come out. 'I found out that he was having an affair with my wife,' I say bitterly. 'I beat him up pretty badly and Elise called the police.'

'In light of that incident, you were nervous about asking the authorities to revisit the custody agreement?'

'Yes. I thought they'd look at the petition and think I was doing it to get back at Elise.'

'So.' Eric faces the jury. 'You'd already tried to get Elise to participate in her own rehabilitation, and it didn't work. You saw obstacles lying in front of you if you took legal action. What did you do next?'

'I had run out of options, the way I saw it. I couldn't leave Bethany there, and I couldn't let this keep happening. I wanted my daughter to have a normal life – no, a better than normal life. And I thought that maybe if I got her as far away from all of this as I could, we could both start over. I thought maybe she was even young enough to completely forget that this was the way she'd spent the first four years of her life.' I look up at you, watching me with haunted eyes from the gallery. 'As it turned out, I was right.'

'What did you do next?'

'I took Beth and drove to my condo. I packed as much stuff as I could into the car, and then I started to drive east.'

Eric guides me through a narrative of flight, a web of lies, an outline of how to reinvent oneself. I answer more of his questions – ones about life in Wexton, ones that dovetail with the spot where he began to overlap with our lives. And then he reaches the end of this act, the one we have practiced. 'When you took your daughter, Andrew, did you know what you were doing was against the law?'

I look at the jury. 'Yes.'

'Can you imagine what would have happened to Delia if you hadn't taken her away?'

It is a question Eric's not expecting to get in, and sure enough, the prosecutor objects.

'Sustained,' the judge says.

He has told me that this will be the last question, that he wants to leave the jury thinking about the answer to the question I am not allowed to give. But as Eric heads toward the defense table again, he suddenly stops and pivots. 'Andrew?' he asks, as if it is just the two of us, and something he's wanted to know all along. 'If you had the chance, would you change what you did?'

We haven't rehearsed this answer, and maybe it's the only one that really matters. I turn, so that I am staring square at you; so that you know, all my life, anything I've ever said or buried beneath silence was just for you. 'If I had the chance,' I reply, 'I'd do it all over again.'

IX

But what do you keep of me?
The memory of my bones flying up into your hands.
– Anne Sexton, 'The Surgeon'

Eric

Maybe I'm not going to lose this case, after all.

It's clear Andrew's broken the law – he has admitted it, as well as a lack of remorse – but he's got a few sympathetic jurors. One Hispanic woman, who started crying when he talked about Delia growing up, and one older lady with a tight silver perm, who was nodding along with pity. Two, count 'em, two – when it only takes one to hang a jury.

But then again, Emma Wasserstein hasn't attacked yet. I sit beside Chris, my nails digging into the armrests of the chair. He leans closer to me. 'Fifty bucks says she goes for rage.'

'Lying,' I murmur back. 'She's got that one in the bag already.'

The prosecutor walks toward Andrew; I try to will him faith and composure. *Do not fuck this up,* I think. *I can do that myself.*

'For twenty-eight years,' Emma says, 'you've been lying to your daughter, haven't you.'

'Well, technically.'

'You've been lying about who you are.'

'Yes,' Andrew admits.

'You've been lying about who she is.'

'Yes.'

'You've been lying about all aspects of your former life.'

'Yes.'

'In fact, Mr. Hopkins, there's an excellent chance that you're lying to all of us right now.'

I feel Chris stuff something stiff into my hand; when I look down, it's a fifty-dollar bill.

'I'm not,' Andrew insists. 'I have not lied in this courtroom.'

'Really,' Emma says flatly.

'Yes, really.'

'What if I told you I could prove otherwise?'

Andrew shakes his head. 'I'd say you're mistaken.'

'You told this court, under oath, that you came home to get a security blanket for your daughter . . . and you found Elise Matthews drunk, lying amidst vomit and broken glass and dog feces. Is that correct?'

'Yes.'

'Would it surprise anyone in this courtroom to learn that Elise Vasquez is allergic to dogs? That she never owned one, either while you were living with her or anytime afterward?'

Oh, shit.

Andrew stares at her. 'I never said it was her dog. I'm just telling you what I saw.'

'Are you, Mr. Hopkins? Or are you telling this court what you want *them* to see? Are you painting this situation to be worse than it really was, to justify your own heinous actions?'

'Objection,' I mumble.

'Withdrawn,' Emma says. 'Let's give you the benefit of the doubt, then; let's say your memory of the state of the house is flawless, even after almost thirty years. However, you also said that after finding your wife in this state, and feeling unfairly persecuted by the authorities, you went back to your condo and packed as much as you could into your car, and started driving east with your daughter. Do I have that right?'

'Yes.'

'Would you classify your decision to abscond with your daughter as impulsive?'

'Absolutely,' Andrew says.

'Then what made you close out your bank account on the previous Friday morning, a full day before you picked Bethany up for her custody visit?'

Andrew takes a deep breath, just like I've told him to. 'I was in the process of switching banks,' he says. 'It was a coincidence.'

'I'll bet,' Emma remarks. 'Let's talk about your good intentions for a moment. You said you brought your daughter to Harlem with you, to a crack house, when you purchased those identities?'

'Yes, I did.'

'You brought a four-year-old along to watch you commit a crime?'

'I wasn't committing a crime,' Andrew says.

'You were purchasing someone else's identity. What do you think that is, Mr. Hopkins? Or is your set of laws different from everyone else's?'

'Objection,' I interrupt.

'Were there drug addicts at that crack house?' Emma asks.

'I assume so.'

'Might there have been needles on the floor?'

'It's possible, I don't really remember.'

'Were there individuals with guns or knives?'

'Everyone was busy doing their own thing, Ms. Wasserstein,' Andrew says. 'I knew it wasn't Disneyland when I went in there, but I had no alternative.'

'So let me get this straight: You ran away with your daughter because you were worried about her safety . . . and took her less than a week later into a crack house to become an accessory to a crime?'

'All right,' Andrew admits heavily. 'I did.'

'You never called Elise to let her know that her daughter was healthy and happy, did you.'

'No. I haven't had any contact with her.' He hesitates. 'I didn't want her to be able to track us down.'

'You also never told your daughter that her mother was alive and well in Phoenix?'

'No.'

'Why is that, Mr. Hopkins? Your daughter turned eighteen over a decade ago – she wouldn't have been returned to her mother's custody then, no matter what. The danger, as you perceived it, was over. If your motive for abducting Bethany was to keep her safe, and eventually her safety was a sure thing, you had no reason to hide her whereabouts from your ex-wife anymore, did you?'

'I still couldn't tell her.'

'Because you knew you'd committed a crime, didn't you. You knew you had broken the law.'

'That's not the reason,' Andrew says, shaking his head.

'You were hiding the fact that you had kidnapped her, and would most likely have to face the legal consequences.'

'*No,*' Andrew explodes, too loud. I take the fifty-dollar bill and push it across the table toward Chris.

'Then why, Mr. Hopkins?' the prosecutor asks.

'Because Elise had to stay dead for us to have the lives that we were leading. Delia and I, we were happy. If I told her the truth, I might have lost that. I didn't want to take that risk.'

'Oh, please,' Emma slaps back. 'The only risk you couldn't take is the same one you face right now – the risk of everyone finding out who you really are, so that you'd be sent to prison.'

Andrew stares her down. 'You have no idea who I am,' he says.

Emma walks toward the prosecutor's table. 'I think you're wrong, Mr. Hopkins. I think I know exactly who you are. I think you're a man with a hair-trigger temper, who lies like a rug and acts rashly whenever the situation calls for it.'

'Objection!' I say.

But Andrew isn't even listening to me anymore; he's focused on Emma, walking toward him. 'Isn't it true, Mr. Hopkins, that you've gotten in trouble for letting your emotions run away with you before?'

'I don't know what you mean,' he replies.

'You assaulted Mr. Vasquez after you found out your wife was having an extramarital affair, is that correct?'

'Yes.'

'You were angry when you found out, weren't you.'

'Yes.'

'He was there with *your* wife, *your* daughter, wasn't he.'

'Yes,' Andrew says, his voice taut as a wire.

'You weren't going to let him get away with it, were you?'

'No.' I try desperately to catch Andrew's eye, to center him, before he buys into the anger that Emma's building in him. But this is an Andrew I haven't seen before. His eyes are darker and harder than I have ever seen them; his face twists. 'I saw what he was doing.'

Emma steps directly in front of Andrew. 'So you decided to beat him unconscious, Mr. Hopkins? You assaulted a man in front of your three-year-old daughter?'

'I didn't—'

'You saw something you didn't like, something that you considered a personal slight, and instead of weighing the alternatives you decided you were the only one who could possibly fix it, no matter who got hurt and how many laws were broken.'

'You weren't—'

'You broke the law then, and you did it again when you kidnapped Bethany, Mr. Hopkins, isn't that the truth?'

By now, Andrew is shaking so hard I can see it even from where I'm sitting. 'He was abusing my daughter. That sonofa-bitch was doing it then, and he was still doing it six months later when I took her away from him.'

If the courtroom ceiling had plummeted at that instant, I couldn't have been more shocked. The entire corps of us is stunned into silence by this admission – Emma, the judge, myself. I turn to Delia, searching her out in the frantic gallery, and find her by the white oval of her face. 'Objection, Your Honor,' Emma shouts, the first to recover. 'We've had no evidence to support this claim.'

I know I am supposed to be doing something, but I cannot take my eyes off Delia, who begins to wilt into her chair, like the stalk of a milkweed pod after its heart has been blown away. Beside me I am vaguely aware of Chris Hamilton approaching the bench. 'Of course there was no evidence, Judge. If there were, our client would have been able to present it to the authorities at the time, and we wouldn't all be sitting here. Instead Mr. Hopkins had to *react*—'

The judge bangs his gavel, screaming for order. Across the gallery, I see Fitz put his arm around Delia's shoulders and whisper something to help her keep herself together. I turn to face the spectacle. 'Your Honor, I request a recess with my client.'

'No way,' Emma argues. 'He's not going into a private conference room. If the defendant said or did something that counsel didn't know was coming, he can deal with it here and now.'

'Mr. Talcott,' the judge says, 'I don't know what's going on here. It seems to me that you don't either. I urge you to prove me wrong.'

I look at Andrew, and remember the time he taught me how to do a card trick. It was a simple one, a sleight of hand, but you would have thought from my reaction when I'd mastered it that I had just become David Copperfield. Andrew had laughed at me. 'It's all just smoke and mirrors,' he had said.

Now, I am the one with the tricks up my sleeve. I break the first rule of direct examination: I ask a question the answer to which I don't know, and don't want to. 'Andrew,' I say. 'Tell us about the abuse.'

'I thought Elise was having an affair. And I came home early, thinking I could catch her . . .' He closes his eyes. 'When I got there, and I looked in the window, Elise was asleep on the bed, alone. But in the living room . . . Beth was watching television. He had her on his lap . . . and he was scratching her back. But then his hands went underneath her skirt . . . and . . .' Andrew bends down, his shoulders heaving. 'He had his hands on her. He touched my daughter. And every time Elise got drunk, or fell asleep, he was going to be there doing the same thing. I beat him up. But that wouldn't stop it from happening again.'

There is noise in the gallery; I am not brave enough to look in that direction and risk seeing Delia's face yet. Andrew buries his face in his hands; I wait for him to regain his composure. When he lifts his head, his eyes are red and raw and hold every member of that jury accountable. 'Maybe I kidnapped my daughter. Maybe I broke the law. But you can't tell me that what I did was *wrong.*'

My head is a kaleidoscope of questions – not about this case, but about the woman ten feet away from me, whose life has just been ripped out from underneath her once again. 'The defense rests,' I murmur.

Before I can even make it back to my seat, though, Emma stands up again. 'The prosecution would like to recall Delia Hopkins.'

I turn around. 'You can't.'

'On what grounds?'

On the grounds that I love her.

No one comments when Fitz walks Delia all the way to the bar, and opens the gate to let her inside. She moves slowly, precariously. When she sits down on the edge of the chair, she does not look at her father, and she doesn't look at me. She is full of ghosts; I can see them peeking from the windows that used to be her eyes.

'Ms. Hopkins,' Emma says, 'do you have any recollection of being sexually abused by Victor Vasquez?'

Delia shakes her head.

'Let the record reflect that the witness has given a negative response,' Emma says. 'Nothing further.'

The judge glances at me. 'Mr. Talcott?'

I start to shake my head – I would rather be eviscerated with a butter knife on the bench right now than cross-examine Delia – but Chris Hamilton grabs my arm. 'If you don't detonate this bomb,' he whispers, 'we are screwed.'

So I get to my feet. *Forgive me,* I beg silently. *I am only doing this for you.* 'You *really* don't remember being sexually abused by Victor Vasquez?'

She looks at me, surprised. The last thing she would expect

from me right now is this tone of voice, this mockery. 'I think it would be hard to forget something like that,' she says.

'Maybe,' I say coolly. 'Then again, you don't remember being kidnapped, do you.' I turn away from Delia before I can see how much more damage I've done.

As it happens, Emma is the one who needs a hiatus; the prosecutor's water breaks about five minutes later during a recess. She is taken to the hospital by ambulance, and court is adjourned for five days.

I find Delia and Fitz taking refuge in a conference room upstairs, away from the frenzied sea of media that has doubled in size, it seems, since this morning. She still looks unsteady, but by now, she is angry, too. 'How could you do this to me?' she accuses. 'You made this all up.'

Shaking my head, I walk toward her. I am struck by the sense that although she looks just like Delia should look, she is a soap bubble, and if I get too close she will simply disappear. 'I give you my word, Dee, this was not some defense ploy. I didn't know this was going to happen.'

When she tilts her face up to mine, it breaks my heart. 'Then why didn't I know it ever *had?*'

Because I am a coward, I choose not to answer. 'I have to go to the jail,' I say gently. 'I need to speak to your father now.' With a squeeze of support to Delia's shoulders, I leave the conference room. I hurry across the street to the Madison Street Jail, and I ask to see Andrew.

I should have hired an investigator to depose him instead of doing it myself, then I would have been able to impeach him with his own testimony and salvage this trial. I don't say a single word, just wait for him to sit down and initiate conversation. 'What happens now?' he asks finally.

'Well,' I suggest, 'how about you tell me what the hell that was all about?'

He knots his hands on the scarred table, his thumb tracing the graffiti that reads TUPAC 4EVA. 'What kind of man goes after a woman who's married, a woman who's an obvious drunk, and who has a little girl? You do the math, Eric.'

'Andrew,' I explain, frustrated, 'you can't throw a smoking gun down at the end of a trial. Why didn't you mention this before? It would have been a perfect defense.'

'I managed to keep this from her all these years, so that she could have a normal life.'

I scrub my hands through my hair. 'Andrew, there's no evidence here. *Delia* doesn't even remember it happening.'

But even as I say it, I'm remembering the smallest of details, the clues that I should have picked up on. Like when we first talked about Victor and the assault charge: *I saw him,* Andrew had said, *I watched him kiss her.*

Elise? I had asked, and he'd hesitated for a half-second before he nodded.

Or the medical records Delia and I had read together: Focused on the fact of the scorpion sting, I never really considered the physician's comment about the patient fighting when her clothes were being removed for treatment. Or the fact that a four-year-old girl had a urinary tract infection.

'What happens now?' Andrew repeats.

What happens now is that Emma will come back from her labor and delivery and file a motion to get Andrew's revelation excluded. The judge will be inclined to agree. The jurors – already dubious, because who drops a bomb like this one at the last minute but a liar? – will be asked to disregard the testimony. And Andrew, who literally confessed to kidnapping on the stand, will be convicted.

I don't want him sitting here for five days, thinking about going to prison; I can protect him from his own future for at least that long. So I look him in the eye and lie to him. 'I don't know, Andrew.'

It isn't until I have left the jail that I realize I'm no better than he is.

By the time I get home, it is twilight. Delia sits on the steps of the trailer, stroking Greta. 'Hey,' I say, kneeling down in front of her. 'Are you okay?'

'You tell me,' she says, brittle, brushing her hair away from her face. 'Since I don't seem to have any clue at all about myself.'

As I sit down next to her, Greta gets up and moves away from us, as if she knows I've taken over the helm of support. 'Where's Sophie?'

'Napping.'

'And Fitz?'

'I sent him home,' she says. She draws her knees up and wraps her arms tight around them. 'Do you know how many people I've come across on a job, who tell me they didn't even know they were off course until it was too late? Hikers who take a wrong turn, novice campers who misread a map – they all say they thought they were somewhere else.' She stares at me. 'I never really believed them, until now.'

'Sweetheart, listen—'

'I don't want to listen, Eric. I don't want to be told anymore who I used to be. I want to fucking remember it myself.' Tears swim in her eyes. 'What is *wrong* with me?'

I reach out, intending to draw her into my arms, but as soon as my hands slide across her shoulder blades, she stiffens.

He was scratching her back . . .

His hands went underneath her skirt . . .

She looks up at me with tears in her eyes. 'Sophie,' she says. 'She was with him, alone.'

'You got there first,' I tell her, because I need to believe it myself. She ducks her head, lost in thought. 'I'll be inside if you need me.'

She tucks her hair behind her ears and nods. But then, it's never the finding part that's been a problem for Delia. It's coming to terms with being lost.

It's choice that makes us human: I could put this bottle down at any time, or I could continue till it's empty. I can tell myself

I know exactly what I'm doing; I can convince myself that it will take much more than a few drinks to slide down to a pit I cannot climb out from.

And, oh, God, the taste of it. The sooty smoke in the back of the throat; the burn on the flesh of my lips. The stream of it through the baleen of my teeth. After a day like this one, anyone would need to unwind a little.

Tonight, the moon is jaundiced and scarred. It's so close to the roof of Ruthann's trailer that for a moment I imagine that the corner of the roof might prick it, send it flying like a pierced balloon.

Why do they call it a mobile home, if it never goes anywhere?

'Eric?' A sliver of light splinters my arm, then my leg, then half of my body as Delia opens the door. 'Are you still out here?'

I manage to slide the whiskey bottle behind my calf where she can't see it.

She sits down on the step behind me. 'I just wanted to say that I'm sorry. I know this isn't your fault.'

If I answer, she'll smell the booze on my breath. So instead, I just hang my head, and hope she thinks I'm overwhelmed.

'Come inside,' she says, reaching for my hand, and I'm so grateful for this that when I stand up I forget what I've been hiding, and the bottle rolls down the steps.

'Did you drop something?' Delia asks, but as her eyes adjust to the darkness, she sees the label. 'Oh, Eric,' she murmurs, a boatload of disillusion in those broken syllables.

By the time I shake myself out of my stupor enough to follow her inside, she's already hauled a sleeping Sophie into her arms. She whistles for Greta, and grabs her car keys from the counter.

'For God's sake, Delia, it was just a little nightcap. I'm not drunk, look at me. *Listen* to me. I can stop whenever I feel like it.'

She turns around, our daughter caught between us. 'So can I, Eric,' she says, and she walks out the front door.

I don't call her back when she gets into the Explorer. The taillights dance down the road, the sideways eyes of a demon. I sit down on the bottom step of the trailer and pick up the bottle of whiskey, which is lying on its side.

It's half full.

Fitz

It takes a while to get Sophie settled in my motel room, with Greta curled on the edge of the bed like a sentry. Then, using the tiny immersion heater that shares a plug with the hair dryer in the bathroom, I boil water for tea. I bring a cup of it out to Delia, who is sitting outside the motel room on one of the plastic lawn chairs that overlook the parking lot.

'Let's see,' she says. 'In less than twelve hours' time, I found out that I was abused as a child and that my fiancé's fallen off the wagon. I figure I'm due to come down with cancer any minute, don't you think?'

'God forbid,' I tell her.

'Brain tumor.'

'Shut *up.*' I sit down beside her.

'All those things he was saying in the courtroom,' she says. 'Didn't Eric even listen to himself?'

'I don't know if he wanted to,' I admit. 'I think he would have rather believed he was who you wanted him to be.'

'Are you saying this is *my* fault?'

'No. Not any more than the other is your father's.'

Her mouth snaps shut, and she takes a sip of her tea. 'I hate it when you're right,' she says. And then, more softly: 'How can you be a survivor, when you can't even remember the war?'

I take the cup out of her hand and spread her palm flat on top of mine, then turn it over as if I am about to read her future. I trace the life line and the love line; I trail my fingers over the cords of her wrist. 'None of it changes anything,' I tell her. 'No matter what your father said up there. You're the same person you were before he said it.'

She pushes me away. 'What if you found out that you used to be a girl, Fitz? And that you had operations and everything and you don't remember a single bit of it?'

'That's just crazy,' I reply, my masculine pride kicking in. 'There'd be scars.'

'Well, don't you think I have those, too? What else do you think I've forgotten?'

'Alien abduction?' I joke.

'No, just a plain human one,' she says bitterly.

'Would you like my childhood memories, instead? How about the one where my father leaves my mother for a month when he can't stop gambling in Vegas? Or the one where she holds a kitchen knife up to him and tells him he will never, ever, bring his whore to her house again. Or maybe you'd like the one where she swallows all her Valium, and I get to call nine-one-one.' I stare at her. 'Remembering misery is not all it's cracked up to be.'

Chagrined, she looks into her lap. 'It's hard to know what to trust, that's all.'

Her words make me run cold. 'Delia, I need to tell you something.'

'You used to be a girl before the operation?'

'I'm being serious,' I say. 'I knew that Eric was drinking again.'

She draws back slowly. 'What?'

'I was there two days ago, and I found a bottle.'

'Why didn't you tell me?' Delia says, stung.

'Why don't any of us tell you anything?' I respond. 'We *love* you.'

My statement startles a hawk out of the blanket of the night; it takes to the sky with a cry. Delia turns my words over in her mind, and then glances up at me. 'How is my book coming?' she asks quietly.

'I haven't worked on it,' I say, though my throat has gone narrow as the eye of a needle. 'I've been busy.'

'Maybe I could help you with it,' Delia suggests, and she kisses me again.

She unspools in my arm, and although I understand she is trying to lose herself, I've been waiting too long for her to allow that to happen. I sink my fingers into her hair and unravel her ponytail; I tug at the buttons of the pajama top she arrived wearing. I sign my initials on the small of her back.

When she starts to unbuckle my belt, I grab her wrist. We can't go into the room where Sophie's sleeping, so I haul her into the backseat of her rental car, parked two feet in front of us. It seems ridiculous, adolescent, and in a way, perfectly fitting. Our knees knock against the windows and our feet get in the way, and because it is Delia, we even laugh. When we are both lying sideways on the seat and she reaches into my boxers, so that the ridge of my erection meets the silk of her palm, I actually stop breathing. 'I'm a natural redhead,' I say, my voice shaking.

'That wasn't what I was checking.'

'Delia,' I ask, because even if she doesn't know herself all that well, I've made a life study of it, 'are you sure you want to do this?'

'Are you sure you want me to think twice?' she answers, and then she lowers her mouth onto me.

There is a tremendous tide in me I didn't know I had; it pulls me by the blood to surge against her, to cry out when her fingernails rake the insides of my thighs. When I twist so that I'm braced above her, I wait for her to open her eyes, to know that this is me. I slide into the violet heat of her. I pick the rhythm between our pulses. We move as if we've been together forever, which, when you think about it, we have.

Afterward, the moon rounds on the roof of the car like a lazy cat, and Delia dozes in my arms. I don't let myself fall asleep; I've dreamed this enough already. This is how my story starts; this is how hers will end, if I have anything to say about it.

An hour or so later, she stirs, stretching against the length of me. 'Fitz?' Delia asks. 'Have we ever done that before?'

I glance down at her. 'No.'

'I didn't think I'd forgotten,' she says, but she's smiling against the curve of my neck.

She falls asleep this time holding my hand, Eric's diamond ring cutting into my palm like the wounds of Passion from the Crucifixion. I would do that for her, I realize. Die. Be reborn.

Delia

When we were kids, Fitz was unbeatable at Scrabble. It would drive Eric crazy, because he wasn't used to being bested by Fitz in much of anything. But Fitz had an uncanny memory, and once he saw a word, he wouldn't forget it. 'There is no such word as *linn*,' Eric would argue, but sure enough, Webster's defined it as a waterfall.

Personally, I thought it was sort of amazing that anyone twelve years old would know that a *pyx* is a container for the Host during communion. But Eric wasn't used to being second-best, so he commissioned me into teaching him the dictionary.

We worked our way through the letters with the same incredible focus that Eric applied to anything, when he was inclined. I'd make up vocabulary tests for Eric, and quiz him when he ate dinner over at our house. 'At the very least,' my father used to say, 'you two are going to ace your SATs.'

Three weeks after we'd taken on the English language, it rained on a Saturday. 'Hey,' Fitz suggested, like usual. 'Bet I can whip you in Scrabble.'

Eric looked at me. 'Huh,' he said. 'What makes you think that?'

'Um . . . the five hundred and seventy thousand other times I've kicked your ass?'

Fitz knew. The moment Eric laid down the letters *J-A-R-L* and then casually mentioned that it was a term for a Scandinavian noble, Fitz's eyes lit up. Our board was full of words like *larum* and *girn* and *ghat* and *revet*. Finally, when the score was almost tied, Eric set out *valgus*. Fitz started to laugh. 'I don't think so.'

Triumphant, Eric passed him the dictionary. He waited until Fitz found the right page. *'Turned abnormally outward. Twisted.'*

Fitz shook his head. 'You got me, but you still lose.' And he set the word *fungible* on a triple word score, pulling into the lead.

'What does it mean?' I asked.

'It's us,' Fitz said. 'Look it up.'

I did. I liked the word; it sounded like something you could punch into position, like a soft pillow, or hold on the roof of your mouth. I expected it to mean inseparable, brilliant, loyal – any of a hundred adjectives I could apply to us as a trio.

Fungible, I read. *Interchangeable.*

In the morning, while Sophie is still fast asleep, I shower in Fitz's motel bathroom. He comes in as I am brushing my hair. Without saying a word, he takes the comb out of my hand and tilts my head back. He works through the knots first, and then makes long, sweeping strokes from the crown of my head to the ends. Our eyes meet in the mirror but neither of us speaks; we are afraid that whatever words we pick won't be able to bear the weight of what's happened.

'Do you want me to come with you?' he asks.

I shake my head, still attached by a rope of a loose ponytail to his fist. 'I need you to take care of Sophie.'

I have told him I need to talk to Eric; I just haven't told him I'm stopping somewhere else, first.

As I drive, I relive what it was like to sleep in Fitz's arms last night. As much as I would like to credit this, too, to a memory lapse, I know it isn't.

I can't blame Eric's drinking, either.

What I did was a mistake, because I am engaged to Eric.

But what if *that* was the mistake?

I met Fitz and Eric at the same time. We have all been friends for years. But what if the way I remember my relationships evolving with the two of them is different from the

way it actually was? What if the things I've chosen to recall
got twisted, somehow, during the re-creation?

What if last night wasn't wrong . . . but finally, remarkably,
right?

'I swear to you,' my mother says urgently, 'Victor never would
have done any of that.'

We are sitting on her patio, under a mister meant to coun-
teract the blistering heat. As the water sprays out of the tiny
nozzle heads, it immediately evaporates. It makes me think of
those first years of my life, the ones that disappeared before I
ever had a chance to really see them.

'You know what?' I say wearily. 'I really don't know who
I'm supposed to believe anymore.'

'How about yourself?' She shakes her head. 'Did you ever
think that maybe the reason you can't remember any of . . .
that . . . is because it never happened? I know I'm the last
person you'd turn to for credibility, Delia, but your father . . .
he wasn't *here*. You used to follow Victor around in the backyard, helping him plant his gardens – you followed him like a
puppy. You wouldn't have done that if he'd been hurting you,
would you?' She sighs. 'Maybe your father thought he saw
something, even though he didn't. Maybe you said something
one day that didn't make sense to him. But maybe he was just
jealous, because there was another man spending time with
you, and he was afraid you'd found a replacement.'

I realize, suddenly, that everyone is a liar. Memories are like
a still life painted by ten different student artists: some will be
blue-based; others red; some will be as stark as Picasso and
others as rich as Rembrandt; some will be foreshortened and
others distant. Recollections are in the eye of the beholder; no
two held up side by side will ever quite match.

In that moment, I want to be with Sophie. I want to take
off our shoes and run through the red sand; I want to hang
upside down from the monkey bars with her. I want to listen
to the jokes she makes without punch lines; I want to feel her

sidle closer to me when we come to a street crossing. I want to make new memories instead of search for old ones.

'I have to go home,' I say abruptly. My mother gets to her feet, but I say I will let myself out. She hesitates, unsure, and then leans forward to kiss me good-bye on the cheek. We don't quite connect.

I head through the side gate and walk along the crushed stone path toward my car. I have just unlocked the door when a truck drives up. Victor steps out, and we stare at each other, palpably uncomfortable. 'Delia,' he says. 'I didn't do what he said.'

I look at him, then open my car door.

'Wait.' He pulls off his baseball cap and holds it in front of him. 'I never would have hurt you,' he says earnestly. 'Elise couldn't have children – I knew that – and it was a blessing that she already had one I could share. I know you can't remember, but I can.'

He is looking right at me with his solemn, dark eyes; his mouth trembles with his conviction. I try to imagine following him around as he plants, dropping small white stones in mounds around the cacti. I begin to hear, in my mind, the names of some of the flora and fauna in Spanish: *el pito, el mapache, el cardo, la garra del Diablo* – woodpecker, raccoon, thistle, Devil's Claw.

'You were like my daughter, *grilla*,' he says, uneasy in the silence. 'And I loved you like a father, nothing more.'

Grilla.

I am watching him plant the lemon tree. I've gotten tired of dancing around it. I want to make lemonade, already. How long will it take? *I ask him.* A while, *he answers. I sit down in front of it to watch.* I'll wait. *He comes over and takes my hand.* Come on, *grilla, he says.* If we're going to sit here that long, we'd better get something to eat. *He swings me up onto his shoulders. He clasps the backs of my legs, to steady me. His hands are butterflies on the insides of my thighs.*

With trembling fingers, I fumble for the latch of the car door. 'Delia?' Victor asks. 'Are you all right?'

'That word: *grilla,*' I say, my voice coming out a faint whistle. 'What does it mean?'

'*Grilla?*' Victor repeats. 'Cricket. It's a . . . how do you say . . . term of endearment.'

From a distance, I feel myself nod.

It's not a surprise to find Eric asleep; it is only nine in the morning. I find him on the bed inside the trailer, with the empty bottle beside him. He is naked, wrapped partly in a sheet.

I reach down and pull it off him. He scrambles upright, wincing when the light falls into his bloodshot eyes. 'Jesus Christ,' he murmurs. 'What are you doing?'

For a moment, it is three years ago, and this is one of the hundred times that I came into a room to find Eric after a night of drinking. Back then, I would have put on a pot of coffee and dragged him into the shower. Three years ago, I had a whole host of techniques for immediate sobriety. And yet none of them ever got him to react as quickly as the method I employ today. 'Eric,' I announce, 'I remember.'

X

'Memory is the only way home.'
– Terry Tempest Williams, as quoted in
Listen to Their Voices, Chapter 10,
by Mickey Pearlman (1993)

Eric

Memory has had a spotty record in the United States court system. For a while, recovered memory was all the rage – adults went to therapists, who planted seeds for trauma that didn't really exist. Hundreds of people came out of the woodwork to accuse child-care workers of abuse and Satanism, and their recollections were allowed as evidence and treated as fact. In the mid-nineties, however, the tide began to turn. Judges steered clear of recovered memories, saying they weren't valid unless they were supported by independent evidence.

We happen to be twenty-eight years late for that.

Still, it's new evidence, and I'll be damned if I'm not getting it in. Delia has given me a list of the memories, the ones that are coming fast and furious now that the wire has seemingly been tripped: the lemon tree, in its entirety. A pair of boxers Victor used to own with blue fish printed all over them. Having him sit on the edge of her bed and lift her nightgown to rub her back. Victor asking her to pull down her underwear and touch herself.

I have to treat it the way I would any other evidence. If I think too hard about it, I want to kill someone.

I send Emma flowers at the birthing center of the hospital. The card reads 'Delia has started to remember the abuse. Consider this notice of my intention to bring these memories into the trial.' Two days later, she moves for a 702 hearing, to address the scientific reliability of the evidence.

We are in the courtroom, but it's a closed hearing, just the judge and the attorneys; no media or jury. Emma wears a maternity dress, but it's pouchy and bunched at the stomach.

Alison Rebbard, Emma's expert witness, is a memory expert affiliated with a string of Ivy League universities. She has a thin face accented by pink, wire-rimmed glasses, and she's used to sitting in a witness box. 'Dr. Rebbard,' Emma asks, 'how does memory work?'

'The brain can't remember everything,' she says. 'It just doesn't have the storage capacity. We forget most of what occurs, including events that were probably significant at the time. Now, the things that *do* stick . . . well, they aren't like images on a videotape. Only minimal bits of information are recorded, and when we recall it, our mind automatically fleshes out the recollection by inventing details based on previous similar experiences. Memory is a reconstruction; it's contaminated by mood and circumstance and a hundred other factors.'

'So, a memory might change over time?'

'It most likely will. But interestingly, it seems to retain its mutations. Distortions become part of the memory in subsequent recalls.'

'Are some memories true, then, while some are false?' Emma asks.

'Yes. And some are a mixture of books we've read or movies we've seen. One of my studies, for example, focused on children at a school that was attacked by a sniper. Even the kids who weren't on school grounds at the time had a recollection of being there during the attack . . . a false memory that was probably inspired by the stories they heard from their friends and on the news.'

'Dr. Rebbard,' Emma asks, 'is there a general agreement about when a child is capable of retaining traumatic memories?'

'Overall, we say that events that happen before age two won't be remembered past childhood; and memories before the age of three are rare and unreliable. Most researchers believe that serious abuse after the age of four *will* be remembered into adulthood.'

'Delia Hopkins has not been seeing a therapist, but has been experiencing recovered memories,' Emma explains. 'Would that surprise you?'

'Not given what you've told me about this case,' Dr. Rebbard says. 'The preparation for this trial and the testimony itself would force her to relive hypothetical scenarios. She's wondering why her father might have taken her; she's wondering if there was something in her past that might have precipitated it. It's impossible to tell whether she's actually remembering these things or if she only wants to remember them. Either way would explain a period of her life she doesn't understand, and would most likely vindicate her father's behavior.'

'I'd like to address the particular memories that Ms. Hopkins claims to have recovered,' Emma says, and I jump up.

'Objection,' I say, 'this hearing is only about admissibility, Your Honor. It would be premature to have the State's expert judge the reliability of memories without hearing the actual testimony of the memories and how the witness experienced them.' Or in other words, *you have to let my evidence in first.*

Judge Noble looks at me over his half-glasses. 'Is Ms. Hopkins here to testify?'

No, because she's barely speaking to me.

'Not today, Your Honor,' I say aloud.

'Well, that's *your* problem, son. We're going to allow your offer of proof to stand as to what she might testify to in open court, and I'm going to allow Ms. Wasserstein to proceed.'

Emma approaches the witness stand. 'In the first alleged memory,' she says, 'Ms. Hopkins remembers Mr. Vasquez wearing boxer shorts printed with blue fish. In the second alleged memory, Mr. Vasquez is coming into her bedroom at night and stroking her back. In the third, he asks her to remove her underpants and touch herself. Is this damning evidence, in your opinion?'

'Often we'll see a subject come to a therapist with a few disconnected traumatic images, sort of like bits of a black-and-white photo. These are what we'd call deteriorated memories.'

'Isn't it possible, Doctor, that Ms. Hopkins remembers seeing Mr. Vasquez in his boxers because, like every other child on the planet, she walked in on him in the bathroom?'

'Absolutely.'

'And what if the reason he was in her room at night was not to harm her, but to comfort her after a nightmare?'

'Very plausible, as well,' Rebbard agrees.

'And as for the third, what if there was a medical reason for the request – for example, if the child had a yeast infection and Mr. Vasquez wanted her to apply cream to the area?'

'In that scenario,' Dr. Rebbard points out, 'he's going out of his way to *not* touch her. The point here is that we don't have the whole memory, the whole story. Unfortunately, neither does Ms. Hopkins. She's looking at a striped tail and screaming because it must be a tiger, when in actuality it might be a house cat.'

I don't have an expert witness; I couldn't have afforded one even if I'd had the foresight to find one. Instead, I've spent the past two days poring over psychiatric texts and legal briefs, trying to find what I can to trap the State's expert during cross-examination.

I approach Dr. Rebbard with my hands in my trouser pockets. 'Why would Delia want to make up a memory that's so painful?'

'Because the fringe benefit outweighs that,' the psychiatrist explains. 'It becomes a hook for the jury to hang its hat on, and acquit her father.'

'Repression is defined as the selective forgetting of materials that cause pain, isn't that true?' I ask.

'Yes.'

'It's not a voluntary act.'

'No.'

'Can you explain dissociation, Doctor?'

She nods. 'When a person is in a state of terror or pain, perceptions get altered. Attention is focused on the present moment, and surviving. When attention becomes that narrow, there can be great perceptual distortion, including desensitization from pain, time slowing down, and amnesia. Some psychiatrists believe that removing the anxiety can lead to remembering what happened,' she adds, 'but I'm not one of them.'

'Even though *you* don't believe it, however, dissociative amnesia is a valid psychiatric condition, isn't it?'

'Yes.'

'In fact, the *DSM-IV*, the bible of psychiatric diagnosis, even lists it.' I lean down to the defense table and read aloud. '"Dissociative amnesia is characterized by an inability to recall important personal information, usually of a traumatic or stressful nature, that is too extensive to be explained by ordinary forgetfulness." That seems to describe Delia Hopkins, doesn't it?'

'Yes.'

I continue reading. '"It commonly presents as a retrospectively reported gap in recall for aspects of the individual's life history." Again, that's a bull's-eye.'

'Apparently.'

'". . . in recent years, there has been an increase in reported cases of dissociative amnesia that involves previously forgotten early childhood traumas." Bingo.' I look up at her. 'This manual only lists diagnoses that have come from years of empirical data and clinical observation, right?'

'Yes.'

'And it's considered a conservative document?'

'Yes.'

'You use this manual professionally, don't you?'

'Yes, but as an analytic tool, not a legal one.' She tilts her head. 'Do you know when the *DSM-IV* was written, Mr. Talcott?'

I freeze and scan the front of the book. 'Nineteen ninety-three?'

'Right. *Before* the rise of repressed memory therapy led to hundreds of false convictions of sexual abuse.'

Ouch. 'How does a triggered memory differ from a recovered memory, Doctor?'

'There's a school of thought that says memories of traumatic moments are just as abnormal as the moments themselves, and don't have the same associations that other memories do, which means they're harder to bring front and center in the mind. But by the same reasoning, trauma-specific clues might be able to trip those memories.'

'So a triggered memory isn't planted, so to speak. It really does exist, and has just been waiting for the right time to break free.'

'That's right.'

'Can you give an example?'

'A subject might hear a gun go off in close proximity, and then suddenly remember a gunshot years ago that killed his father when he was standing next to him.'

'Isn't it true that this scenario is closer to the way Delia Hopkins has recovered her memories, Doctor?' The psychiatrist nods. 'And isn't it possible, Doctor, that there is a place memory can go, until it's ready to come forward again – for whatever reason? That recovering a memory might not be a re-creation but . . . a search-and-rescue mission?'

The words remind me, of course, of Delia. 'I suppose so, Mr. Talcott.'

I take a deep breath. 'Nothing further.'

Emma stands up again. 'By the defense's own reasoning, if Ms. Hopkins was recovering memories of traumatic childhood events when there was a trigger, such as courtroom testimony, wouldn't it make sense that she'd react the same way to similar triggers?'

'Theoretically,' Dr. Rebbard agrees.

'Then why didn't she have a barrage of recollections about her abduction?' Emma poses, as I object. 'Nothing further.'

I'm already approaching Dr. Rebbard again. 'What if it wasn't traumatic?' I ask.

'I'm not sure I understand . . .'

'What if, to Delia, the kidnapping wasn't something frightening? What if she considered it a relief, a way out from the sexual abuse? In that case, Dr. Rebbard, a memory of the abduction *wouldn't* have been triggered by her father's testimony, right?'

This time Dr. Rebbard gives me a full smile. 'I suppose not, Counselor,' she says.

Emma is showing me pictures of her son when the judge comes back with his ruling. 'The issue here is whether we can forget events that took place,' Judge Noble says, 'and if we can remember events that never took place. This topic, of course, is a highly charged one. No matter how I rule, and no matter what we say to the jury, we're going to be dealing with a situation where the jurors are going to have a hard time separating their feelings from the events being discussed.' He looks at Emma. 'The greatest tragedy of this trial would be to believe another lie from Andrew Hopkins. And as it stands, the evidence is not reliable enough to justify inclusion.'

Then he turns to me. 'I'm making a legal decision here, but I can't make the emotional ones. I'm damn sure my decision isn't going to make you very happy, son. But I want you to remember that even though I can rule out what happens from this point forward, I can't take back what's already been said. Maybe in New Hampshire those judges don't tell it like it is, but here in Arizona, we do. And I want you to know, Mr. Talcott, you may think your case hinges on this evidence, but I expect you're gonna do just fine without it.'

He gets up and exits; Emma behind him. I sit for a few moments in the empty courtroom. If this were like old times, I would go home and tell Delia that I'd lost the hearing. I'd repeat, verbatim, what the judge had said, and I'd ask her to interpret it. We'd dissect my performance until she finally threw up her hands and said we were going nowhere with any of this.

She will not be back tonight, I suppose. And we're still going nowhere.

Andrew

Delia is the last person to enter the courtroom before the doors are shut. She is wearing a yellow dress and her dark hair is pulled back off her neck; it reminds me of a long, lovely sunflower. I have so much to say to her, but it is better done afterward, anyway; when I will likely have yet another reason to tell her I'm sorry.

Beside me, Eric gets to his feet to address the jury. 'You know what love is, ladies and gentlemen?' he asks. 'It's not doing whatever the person you care for expects of you. It's doing what they *don't* expect. It's going above and beyond what you've been asked. That's what Andrew Hopkins should be charged with, you know. That's what he would plead guilty to, hands down.

'The prosecutor is going to talk to you about obeying rules. She's going to use words like "kidnapping." But there was no kidnapping here; there was no force. And as for rules, well, you know there are always exceptions. What you might *not* know, however, is that the same thing applies to the letter of the law.'

Eric walks toward the jury. 'The judge is going to tell you that if you find that Andrew had committed all the elements of kidnapping beyond a reasonable doubt, then you should convict him. Not that you *have* to . . . not that you'd *like* to . . . but that you *should* find him guilty. Why doesn't the judge say that you *must* find him guilty? Because he can't. You, as jurors, have the ultimate authority and power to convict or not to convict – no matter what.'

'Objection!' Emma Wasserstein steams. 'Bench!' The two

lawyers approach the judge. 'Your Honor, he's telling the jury they can nullify the whole charge if they want to,' the prosecutor complains.

'I know,' Judge Noble says evenly. 'And there's nothin' I can do about it.'

When Eric turns around, he's stunned; I don't think he expected to get away with this. He swallows and faces the jury again. 'The law is very deliberate, and it chooses its words carefully. And sometimes, on purpose, it opens the door for that gap between rule and reason. You have a choice to make, ladies and gentlemen. Some choices are not made lightly. Not the ones Andrew made, not the ones the law makes, and, I hope, not your own.'

Emma Wasserstein is so angry I expect to see sparks flying from her shoes. 'Mr. Talcott has apparently been spending too much time with his client,' she tells the jury, 'because he's just lied to you. He told you this isn't kidnapping, because there was no force involved. Well, nobody asked Bethany Matthews if she wanted to go. Maybe he didn't tie her up with duct tape and throw her in the back of his van for the ride to New Hampshire, but he didn't have to. He told a poor, innocent child her mother was dead. He told her that she had nobody but him. He did so much damage to this child in an effort to wrestle her out of her mother's home that he might as well have bound and gagged her. This was emotional duct tape, and Andrew Hopkins was a master.'

She turns to look at me. 'But he didn't just affect the life of one victim. This rash, selfish act claimed two – Bethany Matthews, and her mother, Elise, who spent twenty-eight years waiting to see the child who'd vanished. This rash, selfish act gave Andrew Hopkins everything – the child, full custody, and freedom from punishment . . . until now.'

Emma moves toward the jury box. 'For you to find Andrew Hopkins guilty of kidnapping, you must agree that he took a child without having the authority to do so, and that he did this with force. Andrew Hopkins himself even said on the stand that he had indeed kidnapped his daughter. You can't get much clearer than that.

'Yet, as Mr. Talcott said, rules don't always fit. Mr. Talcott pointed out that the law says you should convict, if all these conditions are met, but that you don't *have* to. Well, let me tell you why that's not quite as simple as he's making it out to be.' She walks over to Eric. 'If we lived in a world where rules were trumped by emotions, then we'd be in a very uncomfortable place indeed. For example, I could do this' – without hesitation, Emma picks up Eric's briefcase and moves it to her own table – 'because I like it better than mine. And if I could convince you from an emotional standpoint that I have good reason to like it better than mine, then hey, you would be justified in saying I was allowed to steal that briefcase.'

She walks back toward Eric and picks up his glass of water, drinks it down. 'If we lived in Mr. Talcott's world, I could come over here and drink his water, because I'm a nursing mother and I deserve it. But you know what? That kind of world would also be the place where rapists could do what they wanted because it was what they felt like at the time.' She approaches the jury again. 'It would be the kind of world where if someone was overcome with rage, it would be okay to commit murder. And it would be the kind of world where, if someone could convince you it was really just an act of heroism, he could steal your child away from you for twenty-eight years.'

She hesitates. 'I don't live in that world, ladies and gentlemen. And, I bet, neither do you.'

While the jury is deliberating, Eric and I hole up in a tiny conference room. He orders corned beef sandwiches from a kosher deli and we chew in silence. 'Thank you,' I say after a moment.

He shrugs. 'I was hungry, too.'

'I meant for representing me.'

Eric shakes his head. 'Don't thank me.'

I take another bite; swallow. 'I'm counting on you to take care of her.'

He looks down at his hands, then sets down his sandwich. 'Andrew,' Eric replies, 'I think it might have to be the other way around.'

We are called back for a verdict in less than three hours. As the jury shuffles in, I try to read their faces, but they are inscrutable, and none of them meet my eye. Is that a sign of pity? Or of guilt?

'Will the defendant please rise?'

I do not think I have ever been as aware of my age as I am in that moment. It is nearly impossible for me to stand; I find myself leaning against Eric even when I try to remain straight and brave. When I cannot bear it any longer, I turn my head and look for Delia in the gallery. I hold on to her face, a focal point while the rest of the world is going to pieces around me.

'Have you reached a verdict?' the judge asks.

A woman with tight red pincurls nods. 'We have, Your Honor.'

'What say you?'

'In the case of *The State of Arizona* versus *Andrew Hopkins*, we find the defendant not guilty.'

I am aware of Eric crowing with delight, of Chris Hamilton slapping us both on the back. I try to find enough air to breathe. And then Delia is there, with her arms around me and her face pressed into my chest. I hold tight and I think of something Eric said, just after his closing statement. *It's not a real defense,* he murmured, *but sometimes that's all you've got.*

Sometimes it even works.

There is a commotion as the reporters vie for Eric's sound bite. Gradually, the crowd falls back to allow Emma Wasserstein passage. She shakes Eric's hand, and Chris's, and then leans forward to give Eric's briefcase back to him. But as she does, she comes close enough to whisper to me. 'Mr. Hopkins,' she says, a truth meant only for me, 'I would have done it, too.'

Fitz

I am trying to find a back exit that we might use to escape when Delia appears and throws herself into my arms. I'm still not used to that; immediately every conscious thought or rational plan flies out of my head while I just enjoy the feel of her. 'Congratulations,' I say into her hair.

'I want to tell Sophie,' she announces. 'I want to tell her and then I want to drive straight to the airport and get on the first plane to New Hampshire.'

And what happens then? Delia, so happy about the verdict, hasn't even touched down close enough to ground to remember all that's been left behind. It's nice to know that the atomic bomb missed your house, but you will be cleaning up the rubble for some time before your front path is clear.

As it turns out, I don't want to write the story of her life. I want a series.

'Stop thinking,' Delia says, the same advice I once gave to her. She sweeps forward and, jubilant, kisses me, which is just when Eric turns the corner.

She can't see him; I'm the one facing the opposite end of the hall. But she breaks away from me when she hears his voice. 'Oh,' he says quietly. 'It's like that.' He looks at me, and then at Delia. 'I was trying to find you,' he murmurs. 'I was . . .' He shakes his head and turns around.

'Stay here,' I tell Delia, and I hurry after Eric. 'Wait up.'

He stops walking, but he doesn't turn around.

'Can I talk to you?'

Eric hesitates, but then he slides down the wall to sit on the floor. I sit down beside him. In spite of my facility with language, I can't think of a single word to say to make this better.

'Let me guess,' Eric says. 'You never meant for it to happen.'

'Hell, yes, I did. I've wanted her since you two started dating.'

Surprised, Eric blinks at me, and then even laughs a little. 'I know.'

'You did?'

'For God's sake, you're about as subtle as Hiroshima, Fitz.' He sighs. 'At least I didn't lose the girl *and* the case.'

I look down at the floor. 'Incidentally, I never meant for it to happen.'

'I should beat the crap out of you.'

'You can *try*.'

'Yeah,' Eric says quietly. 'I just might do that.' Then he glances up at me. 'If I can't take care of her myself, there's no one else I'd want to take my place.' He hesitates, and when he speaks a moment later, his voice is heavy with hope. 'I'm going to clean up,' he vows. 'This time for good.'

'I want you to,' I tell him. 'I'd like that.'

Eric will be with us – maybe not as often, maybe not even in the same neighborhood, maybe not for a while. But we are three; none of us would have it any other way.

He smiles, his hair falling over his brow. 'Be careful what you wish for,' Eric says. 'I've learned my fair share about abduction.'

We sit for a few more moments, although there's really nothing left to say. This is new to me, too, an entire conversation that takes place in silence, because the heart has its own language. I will remember what Eric says even though he doesn't say a word. I will tell it to her.

Delia

There is one other person who hangs back in the court-room, unwilling to face the storm of media that is waiting on the other side of the doors. My mother waits at the end of the aisle, her hands clasped in front of her. 'Delia,' she says. 'I'm happy for you.'

I stand a foot away from her, wondering what I am supposed to say.

'I guess you'll be going back home, then.' She smiles a little. 'I hope we can stay in touch. Maybe you'll come back for a visit. You're always welcome to stay with us.'

Us. At the mention of Victor, something shuts down inside of me. Eric says that we can try to press charges against Victor if the statute of limitations hasn't run out yet, that this would be a whole new trial. As much as I want him to pay, there is a part of me that wants to just put it behind me. But even more, I want my mother to believe me. I want her, for once, to take my side instead of her own.

'He hurt me,' I say baldly. 'I *did* remember. But *you* don't . . . so it couldn't have happened, right?'

She shakes her head. 'That's not—'

'True?' I finish, the word bitter on my tongue before I swallow it. 'I wanted you to be my mother. I wanted one so badly.'

'I am your mother.'

I think of what would happen if someone, anyone, touched Sophie. It wouldn't matter who it was – Victor, the man in the moon, Eric – I'd kill him. An icicle through the heart, a car filled with carbon monoxide. He would not take another breath if he touched my daughter; I'd find a way to hurt him that didn't show, just like he'd done to her.

And if Sophie was the one who came to tell me about it, I'd listen.

In this way, I am different from my mother. And for that, I'm incredibly grateful.

When I look up at her, I don't feel regret or sadness or even pain inside; I just feel numb. 'I wish I could tell you that I know you did the best you could,' I say softly, 'but I can't.'

As a child, what I was missing was so much bigger to me than what I had. My mother – mythic, imaginary – was a deity and a superhero and a comfort all at once. If only I'd had her, surely, she would have been the answer to every problem; if only I'd had her, she would have been the cure for everything that ever had gone wrong in my life. It has taken me twenty-eight years to be able to admit that I'm glad I did not know my mother until now. Not because, as my father suspected, she would ruin my life, but because this way, I did not have to bear witness as she ruined hers.

My mother's sorrow is so powerful, it cracks the clay tile beneath her feet; it makes the water in the fountain behind us overflow. 'Delia,' she says, as her eyes fill with tears. 'I'm trying.'

'Me, too.' I reach for her hand: a compromise, a good-bye. Maybe this is as good as it gets.

Eric and I sit in the anteroom of the Madison Street Jail while we wait for my father's paperwork to be completed. I am careful to keep an inch of space between us, even when we are cramped tight by others. It shifts with us, and keeps me from brushing up against him. Once that happens, I will not be able to keep myself from falling apart.

We watch a parade of felons: prostitutes who try to come on to the detention officers; gang members bleeding from open wounds; drunks who sleep in the corners and sometimes cry in their sleep. 'You know,' he says, after 'a few minutes, 'I might just stay here for a while.'

'In *jail?*'

'In Arizona. It's not so bad, really. And I've got at least one judge who likes me.' He shrugs. 'Chris Hamilton offered me a job.'

'Really?'

'Yeah. Right after he chewed me out for not telling him I'm an alcoholic.'

I stare down at my hands. 'That's not why I did it, you know.'

'That's exactly why you did it,' he corrects. 'And that's why I love you.' He reaches into his pocket and pulls out a piece of paper with an address scrawled across it. 'This is the closest AA meeting. I'm going there tonight.'

My eyes fill again. 'I love you, too,' I say. 'But I can't carry your baggage.'

'I know, Dee.'

'I'm not sure what I want right now.'

'I know that, too,' Eric says.

I wipe my eyes. 'What am I supposed to tell Sophie?'

'That I said this was the best thing for her mother.' He takes my hand and traces his thumb across my knuckles. 'For God's sake, if I learned anything during this damn trial it's that the only way someone can leave you is if you let them. And I'm not doing that, Dee. It may look like that today, or tomorrow, or even a month from now, but one day you're going to wake up and see that this whole time you've been gone, you've only been headed back to where you started. And I'll be there, waiting.' He leans forward and kisses me once, feather-light, on the lips. 'It's not like I'm not letting you go,' he murmurs. 'I'm just trusting you enough to come back.'

When he stands, he is tall enough to block the line of the sun. He is all I see, for a moment, when he walks out the door.

★

We leave the jail and head onto the highway. But instead of going back to Fitz and Sophie, I pull off at the first exit and veer to the side of the road in a cloud of dust. For the first time I allow myself to look at my father, really look at him, since this trial has begun.

The bruises on his face are healing, but his nose is never going to be straight again. His hair is still tufted and spotty from the shave. He sits with his arms crossed tight, as if he doesn't quite know what to do with all the space in the front seat, and even when the grit gets unbearable, he will not roll up his window.

'You probably have some questions for me,' he says.

I look away, over the flat of the desert. There are wild boar out there, and coyote, and snakes. There are a thousand dangers. You can trip on a garden hose and wind up in a coma; you can eat a bad mushroom and die. Safety is never absolute, no matter what precautions you take. 'You should have told me about Victor.'

He is quiet for a full minute, and then he rubs his hand over his jaw. 'I would have,' he says. 'But I honestly didn't know whether it was true.'

My mouth drops open and I cannot move, cannot breathe. '*What?*'

'I didn't have any proof, just . . . a *feeling*. I couldn't risk leaving you there with him, but I also couldn't take a hunch to the cops.'

'What about what you saw through the window?'

He shakes his head. 'I don't know if I really did see that, Delia, or if I just convinced myself I did, over the years. The more time that passed, the more I wondered if I'd jumped to the wrong conclusions. And I needed to think I hadn't, because that way I could justify running away with you.' He closes his eyes. 'It turns out that if you want something to be true badly enough, you can rewrite it that way, in your head. You can even start to believe it.'

'You lied on the witness stand?' I manage.

'It just . . . came out. And when it did – even when I realized that it could be the thing that saved me – I felt awful. But
then I thought maybe you'd forgive me,' he says. 'I'd spent
almost thirty years being someone I wasn't, for you. So maybe
you wouldn't mind spending a week being someone you
weren't, for me.'

I do not tell my father about the memories I've had of
Victor; memories that were never heard in that courtroom;
memories that would validate his intuition from so long ago.
I don't think about what I know, and what I've painted over
in my mind. There isn't one truth, there are dozens. The challenge is getting everyone to agree on one version.

So I ask the only question, really, that's left. 'Then why did
you take me?'

My father looks at me. 'Because,' he says simply, 'you asked.'

*I am sitting in the front seat of the car, with my toes up on the
dashboard. I close my eyes so the ribbon road in front of us vanishes,
and I pretend it would be this easy to disappear.* Please Daddy,
I say. Don't take me home yet.

When I open my eyes, it has started to rain. Fingers drum
on the roof, and I roll up the windows of the car. What if it
turns out that a life isn't defined by who you belong to or
where you came from, by what you wished for or whom you've
lost, but instead by the moments you spend getting from each
of these places to the next?

I glance at my father and ask him the question he asked me
exactly a lifetime ago. 'Where would you go, if you could go
anywhere?'

His smile lights me. I drive east, toward Sophie, toward
home. I follow a procession of telephone poles that stand with
their arms outstretched, marching toward the horizon line.
They keep going, you know. Even when you can't see where
they're headed.

Jodi Picoult's stunning novel
The Pact is available in
paperback July 2005